About the Author

Claudia loves to write about ordinary women who find themselves in extraordinary situations and to date, has written about three love affairs, five crazy mothers, two fractured sibling relationships, one cancelled wedding, a recovering alcoholic, two stately homes, one vicious stepmother and not forgetting countless failed 'goes' at online dating.

As a bestselling author, Claudia has published sixteen novels, four of her books have been optioned, two for movies and two for TV. Her books regularly reach number one in Ireland, they're widely translated, and in the UK, she's a *Sunday Times* bestseller.

In 2018, she published *The Secrets of Primrose Square* and the stage adaptation marks Claudia's debut as a playwright.

During Covid lockdown, the book was one of the top ten downloaded books across all genres, both in Ireland and the UK.

🐦 @carrollclaudia

📷 @claudiacarrollbooks

The
love
algorithm

Claudia Carroll

ZAFFRE

First published in the UK in 2022 by
ZAFFRE
An imprint of Bonnier Books UK
4th Floor, Victoria House, Bloomsbury Square, London, England, WC1B 4DA
Owned by Bonnier Books
Sveavägen 56, Stockholm, Sweden

A CIP catalogue record for this book is
available from the British Library.

Trade Paperback ISBN: 978-1-83877-831-6

Also available as an ebook and an audiobook

1 3 5 7 9 10 8 6 4 2

Typeset by IDSUK (Data Connection) Ltd
Printed and bound in Great Britain by Clays Ltd, Elcograf S.p.A.

Zaffre is an imprint of Bonnier Books UK
www.bonnierbooks.co.uk

To my fabulous mum, Anne Carroll.
This one's for you.

Chapter One

She was nervous. He was hungry. She'd had her hair done specially. He seemed far more interested in the menu than he did in her. She was wearing a brand-new dress. He was in trainers. She didn't want to drink. He ordered a full bottle.

'So, tell me all about yourself,' she said, reminding herself to smile and maintain eye contact, as all the dating websites advise you to do on a first date. *Remember to sit forward and show interest in the other person. Don't be a conversation hogger, but do ask pertinent questions. Create a strong first impression, and prepare some interesting first-date topics in advance.*

'You want to know how I am right now? Bloody starving,' was his blunt answer as he scanned up and down the menu, all eight pages of it. It was an expensive restaurant, with white linen tablecloths, cut-crystal glasses and a sommelier. And he was the one who'd chosen it, which she thought augured well. Statistically, men who were prepared to expend on a date were 72 per cent more likely to end up in a serious, committed relationship within six months. Fact.

'So tell me, whereabouts do you work?' she asked politely.

There was a lengthy silence which wore on, until eventually the penny seemed to drop with him that it was not a rhetorical question.

'Ehhh . . . sorry . . .? So . . . what were you saying there?' he stammered distractedly, looking up from the menu. 'Oh, right – OK, so I work in sports management for a big multi-national. I'm pretty senior in the company, actually.'

His profile specified that he'd played rugby at club level, and he looked every inch of it: a physically huge, hulking man in every way. He must have stood at about six-four with hands the size of shovels and the thickest neck on any human being she'd ever seen.

'Sounds great! Tell me more.' She smiled agreeably, but by then she'd already lost him back to the menu.

'Tell you what,' he replied, 'the starters here look really good. How about we order a few of those, then we can share?'

Appear compliant and agreeable on any first date, she'd seen on a Ted Talk before setting out that evening, so that's what she did, she nodded and agreed. She wasn't remotely hungry, but she knew that low blood sugar driven primarily by hunger led to a 45 per cent decrease in social skills. Maybe, she hoped, this date would get off the ground properly once he'd eaten.

He ordered for both of them – an astonishing four starters in total: the chicken skewers, pork falafel, beef carpaccio and smoked salmon.

'I'm vegetarian,' she gently reminded him. This was clearly specified in line three of her dating profile – had he just forgotten?

'Oh yeah,' he said to the waiter who was scribbling down their order. 'Better throw a few greens in there for herself, OK?'

Sure enough, when the food was served, exactly 80 per cent of it was entirely inedible to her, leaving her with no option but to pick at a watery-looking garden salad. This did not seem to bother her date though, who ate like a man on death row. And that was before he got started on the wine list.

The first bottle of wine he'd already milled his way through long before their starters had even been cleared. It was ferociously expensive, and she nearly choked on an asparagus spear when he called the wine waiter over and ordered the same again.

'But I'm driving,' she spluttered.

His response? 'You've got a car? Great. Maybe you can give me a lift into town when we've finished eating? A few of the lads are meeting up in the Capitol bar and I said I'd stick my head in when we're done here. Oh, and don't worry about the vino – my treat, I'll take care of it.'

Well, at least that's something, she thought.

Then he couldn't decide between entrées, so he decided to order two: a filet mignon and a tuna steak. 'This way, I can make my own DIY "surf 'n' turf",' he said. 'Hey, I'm a big guy, gotta get the old protein into me.'

Not only that, but the amount of side dishes he'd ordered filled the entire table to groaning. Food, food and more food just kept rolling out of the kitchen, and while he horsed hungrily into it, she picked at a mushroom risotto and valiantly tried to steer this date back on track.

'So tell me what you like to do when you're not working,' she asked, even though she had done her research on him thoroughly beforehand. Just like she did on everything throughly. 'I can see that you enjoy eating out, and I know you're a sportsman, but what other hobbies and interests do you have?'

Regular theatregoers scored particularly high with her here. As did any potential partner who'd visited an art gallery or exhibition in the past six months. Extra points for raising the topic of books, particularly if any date was prepared to discuss what he was reading at the moment. Top marks if this happened to feature something on the Booker Prize list.

'Well, work takes up most of my time right now,' he shrugged, speaking with his mouth full of tuna and pommes frites, a sight too disgusting for words. 'Any free time I do get, I'm either at club matches, or else the big international games. Did you happen to see Ireland versus France last weekend?'

She was about to reply that no, actually, she hadn't. She wasn't particularly interested in rugby, or soccer either, for that matter. As he'd have known if he'd bothered reading her dating profile properly. But just then, as soon as he'd finished eating, abruptly and without even excusing himself, he got up to go to the gents.

She sighed deeply, taking the chance to sit back, have a sip of water and reflect on how the evening was going so far.

It was only when he'd been gone for a good ten minutes and still hadn't returned that she began to wonder where he'd got to. The probability of him having bumped into an acquaintance she gave a low 15 to 20 per cent. So what was keeping him? A binge then purge eater, she wondered, as the minutes ticked by? No; statistically, bulimic men in his age category only accounted for 0.1 per cent of the population. More than likely he'd taken a call and was outside somewhere on his phone. Rude beyond words, but then in her long and bitter experience, rudeness seemed to be a factor in approximately 67 per cent of all her first dates.

'OK if I clear away now?' their waiter asked, and she nodded yes.

He'd been gone a good fifteen minutes now, and still no sign of him. Annoyingly, she didn't have his mobile number, as they'd been direct-messaging via the dating app they'd met up on, so she tried contacting him on that instead.

Everything all right? Where did you disappear off to?

Still no response. She tried again – still nothing. Should she just pay for herself, then walk out, she wondered? But she quickly dismissed the thought. Apart from anything else, it would be a rotten thing to do to the restaurant staff. The waiter came back with dessert menus, which she waved away.

'May I bring you some tea? Coffee?' he asked her instead.

'I think just the bill, please,' she said. Moments later, the bill arrived, elegantly secured in a leather-like wallet and discreetly placed in front of her.

She opened it up. Glanced down at the total. Took it in. Processed it. Tried not to panic. Snapped it shut again, and did her best to act as if this was not a problem for her.

Nine hundred and twenty-one euro. *Nine hundred.* Almost a month's mortgage payment on a dinner for two, and she'd hardly eaten a scrap. The wine alone was an astonishing two hundred and thirty *per bottle*. Wine that she hadn't even sipped. By her calculation, the head of lettuce and minuscule portion of risotto she'd consumed should have cost approximately seventy-five euro, even in an upmarket restaurant like this.

She willed herself to remain calm. A sudden spike in blood pressure, she knew, led to a 45 per cent increase in poor decision-making, and right now, she needed her wits about her. He'd be back, of course he would, and he'd split it with her, as she had assumed all along would be the case. It would still end up costing her considerably more than she rightfully should be paying, but still. It was better than nothing. She was a financially independent woman; she earned well; she had credit cards; she always, always paid her own way. Particularly on any first date, where dividing bills fifty-fifty was par for the course.

'May I bring you the card machine?' the waiter asked, by now hovering in a most irritating way. Did he perhaps suspect that all was not well?

She tried to remain cool and collected.

'I'll just pop to the ladies first. May I ask if you've seen the gentleman I was dining with? I assume he's still in the bathroom? Or else taking a call outside?'

'I'm afraid I haven't, Madam,' her waiter replied smoothly, tactful enough not to embarrass her. 'Also, just to remind you Madam, if I may, that your table is booked as a time limited reservation.'

It was crowded at the bar, and she was aware of multiple eyes boring into her, the middle-aged single woman hogging a precious table for two.

She went downstairs to the bathroom to splash cold water on her face and check for herself whether he was down there or not, even though she knew in her heart of hearts that the probability of the waiter lying was close to zero. She even slipped outside onto the street, to double-check that he wasn't there either, perhaps indulging in a sneaky cigarette as, she knew, 23 per cent of the population did.

It was at this point that she had to remind herself of the principle of Occam's razor, in Latin sometimes known as *lex parsimoniae*.

That the simplest explanation is usually the correct one.

Like it or not, he'd done a runner. Which made it worse, far, far worse than being stood up. In this case, clearly he'd arrived, taken one look at her, decided she wasn't for him, but figured what the hell, he'd stay for dinner anyway, consume as much as he was capable of, then stick her with the bill and vanish into thin air.

It was cruel beyond words. It beggared belief. It was unthinkable. But with the waiter hovering beside her, credit card machine in hand, she did what had to be done. Swallowing her pride, she handed over her card, paid the bill and somehow managed to leave the restaurant with her head held high.

By no scientific or mathematical law that she was aware of, she thought on the drive back home, could it possibly get any worse than this.

She had officially hit rock bottom.

Chapter Two

Iris

Her name, by the way, was Iris Simpson, and if all her years of unsuccessfully scouring the dating coalface had taught her anything, it was this.

You wanted to meet a partner? Then you had to be optimistic. You had to trust in the triumph of hope over experience. You had to strategise, you had to be brave, you had to be prepared to make the first move and not take it too personally if you were rebuffed. You had to put real thought into writing the perfect profile – that went without saying. But above all, you absolutely had to believe in your heart of hearts that dating was purely and simply a number-crunching game. The greater the number of dates you went on, the higher your chances of securing a partner. Simple as that.

Numbers, fortunately, happened to be Iris's particular area of expertise.

♥

She had tried contacting her 'date' from the previous night, to shame him out of it, if nothing else, only to real-ise that the bastard had gone and blocked her. So at her desk at work the following morning at Sloan Curtis, the firm where she was a senior manager, she fired off a furious missile to the dating agency who'd dared to match her up with a con man and petty larcenist.

This, she wrote, *is the standard at a highly respected, not to mention expensive dating agency? This is who you 'match' me with? Don't you have any kind of screening process for your members? My date last night*, she typed away crossly, *was a thief, and the only common ground between us appears to be that he and I live in the same city, we're both in our forties and we're both single.*

Well, shame on you, she tapped away, her fingers flying over the keyboard. *If you think this standard of 'matching' is acceptable, then you're an utter disgrace to your profession.*

It was highly unusual for someone like Iris to allow emotion to cloud her thoughts, but on this one occasion, she allowed it. Not only did she demand an apology and a thorough investigation from the agency, which went by the most inappropriate name of True Love Guaranteed, if you could believe that for bitter irony, but she also threatened to take them all the way to the district court unless they refunded her the full amount of her joining fee. *Should you fail to do this*, she punched into the keyboard for good measure, *then rest assured I won't hesitate to air this matter on the wider social media platforms, the court of public opinion.*

Which, naturally, she had no intention of doing. Iris was a deeply private person, and the humiliation of the previous evening was quite enough to last her a lifetime, thanks all the same. Her only consolation was that no one, literally no one, would ever know. Mainly because who would Iris tell? Who was there in her life who'd be even vaguely interested?

The actuarial firm where Iris worked was particularly hectic that Friday morning, and as usual, her colleagues were busily hustling and bustling, juggling phone calls, zipping in and out of meetings and frantically trying to make project targets at their individual desks. All the normal day-to-day business that went with being one of the largest data-processing firms in Dublin. Most unusually though, Iris just let the buzz happen around her, closed her office door, sat back and allowed herself a rare moment to gaze out of the window and down on to the city centre streets below. It was utter gridlock down there: buses, taxis, cars and bikes all squeezed into one narrow lane of traffic and all angrily trying to work their way through the Friday rush hour.

Car horns blared in the dim distance as her thoughts began to wander.

I wouldn't mind, she thought, *but it's not like I haven't done my homework here. It's not like I haven't prepared.*

Iris was now of an age where she could claim to have been online dating for almost as long as the whole concept had been in existence. Since the millennium, in other words. All those years ago, back when she was a young, fresh-faced, hopeful college graduate, top of her class and the gold medal student, with tech firms headhunting her, tantalising her with incredibly generous salaries; doing everything they possibly could to get her to sign on the dotted line.

Nor had Iris been idle in the intervening time. OK, so she may not have found the holy grail of a life partner – certainly not yet – but she had at least worked out precisely what it was she did and didn't want from any potential future relationship, in a way that appealed to her clear, mathematical mind.

Online dating, she knew, functioned on algorithms. Simple as that. You fed in your personal information, the dating website would process it then yield results, based solely on the information you had given it in the first place.

Iris's input, like most people's, had closely resembled her CV. She took care to reference her applied mathematics degree from Trinity College (in which she took a first, thanks very much for asking); her postgraduate degree from Oxford and her years of experience working in a high tech job, that had flourished for her over the years.

Was all this stellar success a bit too intimidating to a guy, she occasionally wondered? Nonsense. She was proud of all she'd achieved. Besides, surely this would appeal to the right man? Surely he'd be proud and supportive of her too?

So that was work and career taken care of nicely, or so she'd assumed. Then, under the 'hobbies' section on any dating site, she would list her skills with JavaScript and her fluency in Mandarin. Not terribly sexy, admittedly, but Iris was anxious to illustrate exactly how it was that she liked to spend her free time.

To lend a more personal flavour, she'd also write about her great love of long-haul travel; after all, it was no harm to show that you were broad-minded and cosmopolitan.

Maybe even up for moving to a different country, should the right man come along. Make no mistake, Iris was a deeply committed and serious dater.

Last of all, she would painstakingly outline, in crystal-clear terms, what it was she was looking for in a relationship, as well as her absolute deal-breakers, so as to save everyone's time.

I'd like to meet someone urbane, smart and successful, she'd invariably post in her online profile. Someone who wanted marriage and possibly even a child before it was too late, just as she did. Someone who aspired to the same lifestyle as her. Someone who was culturally attuned, exactly like she strove to be. Someone professional, who enjoyed their work. Someone who was widely travelled and who intended to travel even more, but categorically never on a cruise ship or to any resort that boasted an 'all-inclusive buffet'.

Iris's idea of an all-round wonderful holiday was a trip to Italy to witness the spectacle of an outdoor opera among the ruins at the Arena di Verona. Or go to France for a walking tour of the great historical battlegrounds from the First World War; the Somme being one that particularly appealed to her. A good, hefty, outdoorsy walking tour of a battlefield – now who could possibly fail to be suitably enticed by a holiday like that? So why was it that Iris had had absolutely no takers? No one even commenting on how interesting that sounded?

In all these years, she thought, as she continued to stare blankly out of the office window, she had unfailingly done everything these websites requested of her.

Every single thing. She'd been honest about her age and income. She was upfront about her plans for the future. Moreover, she would always post a fresh, up-to-date photo, with absolutely no sneaky blurring for a flattering soft-focus effect and without, God forbid, any sort of filter.

There was a large twenty-something cohort fresh out of college working at Sloan Curtis, and it seemed to Iris that they were forever taking selfies to post on those Gen Z dating sites – Bumble, Hinge, and what have you – then filtering them up to the most insane levels, so that every single one of them ended up looking as though they were made of wax. Honestly, Iris thought, shuddering at the very idea. Why bother? What was the point in pretending to be someone you weren't? Someone like her simply didn't believe in playing games. Quite apart from anything else, she didn't have the time.

A misleading photo, she knew from bitter experience, accounted for a whopping 95 per cent of poor outcomes on a first date. You had to be honest about who you were and what you looked like from the get-go, otherwise your prospective date would take one look at you and instantly feel cheated and let down. As she herself had on occasions too numerous to detail.

Oh, at this stage, Iris had seen it all. Men who actually used their wedding photos as a profile shot, with brides crudely chopped out. Elderly men, clearly in their seventies if they were a day, who posted photos and swore blind they were 'early forties'. Men whose photos were taken from such a distance you failed to see any of their features at all. Worst

14

of all were the ones who posted group shots, so you were expected to guess whose photo you were actually meant to be looking at. Really, who did these people think they were kidding? Were there any serious daters left out there?

Iris, on the other hand, had always prided herself on being completely straight about her appearance. Her most recent photo was a selfie, taken at her desk, where she seemed to spend 90 per cent of her time anyway: tall, pale, whippet-thin and unsmiling – mainly because she wasn't the smiling type, and to photograph herself with a fake grin plastered across her face would have constituted false advertising. She'd removed her sharp, black-rimmed glasses for the photo and was dressed in her trademark 'uniform' of neat black wool trousers, well cut and flattering, along with an elegant black cashmere turtleneck, with her shoulder-length dark hair slicked back into a simple, tidy, low bun. OK, so maybe there were a few more grey hairs in there than she'd have liked, but when did someone like her ever get the time to go to a hairdresser?

The years wore on and on, and she still hadn't managed to find her perfect match, yet Iris refused to be ground down. Negativity was absolutely not for her; she was very much a solution-orientated person. So instead, she began to look at each fresh date as research. She compiled data. She crunched numbers. She went home after every single date and got straight onto her laptop to make notes of her results and observations. And over time, she distilled the whole concept of meeting a partner online into one simple formula, which could essentially be pared right down to the following.

For some unknown reason, men with poor vocabulary accounted for 45 per cent of 'matches' presented to her online. Not exactly what you might call a turn-on. All it took was one ungrammatical post, one apostrophe in the wrong place, one 'your' instead of 'you're', and she automatically discounted them. Men who consumed more than four units of alcohol on a date accounted for 62 per cent. Men who played golf an astonishing 54 per cent, in spite of Iris's utter loathing of the sport.

And all the time, she kept coming back to numbers, numbers, numbers. Iris lived in a city with a population of 1.98 million, which yielded an approximate figure of nine hundred and fifty thousand men. So surely there had to be someone in her locale who fulfilled everything she was searching for in a partner? Why, she often wondered, had the whole world of online dating brought her absolutely zero per cent success? Particularly when it wasn't like there was a shortage of men out there?

Throughout her entire dating history, Iris had had lots of first dates, but a disproportionately small number of them had turned into actual relationships, and those that did tended to peter out very quickly. So here she was, at the grand old age of forty-two, and in a sobering moment having to admit that her longest and most successful relationship had been with a balding dentist called Angus, who was ten years her senior and who she'd been seeing for exactly eighteen months. All was well, until one particular week when, without even telling her, Angus applied for a job all the way over in Whakapapa, New Zealand, was offered the post right away, and before the month was out, had emigrated out of the country and out of her life. Gone, lock, stock and barrel. Just like that.

It seemed to Iris, at the time, that he quite literally couldn't get far enough away from her.

Then she dated a scientist called Barry, who worked in a research lab and who still lived at home with his mother. Nothing wrong with that, except that mother and son enjoyed such an incredibly close relationship, Barry would frequently bring his mum out on dates with him and Iris, like some kind of permanent chaperone. For a time, Iris held out great hopes that this one might actually go the distance. After all, men who loved and respected their mothers, she knew, accounted for a surprisingly low 12 per cent of divorce cases in Ireland. Her feelings for Barry ran deep, and for once, seemed to be reciprocated. They'd even had the 'I think I love you' conversation, for God's sake.

That was until one particular night at the theatre, when she returned to her seat after the interval only to overhear the mother talking about her behind her back.

'Why do we always have to go out with *her*, Barry love?' she was moaning. 'She's so up herself. If she starts quoting any more statistics at me, I swear I'll clobber her. Did you hear her giving out yards about the wine here, just because it was served in plastic glasses? That Iris one is an out-and-out snob, if you ask me. You could do much better for yourself, pet. I'm sorry, but I just can't take to her, and I never will.'

Within a matter of days, Barry had started ghosting Iris and not even bothering to return her calls. In a matter of months, she'd heard on the grapevine that he was currently seeing a fellow lab technician and planning a trip to Lourdes with her and the mother. Frankly, Iris thought, the best of luck to them.

The least said about her most recent partner, Tim, who worked in aviation management out at Dublin Airport, the better. Iris had been seeing him for several weeks, and was just beginning to wonder why roughly 70 per cent of their dates involved him drinking heavily, very heavily, sometimes to the point of oblivion.

But Iris was nothing if not a problem-solver, and so she took it on herself to try to 'fix' Tim. You're drinking to excess, she helpfully pointed out to him during the course of one of their pub dates. Just like all of their dates seemed to centre around loud, heaving, stinking bars. You're drinking way above seventeen units per week, which is recommended for men under the official drinkaware.ie guidelines. Why would you want to jeopardise your health like that? she asked him, genuinely puzzled and deeply concerned.

That conversation had taken place over a year ago now and that, quite literally, had been the last Iris was ever to see of Tim. Given the choice of her or a pint of Guinness, Guinness had won the day. Her out, pints in, simple as that.

The traffic gridlock continued down on the street six floors below her as she sat there alone in her office, utterly focused on the problem.

And the more she thought about her online dating life, the angrier she began to grow. After all this time and effort, she thought, what was wrong? She knew of so many people, work colleagues predominantly, who'd had staggering success meeting partners online. She'd heard of one or two engagement parties, and a sizeable number of weddings, too, where the bride and groom, or in one particularly fabulous case, the groom and groom, had all met online.

So many people she knew were now happily matched and married.

Why not her?

Clearly there was a problem here, and Iris vowed not to rest till she had drilled it right down to its bare essence.

Algorithms, she decided. It all lay in algorithms. All of her dating life, she had blithely trusted in these completely random algorithms, time and again confiding her most personal, intimate details to them. Yet the cold, hard fact was that every single one had failed her.

When work eventually finished up for the day and yet another weekend rolled around, Iris found herself still giving this much, much thought. Well into the following week, it consumed her around the clock.

Generally she was the first into the Sloan Curtis office every morning, arriving bang on seven thirty sharp, and she was the last home every night, well past 10 p.m. most nights. She still kept up that gruelling schedule, but in what little free time she had, all she could think about was the sheer volume of dating websites out there, and why they yielded results for some but not others. Why did a lucky few hit the romantic jackpot, and not people like her? Some put it down to 'fate', but that Iris immediately dismissed as arrant nonsense.

Fate be damned, she thought. Algorithms, they were the real culprit here. One hundred per cent of them seemed absolutely rubbish to her. Had their creators perhaps scribbled them out on a square of loo roll, then randomly turned them into useless apps that generated vast fortunes for the developers, while leaving countless users like Iris disappointed, disheartened and ready to throw in the towel?

So, she thought, instead of investing all her hopes in a succession of failed algorithms to find her future life partner, why not create her own? After all, she'd been coding ever since she was in secondary school, she could practically do it standing on her head. What was to stop her?

The more Iris thought about it, the more excited she grew, as her energy levels began to surge and the idea really took root. Creating an algorithm, she knew, took approximately two thousand, two hundred and fifty-five hours of time, as extensive research had proven over the years. A mere matter of months. It was early April now, and if Iris was to take up the challenge and devote herself wholeheartedly to working on this as and when she could, there was no reason why she couldn't come up with her very own dating algorithm – and possibly an app to go along with it – by summer. Not that Iris had a whole lot of free time, given the insane hours she was required to work.

And yet, she thought, *and yet. Wasn't this worth it? If I can find the time for all these disastrous first dates, then why can't I find the time to design a dating app with a difference?*

After all, what was an algorithm when you pared it right down to its core? Nothing more than a simple formula.

Exactly the same as following a recipe in the kitchen. You wanted to bake a cake? Then you worked from step A through B, C and D, etc., until you were finally done, had achieved your goal and were now looking at a lovely jammy Victoria sponge. An algorithm was to your computer what a cake recipe was to your kitchen.

How hard could it be? Besides, Iris thought, perhaps she could actually do a bit of good here. Maybe, just maybe, she could make a difference in the lives of scores of other women out there, women who were just like her. Middle-aged professional women, who had devoted their lives to their careers, just like her, who had scant family to speak of and who were . . . she hated to use the word, but in this instance she'd allow it . . . lonely.

Iris thought back to that last, horrific date she'd been on which, let's face it, she'd still be paying off on her credit card for some considerable time to come.

Then she shuddered. If she could at least prevent one other human being from going through an experience like that, then wasn't it all to the good?

But her dating algorithm needed to be different.

It needed to stand out from the field.

And most critically of all? It needed to bloody well work.

Chapter Three

Kim

'You swiped right on me? Seriously? This must be my lucky day! I mean, like . . . like . . . just look at you. I'm seriously punching above my weight here!'

'Wow,' said Kim, beaming. 'This date is only about three minutes old and already it's the best one I've had in months.'

'So tell me all about yourself, Kim,' he asked, smiling broadly, taking care to use her name, just like you were supposed to.

'And, right there, you see what you just did?' she said, shaking her head teasingly and knocking back the dregs of the vodka and cranberry juice she'd ordered for herself while she was waiting for him. 'You just got docked a point for asking a really boring question. "Tell me all about yourself"? Seriously? That's an aul' one question. I knew there'd be a catch with someone as attractive as you. Good-looking guys? There's always something!'

'Ahh, shite,' he said, twinkling down at her, because that was the other thing about this fella, he was very, very tall. Like, giraffe tall, with the loveliest twinkly brown eyes. Maybe not what Kim would call conventionally fit, but a definite cutie. 'So, tell me how I redeem myself back into your good graces, O gorgeous one,' he asked, half joking, mock serious.

'Well, you can haul yourself up to that bar, and mine's a large vodka and cranberry juice, ta very much,' she grinned, holding up her by now empty glass and waving it under his nose.

'Consider it done,' he smiled, before milling his way through the packed Friday-night crowd to nab a space at the bar.

Was that her third or her fourth vodka so far tonight, Kim wondered? Ah, so what if it was, who the hell was counting? She'd gone for 'just the one' with her gang of pals from Sloan Curtis earlier, her 'sesh pigs', as she called them, and they were having such a laugh in the bar around the corner from the office, that at one point she'd seriously considered standing her date up for the night.

'But you can't just leave him hanging there,' her best friend Hannah had said. But then Hannah was kind and conscientious like that. 'I'd hate it if some randomer did that to me. Come on, Kim, there's a lady buried there somewhere deep inside you – you can do it, you can at least have a drink with this guy and see what he's like. One little drink isn't going to kill you.'

'But the craic is here, with you lot,' Kim had protested. 'This is just a date – sure I go on ten of them a week. What's another cancelled date? Who's even bothered?'

'You have to go,' Hannah insisted. 'At best, he could turn out to be "The One".' And at worst, you'll have a hilarious story to tell us all at work tomorrow morning. The more disastrous your dates, the funnier your stories. Same as always.'

So now that Kim had actually made it here, to yet another packed, jostling pub, and now that she'd got a full-on head-to-toe look at her date, she had to admit that turning up was actually a pretty good idea, all things considered.

I'd give him a rock-solid 6/10, she WhatsApped Hannah. In fact, most unusually, he was even nicer looking in the flesh than he was in his profile pic. **Lovely tight buns**, she added in her text. **A gym bunny, defo. Abs, arse, pecs, he's packing it all**. As proof, she took a quick, surreptitious photo of him when he was up at the bar, so she could show everyone at work tomorrow just how cute he was. Brighten up a boring morning at the office, if nothing else.

Then she took a selfie to make sure she wasn't looking too pissed and bleary-eyed beside him. Holding up reasonably OK, she thought, double-checking it like it was a mirror, although she had a few zits too many on her freckly round face than she'd have liked; the result of too many late nights and a diet that consisted mainly of oven chips and vodka. Briefly, she wondered if she should lash a bit of concealer over her spots, now, when she had the chance. But then decided, what the feck. Kim wasn't the make-up type, and any fella could take her as he found her. She flicked out her short, croppy, light brown hair with blond streaks long since grown out, checked she didn't have spinach stuck in the gap between her front teeth from a panini she'd had at lunchtime, then sorted out an uncomfortable wedgie in her knickers when no one was looking. And that's me, she thought, good to go, hot to trot.

Be safe and enjoy, Hannah texted back. **See you at work tomorrow. I'll bring the coffees and you can tell me everything. Don't be late for the Dreadnought Iris!**

Kim giggled as she put her phone away. Dreadnought Iris was the nickname they'd given to their supervisor in work, and it suited the woman down to a T. This Iris one was a weapon, pure and simple, and Kim often thought that was a lot of the reason why she went out on the lash as much as she did; purely because the Dreadnought Iris was down on her so much. Well, she had to let off steam some way, didn't she?

Her lovely, handsome date wove his way through the crowds, that were predominantly made up of twenty-somethings, just like he and Kim. He got back to their table with the drinks and handed Kim over her vodka with a jokey little bow.

'To your satisfaction, I hope, milady?'

On and on the chat went, light-hearted, messing, meandering and fun.

'So, whereabouts do you work?' he asked.

'Oh, for feck's sake . . . quick! Subject change required urgently,' Kim said, with a mock-dramatic eye-roll. 'Trust me, you don't want to know the first thing about where I work. What I do is as boring as arse. It's one of those jobs that's designed to suck your soul from your body and leave you an empty shell, dead on the inside.'

'You really hate it that much?' he said, raising a sexy, slanty eyebrow.

'Yup,' she nodded, 'I really hate it that much. I only do it 'cause the money is decent so I can help out my mother, plus I'm saving up so I can travel.'

'If you really want to know about a boring job,' he grinned, 'then let me tell you all about mine. You'll either fall asleep in five minutes flat, or else run screaming out of here. Guaranteed.'

'You go first,' said Kim.

'No, you go first.'

'You'll be sorry you asked,' she said, sticking her two fingers down her throat, fake-vomiting. 'But if you really want to know, then I'm an actuary. I work for a scarily intimidating company in the Financial Services Centre, and there you go, I can already see your eyes glazing over – told you it was deadly.'

'Sorry . . . you work as a . . . what?' he asked, looking puzzled. Kim took a big gulp of her vodka and spluttered laughing.

'Excellent question,' she said. 'I haven't the first clue either, and it's all I've done ever since I graduated. Basically it's to do with numbers and it's a gobshite job and I can't believe they hired me and my supervisor is down on me like a ton of bricks, and I keep waiting for her to find out that I haven't a bull's notion what I'm at, really. So in the meantime, I just faff around the office and try to look busy, then numb the boredom by coming out on nights like this and skulling back the vodkas with the gang. Who are all great, by the way – they're by far the best part of what I do.'

'I bet your job isn't that boring at all, and that you're far from rubbish at it,' her date said kindly. 'I bet you're miles better at it than you think you are.'

Jesus, this guy was so nice! *Thank God I turned up*, Kim thought. Thank Christ she'd had the good sense to listen to Hannah.

She slugged back another gulp of vodka and took a good, long, hard look at her date in all his handsomeness.

'You're lovely,' she slurred at him. In fact, there was probably an 80 to 85 per cent chance of her shagging him later on that night. Had she just said that out loud? She hoped not, but then figured, so what if she had? Who was bothered?

'You're lovely too,' he twinkled back at her. 'You know that gap between your front teeth? It's just the cutest thing I've ever seen. Never get it fixed, do you hear me?'

The night wore on and this date just kept getting better and better. This was like the dream date; this was turning into the holy grail of dating.

By midnight, when the pubs were spilling out onto the street, Kim was dragging him on to a club, with the 80 to 85 per cent probability of sex on the horizon now a very firm 100 per cent. *Am I wearing sexy underwear*, she wondered? *Ah, so fecking what if it's a bad knicker day.* Who even cared? She certainly didn't give a shite.

'Come on, let's just have one for the road,' she garbled a bit drunkenly, as they reached the top of a queue to get into Boujis nightclub just off Grafton Street.

'Howaya, Kim,' a bouncer with a shiny bald pate and absolutely no neck at all greeted her. 'Another late one for you, yeah?'

'We're only here for a quick one, Joe,' Kim grinned at him. 'Then we'll be on our way – no late nights tonight, I promise.'

'Jaysus,' he said, rolling his eyes. 'If I had a euro for every single time I heard you say that, I'd be a wealthy man.'

♥

Inside the club's plush, velvety interior, they grabbed a booth and ordered another round.

'Better go easy,' her date said, asking for a fizzy water for himself this time. 'I've got work in the morning. You know how it is.'

'So have I,' Kim shrugged, necking back her vodka as soon as it arrived. 'But we've a fantastic Nespresso machine in the office. Trust me, if you have Solpadeine for breakfast and keep mainlining enough Nespressos until you get the shakes, you'll feel no pain.'

'Solpadeine for breakfast?' he smiled. 'Seriously?'

'My nickname is Solpachina,' she told him straight-faced, and he roared laughing.

God, Kim thought happily, *is there anything sexier than a man who laughs at your gags?*

'Do you have your own flat?' she asked apropos of nothing, leaning in a bit closer to him.

'Why do you want to know?' he said, baffled.

'Long and bitter experience,' she explained, maybe slurring her words just a tiny bit. 'If we go back to mine, it can be a bit of a passion-killer when you're in the throes of wild, abandoned sex on our living room floor, to the backing track of my mother upstairs snoring her head off. Or worse, if she decides to come downstairs because she forgot her teeth or something, at a critical moment, let's just say, when you're lying bollock-naked on her good IKEA rug. That's why.'

Bit upfront, maybe? Ah, what the hell. This date was going far too well to get hung up on minor details like where to have the shift on a first date. There were no rules anymore when it came to sex and dating, were there? At least, none that Kim gave a shite about.

'You still live at home?' he asked her.

'Course I do,' she shrugged. 'Same as everyone else I know. We're all working, but have you copped the price of rent in this town? A thousand quid a month for a matchbox in some co-living dump? Feck that, my friend. And you know, apart from it being a bit awkward if I bring a fella home late at night, living at home is pretty cool, really. I never have to wash a thing, and the freezer is always full of oven chips and Cornettos. What's not to like?'

'Then, in answer to your question,' he said sexily, 'yes, I do have my own flat.'

Kim nodded and snuggled in tighter to him, wishing he'd just shut up and kiss her properly now. 'I'm not from Dublin originally, you see,' he went on to explain, 'I'm from Cork. So I've no choice but to be one of those eejits who forks out a fortune for a shoebox. Or in my case, a shoebox with a wonky boiler and a grand scenic view over the M50.'

'You're a Corkman?' said Kim, poking him playfully. 'I thought I heard an accent somewhere in there! Whereabouts in Cork are you from?'

'Ahh, tiny town in West Cork, you'd never have heard of it,' he smiled down at her, so, so much taller than her, even when he was sitting back against a sofa.

'You never know, I might have,' she said stoutly. 'My mum is a proud West Corkwoman too, I'll have you know. We spent all our summers down there when I was a kid. In this gorgeous little fishing village called Union Hall.'

'You're kidding!' he said animatedly. 'That's exactly where I'm from!'

'No actual way,' Kim laughed. 'Seriously?'

'Dead serious,' he said. 'My dad is the headmaster of the local school, and my mother works in the post office. What's your mum's name?'

'Her maiden name was O'Sullivan,' said Kim. 'But she changed it to Bailey when she married Dad.'

'This is bonkers,' he laughed delightedly. 'I'm an O'Sullivan, too. Don't suppose your mum is anything to do with the gang of O'Sullivans that run the pub down there on Main Street?'

Kim shook her head in disbelief.

'She *is* one of the O'Sullivans who have the pub on Main Street! Her brother Tom runs the pub to this day!'

But now he went a bit quiet and started looking at her very, very weirdly. Was Kim imagining it, or had the whole mood between them seemed to shift? Mind you, she'd knocked back at least six or seven vodkas by then, so there was every chance she *was* imagining it.

'Then your mum,' he said slowly, very, very slowly, 'is Connie O'Sullivan. She has to be.'

'Yeah,' said Kim, 'that's her.'

'In that case,' he said, 'your mum and mine are first cousins.'

♥

The following morning at the office, a killer hangover notwithstanding, Kim had an absolute field day with the story, milking it for all it was worth, wringing every last laugh out of it.

'And it turns out we're cousins!' she said, to hilarity around the main office, where she was holding court. 'Actual blood relatives, can you believe it?'

The office was light, bright and open-plan, with modern, airy, floor-to-ceiling windows, glass surfaces everywhere you looked, and just then, a cluster of about five or six of Kim's work buddies were all gathered around her desk, sniggering and goading her on to tell them more.

'Eughhh!' said Emma from Risk Assessment, pulling a disgusted face and looking like she was about to dry-retch. Emma had the deepest contralto voice you ever heard, she only ever wore black, day and night, winter or summer, and her little office rebellion was to wear Doc Martens along with her work suits. Somehow she got away with it, too; Kim could never fathom out how.

'It's not incest if you're second cousins,' someone else piped up.

'Still, though,' Emma insisted in that low, gravelly voice, 'it's . . . bleuuhhh!'

'Bloody hell,' Hannah blinked, wide-eyed. 'What are the odds?' Petite, blonde and with a round, open, smiley face, Hannah was Kim's closest pal and probably the nicest person on the planet. She was from Donegal, and as she was renting in Dublin and had no family in the city, Kim's mother was forever inviting her over for Sunday dinners and fretting about whether she was getting her five a day or not.

'Are you joking me?' Kim said to her. 'In a country like this, with Dublin basically like a very big village? It's actually amazing it doesn't happen more often.'

'Just as well you found out on your first date,' Hannah said wisely, in that soft Donegal burr. 'Could you imagine if you'd married him and gone on to have kids? This is why they make you do blood tests in the States before you tie the knot.'

'Do you want to know what the real killer is?' said Kim, rolling her eyes. 'He's so bloody gorgeous – you should see him. He's a slow burner, but the total package. A real Mr Nice Guy. For the whole night, I kept thinking, this is exactly the kind of fella my mother would love, and now I know why. Because he's related to her.'

More guffaws from the crew gathered around her.

'Makes for a cracking story, though,' said Greg from Statistics, arms folded, all ears, having a great old time. But then everyone had a great old time whenever Kim was around. She was just one of those people. Always up for a laugh and never afraid to be the butt of her own joke.

'It's right up there with the time you went on a date with Limo Man,' Hannah giggled. 'Do you remember that one?'

'Who was Limo Man?' someone else asked.

'Ahh, Jesus, don't remind me!' Kim said, facepalming.

'Go on, tell us,' said Greg. 'This sure as hell beats having to work for a living.'

'OK, long story short,' said Kim, although her dating stories were never, ever short. Generally she found that the longer they were, the more laughs she wrenched out of them, so what was the harm?

'Limo Man was this guy I met online,' she said to the gang, 'and anyway, this night, he arranged to collect me straight from here after work in a big black stretch job, the whole works.'

'I'll never forget it,' Hannah chipped in, for the benefit of anyone who hadn't heard this one from Kim's Greatest Dating Disasters before. 'There was me, hanging out the window with my eyes on stalks. Thought you'd seriously scored the jackpot with that one, Kim!'

'So I said to him, "are you a limo driver, is that what you do?"' Kim went on, warming into her story. 'So he says, no, the stretch is just for work. So we went for a few scoops and we were getting on brilliantly, and then he had this great idea that we'd get some takeaway grub and drive up the mountains, so we could have a bite to eat in the limo, looking out at the stars. I thought, brilliant, sounds dead romantic.

'Next thing, he looked at his watch and asked if we could drop by where he worked first, that it would only take five minutes – he just had to pick something up he needed for the morning. Course, I said, no problem, but then I nearly died when he drove us into the car park of an undertaker's. So he ran inside and next thing, he and three others came out carrying a huge big mahogany coffin, and they loaded it up onto the back of the stretch limo, all set for a funeral first thing the following day. Then he drove us on to McDonald's, like this was the most normal thing in the world, ordered all around him, then took us up to the Hell Fire Club and sat there stuffing his face with chicken nuggets and fries – and that was our romantic date. Him, me and the dead body in the back of the car.'

'Oh God, Kim,' Emma said, face buried in her hands, 'how do you pick them?'

'That's nothing!' Hannah said over the clamour of laughter. 'Kim, tell them about the time you went on a date with some randomer and the cops pulled you over!'

'What's that one?' asked Greg.

'Ahh, don't remind me,' Kim said dramatically, slumping to the floor to pretend she was hiding under the desk, but then instantly springing back up again, because feck it anyway, it was a great story.

'So anyway, this was a guy I met on FixedUp . . .'

'Where else?' someone chipped in.

'. . . and he'd literally only just picked me up in his car,' Kim went on, 'when he asked if I fancied going to this great restaurant he knew a bit outside Dublin, down in Avoca village. I thought, fine by me, sounds lovely and romantic. So the two of us are chatting away, getting on like a house on fire, when next thing, he gets pulled over by the cops. And the guy completely overreacts – I shit you not, he starts panicking and sweating and going seriously apeshit. "But you haven't done anything wrong," I said to him. "We haven't even had a drink yet, and you weren't

34

speeding. It's probably just a random road check, so just show them your licence and sure you'll be fine." But it was worse than I thought, far, far worse. Turns out the cops were alerted by this guy's car reg because – are you all ready for this?'

Eager nods from the gang, who were hanging on her every word.

'He'd done time on a drugs charge, for dealing, can you believe that? Anyway, he was out on remand, but had broken his parole. So there was a warrant out to rearrest him and of course, the minute the cops pulled him over, they clapped him into handcuffs, and that was the last I saw of my date. They took his car off to the pound and I ended up getting a lift home in the back of a squad car.'

There were very satisfying gales of laughter from all around Kim, and she even got a tiny ripple of applause.

'It could only happen to you, Kim,' said Hannah, wiping tears of laughter from her eyes.

Then a different voice rang out, cold and clear.

'And what is it precisely that could only happen to you, Kimberley?'

Total silence all around Kim's desk, absolute pin-drop silence.

There, right in front of them, stood the Dreadnought Iris, all five foot ten of her, skinny as a toothpick, sticking her long, beaky nose in where it wasn't wanted, as per usual. The school headmistress, come to break up a gang of unruly kids.

'Kimberley?' Iris insisted, icily calm. 'I believe I asked you a simple question?'

'Oh . . . nothing,' Kim said, as the others fast fled back to their desks. 'We were just discussing . . . emm . . . the Databank Insurance report . . . that's all.'

'You find something amusing about Databank's Insurance report? Anything you'd care to share?'

'Absolutely nothing, thanks, Iris,' Kim replied, feeling like a bold schoolgirl about to get detention. 'All is in order, and I'll have that insurance proposal on your desk by close of play this evening. That's a promise.'

'Kindly see to it that you do,' said Dreadnought Iris, before sweeping back to her own desk.

The minute her back was turned, Kim gave her the fingers, to more muted titters from her pals dotted around the office.

For feck's sake, she thought, slinking back down onto her chair again. What was it about the Dreadnought Iris that made her feel ten years old? Why did the woman have to be such a fecking weapon?

Chapter Four

Iris

It was well past nine at night, and Iris was still chained to her desk, working, researching, beavering, compiling. Most unusually for her, however, she wasn't doing her normal actuarial work. This time she was focusing on a project of a more personal nature.

Her first challenge? To run an exhaustive – and by that she really did mean thoroughly exhaustive – analysis of every single dating website out there, mainly so she could evaluate a) precisely what it was that they were doing wrong, and b) how she could make her own algorithm completely standout unique.

A USP, that's what she was after.

As Iris knew only too well, there were literally thousands of dating websites online, and at this stage, there was precious little that a long-term serial dater like her couldn't have told you about each and every one of them.

For a start? They had to be pay-to-use or else you were just wasting your time. If a potential partner wasn't prepared to invest a small nominal fee into meeting 'The One', then what was the point? To Iris's clear, logical mindset, serious daters were prepared to pay; messers and time-bandits just coasted along on the freebie sites, purely in it for the 'lols', as her younger colleagues might say. A most repugnant phrase, in Iris's opinion, but one which seemed to have gained considerable currency among that Kim Bailey and her cohorts around the office.

Kim Bailey. For a moment, Iris allowed her mind to wander, as she took a gulp of water from the bottle in front of her and thought back over the events of the day. Kim Bailey, bleary-eyed and stinking of stale booze first thing that morning, holding court among all the junior members of staff, the centre of attention as per usual. Honestly, the girl seemed to confuse this office with some class of a stand-up comedy cellar. How someone like her ever managed to get a job at a reputable firm like Sloan Curtis completely beggared belief.

Mind you, Iris was monitoring Kim Bailey's work like you wouldn't believe, watching and waiting for the day when the party lifestyle the girl seemed to be enjoying would inevitably catch up with her. Which it surely would. A question of when, not if. And then she'd be out on her ear, and the best of good luck to her.

But then a random thought struck Iris, just before she knuckled back down to her own work.

Online dating. Before she'd broken up Kim's little comedy routine earlier, the girl had most definitely been telling tales about online dating.

Interesting.

Snapping out of it, Iris went straight back to the task at hand, making notes, copious amounts of notes. For weeks now, working till all hours every night, she'd been writing, scribbling and compiling information like a woman possessed. She constantly asked herself the same question over and over again: what was the one single uniting factor that every dating website out there had in common?

First, of course, any website required a new user to register a profile, whereupon, in theory at least, that user's compatibility score would be ranked against any potential matches. As far as Iris could see, each individual website seemed to have its own marketing strategy, and consequently, its very own tailor-made market. MatchedUp.com, for instance, appeared to be for 'getting back out there again'. Divorcees and people just emerging out of long-term relationships tended to feature predominantly here, as Iris knew to her cost. On the plus side, these users tended to be serious daters, but on the flipside, they'd frequently been hurt badly and were left carrying a considerable amount of baggage.

To this day, Iris could vividly recall being on a date with a guy she'd met on that particular site who appeared to be perfect for her on paper, but who turned out to be a newly separated dad with a six-year-old daughter. Naturally the poor child was confused, upset and angry at the fact that Mum and Dad were no longer together; who could blame her? However, matters were not helped when her father decided it would be a good idea to bring her along on one of his very first dates with Iris. They were at the zoo, as it happened, and every time her dad zipped off to buy tickets or ice creams or treats, the little girl would turn angrily on Iris.

'Who are you, anyway?' she'd ask crossly. 'Why are you even here with us? You're not my mum! I don't like you, you look mean. You look like the wicked witch in

Maleficent. I hate you! Why can't you just go away? I want my dad all to myself!'

A perfectly understandable position to take, in Iris's view.

Then there was a site by the name of Elite Over Forties, who charged a premium amount to join, far more than any other site out there, and who based their entire marketing strategy on the hook 'friends first, then maybe more'. Likewise, Make New Friends, which again was perfectly fine if you'd just moved to a new city or country and wanted to expand your social horizons. But where did that leave a user like Iris, she wondered, a committed dater who at least wanted to know, when embarking on a relationship, that it had the potential to go the distance? What if you were after a proper life partner, and not a new friend, thanks all the same?

Mature Singles, meanwhile, was marketed at users aged sixty plus, and appeared to be predominantly composed of widows and widowers who were seeking out companionship, really, more than anything else. At one point, thinking she had nothing to lose, Iris had gamely given it a whirl, but sadly without success.

'I'm looking for someone to go to the bingo with,' a potential date had said to her. 'And maybe to a nice tea dance on a Sunday afternoon. Nothing too late, mind you, I like to be home in time for the Angelus.'

Now Iris was nothing if not an equal opportunities dater, and firmly believed in giving every man out there a chance, no matter what his age. This, however, was a bridge too far, even for someone like her.

Then there were a whole plethora of websites which were quite strict about targeting college graduates only. They actively touted it and bragged about it, almost like it was some kind of entry policy in a nightclub. Initially, Iris had high hopes here, given the maths degree and Masters from Oxford she herself was the proud holder of. Sadly though, over the course of several none-too-pleasant experiences, she quickly learned that this lot tended to be by far the worst when it came to out-and-out cheating. Almost as if the fact that they were high achievers in all other walks of life conferred a sense of entitlement on them, a *droit de seigneur*, giving them a free pass to do whatever they wanted with whomever.

Oh, these men were quite open about it, too, with no qualms whatsoever. Iris had lost count of the nights she'd sat at a table opposite a guy whose conversation went along the lines of, 'now don't be put off by my wedding ring, my wife and I are actually separated. We still live together, of course, but that's only for the kids.'

Really, who did these people think they were fooling?

Lastly, of course, there was probably the mother of all online dating apps out there – the mighty FixedUp.com. To be avoided like the Black Death, in Iris's view. As far as she could see, FixedUp appeared to be 10 per cent about age, 40 per cent about geographic location and a whopping 50 per cent about looks, looks and looks again.

Its algorithm, as far as she could glean from a perfunctory glance, appeared to run on a similar system to the Elo rating system – exactly the same method used to calculate the skill levels of chess players. You rose in the ranks based on how many people swiped right on ('liked') you, which in turn was weighted based on who the swiper was. It sounded complicated, Iris thought, but in reality, this was exactly like being sixteen and back in co-ed school again. The most popular guys got to pick and choose the most popular girls, and vice versa, whereas everyone else had no choice but to make do with who and whatever came their way. FixedUp may have pretended that their 'personality quiz' counted for something, but they were kidding no one.

So what about users like me, Iris wondered, who aren't exactly supermodel material? In her long and bitter experience, your self-esteem took a battering when no one swiped right on you, and if you had a single brain cell, you got the hell out of there and deleted this particular app ASAP.

Much later on that same night, Iris was still at her desk in the office, working away and utterly absorbed, when a door slamming directly behind her firmly jolted her back to where she was.

'Look at you Iris, the last to leave, as ever,' said Paul, the company CFO, as he pulled on a thick overcoat and grabbed an umbrella, finally on his way home.

Iris looked blankly up at him, probably the first time she'd torn her gaze away from her desk all evening.

'It's almost ten o'clock,' Paul said, looking at her with sympathy. 'Isn't it time you called it a night? You've been here since the crack of dawn, even earlier than me.'

To her astonishment, when Iris glanced out the window, it was pitch-dark outside. Night already? She'd barely even noticed.

'Oh,' she said, coming back to her surroundings. 'I'm just . . . working on a project here . . . I'd lost all track of time.'

'You probably shouldn't stay too much later, though,' Paul said, looking at her a bit worriedly. 'Security will be trying to lock up shortly.'

'Ten more minutes,' Iris said. 'Promise.'

'You know, at this rate we'll have to promote you to the board of management,' he added cheerily before heading for the lift. 'Well, have a good evening, see you bright and early.'

As he walked away, Iris's gaze drifted after him. Paul was exactly forty-nine, she knew, married with three kids, who he bragged and boasted about every chance he got, and with the kind of lifestyle anyone would crave. On the surface, Paul appeared to have it all: the six-figure salary, the fantastic career, an address in the most desirable part of the city, as well as a holiday home down in Wexford. On top of all that, he was a perfectly likeable person – he and Iris had always got on well, and appearance-wise, he was what anyone would consider attractive. Were he single, and not a happily married man, someone like Paul would be classed as a 'catch'.

But on the algorithm that Iris was slaving over every hour God sent? Given the calibre of user she was hoping to attract to this particular site?

He'd score a paltry six out of ten, max.

Chapter Five

Connie

'*Take me up the mountains and shag me sideways?*'

'Oh, you dirty, filthy-minded aul' bastard! Honestly, is this what passes for a gentleman on a website like this? Revolting carry-on altogether. Shame on you.'

Connie had spent the whole evening on her iPad, tap, tap, tapping away on the GreyingDater website and honestly, some of the fellas who'd 'matched' with her would nearly turn your stomach. Sure look at this aul' eejit here, she thought disgustedly. A farmer in his late seventies, and in the very first personal message he'd sent Connie, there was no hello, no how are you, not a bit of it. Instead he was straight down to brass tacks, inviting her up to his secluded farm in the back of the beyonds 'for fun and games. Be prepared to be ridden ragged!'

The dirty, filthy-minded article.

Connie had only been on this rubbishy aul' dating site for about a week and so far, she'd been approached by the greatest shower of chancers you ever came across. The very first fella was a man in his late sixties, who told her straight out that his wife would be out of the house between 9 a.m. and 5 p.m. weekdays, 'so you can call around to me for a bit of the other, when she's working behind the tills in Spar. She'll never know a thing!'

What a charmer, Connie thought wryly. God love the poor wife; don't I just wish I could ring her up and tell on him? Serve him right.

And then there was another halfwit who went by the username **Ever Done It In The Back Of An Audi?** Seriously. Connie nearly passed out when she saw it; she took one look at the name and that was the end of your man.

What in God's name had happened to the whole world of love and romance, she wondered, abandoning her iPad and letting her thoughts meander. OK, so she'd been 'off the market', as they say, for a very, very long time, but had things really changed all that much in the meantime?

She thought back to how she'd first met her late husband Jack, the love of her life. All the way back in the 1970s, when she was just a young one, no older than her daughter Kim was now. Back in those days, certainly down in West Cork, where Connie was from, you went to discos and parties and if a fella liked the cut of you, he asked for your phone number, simple as that. No messing around with multi-dating and all the nonsense that went on these days. Then you'd wait and hope and pray that he did ring, and if you were anything like Connie, you had your whole family demented asking them twenty-four hours a day, 'Were there any messages for me when I was out? For the love of God, will you all start writing down messages?!'

It was impossible to try to explain to the likes of Kim and her friends that back then, you had one landline in your house, shared by seven people, and that's if you were lucky. Answering machines? Sure they were only for millionaires.

Anyway, Connie had first met Jack at a tennis club dance in Skibbereen, not far from the small town where she grew up in West Cork. He'd asked her up to dance for a proper slow set (to a beautiful song called 'I'm Not In Love' by 10cc,) and that was the end of that. She knew, she just knew that this lovely, funny, kind-hearted fella was the one for her.

Jack was only starting out as an apprentice electrician back then, but he was hard-working and driven, and on the brink of moving to Dublin to get even more work and grow his little business, when he met Connie. So when they first got engaged and then married, of course she upped sticks and moved with him. Poor old Jack, Connie thought, as her eye drifted onto a photo of the two of them taken at Kim's graduation nearly five years ago now. How handsome he looked in the photo, and how proud they'd both been of their only child that day. And there was Kim in the middle of them, with that cheeky little gap-toothed smile and the big, roundy faceful of freckles on her. Kim had only gone and got a first-class honours degree in applied and computational mathematics, whatever the hell that was, Connie hadn't a clue then and still hadn't now. Sums, she'd tell anyone who asked. 'Ah, you know our Kim,' she'd laugh, 'she's a demon for the aul' maths!'

All she knew was that her daughter never seemed to do a single tap of work the whole way through school or college, just spent her whole time going out to parties and nightclubs and what have you. Yet she still flew through all her exams and had now landed a great job for herself in a company with a funny name down in the International

Financial Services Centre along the quays, where she did something to do with maths and numbers all day long.

In fact, that graduation photo of Connie and Jack had been taken shortly before he died, Connie thought sadly, still staring at it as yet another pang of grief came over her. One of the very last happy days they'd had as a family before Jack passed away. A sudden, massive aneurysm and the poor man was taken from her in a blink, just like that.

'Even if he'd done a CAT scan on the very morning he died,' the family doctor had tried to reassure Connie at the time, 'nothing would have shown up. There's no early-warning system for something like this, it's just . . . most unfortunate, that's all.'

If this was meant to be some kind of a comfort to her, she'd thought bitterly, then it was well wide of the mark. She honestly thought she'd never get over the shock of losing Jack. Nothing worse than a sudden death, that's what everyone told her, and weren't they right? It had been a dark, awful time for her – and it still was, to be perfectly honest.

Grief never really went away, did it? It just got a bit more bearable; that was the best you could hope for. Grief took everything from you – sure any zest for life Connie might have had was long gone. These days, she never wanted to go anywhere, see anyone or do a single thing – in a strange, funny way, going out almost felt like she was betraying Jack. If she had a good time or, God forbid, laughed, it was even worse; all she could think was, 'Jack would have loved this. He should be here with me, enjoying all this. Not sitting in his little urn above the telly.'

Only for Kim, she'd be a goner.

Kim was such a great girl, she thought fondly; a real live wire as Jack used to proudly brag, 'Small in stature, but big in personality!' Wasn't he always showing off her great exam results to anyone who even crossed the threshold of their house? The neighbours must have been well sick of us back then, Connie thought, with a wry little smile.

She would have loved a bigger family, but Kim was to be their only child, not arriving until Connie was well into her forties, beyond the age where she even thought she could have children. Truth be told, she was four months gone before she even realised she was pregnant at all; she'd mistakenly thought this was the menopause, or perimenopause, or whatever the hell you called it.

Then along came Kim, her 'rainbow baby', as all the medics called her. Her miracle child. For Connie and Jack, Kim was the light of their lives, and now that Jack was gone, the girl had been an absolute angel. The sacrifices she'd made in her own life, just to make sure that Connie was safe and minded and looked-after! Sure, what daughter would have done more?

Kim was only twenty-six, and with her highfalutin job she could easily have moved out of the family home and got herself a nice little flat somewhere. But she didn't; she stuck with her old mammy and was a huge help when it came to paying all the household bills, even handing Connie over a few quid every week, now that money had got so tight.

'Buy yourself something nice, Ma,' she'd often say, shoving an envelope stuffed with cash Connie's way, and

Connie was always so grateful to her. Towards the end of his life, poor old Jack had made a few investments that hadn't gone too well, to put it mildly, so she only had her tiny widow's pension to fall back on – the money Kim brought in was what kept the show on the road.

In fact, it was Kim who'd first encouraged her mother to join up with a dating site in the first place. 'Come on, Ma,' she was forever nagging, 'you have to get back out there again! Sitting home looking at the four walls night after night is going to melt your brains if you keep it up for much longer.'

Truth to tell, Connie wasn't all that pushed, really.

'I'm not taking no for an answer, Ma!' Kim kept insisting. 'At your age, it's about companionship more than anything. You need to meet new people and start enjoying your life again.'

'But I've got plenty of friends, love,' Connie had protested weakly.

'Never any harm to widen your circle though, is it?' said Kim, who had the biggest social circle of anyone Connie had ever met. Honestly, the girl was out seven nights a week, and she seemed to exist on about two hours' sleep a night. Where she went, Connie hadn't the first clue. And where did she get her energy? She seemed to live off takeaways, scraps of oven chips, the odd Cornetto and not much else.

'You should be going off on holidays and cruises and playing golf and in active retirement groups,' Kim would harp on at her, time and again.

'But I hate golf,' Connie would protest.

'That's not the point, Ma, it's about making a fresh new start in your life. You're only seventy-one, and by today's standards that's really young. Dad wouldn't want to see you like this, cooped up at home, doing nothing and going nowhere.'

'Excuse me, missy,' Connie had said to her, mock annoyed. 'Are you calling your mother a big aul' mopey-drawers?'

'Course you're not a mopey-drawers,' Kim had said gently. 'But still, Ma. Here you are, home alone, night in, night out. When was the last time you went out properly? Even just to see a show or go to a movie with one of your pals? You're stuck in a rut, and we need to get you out of it. There has to be more to life than this, doesn't there?'

♥

Just then, another message pinged through for Connie on that aul' GreyingDater website. A Nigerian prince, this time, saying he had a legacy he wanted to leave to her, and if she'd kindly forward on her bank details, he'd transfer her the cash. Honest to God, what class of a roaring eejit did these scammers take her for?

She didn't bother reading any more, just flung the iPad away in disgust and went into the kitchen to make a nice soothing mug of tea. Kim could lecture her all she wanted about 'getting back out there again', but she'd had quite enough of all the eejits and messers and con artists who were approaching her, thanks all the same. Besides, she liked being at home with her own company; what was so wrong with that?

Mug in hand, she went back into the living room and turned on the TV. Nothing; only boring aul' soap operas were on, and she wasn't following any of them. She glanced at her watch; it was just gone seven and it was a grand, mild, sunny spring evening. Too early to go to bed, and yet what to do with the whole night stretching ahead of her?

The house seemed even lonelier now that Kim was out, and God knows when she'd be home again – not till the wee small hours, probably. Kim would often leave the house at the crack of dawn, then go out straight after work and not get home until well past midnight. Sometimes Connie only got to see her daughter when they bumped into each other on the upstairs landing, when Connie was going to the loo in the middle of the night and Kim was only just crawling home, with more than a few drinks inside her. The girl would crash out on her bed for a few hours, still in her 'going out' gear, then spring out of bed at six the next morning and bolt out the door to do it all over again.

Bored off her head, Connie snapped off the telly and flung the remote control down onto the sofa beside her. She could always ring her pal Betty to see if she fancied a walk, or else maybe just popping over for a nice glass of wine and a chat. But then, as Betty was always at pains to tell her, 'I'm a working girl these days, you know, and I can't just drop everything to go out and socialise midweek, with an early start in the morning. Maybe we can meet at the weekend? If I'm not too exhausted, that is.'

Honest to God, the way the woman went on, you'd swear she was up there running the EU with Ursula von der Leyen, and not volunteering in a local charity shop.

Connie would dearly have loved a job herself, not only to bring in a few extra quid, but also to pass away the days, which all seemed so long to her now. When Jack was alive, she'd worked as a waitress in Flynns hotel in town; she was there for decades, as were most of their loyal staff, and she'd loved every day of it. Not great money, but the tips were good and the camaraderie among all her co-workers was brilliant. Connie used to love bouncing in and out of the hotel, mainly for the chats and the laughs they'd all have. Honestly, most of the time it felt like being paid to hang out with your pals, rather than putting in a day's work.

But then the hotel had been sold off a few years ago, Connie and her pals were made redundant and it was heartbreaking. No one seemed to care that the staff had just been left high and dry. They had a miserable little farewell party just before the hotel doors closed for good, and apart from Jack's funeral, Connie honestly thought it was one of the saddest days of her whole life.

Of course, she'd tried very hard to get work somewhere else, even just a few part-time hours a week, anything at all, really. But she was quite rudely told that she was well past retirement age, so that was the end of that.

Here I am, she thought sadly, home alone with a pot of tea and a packet of Jaffa Cakes with the whole night stretching ahead of me and nothing to do but watch boring old telly and a load of repeats. Same as the night before and the night before that, too. And what had she to look forward to for the rest of the week? Doing the big shop in Tesco's at the weekend? Party on, as Kim would say, rolling her eyes.

Was this it, she wondered? Was this all that life had in store for her from here on in?

She sighed deeply, picked up her iPad again, put on her reading glasses and reluctantly went back onto the GreyingDater website. Maybe Kim was right. Maybe there was more to life than this. Maybe it was finally time to get back out there again.

Dear Blue Eyed Garsun, she wrote, finally getting around to answering one of the many messages she'd been sent. *Very nice to hear from you. Like you, I'm widowed, so I can sympathise with you on your sad loss. However unlike you, I'm only on this site to make new friends, not to 'reawaken your inner sex beast', as you so romantically put it. Honestly, what would your late wife say if she saw what you were up to, and her only gone three months? Where's your sense of shame?*

Chapter Six

Iris

1. What is your idea of perfect happiness?
2. What is your greatest fear?
3. What is the trait you most deplore in yourself?
4. What is the trait you most deplore in others?
5. Which living person do you most admire?
6. What is your greatest extravagance?
7. What is your current state of mind?
8. What do you consider the most overrated virtue?
9. On what occasion do you lie?
10. What do you most dislike about your appearance?
11. Which living person do you most despise?
12. What is the quality you most like in a man?
13. What is the quality you most like in a woman?
14. Which words or phrases do you most overuse?
15. What or who is the greatest love of your life?
16. When and where were you happiest?
17. Which talent would you most like to have?
18. If you could change one thing about yourself, what would it be?
19. What do you consider your greatest achievement?
20. If you were to die and come back as a person or a thing, what would it be?
21. Where would you most like to live?

22. What is your most treasured possession?
23. What do you regard as the lowest depth of misery?
24. What is your favourite occupation?
25. What is your most marked characteristic?
26. What do you most value in your friends?
27. Who are your favourite writers?
28. Who is your hero of fiction?
29. Which historical figure do you most identify with?
30. Who are your heroes in real life?
31. What are your favourite names?
32. What is it that you most dislike?
33. What is your greatest regret?
34. How would you like to die?
35. What is your motto?
36. What is the last cultural experience you had?
37. Describe what is, for you, a perfect date.
38. Describe your relationship with your parents.
39. What would instantly put you off a date?
40. How long was your longest relationship?

Well, now, Iris thought, feeling particularly proud of the work she'd done so far. *This should most certainly sort out the messers from the more serious candidates.*

Forty questions, all requiring forty incredibly well-thought-out answers. Nothing less would do. And it all went back to Marcel Proust, thank you very much. In the late nineteenth century, the series of questions Iris had based her whole dating algorithm on was actually a parlour game Proust had invented, very popular among well-to-do Victorians, apparently. Hard to believe, but evenings spent sitting around the fire posing questions like these were what passed for a great night's entertainment in the age of gaslight and horse-drawn carriages. *Mind you, an evening of parlour games certainly couldn't be much worse than some of the nights out I've had recently*, she thought ruefully, thinking back to that last dismal date she'd been out on almost six weeks ago, in early April.

The less said about that, the better.

Iris had worked bloody hard on this project, and the next step now was to road-test it properly. She'd designed it painstakingly, methodically working out an algorithm that she confidently predicted would match up users based on personality similarities with over 84.8 per cent accuracy. So of course, what she really needed was to discover where all the flaws and weaknesses were, so that each and every one could be ironed out. Every single dating app out there had its fissures, and she needed to know precisely what hers were.

Other than that, though, she figured that her app was in pretty good shape, all things considered. As always, Iris had been nothing but thorough from day one. She'd already bought a domain name and everything, and planned on posting her brand-new app, along with its freshly designed algorithm, to both Apple and Android just as soon as she possibly could. After all, why not? Why not just 'put it out there', and see what users could possibly be attracted? Best-case scenario – maybe her app would improve the lives of others. And what was wrong with that?

Iris, being Iris, had done her homework thoroughly. She knew only too well that there was a whole publishing process involved here. Of course, it went without saying that she'd have to get pre-approval from one of the big tech giants. After all, she wanted her app to reach the widest possible market, and this was by far the best way to go about it. Due diligence would have to be applied, from any reputable tech company's point of view, and given the hundreds and thousands of wannabe app designers who targeted them on a daily basis, you could imagine the sheer length of time that was bound to take. Weeks, in most cases, and woe betide if there was as much as a single technical glitch in your app; in which case, you would be instantly rejected.

This is for all the people like me out there, she'd remind herself every time she felt too exhausted and bone-weary to put in a few more hours of work. *This is for the unloved. This is for the ones who rarely get any messages or replies whenever they sign up to any new dating site. This is for the people who get stood up regularly. For the disheartened and the disillusioned. For the ones who've hit their forties and who've had enough of all this dating nonsense and who are finally ready to throw in the towel. For the ones who've lost sight of their end goal and who are starting to believe that there's no one out there for them, no one at all.*

This is for you, Iris thought, night after night as she forced herself onwards, ever onwards. *I'm doing all this for you, even if it kills me. This is going to work, and this is all for you.*

Apart from eating, sleeping and going into the office, working on the app had become her 24/7 obsession. She'd had no break, no time out, no nothing. Since she started work on the project, she hadn't even stepped out the door at weekends, not even to go to her beloved gym classes, which normally she disciplined herself to attend religiously. In fact, now that Iris thought about it, what other kind of a social life did she have to speak of? What social outlets did she have, otherwise? When did she really ever get invited anywhere, by anyone?

Not that she was someone who allowed herself to wallow. That did absolutely no good for anyone, ever. Iris had lived her life in a tough school for the emotions, and so Christmases, New Year's Eves and birthdays spent by herself weren't that much of a challenge to her really. Certainly not now that she was so used to them.

And she was used to an awful lot more besides. She was used to coming into the office on a Monday morning and overhearing all the chat about whatever fabulous party everyone else had been at over the weekend. She was used to everyone – and by that, Iris really did mean everyone, from board level down to the newest, lowliest and humblest intern – being invited to thirtieth, fortieth, fiftieth birthday parties, weddings and, more often in this fine spring weather lately, just casual, relaxed weekend barbecues in some colleague or other's garden. Lovely, celebratory gatherings that everyone had been asked along to – literally everyone except her, that is.

She genuinely didn't understand why no one seemed to like her or why she was so deeply unpopular. All she knew was that it was ever thus, right back to when she was in primary school. People seemed to get the wrong idea of her . . . or maybe she just rubbed them up the wrong way? Who knew? She was a grown adult at Oxford University before she really found true friends who she connected with. Before she 'found her tribe', as it were.

But a partner, Iris knew deep down, was the perfect antidote to all of this. A perfect, wonderful partner, who hopefully 'got' her, just as she would hopefully 'get' him, whose life blended in perfectly with hers, who supported her in her work and who celebrated all her milestone achievements, just as she would his; wouldn't that just make life worthwhile?

There was still much, much work to be done. But at this exact point, Iris felt a fresh surge of energy and pride at how well the project seemed to be shaping up. There was just one critical outstanding thing she needed to finally get her up and running.

Test pilots. The dating equivalent of guinea pigs. Two, preferably, would be ideal. First, one in their twenties, to test out the younger end of the market, and secondly, another older 'guinea pig', significantly older, if possible, to try out the sixty-plus age bracket. It had to happen the minute Iris's app went 'live', so that any and all teething problems could be dealt with efficiently and quickly, before – hopefully – users signed up in larger numbers.

Of course, in an ideal world, all of this would be done long before the app launched, but there, unfortunately, Iris hit her very first roadblock. She needed real live actual users on her dating app interacting with other real live actual users, because that's how the world of dating worked, didn't it? Of course, she could spread the word around the office and invite her colleagues to sign up free of charge, but then what good would that do? In that case, you'd be stuck with people who knew each other too well trying to flirt with each other on a dating site, and that would be mortifying for all concerned.

No, she decided, having given this conundrum a lot of thought. The only way for her to get accurate feedback on her site was to launch it, and in those precious early days, engineer it so she had her 'dating guinea pigs' already on the app from day one, testing it out for her in the way the site was designed to be used. That way, at least, any issues which arose she could stamp out right away, hopefully before the site really started to attract a respectable amount of users. Hopefully.

Romantic 'test pilots'. Finding them might have sounded like a simple enough task, but was actually far from it. Who to ask? Where to turn? Iris racked her brains, and this worried her late into the night. Could she possibly ask someone within her own family? Don't be funny, she thought, immediately dismissing the thought. Her mum had passed away when she was just a teenager, and as for her dad, she'd never really got on with him to start with. In the intervening years, he'd married for a second time and moved to the South of France, where he certainly never troubled her too much by keeping in contact.

Whole years went by with just a Christmas card from her father, and aside from that, nada, nothing. Iris had never even met his new wife; she'd been away acing her Oxford postgraduate exams at Magdalen College when the wedding took place. And that's how it all panned out in the Simpson family; her dad went ahead with his small registry office wedding in Nice, or so Iris heard, with her new stepmother's two daughters acting as witnesses. Meanwhile, Iris herself went through the rituals of her graduation subfusc without anyone there to support her, the only person in her entire year who had to be told exactly what subfusc meant in the first place. (The dark colours of a gown and mortarboard, apparently.)

'You're absolutely fine by yourself, Iris,' her dad had said to her over the phone, on the morning of both his wedding and her graduation ceremony. 'You don't need me there with you, you don't need anyone. You're the most independent person I ever met. You're the human equivalent of a self-cleaning oven. Always were, always will be.'

Other graduates were gifted holidays, cash, even brand-new cars to mark this huge milestone in their lives; Iris got a three-minute-long phone call, comparing her to a self-cleaning oven.

Hard to believe, she sometimes thought, that somewhere out there I have a stepmother and two stepsisters, who I literally couldn't pick out of a police line-up.

And that effectively summed up her family for you.

The answer, or at least, part of the answer to the guinea pig conundrum came to Iris one sunny lunchtime in late May out of a clear blue sky.

It was one of those days when, come 1 p.m., most of the Sloan Curtis staff had drifted out onto a particularly inviting rooftop terrace which the office proudly boasted, and which was often used for corporate functions. It was a glorious afternoon, and as Iris stepped out onto the rooftop, no one invited her to join their table, so as usual, she took a quiet seat all alone in the shade, unnoticed by anyone. All she had with her apart from her laptop was a bottle of sparkling water and a light, protein-based lunch consisting of lean chicken breast and a side of leafy kale. But then Iris was nothing if not pragmatic when it came to food, seeing it fundamentally as fuel to keep her working the kind of hours she did. She didn't mind that no one greeted her or even looked up at her; she'd only come out here to clear her head, get some fresh air and do a little more work on her algorithm project.

From where she sat, she could hear the cheerful, raucous sounds of the younger team members, squished in together at one of the long wooden bench tables, laughing, messing about, stuffing their faces with sandwiches and joshing with each other, full of the joys of this fabulous early-summer's day.

Quelle surprise, Kim Bailey was the centre of attention. How in God's name, Iris frequently wondered, did the girl manage to do that? Always at the heart of the gang, always the focal point, always telling stories that effortlessly entertained every single person present? What made it particularly noteworthy was that Kim's gang of co-workers, Iris knew from bitter experience, were a particularly difficult crowd.

She herself was their direct line manager and had a tough enough time holding this lot's attention in important meetings. She'd frequently try to communicate a vital facet of data-processing info to them, only to look out over a sea of eyes glazed over, staff doodling on their notepads or else twitching, fidgeting, gazing out of the window – basically looking anywhere except at her.

So what on earth, she wondered with a sudden pang, was Kim Bailey's secret? Or was this what real charisma looked like close up? Half of Iris wanted to cut the girl down to size, and yet the other half was . . . well, if she was being brutally honest with herself, there was only one word for it. Envious.

Iris sat quietly with a bird's-eye view of what was going on, watching with interest as Kim Bailey wove her tale, skilfully building to a crescendo, yet somehow managing to gain more and more laughs along the way. Honestly, there were stand-up comedians out there who hadn't a bald patch on this girl.

But then Iris overheard exactly what it was that Kim was saying and suddenly her attention completely shifted.

'So do you remember yer man I actually managed to have a reasonably normal first date with last week?' Kim was asking everyone.

'Remind me again which one he was?' said Greg from Statistics, a tall, sports-mad guy, who frequently took leave from work so he could run marathons. So bulked out was this Greg, in fact, that Iris had long suspected anabolic steroids were involved.

'Yeah!' laughed Hannah Davison from Purchasing, that innocuous Donegal girl who Kim seemed to be so utterly inseparable from. 'There's such a high turnover in your love life, Kimmy, it's easy to get confused!'

More laughter around the table, which Kim silenced with just a wave of her wrist. 'This was the same fella I met in Grogans last week,' she said, her voice ringing out loud and clear, 'and for once, I actually had this perfect night with him – we chatted the night away and got on like a house on fire. It was actually hilarious, I kept having to touch the guy like he was some kind of unicorn. He really seemed to be that rare thing – a halfway decent guy, who was funny and attractive and normal. I mean, when does that ever happen? To me, anyway?'

'Ahh, now, Kim,' her best friend Hannah said over muted laughter, as the whole gang sat waiting for the big punchline. And with Kim Bailey, there was always, always a big punchline. 'Your stories are only funny when they go arseways. When does Unicorn Man turn out to be a cross-dresser, or else a serial killer? Or maybe someone who strangles kittens at birth?'

'Wait till you hear, I'm only warming up,' said Kim, and in spite of herself, Iris was keenly tuning in. She disguised it by burying her face deep in her laptop, but in actual fact, she was listening attentively to every word.

'Anyway,' Kim went on, 'he asked to meet me yesterday evening in the National Gallery.'

At the mention of the National Gallery, even Iris sat up, impressed. If any date asked *her* to meet him at the gallery, frankly she'd have thought they were off to a pretty promising start. Mind you, she would have thought a cultured man was a bit wasted on the likes of Kim Bailey, but like everyone else, she sat quietly and waited for the Big Finish.

'Well, the last time I was at the gallery was on some kind of a boring school trip years ago,' Kim was saying to her adoring little fan club. 'All I can remember about it is sneaking outside in the pissing rain for a quick tin of cider with the rest of the dossers in my year. My idea of art, then and now, is to lash a coat of paint on my mother's hall door for her.'

Predictable titters at that.

'So anyway, me and Unicorn Man meet at the main entrance yesterday evening,' Kim went on, 'and, at his insistence, we start off in the portrait section – he's the one leading the way, mind you, I'm only trailing after him, wondering if there's a bar in there somewhere. And by the way, in case any of you are wondering, the answer is no.'

Yet more laughs. Really, Iris thought. Boasting about being uncultured, bragging about treating a national treasure like the National Gallery as some kind of bar extension. Was this really the standard of employee here? And every one of them on fantastic salaries, too. From here on in, she decided, making a firm mental note, that she'd mention to the board of management, screening at interviews needed to be significantly more thorough.

'So after a while,' Kim said, 'I notice all this guy is doing in room after room is videoing some of the paintings. Not all of them, mind you, just a select few. "Wow, you're some keen art lover," I said to him, but then I notice that the only paintings he's snapping and videoing are all the nudey ones of big-busted women. Any portrait of a man, or a fully clothed woman, he just sails past, almost like they're invisible to him.

'So I ask him straight what he's up to. "Do you not see the jugs on this?" he says to me, as we're standing in front of one of those Pre-Raphaelite jobs, you know, where you've got a nude woman reclining. I thought I'd misheard him, so I say, "I'm sorry, what did you just say?" And on he goes about how full-breasted women are what do it for him, and that's what he really loves about all these Renaissance paintings.'

Different period entirely, Iris mentally corrected her. The Pre-Raphaelite movement lasted from the 1850s through to the end of the nineteenth century. The Renaissance was, in fact, three hundred years earlier.

Ignorant girl, she thought crossly.

'So then he comes to a painting of these two leggy girls in ballet dresses,' Kim went on to a rapt audience, 'and honest to God, the guy starts salivating over them. "Get a load of this," he says, "Legs AND big knockers. My ideal woman."'

Two Ballet Dancers in a Dressing Room by Edward Degas, Iris thought. She could even have told you precisely what room it was hanging in in the gallery, but like everyone else, was holding out for the end of the tale.

'Now there's all these long benches in the gallery,' Kim is saying, 'for anyone who fancies a little sit-down to admire all the art and whatever you're having yourself. So he walks on ahead of me, into a roomful of even more nude women, and no kidding, he's sitting gaping at all the boobs on show, camera out, the whole works. Now as you are no doubt aware, I've met more than my fair share of loonies, weirdos and pervs over the years . . .'

Indeed we are all well aware of that, thank you very much, Iris thought waspishly. *You remind us of that every single day.*

'But this tulip is by far the worst yet,' Kim said. 'So here we are in this beautiful, long, elegant room, we're the only two people in it, and there's my wack job date, staring at a reclining nude, with his hand in his trousers, like, deep down in his trousers. Like very, very, very deep down . . .'

'Oh, dear Jesus, don't tell me . . .' says her pal Hannah, shoving away the remnants of a half-eaten egg sandwich in disgust. 'I think I can guess what's coming.'

'And I am not making this up,' Kim says, 'but the guy is actually, I believe the politically correct term is "pleasuring himself", right slap bang in the middle of a public space. Well, my stomach turns and I say to him, "Hey, perv boy, you are aware that there's CCTV cameras pointing at you?" And do you know what he says back to me? "This is art appreciation, baby, and if you had any sense of artistry, you'd join in."'

A wave of catcalls and disgusted groans from around the table.

'I am NOT making this up!' Kim said, over the racket. 'Can you believe it? Well, I'll tell you, I was out of there like a hot snot—'

Now there were raucous guffaws and gales of laughter as someone shouted, 'Tell me his name, Kim, so I can keep an eye out for him on the nine o'clock news, being dragged into court on sex offence charges!'

By then, though, Iris's thoughts had moved on as an idea began to form.

Maybe, she thought, as she looked at Kim with fresh new eyes. It would be mortifyingly embarrassing asking her, but then on the other hand, where else was she going to find anyone more suitable for her purpose?

And really, when it came down to it, what other choice did she have?

Chapter Seven

Kim

A performance evaluation review?

Well, this stinks to high heaven, Kim thought, when she first got the message saying she was to report to Iris's office immediately after she'd finished up work for the day. She wasn't due a review for months, for starters. Was she about to be given the third degree over some huge financial analysis case she'd made a major mistake on? Kim was working on several just at the moment, and of course, she might have slipped up somewhere along the way, without even realising it. Nothing would be beyond the eagle-eyed Dreadnought Iris to spot – and subsequently give you hell over.

Still, this was weird beyond words. For one thing, Kim thought she was on target with most of her work reports. Her clients seemed reasonably happy, and she certainly wasn't aware of having neglected anything that might come back to bite her in the arse. So why did the Dreadnought Iris want to see her so urgently?

Her heart sank as the most likely reason struck her. Because maybe, once or twice maybe, she'd come into work stinking of booze and, ahem, maybe not as . . . fresh-faced . . . as she might have been. Kim certainly hadn't been unpunctual, mainly thanks to her mother yanking her out of bed at seven every morning on the dot, but . . . well, still. The Dreadnought Iris was famous for missing absolutely nothing; if the old witch could find fault with you somewhere along the way, then she surely would.

As the time drew nearer, Kim mentally prepared herself and girded her loins. In fact, the more she thought about it, the more it made sense that this was a bollocking for living such a party lifestyle, when the Dreadnought Iris expected every single employee to be just like her: married to their job, first in and last home every single day.

And she probably won't be happy till I end up exactly like her, Kim decided, when the end of the day finally rolled around, as she did the 'walk of shame' all the way down the office with every single eye sympathetically following her, before steeling herself to rap on Iris's office door. *Just as sour, wizened, cranky and miserable as she is.*

'You wanted to see me?' Kim asked, nervously sticking her head round Iris's door.

'Ahh, there you are,' said the old she-devil, whipping off those horrible oversized pointy glasses she always wore and swivelling her office chair away from her desktop computer. 'Come in and sit down. You might want to close the door, too. This is very much a private conversation.'

Kim did as she was told, thinking, *bloody hell*. The only other time she was ever invited to sit down in Dreadnought Iris's office was on the day she was interviewed for the job.

Silence. Iris even got up and paced over to the window, staring down on to the street below. Still more silence.

Fuck, fuck, fuck, Kim thought. *My arse is so fired here. Why else would she be acting like this? Like she's grasping for the right words to say to me?*

'Look, can I just say one thing in my defence here,' Kim began, grabbing the bull by the horns, attack, she figured, being the best form of defence. 'If this is about the McKinsey report, I know I mightn't be as far along with it as I'd hoped by now, but it's only because Risk Management came back to me with a whole load of further questions that they wanted answered, so that added two full days onto the project. I'm happy to work late nights this week to get it finished, if you're under time pressure over it?'

'This has nothing whatsoever to do with the McKinsey report,' Iris interrupted. 'In fact, this has nothing to do with work at all.'

'So . . . so I'm not fired then?' Kim asked tentatively.

'No,' said Iris, swivelling round on her black stiletto heel to look at Kim in blank surprise. 'Why would you assume that? Of course you're not fired. Your work is on time and on target, it's completely accurate and I know the board have no issues with you, so therefore neither do I. I repeat; this isn't about work.'

'Oh,' said Kim, feeling almost light-headed with relief. 'Right. I see.'

'This,' said Iris, swivelling back to the window, 'is a matter of a far more personal nature.'

OK, so now Kim was really, seriously flummoxed. Still more silence, and now the Dreadnought had her back to the window, and was rocking on her heels, pursing her lips and looking like she was choosing her words very, very carefully.

'I happened to overhear your conversation at lunchtime today,' Iris said straight out. 'As you were telling your colleagues about, let's just say, a date you'd been on at the National Gallery that went wrong. Very badly wrong.'

'You heard that?' Kim said, not having a clue where this was going. Was this some kind of new work policy, maybe? No more discussing your private life in the office environs anymore, for fear it might momentarily distract you from the life-or-death business of financial analysis, risk assessment and uncertainty evaluation? Knowing fecking Iris, Kim thought ruefully, you wouldn't be surprised.

'Of course, I wasn't in any way eavesdropping,' Iris said, slowly stepping away from the window and sitting back down again at her desk. 'Far from it. Your personal business is very much your own. Let's just say that your voice rang out loud and clear, and it was very hard not to overhear you when you were in full flow – put it that way.'

Kim's mind raced. Her mam was always telling her she had a voice like a foghorn – could this be what it was about? A possible new office directive, maybe? At all times, speak in dulcet, ladylike tones? Iris herself barely spoke above a low-pitched whisper; you almost had to strain to hear the woman. Was that the new way you were expected to interact around the place from here on in? Was it because she was spinning a yarn about that pervert who she'd caught masturbating right in the middle of the National Gallery, and her crudeness had somehow caused offence, maybe to a few of those fluttery-looking aul' fellas on the board of management?

'It's not the first time it's happened,' Iris went on. 'I have often, on occasion, chanced to overhear you enlivening office discussions with tales from the more colourful aspects of your personal life. Naturally, of course, you are perfectly entitled to do this. My reason for calling you in here this evening was to see if perhaps you and I might share some common ground.'

Common ground with *Iris*? Kim's head started to spin. She doubted it very much, but said nothing, just looked longingly over at the door, wondering when this excruciating talk would be over.

Then Iris sat forward, hands clasped in front of her on her desk, like the prime minister about to do a televised address to the nation. She even had that 'fake sincere' look on her face, which only freaked Kim out even more.

'You see, I too have had occasion to regret how difficult it is to find a suitable partner online,' she said, as the disbelieving part of Kim's brain madly tried to process what she was hearing.

'You . . . do online dating too?' Kim half stuttered.

Iris raised an eyebrow at her in vague surprise.

'Yes, I do,' she replied. 'You imagine that because I'm significantly older than you that perhaps all this has passed me by?'

'Oh, no, no!' Kim rushed to dig herself out of the hole. 'Not at all! It's just . . . well . . .'

'Well, what?' Iris had taken off her glasses now and was looking directly at Kim, borderline hurt. 'You think because I work such long hours that I don't want to have a private life, same as everyone else?'

'Not at all,' said Kim. *No, it's just that I never in a million years thought of you with a boyfriend or husband or a normal family life*, is what she wanted to say. *I assumed, like everyone else in here that you went home at night and drank the blood of orphans around a bonfire, cackling.*

'Anyway, the reason why I brought you in here is this,' Iris said crisply. 'Now that we've established we're both single people who are searching, perhaps we can be of mutual benefit to each other.'

I seriously doubt that, Kim thought, but she stayed silent.

'You and I certainly appear to share a common goal,' Iris went on, 'that of finding happiness with a partner. But preferably a decent partner. From what I've heard you saying, it certainly sounds like you've come across more than your fair share of time-wasters. Well, snap. So have I. My stories may not perhaps be quite as colourful as yours, but still, I can sympathise.'

A horrible, horrible thought began to form at the back of Kim's mind, and once it had lodged there, it wouldn't budge. She started to feel sick to the pit of her stomach at the idea; nauseous beyond words. Mind you, that could also have been the tuna roll with a side of Tayto Cheese and Onion, washed down with two Solpadeine she'd had for lunch earlier as a hangover cure. There was no telling.

Still that thought kept at her. Was Iris queer, or bi, and did she fancy her, and was this whole long-winded preamble about private lives and being long-term single maybe Iris's way of asking her out on a date?

Sweet God, wait till I tell the others, Kim thought.

'So . . . em . . . how can I help you, Iris?' she began to say, choosing her words very, very carefully.

'By going on dates,' Iris replied. 'Lots of dates. Multiple dates. You're of course under no obligation to do so, but rest assured, you would be helping me out enormously.'

This is it, Kim thought, *the scariest woman I ever met in my whole life is asking me out*. What to do, what to say, how to let Iris down gently and kindly? How to explain that she was, in fact, straight? Preferably without getting sacked?

'I would be glad to pay you a small fee for doing this, of course,' Iris went on.

It gets worse, Kim thought, as the palms of her hands actually began to pump sweat. *Way, way worse*. The really weird thing, though, was that Iris was acting so bloody normal about it. Pay her a fee to go on dates? What did the woman take her for anyway?

'But in return, I would need to ask you for feedback,' Iris said, matter-of-factly.

'I'm sorry . . .?' Kim said, flummoxed. 'You want to pay me to go on dates with you, then give you feedback? But . . . why, exactly? Is it that you want to practise your dating skills on me?'

Iris stopped dead in her tracks. Then she looked at Kim for a moment, before putting her pointy glasses back on again, sitting back and sighing deeply, shaking her head.

'Perhaps,' she began to say in that deathly quiet voice, like she was explaining algebra to a five-year-old child, 'I should have explained myself a little more clearly.'

Chapter Eight

Connie

'Well, I've heard some mad aul' stuff in my time,' Connie was saying, 'but this really beats Banagher. Are you having a laugh at my expense, Kim? Is this one of your jokes?'

'I know it sounds nuts, but I'm being deadly serious,' Kim replied, sitting opposite her mother at their long pine kitchen table in their little red-brick terraced house, with its walls that could probably have done with a fresh lick of paint, a plastic tablecloth covering the table and flowery curtains on the windows, straight out of IKEA. She was horsing into a big feed of oven chips, rashers, fried egg and beans, with a clatter of toast on the side; a 'café tea', Connie always called it. Sure it was rare enough that she and Kim ever got to sit down together to eat any kind of dinner at the same time, wasn't it? She might as well load the calories into her while she got the chance.

Wait till you see, Connie thought to herself. The girl would probably be straight back out the door again in jig time, same as always – home for twenty minutes max. Just long enough to get out of her neat little work suit, that she looked so pretty in, by the way, and change into one of those godawful low, strappy tops with glitter and sequins and all sorts of cheap aul' tat pasted on them.

Honestly, she thought, the more tarty the clothes, the more Kim seemed to love them. It could be below freezing outside and she'd still go out in a bra top that was barely the size of a facecloth, along with a pair of those awful leather trousers, or else a skintight minidress that did absolutely nothing for her. And off Kim would go, plastered with fake tan and heavy make-up that she was so much better without. Away gallivanting, God only knew where or with who, till stupid o'clock in the morning.

'Well, I don't think too much of the way that dreadful boss of yours spoke to you today, love,' Connie said, pouring herself out another big mug of tea, because you couldn't have a fry without the pot of tea. 'You read about this kind of thing in the papers all the time. Workplace harassment, that's what they call it. But you have rights here too, Kim, never forget that. What's to stop you going over Iris's head and telling someone more senior than her what just happened? That she called you into her office to give you a hard time about your private life?'

'No, Mam,' Kim tried to say with her mouth stuffed with chips and baked beans, 'you're getting completely the wrong end of the stick here—'

'If I had two minutes on my own with that Iris one,' Connie fumed, in full flight. 'I wouldn't be long sorting her out, I can tell you.'

Connie had actually met Iris once, over a year ago now, at a corporate garden party the company hosted for all the Sloan Curtis staff. Kim had asked Connie along as her guest, which excited Connie no end, and a wonderful evening it was too.

It was held in the beautiful botanic gardens, the weather was fabulous and the hospitality was unbelievable. Free everything, sure Connie couldn't believe her luck. Free bar, free champagne, even those funny-looking cocktails with mad names that the young ones seemed to love were all free. Not only that, but there were a few takeaway vans serving food for the entire evening, including a vegan one, a sushi one, an ice cream one and a good old-fashioned chipper van.

Everyone had got well and truly merry on the freebie champagne, Connie herself included. 'I could get used to this great lifestyle!' she still remembered saying to that Iris one, as they ended up side by side together, stuck making small talk.

To this day, she'd never forget the withering look Iris had shot back at her in return.

'Yes, but kindly remember that hospitality closes in precisely thirty minutes,' she'd said, as snooty and superior as any of the awful nuns who'd taught Connie in years gone by. Then she gave this pointed look to the glass of champagne that, if the truth be told, Connie just might have been sloshing about a bit over the grass.

'Also,' Iris said, eyeing up the now empty glass, 'there is a strict two-drink limit per guest, you know.'

Well, Connie had never felt so mortified in her whole life. She went bright red in the face and glanced around for Kim for a bit of back-up. But of course, Kim was way over by the marquee, in the middle of a gang of her pals, telling some class of a funny story and making them all roar laughing.

Just then, in the nick of time, Kim's dotey friend Hannah came over to rescue Connie. She had been a total sweetheart, steering Connie over to a park bench for a quiet little chat and telling her that Iris was only a wizened aul' wagon and that no one liked her anyway, and that her nickname was the Dreadnought Iris for a very good reason. Not only that, but Hannah even went and queued and got two singles of proper chipper chips from the van, one each for herself and Connie. The pair of them horsed into the chips, had a great chat and in no time, all was well in the world again.

To this day though, Connie only had to hear Iris's name mentioned and her blood ran cold. The snotty cut of her, she thought crossly.

'Ma, I promise you,' said Kim, 'I'm not in any kind of trouble with Iris. All that happened is that somehow, she got wind of the fact that I've been out on my fair share of online dates . . .'

'With eejits, mostly,' Connie interrupted bitterly.

'. . . yeah, and that's what Iris was actually hoping to help me out with.'

'Although if you'd just listen to your aul' mammy,' Connie went on undeterred, 'I'd have you matched up with a grand fella in no time. Someone who we know for a start, from a good, decent home, so you don't get any of your fly fishing carry-on, or whatever you young ones call it.'

'I think you might mean catfishing, Mam.'

'I'm just saying, missy,' she said, 'is that I could have you fixed up with a fabulous fella in jig time, if you'd just trust me. I already have one or two in mind, you know.'

'Oh yeah?' said Kim disbelievingly. 'Like who, for instance?'

'Well, take Betty's son Nigel, now. He's exactly the same age as you and he has a great job in the civil service, permanent and pensionable. Still living at home with Betty, just like you're still living at home with me, so you already have loads in common. And sure he only grew up two streets away from you. Romantic, isn't it? The boy around the corner. And you'd be the girl next door.'

Kim just looked like she was about to gag on a mouthful of baked beans.

'If you'd only give him a whirl,' Connie went on, 'Betty and I think you'd both get along famously. You'd jizz him up a bit, and you never know, he might even calm you down. So much better than going into pubs seven nights a week, to meet total strangers you know nothing about, barring what they tell you online, which I'm sure is lies half the time.'

'Give over, would you, Mam?' said Kim, helping herself to another fistful of chips. 'Betty's son Nigel is not only the most boring man on the planet, but he's a total mammy's boy, too. Everyone around here thinks he's very likely queer, but too terrified of his mother to come out. Can I remind you that you and Betty try to match us up every single Christmas, and it always ends up the same? He starts droning on about his pet topic, the Battle of Waterloo, in mind-numbingly minute detail, and I run away in the opposite direction. Fast.'

'Fine then, madam,' said Connie, folding her arms crossly. 'Stay single. See if I care. But you needn't come crying to me when you're middle-aged and still on your own, that's as much as I'm saying.'

'Anyway,' Kim said, a bit more gently this time, 'I only got onto the subject of dating with you because the thing is, I actually have a bit of news. News that might just involve you too.'

'Me?' said Connie, puzzled.

'Hear me out,' Kim said patiently, shoving away her plate, which, by then, the girl had nearly licked clean. And the little waify size of her, Connie thought. Where did she put it anyway?

'You remember I signed you up to that GreyingDater website?' Kim went on.

'Ahh, here, you needn't remind me, love,' said Connie, rolling her eyes. 'And you can sign me straight back off it again. Greatest waste of time ever, if you ask me. Con artists, Kim love, that's all these online eejits are. Or else total sex perverts. In fact, you can do me a favour and just get that bloody dating site off my iPad altogether. I promised you I'd try out the online dating thing, and I did, and I really, really hate it and now I'm over and out.'

'Yeah, but before I do, there's just one more thing I wanted to chat to you about—' Kim tried to say, exasperated at what a nightmare it was trying to get a word in edgeways with her mother. 'So would you just hear me out for two seconds? Please? Turns out there was a very good reason why Iris wanted to see me earlier. Which involves you, too. If you're interested, that is.'

So now Connie was listening.

'Seems that all this time, Iris has been doing online dating as well as the rest of us,' said Kim, 'except for decades, by the sound of it. And just like you and me, she's met up with her fair share of twats along the way.'

'That Iris one goes out on dates?' said Connie, having a hard time trying to imagine Iris having any kind of a private life at all. The woman just didn't seem like the type, to start with.

'She absolutely does,' Kim nodded. 'Not only that, but she's been through exactly what the rest of us have. Probably worse, if anything, because Iris has been at it for so much longer. She told me she'd had a right few horror stories of her own too, but of course, Iris being Iris . . .'

'Iris being Iris,' Connie said, doing a great impression of her and making Kim smile. 'Sorry, love, you know I try my best to see the good in everyone, but honestly, that boss of yours is in a whole other category altogether. How you and Hannah and all your pals in work put up with her is beyond me. If Iris has been single and on her own for a long time, then it certainly doesn't surprise me. Sure what man in his sane mind would put up with her and all her snootiness and her bossiness? She'd send them running for the hills inside of two minutes.'

'I don't like her any more than you do, Ma,' Kim went on. 'All I'm saying is that this evening she surprised me, that's all. Turns out she's not prepared to take any more crapology from messers online. So I sat there in her office thinking, proper order too. Everyone I know who's been on dating sites has had enough at this stage. Look at your own experience – you've only been at it for a few weeks, and you're already prepared to throw in the towel.'

'So?' said Connie. 'Iris is going to reinvent the whole world of dating, is she? Well, the best of good luck to her.'

'No, Mam, nothing like that at all,' Kim said patiently. 'But she told me she was working on a brand-new algorithm for a new way of dating. It's such a clever idea, too, I only wish I'd thought of it myself years ago and got in there first.'

'Ah here now, love,' said Connie. 'You're speaking a foreign language to me now, so you are. Algo . . . what?'

'Like a computer program, Mam, that's all. But one that knows more about you than you do about yourself. You know, like when you go on Google, and it starts targeting you with ads that you're almost shocked by because of how scarily specific they are to you? That's all because of algorithms.'

Connie had to think about this for a minute.

'Funny you should say that, love,' she eventually said. 'But only today, didn't I get sent an ad for a new pair of bifocals, and the odd thing is that I was only thinking I was due a brand-new prescription and to get new frames. I couldn't understand how the computer seemed to know ahead of me.'

'That's it, Mam. Right there, that's algorithms at work. Or you know when you're on Netflix and you're always saying that you couldn't believe how a movie just happened to pop up that was so perfect for you and so exactly what you were in the mood for, it was amazing?'

'Oh, yes!' Connie smiled now. 'That's always happening to me. It's just great when it does, too. Like you know how

I love Robert Redford? Your dad was always taking me to his movies, and I was so pleased when up popped *Barefoot in the Park* on Netflix for me only the other day. . . .'

Yet again, Kim valiantly tried to get a word in.

'Anyway, Mam,' she said, 'for this to work, Iris needs a few volunteers to try out her new dating site, as soon as she has it up and running properly. Which is where I come in. And you too, if you're up for it.'

'Me?' said Connie. 'If it involves spending any kind of time with that boss of yours, I hope you told her where to go.'

'Did I mention,' said Kim, saving her trump card until the very, very last, 'that we'd both be getting paid for this?'

Chapter Nine

Kim

'Everyone's got an app now, Iris, everyone. Only this morning I got a link asking me to sign up to an app for a tiny little pop-up huckster shop in the train station. Just because I happened to grab a bottle of water there on my way into work. The place didn't exist twenty-four hours ago, and now I'm being invited to join their mobile app. To buy water.'

'Indeed,' said Iris, sitting behind her desk in her light, airy, glass-surrounded office, with its stunning view six floors down on to the quays, utterly absorbed by the screen in front of her. 'Hardly surprising, really. It's now estimated that currently 42 per cent of millennial-owned businesses are using their own apps to drive sales, or else to provide platforms for their customers to use their tools and services.'

Kim nodded, but didn't say anything out loud. *Oh, for feck's sake, Iris*, is what she was thinking in her head though. *Why do you always have to sound like you swallowed a dictionary? No wonder you put any potential partners off you, always so intimidating and superior.* The real irony, of course, was that if Iris would only chill out a bit and relax, it would be such a vast improvement, Kim thought. Because the woman actually seemed OK when she dropped her act and stopped trying to show off how clever she was. *We already know you're the brainiest person in the room*, Kim wanted to shout at her. *No need to keep rubbing it in all the time.*

'The fact that there's such a low barrier to entry for any new app,' Iris was saying, her eyes not budging from her desktop screen, 'does indeed make a successful launch quite challenging.'

'There's, like, literally millions of free apps out there,' said Kim. 'And your one is going to be competing with every single one of them.'

'One point eight million, to be exact,' Iris replied smartly.

'So we need this one to be "sticky",' Kim went on. 'You want users to keep coming back to it time and again, don't you? What we need is for this one to really stand out from the crowd.'

'Naturally I'm aiming for a particularly high active install rate,' Iris replied, completely caught up in tap, tap, tapping on the screen. 'And an equally high retention rate, too.' Then she glanced blankly back up at Kim, who was sitting opposite her, automatically assuming that she hadn't the first clue what it meant. 'You do understand what that means, don't you?'

Kim sighed. She'd loved to have said, '*course I fucking do, Iris, I'm twenty-six, I was practically reared with a mobile in my hand*', but she was in Iris's office after work hours, and bad language and Iris very definitely did not blend.

'Your retention rate,' Kim said politely, 'is the rate of users who install your app, then don't uninstall it shortly afterwards. Which is pretty much the exact opposite to what ends up happening to most apps, particularly the dating ones. You try them out once, and if they turn out to be rubbish, you just delete and move on. Do it myself all the time,' she added, with a shrug. 'Did it just ten minutes ago, in fact.'

'For an app that will charge a nominal joining fee, like this one,' Iris said, sitting back, taking off her glasses and rubbing her eyes, as if they were aching from all the screen time, 'it's perfectly normal to hope for a 50 per cent install rate, which invariably plummets right down to 25 per cent after the first month.'

'Exactly the point I'm making,' said Kim, folding her arms. 'What's going to really make this one stand out? A killer name would be a great start. Any thoughts? 'Cause, as you know, I've been on my fair share of these dating sites, and some of the app names out there would nearly make you vomit.'

'Thank you, Kimberley, for planting that delightful image in my head,' said Iris drily. 'Much appreciated.'

'I'm being serious,' Kim protested. 'Only on my way in here this morning I came across one called Will Dance Privately for You. And, look, here's another beauty, right here,' she added, referring to her phone. 'This one's called, I kid you not, Desperadoes Who'll Date Anything! What a turn-on. I don't think.'

Silence from Iris; just the clacking of her nails as she put her glasses on again and went straight back to her keyboard.

'And another thing,' Kim piped up. 'You need to think about using social media to get the word out there. Can't tell you how important that is for your brand.'

'That,' said Iris, 'I leave entirely up to you. As you can see, I have quite enough to get on with. It would be hugely useful if you could set up Facebook pages as well as both a Twitter and Instagram handle.'

'Facebook?' said Kim, trying not to laugh in her face. 'Seriously? Iris, I'm Gen Z, and to anyone of my generation Facebook is like a dinosaur. The only users you might be able to attract there are your sixty-plus age category. Trust me.'

'And on that note,' said Iris, focusing on Kim again. 'You mentioned that you might have someone that age who'd be willing to come on board? A dating test pilot in that age range would be invaluable to me for feedback.'

'Leave it with me,' said Kim after a pause. 'Let's just say I'm working on it. Oh! And you know what else you need to think about? Your ASO.'

Iris blinked back at her.

'Apple Store Optimisation,' Kim explained. 'Basically, the right relevant keywords in the App Store are what's going to get you noticed in the first place. Drive more users your way. You need a shit-hot title and the right keywords to really make you stand out from the crowd. Take my word for it, the right ASO is basically your secret weapon. And a few killer reviews, too, maybe even five-star ones, will help you out no end.'

'In that case,' said Iris sharply, 'I have no choice but to delegate this side of the project to you. Seeing as how you're "Gen Z", whereas I'm a dinosaur.'

'Oh now come on,' said Kim defensively, 'you know I wasn't calling *you* a dinosaur, I was only making the point that—'

'Well, don't let me keep you,' Iris said briskly. 'If you could have everything I've asked done by this time tomorrow, that would be most useful. Kindly close the office door behind you on your way out. That'll be all.'

♥

'Were you working late again?' Hannah said to Kim, as she finally joined the gang in the bar of the Spencer Hotel, an achingly cool spot which was particularly popular with all the Sloan Curtis gang, as they had happy hour most evenings with beer, wine and cocktails all half price.

The Spencer was just around the corner from the office, right in the heart of the Financial Services Centre, where it seemed every single building was new and glassy and modern, designed by architects out to win major awards. The minute Kim was more or less thrown out of Iris's office earlier, she'd noticed a clatter of missed calls and texts from Greg and the rest of her pals, all along the theme of, 'come on, it's been a shit day and it's drinkies time – WHERE ARE YOU???'

'You never used to work this late before,' Hannah said in that gentle, soothing voice, putting down the glass of white wine she'd been sipping at and looking worriedly over at her pal. 'So what's going on with you?'

Kim peeled off her backpack and jacket and plonked down on the sofa beside Hannah, weighing up whether to tell the gang or not. Then decided, why the feck not? What she'd been working on was hardly the Third Secret of Fatima, now was it? Besides, given the speed she and Iris were going at, in next to no time her friends would be exactly the kind of target market Iris would want to sign up to the twenty-something end of her new dating app. They were all single and already out there dating. They were perfect.

'It's . . . it's a sort of project for outside of work,' Kim explained, 'that Iris is developing by herself. And she roped me in too, because as she told me, in her own Iris-like way, "It has come to my attention that this particular enterprise happens to be your personal area of expertise, Kimberley."'

Kim did a pretty sharp impression of Iris, and no sooner had she launched into it than she had the full attention of everyone around the table.

'So what's your big new project?' Greg from Statistics asked, already changed out of his work suit into his gym gear and trainers, like he was about to sprint out of the door and run a half-marathon any minute. 'Just so you know, it has been noted that you're working late a lot lately, and not coming out on the piss with us as often as you used to.'

'We were all saying it,' said Emma from Risk Assessment, all black eyeliner and Doc Martens and dry sarcasm, while she nursed a margarita, her favourite cocktail. 'Because from where I'm sitting, it certainly looks like we've lost you to the high echelons of the corporate world.'

'And we miss you, Kim,' said Hannah quietly. 'I miss all your funny stories about shitty dates. The shittier the better. I thought you'd suddenly grown a conscience about work and reformed your ways, and now all you wanted to do was work late and suck up to the boss and not be our best friend anymore.'

'As if,' Kim laughed, giving Hannah's shoulder a little nudge. 'That would never happen, and never will. It's far too much craic hanging around with all of you lot, you know that.'

'Seriously, Kim,' said Greg. 'For a while there, we really did think we'd lost you to the dark side.'

'Yeah,' said Emma, staring across the table at Kim. 'You've been staying late at the office every night for weeks now. Since before Easter, in fact. When was the last time you actually came out on the rip with us? You used to organise all our piss-ups, and now we hardly ever see you.'

'So what is this mysterious new project of Iris's then?' said Hannah, puzzled and confused, as Kim called over one of the lounge staff and got another round in for everyone.

'An online course called 101 Easy Ways to Intimidate Subordinates?' Greg piped up.

'Making Grown Men Cry?' sneered Emma.

'A Guide to Bullying?'

'As a matter of fact,' Kim said to the gang, as the whole table seemed to shush, everyone wanting the answer to that one. 'Iris asked me to work alongside her on a new project to do with the whole online dating thing.'

'Iris? Online dating?' said Emma, a bit cuttingly. 'What does that woman want to know about online dating? Or any kind of dating, for that matter?'

'You think maybe she's not entitled to a private life?' Kim asked.

'Oh, come on, you know what I mean,' Emma replied defensively. 'It's just weird wrapping your head around the idea of Iris going out on dates. I mean . . . this is Iris we're talking about. Actual *Iris*. The most terrifying woman on the planet.'

'I always thought of Iris as one of those people who didn't have a private life at all,' said Hannah softly. 'I never thought of her as being, you know, "out there" like the rest of us, searching for the right person.'

'Or in Kim's case, the right person for the night,' Greg joshed.

Kim gave him the two fingers, but ignored him. 'I was well surprised too, I can tell you,' she said.

'It's nearly impossible to imagine Iris with a partner, or any kind of significant other,' Hannah went on. 'I had her down as married to the job. You know the type.'

'Well, it turns out she's not.' Kim shrugged. 'I know, we all think of her as just being a sour, cranky old headwreck with a terrific job, but no kind of life outside the office to speak of. But no, it turns out that all this time, she's been out there dating and trying to meet the right person, just like the rest of us. The only difference is that she has a helluva lot more experience than us, because she's been at it for so much longer.'

'So go on then,' said Emma, 'dish the dirt on this new project. Don't tell me – Iris is going to single-handedly revolutionise the whole world of online dating?'

Was Kim imagining it, or was there a heavy note of sarcasm there? With Emma, there usually was. She chose to ignore it though, as their drinks arrived and she handed over her card to pay. Instead, she took a gobful of the salty peanuts from a dish in front of her and just answered the fecking question.

'Well, you know the way algorithms pretty much determine so much of our lives now?' she explained. 'From the movies and music that we stream to the clothes we buy? Anyway, Iris got completely fed up with the kind of men she was constantly being matched with, because of nothing more scientific than algorithms.'

'God knows what kind of men the algorithms were sending the Dreadnought Iris,' said Greg, grimacing. 'Doesn't bear thinking about it, does it?'

'Now, you see, right there. That's just you being misogynistic,' said Hannah stoutly. 'You're only down on Iris because she gave you a right bollocking over being late with that Flynn Insurance report this week.'

'Well, would you blame me?' said Greg. 'She tore strips off me at our last team meeting. I can't remember ever being so humiliated in my whole life.'

'If it had been a man who gave you a hard time over it,' Hannah persisted, 'I guarantee you wouldn't be down the bar bitching about him afterwards. Come on, Greg, admit it. Don't you think, well, you were in the wrong, and you probably deserved a wee bit of a dressing-down?'

'I actually think fair play to the woman,' said Kim, completely tuning out the brewing tensions around the table. 'I mean, instead of going on rubbish dates and accepting that's the way things are, Iris got up off her arse and did something about it. She only went and designed a brand-new algorithm. With a fancy new app and everything to go along with it.'

'So, what's so different about her algorithm?' asked Greg. 'Why do you think it'll work better than all of the others out there?'

Kim had to think for a minute before answering.

'It's really all in the questions she's asking,' she said, after a pause. 'You know how when you sign up for any new site, they pretty much just take your most basic information, username, age, maybe a bit about hobbies, which most people lie about anyway. After that, it's all down to the photo, as we all know, and photos can be deceptive. Well, Iris is asking questions that go so much deeper than all that shite. You have to really give thought to your answers. You can't fake them. She's asking the kind of in-depth psychology questions that give you a far clearer insight into another human being. She and I have spent weeks having Zoom calls and consultations with this fabulous team at the Psychology Institute, and they've given us such help and insight, you wouldn't believe it. Knock it all you want, guys, but you have to admit, it's a fresh approach. There's nothing like this dating app out there. And I should certainly know, I've tried them all.'

'Sounds to me like you and Iris have got . . . a lot closer in the last while,' said Hannah, looking a bit worried at the thought.

'Nah, no fear of that!' Kim grinned her gappy-toothed smile back at her. 'Yes, she and I have been working side by side on something that has nothing to do with actu-arial work for the past few weeks now. But no, Iris hasn't had a personality change in all that time and no, we're certainly not bosom buddies now, or anything close to it. I have seen a different side to the woman, though. And she's surprising me, that's all.'

'So just to make sure I have this straight,' said Emma in her contralto voice, 'Iris has gone and designed a brand-new dating app? We are talking about the same Iris here? The Dreadnought Iris?'

'One and the same,' Kim nodded. 'And who knows? Maybe it'll work out and be a huge success, maybe it'll crash and burn. But at least she's doing something pro-active. Better than just sitting around whining about only ever meeting up with a load of gobshite losers, isn't it?'

'And where do you come into this?' Greg asked.

Kim gave him a cheeky wink.

'Put it this way: I'm helping out with the digital side of things, but more interestingly, I'll be involved with ironing out any creases in the system in the very early days after we launch. At least, that's the plan.'

'I'd certainly be prepared to give Iris's dating app a whirl,' said Hannah tentatively. 'I've been single for months now, what's to lose?'

'Good on you,' Kim smiled, feeling a fresh surge of fondness for her best friend. 'And just while we're on the subject,' she added, 'there's actually something the rest of you could all help me out with.'

'Don't tell me,' Greg groaned, 'you want me to sign up to the app so I can inadvertently end up being matched with Iris? Jesus, could you imagine? If I walked into a bar and saw her sitting there, I'd have to walk straight back out again. I'd feel it was my moral duty.'

'That's a total case of "the lady doth protest too much",' said Emma witheringly. 'You know what, Gregory dear? I reckon a psychiatrist would have a field day with you and tell you the only reason you're so down on Iris is because deep down you're attracted to her on some level. You're just too thick to realise it.'

'Kindly go and wash your mouth out with soap for even suggesting such a thing,' said Greg mock theatrically, but Kim quickly captured everyone's attention again. As usual.

'A name,' she said firmly and decisively. 'What we need is a killer name to really get this app launched successfully. Something shit-hot. Something fresh and new. Something that catches your eye when you're scrolling through the hundreds and thousands of dating sites that are out there. What, though? I've been racking my brains for weeks now and I keep drawing a blank.'

'Oh God, those dating apps must be a nightmare to name,' Hannah groaned. 'Half of them have the word "love" or "singles" or "cupid" in them and you know what? Seen them all before, and I just tune out. I've been on them ever since I left college and the only guys I keep matching with are all cheaters who call themselves "multi-daters". Like that gives them a licence to go out with several women all at the same time, and make out like there's something wrong with me because I'm an old-fashioned girl who happens to have a problem with it.'

'Couldn't agree with you more,' said Kim, taking a glug of the cider in front of her. 'I'm fed up with the whole thing, too, which is why I'm certainly up for giving Iris's shiny new algorithm a whirl.'

'But you don't have a name yet?' Emma said.

'Nothing decent,' said Kim. 'And my head is melted with it. We need something groundbreaking and original, that really makes users of all ages take a second look. And you're right, Hannah, nothing vomity with "love" or "date" or "single" in there. Been there, seen that. Gotta do better. It's the one thing Iris and I are actually agreed on.'

A silence descended on the table as everyone gave it a serious bit of thought. Kim had just taken another sip of her cider, when it came to her. Just like that, in a flash.

'Guys, sorry about this,' she said, abruptly leaping up from the table, almost knocking her drink over. 'I just . . . remembered something. I have to leave . . . like, right now.'

'Oh, don't tell me,' said Emma, rolling her eyes. 'Back to your new best friend Iris? Back to the office, so you can arse-lick?'

'Give over, would you? It's nothing like that!' said Kim, already pulling her jacket on and scooping up her backpack. 'Look . . . I'll catch you all tomorrow, OK?'

'It's official,' sighed Greg, as she was halfway out the door. 'We've lost her to the darkness.'

'I hope you're wrong,' said Hannah, shaking her head sadly. 'Because whatever Kim is or isn't working on, I just miss my friend.'

On the street outside, Kim fished out her mobile, and as she power-walked straight back to the office, she called Iris's number.

'Kimberley,' Iris answered brusquely, picking up on the very first ring. 'What can I do for you?'

'You're still in work?'

'Yes, as it happens. And I'll be here for at least another hour.'

'Great,' said Kim. 'Stay put, I'm on my way back in.'

'Really?' said Iris. 'You made it clear to me that you'd finished up for the day.'

'Scrap that, I'm working late tonight. Because believe it or not, I think I may have hit on the solution to all our problems.'

Chapter Ten

Iris

It was late one rainy Friday evening, and Kim had gone for a few drinks with that coterie of workmates she seemed to be so inseparable from, when most unexpectedly she burst back into the office, dripping wet, flushed with alcohol and brimming over with excitement.

'Iris, guess what?' she said, practically bouncing off the walls with sheer exhilaration. 'I have it – the perfect name for your app! I don't think even *you* can fault it!'

'And what would that be?' Iris asked. It was well past nine thirty, and she was bone-weary with tiredness. She was just pulling on her raincoat, wondering whether she'd make do with noodles for a late supper, which was all there was to eat back at her house, or else would she splash out and get a takeaway en route home? Decisions, decisions.

What must it be like, she wondered, as she so often did on a weekend night, to be in a normal, ordinary relationship? The kind that so many people took for granted. The kind where you could crawl home, practically sleepwalking from exhaustion, to a loving partner, who'd gone and cooked dinner for you – maybe even waited for you and not touched a bite himself, because he'd wanted to eat with you. Just so he could hear all about your day and chat to you all about his. Did people in loving relationships realise how fortunate they were, Iris often wondered? One thing was for certain, though: after all these decades alone, someone like her would never *not* appreciate such a rare blessing.

'It just came to me now, in the pub,' Kim said breathlessly. 'And I was so excited, I had to run all the way back here to tell you.'

'It's been a very long day,' Iris sighed, taking off her glasses. 'I suggest you tell me quickly, so I can go home. Please.'

'It won't take two seconds,' Kim panted, her hair and jacket soaked right through from the rain. 'Anyway, there I was, minding my own business and having a cider, when inspiration struck. But then booze always has that effect on me . . .'

'Kim! Whatever it is you have to say, I strongly suggest you just say it.'

'OK, OK, OK,' said Kim. 'So, here goes. You know how your algorithm is all about asking each user the right questions, to get the right partner?'

'I am well aware of this,' said Iris wearily.

'And you're basing it on that famous Proust questionnaire? Because it goes so deep and asks the kinds of questions you really have to give a lot of thought to? "No one can cheat these answers, they really have to be thought through properly."'

'Of course I do,' Iris replied, wondering where this could possibly be going. It was so late, she was ridiculously tired, and frankly, if this was just Kim spouting off some drunken nonsense she'd been brainstorming down the pub, then she could really do without it, thanks all the same. God, she could smell the booze from the girl from the far side of her desk. Revolting.

'Well, how about this for a name?' Kim beamed brightly. 'Just one single word. Analyzed.'

'Analysed?'

'Yeah. Analyzed. Good, isn't it?'

Iris said nothing, just stood silently pondering it in her head. Analysed. It was certainly . . . different. She didn't hate it, as she'd hated and instantly dismissed so many other suggestions they'd jointly come up with over the past few weeks. So far, anyway.

'Maybe spelled the US way,' Kim offered, still dripping onto the carpet and trying to sell her idea, 'so it stands out that bit more? I think it'll appeal to all the age categories you're hoping to target, Iris. And it's a play on words, too, because everyone who's signed up to this site really, truly has to be analysed before they can get matched in the first place. So here's the whole baseline for our app: we don't just screen users before dates, we analyse them.

'What do you think?'

More silence. Kim looked hopefully over at Iris, who said nothing, just stood staring into space, completely lost in thought.

'And there's more,' Kim said excitedly. 'If you like the name Analyzed, then how about this? What if our social media logo is a drawing of a human eye, with the app name written underneath it?'

Still no response.

'Iris?' Kim said, worriedly. 'Say something, will you? Even if you hate it, just say something.'

But Iris didn't hate it, far from it. In fact, she'd been in cranky form tonight, but this instantly brightened her whole mood. She liked it, she really, genuinely liked it, and the more she kept repeating the name over and over in her mind, the more it grew on her.

Analyzed. This was it, she thought. This really felt like the start of something. Of what, she didn't know, but of something.

Most definitely something.

Chapter Eleven

Kim

Four weeks to launch

'So here's what I suggest,' Kim was saying, as she and Iris worked side by side together in the office, pulling yet another one of their all-nighters.

'Fire away,' said Iris, glasses on her head, still focused rigidly on the screen in front of her.

'OK, so hear me out,' said Kim, choosing her words very, very carefully. But then, as she'd learned the hard way, you had to approach everything with great caution when it came to Iris, and woe betide if you stumbled over your pitch, or worse, didn't have your facts and figures 100 per cent rock-solid perfect. Iris was eagle-eyed and would pull you up on the tiniest, most minuscule detail, something that may not even have crossed your mind.

'We apply to the big tech giants now,' Kim went on. 'Your Apples, your Androids, all of that malarkey. Because why not? We know the wait to get a response from any of them is a matter of weeks. So in the interim, we keep working on the app as we are now, polishing it and perfecting it. Then the minute we get a response from the giants, we're totally ready to hit the ground running. This way, we can set a launch date for sometime around late June, and our goal is to work towards that. With not a second wasted.'

'I hate to sound pessimistic,' Iris replied, taking her gaze off her computer screen and focusing on Kim now. 'But here's my concern. Supposing the tech giants reject us? What then?'

'Then we have no choice, do we? We go back to the drawing board and we start over. We take their feedback on board, we work on it and we redesign. That's plan B.'

Iris sat back, took a sip of water from the reusable bottle beside her and frowned.

'I dislike plan Bs,' was all she said. 'But then, I dislike failure too. And rejection is something I very much view as a form of failure.'

I've been working shoulder to shoulder with you for weeks now, Kim thought, looking across the desk at her. *You think I haven't noticed?*

♥

Three weeks to launch

'Very Big Moment coming up here! So here we go. Are you ready?'

'Kindly just do it, please. There really is no need to make a fuss or a fanfare.'

Kim rolled her eyes, well used to Iris by now. Jeez, she wondered for about the thousandth time. What did it take to get this woman to lighten up a bit? They were about to submit Analyzed to all of the tech giants and to her at least, this was momentous. To Iris, however, it was just another technicality that had to be got through quickly and efficiently. Like she seemed to get through everything in life.

Working as a team, she and Iris had dotted every single 'i' and crossed every single 't'. No stone had been left unturned. They'd submitted the right version information, as was a prerequisite, their coding seemed flawless, they'd created their App Store listing, they even had an App Store production certificate. Nothing to do now but to trust in the product, hope for the best – and wait.

'But don't you think this is a really special moment?' said Kim, genuinely puzzled at Iris's lack of enthusiasm. 'It's not every day you send off a brand-new app to one of the biggies for approval. This could be the start of something huge! Will we just mark it with a little drink, or something?'

But Iris whipped off her pointy glasses and sighed in irritation. 'Really, Kim, in your world, must every occasion be celebrated with alcohol?'

So Kim had backed down at that and scuttled out of Iris's office with her tail between her legs, as she had to do so often these days. So many times, in fact, she'd lost count.

Two weeks to launch

'Excuse me for a few minutes,' Iris announced out of the blue one Saturday afternoon, when yet again, she and Kim were working in her office, both of them having given up a precious day off to come into work. They were running through the algorithm for about the millionth time, pressure-testing it for any and every possible fissure they may have missed.

'I'll be back shortly,' Iris added bossily, before slipping out.

Kim sat back against the office chair and breathed a big sigh of relief when she had the room to herself. Truth be told, she'd had a late one the previous night, a very late one. She'd gone for a quick drink with Hannah and Emma after work, but then someone, *could have been me*, she thought, suggested going on to the Vice Rooms afterwards. 'Just for the one!' she remembered squealing delightedly as the three of them poured into a taxi outside the Spencer Hotel, in absolutely no rush for the night to end.

Next thing Kim knew, it was ten in the morning on Saturday, her head was thumping, her eyes were bloodshot, she was functioning on about three hours' sleep and for some gobshite reason, she'd arranged to meet Iris at the office that day to put in a few more hours' work. *I must have been deranged*, she thought, dragging herself out of bed, gargling with Listerine to take away the worst of the boozy smell, then knocking back two Solpadeine and somehow hauling herself into Sloan Curtis.

If Iris had noticed anything was up, though, she was far too reserved to say. The two had been working together for about an hour now, and she hadn't said a single word, not even when Kim fumbled over a few figures that she'd normally have been on top of, in the whole of her strength.

Nearly half an hour had passed and Iris was still gone. So where was she anyway? Loo break, Kim guessed, although it wasn't like her to take so long.

Next thing, the office door burst open and Iris swished back in, laden down with a tray of coffee and a pizza from Deliveroo, neatly boxed and smelling garlicky and oniony and bloody mouth-watering.

Silently, Iris plonked the food on the desk in front of Kim, who looked up at her in astonishment.

'What's this?' she asked, puzzled. Delighted, but puzzled.

'Let's just say you seem a tad "tired and emotional" today,' said Iris. 'I've noticed you eating pizza before whenever you've been "slightly less than below par", and I thought you could do with a pick-me-up.'

'You went out and got this? For me?' Now Kim was looking at her, wide-eyed and stunned.

'Just get that caffeine hit into you and eat all the pizza you want. Then we'll get back to the grindstone.'

Wow, Kim thought, gratefully peeling off a pizza slice, and instantly feeling better the minute she'd wolfed it down. 'Thanks so much, I really needed this,' she tried to say with her mouth full. But she'd already lost Iris back to her computer and to the long columns of figures and statistics that were whizzing in front of her eyes.

Just when I think I'm wrong about you, Kim thought, looking over the desk at her. *Then you go and do something like this? Amazing. Wait till I tell the others*, she was about to prompt herself, but then, who'd ever believe her?

One week to launch

'I hate to drag you away from your desk,' Iris said in a low voice, hovering at Kim's shoulder on a rainy, grey mid-morning, when the whole of Sloan Curtis were diligently beavering away. 'So I'm just going to tell you this here. DO NOT overreact, I don't want your colleagues to know what I'm speaking about.'

'Tell me what?' Kim said, looking up at her.

'It appears that we got it.'

For a second Kim had to think, before the penny dropped.

'Jesus. You don't actually mean . . .'

'As of about five minutes ago, the App Store have officially taken on Analyzed. I've just had confirmation.'

Kim clasped her hand over her mouth, to stop her from physically gasping.

'I told you not to overreact!'

'I wasn't overreacting! It's just . . . Iris, this is amazing! If we weren't surrounded, I'd be up on my desk right now doing the happy dance.'

'And while I'm sure that's a beautiful sight,' replied Iris coolly, 'now is neither the time nor the place. Analyzed is ready to go, and that's the main thing.'

'Ready as we'll ever be.'

Chapter Twelve

Iris

Showtime. It was a particularly good, auspicious day, Iris thought, for her app to 'go live', as it were. Her birthday, 29th June. As usual, there were no cards in the post, and the thought of someone sending her flowers or surprising her with an impromptu party actually made her smile with the sheer irony of it. She got a text message from her father in the South of France, wishing her a great day; clearly not sufficiently bothered enough to pick up the phone. On the plus side though, there were more than a few kind texts and emails from her 'tribe' of old college pals. All along the lines of, 'have a wonderful day, spoil yourself rotten and please let's meet up very soon!'

They always said that, and they never did.

Iris had been part of a surprisingly tight-knit little unit of friends back in her happy Oxford days, a quartet consisting of herself and three other women, all of whom had met, quite literally, on day one. All four were high-achieving, straight-A students who'd gained astonishingly high marks in their chosen fields; all were super-competitive and all went on to score coveted places on the college honour roll. The four even had a nickname: The Quad Threat.

On the happy day they'd all graduated, the four had sworn blind that they'd stay in touch. 'We'll always be friends!' they'd vowed. As so often happened though, life somehow got in the way, and work just seemed to take over for each one of them.

Like Ling from Shanghai, a double-maths honours graduate who'd shared rooms with Iris, and who had been snapped up by a top merchant bank based in London. It was one of those spidery, far-reaching companies with tentacles spread across the globe, so Ling had spent the intervening years travelling the world with work. She'd slowly but steadily climbed the ladder and now, to the surprise of no one, she was their Chief Financial Officer, working an eighty-hour week and one of the few women at board level within her company.

Then there was Flora from Perth in Scotland, articulate and highly vocal, who, like Iris, had been a scholarship student, and who had gone on to carve out a career for herself in law, rising through the ranks down at Lincoln's Inn as a barrister, from a humble 'devil' to becoming a Queen's Counsel, and all within the first fifteen years of her career. She'd 'taken silk', as they say, in one of those quirky legal turns of phrase which Iris loved so much. Then, completing her stellar trajectory in the legal profession, Flora had been made a judge only just the previous year, at the ridiculously young age of forty. Flora's glittering success surprised absolutely no one; even back in college, she'd been an absolute whizz at debating and rarely left the Oxford Union hall without the 'best speaker' award tucked securely under her belt.

But Iris's best and closest friend from the quartet had been a mature student called Anna from Belfast, who'd scored a double first in chemistry and applied physics and who'd been the only one of the four who'd elected to stay on at college to study for her PhD. Anna was now Dr Philips, if you don't mind, and had been appointed a lecturer in each of her specialist subjects, the world of academia having effectively swallowed her up whole.

It hadn't occurred to Iris back in those days, but two things had become glaringly obvious in the years since she'd graduated. First, that her three closest friends, just like her, had all been blow-ins. Not one of them had been through Britain's public school system, as had so many of their classmates. They'd arrived at Oxford on exactly the same day, knowing no one and with no personal or family connections whatsoever.

Then there was the most noticeable thing of all about Anna, Iris's particular friend throughout those happy years and probably the closest pal someone like her had ever had. Whereas the others had all been in their early twenties back then, Anna was already forty and had only gone back into full-time education when her marriage broke up and a substantial divorce settlement enabled her to fulfil a lifelong dream of returning to college. So of course today, as Iris was now forty-three, that made Anna sixty-two.

I was looking for a mother figure, Iris now realised with absolute clarity. And who knew? Possibly she still was.

You know I'm just a short flight away from you, Anna emailed Iris that morning, *so why not come over and visit me soon? We're always saying how great it would be to meet up, so why not actually do it for a change? You'd love it here. So much has changed since our day, and yet so much has stayed exactly the same. Here am I,* she wrote, *buried deep in academia. I really need you to visit, so you can remind me of how the outside world actually works. Why not book a flight and just come for a weekend?*

Why not indeed, Iris thought, as she drove through the deserted Dublin streets at 6 a.m. and parked her car in her designated space in the underground car park of Sloan Curtis. What was to stop her? She'd have dearly loved to reconnect with a great old friend like Anna, but somehow work always seemed to get in the way, didn't it?

Were all her college friends single these days, she found herself wondering, as the early-morning news digest that was her current affairs 'hit' for the day went to an ad break. Flora, she knew, was divorced and was now a single working mother down at the Inns of Court with a teenage daughter, but what of the others? Were they all alone and searching, and truth to tell, lonely, just as Iris herself was?

She wondered how they'd each react if she told them that she'd been long-term single, to the point where she'd got so fed up with trying to meet someone she'd gone out there and developed her own dating app. Flora, Ling and particularly Anna were so whip-smart, they could probably have designed an even better app, along with the algorithm to go with it, on the back of a paper napkin during their lunch break. Not even a challenge to them. Would they laugh at her? Ridicule her?

She immediately dismissed the thought. These were good, kind, loyal and supportive women, who'd always looked out for one another. The only thing the four could be faulted for during the course of twenty years was not staying in touch as much as they possibly should have. And maybe, just maybe, her app was something that her old friends might be interested in trying out. They were, if nothing else, precisely the target market Iris had been aiming for. All were smart, successful, professional, educated and cultured – if men as well as women from all walks of life who ticked each of those boxes could be attracted to her app, then it would be game over, she thought.

Game over and job done.

♥

'All set to go live?' Kim asked, sticking her head around Iris's office door as soon as she bounced into work, barging into her office uninvited. She was punctual, of course, but still arriving hours after Iris herself – same as everyone else. 'So how are you feeling today – excited? Nervous?'

I've been awake since about 2 a.m., Iris could have said, but didn't. *I'm nervous. I'm terrified. I couldn't sleep a wink.*

'I'm prepped, primed and raring to go,' was what she did come out with, sounding as much of a bossypants as ever. 'However, we will, of course, wait till after office hours. I hardly need remind you, Kimberley, that we're on Sloan Curtis's time at present, so even to discuss the impending launch would be unethical of us.'

'Oh . . . right . . . of course . . . sorry,' Kim said, looking momentarily downcast. 'I only wanted to wish you good luck, that's all. You've worked flat out, and it's a big day for both of us.'

'I suggest we run through our final checklist after office hours,' said Iris tartly. 'And in the meantime, don't you have the McKinsey file to deliver today? Preferably this morning?'

Kim nodded, looking utterly deflated, and was just about to skulk back out again when from the corner of her eye she seemed to spot something. Right there, where it was plain to see, lit up like a Christmas tree on Iris's desktop screen.

A giant 'Happy Birthday' e-card for Iris, colourful and celebratory with happy-looking cartoon figures dancing across the screen.

'Iris?' Kim said slowly, pivoting on her heel. 'By any chance . . . is today your birthday?'

Iris faffed about a bit and took a sip from the reusable coffee cup beside her, but ducked the question.

'It is, isn't it?' said Kim, smiling. 'Why didn't you say? I'd at least have gone and bought you a card, or something.'

'It's really not necessary,' Iris replied, flushing hot with embarrassment, a most unpleasant sensation. For goodness' sake, why couldn't the girl just drop it?

'Suppose this means you won't be pulling one of your late nights in here tonight, then?' Kim said cheekily. 'I mean, you probably have plans to go out tonight, maybe with your family?'

Silence.

'Or your friends?'

Still more silence, and now Iris was acutely aware that Kim was looking at her with a curious mixture of interest and pity. Whatever it was, it was intolerable and mortifying.

'The McKinsey report?' Iris prompted her. 'At your earliest convenience, please.'

'OK, OK, I'm going,' Kim said, and two seconds later, was gone.

Iris got back to scanning through a list of facts, figures and numbers which she was double-checking for a huge client of the company's – one of their very biggest. She had a momentary stab of something like guilt for being so irritable and waspish with Kim, when clearly the girl only meant well. Kim, she hastened to remind herself, really had been worth her weight in gold when it came to this project. Not even Iris could fault her; she had worked tirelessly with her, side by side, night after night and even occasionally at weekends, too, and her fresh, original take on the whole Gen Z outlook on all matters related to finding a partner online certainly was most refreshing.

After 6 p.m. on launch day, when the office was more or less evacuated for the weekend, Iris began to feel slightly less nervous and a little more in control. This was her time, her best and most concentrated few hours of the whole day, without noise or distractions or conversations or doors banging or endless meetings or phones ringing non-stop. Silence suited her; peace and quiet was good for her.

The quiet lasted for approximately three minutes, before Kim tapped on her office door, calling out, 'You in there? Is it OK if I come in now? Work's over, we're not on office time, and we can do what we like.'

In she bounced, all choppy, highlighted hair falling over her face, already changed out of her work suit and now in a skintight black satin blouse, with what looked like an extra layer of make-up plastered on her.

Going out on the town, Iris thought, taking in the girl's changed appearance at a glance, *just as she seems to do every other night of the week*. Kim had her phone in her hand and waved it right into Iris's face, whizzing round to her side of the desk.

'Just wanted to grab a quick shot of you, as you hit the send key and launch this baby out into the big, bad world,' she grinned delightedly, her enthusiasm infectious. 'Come on then, Iris, go for it! This could well be the day that makes us both millionaires!'

'Although let's remember that financial remuneration wasn't a motivating factor with this project,' Iris said. 'The primary object, may I remind you, was and is to try to help others.'

There it was again, that same punctured look on Kim's face whenever Iris was a bit snippy with her. Christ, she thought, momentarily annoyed with herself. Why was she like this with people? She didn't intend to be so touchy – why did she always come across that way?

She decided it was best to shut up and let Kim take her bloody photo and shake her hand and wish her great success, only drawing the line when Kim asked for a selfie to post on Instagram. *Over my dead body, thank you very much*, Iris thought.

'So here we go,' said Kim happily, 'let's get a photo of you with your finger poised over the key . . . just hovering over send. Come on, Iris, big happy smile!'

Iris sighed and forced a half-grin, which doubtless only made her look fake and insincere.

'How do you feel?' Kim asked, still poking that wretched phone of hers into Iris's face. 'Excited? Proud? Celebratory?'

'Please tell me you're not videoing this. I'm really not in the humour.'

'Oh, right. Sorry,' said Kim, sounding disappointed. 'It's just that this feels like a champagne moment, doesn't it? After all your hard work. Should I run out and buy us a bottle?'

'There's really no need. As of now, we're not quite sure of what exactly it is we've just launched out into the world, so there really is no need to make a big fuss. I'd far rather you didn't.'

'Oh, OK then,' said Kim, looking exactly like a wounded puppy.

'In fact, you appear to be going out for the evening,' said Iris, 'so please don't let me keep you.'

'Well . . . I'm actually due to meet Hannah and the gang over in the Harbourmaster Bar,' Kim replied. 'And I'm dead late. I'm guessing you have plans, too. For your birthday, I mean.'

'Nothing that can't wait. So go on then, off you go.'

'Well, I'll just leave this here for you then, before I head off,' Kim said, filching around in the huge overstuffed tote bag that went everywhere with her and sliding over a neat white envelope, along with a little box of Cadbury's Roses.

'Oh,' said Iris, taken aback. 'What's this in aid of?'

'Sorry – this is so pathetic-looking,' Kim explained. 'I mean, if I'd known it was your birthday, I'd have got you something decent. Like a cake, or flowers. This is only tiny – I just zipped out and grabbed it from the newsagent's down the street at lunchtime. You know how rubbish they are in there. They have next to nothing.'

'Oh,' Iris repeated.

Kim looked at her for a moment, as if trying to make up her mind about something. Then deciding, to hell with it, yes.

'You know, you're more than welcome to join me this evening, if you like?' she said. 'Just for a drink or two? There's only going to be me, Hannah, Emma and Greg, and maybe a few of the lads from Risk Assessment, so you'd know everyone there. If you wanted to, that is?'

'Well . . . em . . . that's . . . em . . . nice of you,' Iris stammered, caught completely off guard.

'Come on, Iris, just come for a little birthday drink? Let us treat you. One drink won't kill you.'

'It's nice of you to offer . . .' Iris began, 'but I'm afraid . . . I can't.'

Why can't I? a voice in her head prompted. After all, she had no plans for her birthday; she was going nowhere and doing nothing. Here was a kind offer – what was to stop her? One quick drink, and no more?

Because it's ridiculous, her sane mind told her, snapping back into action. Kim and her chums were all twenty-somethings, practically children as far as she was concerned. They were all part of a long-standing group of friends who seemed to do everything together. How out of place would it be if their supervisor and line manager just plonked down in the middle of their Friday-night festivities? How awkward for them, and how inappropriate for herself?

'I already have plans, thanks,' she said to Kim, with what she hoped was great finality. *Yes, sure you do*, that same voice in her head nagged at her. *Plans with your laptop, sitting at home on your own, with maybe a sneakily indulgent glass of Sauvignon Blanc and, as a special treat, a takeaway from YO! Sushi.*

Wow. How popular and in demand are you?

'Well, Happy Birthday then,' Kim smiled warmly, on her way out. 'You know I'm around over the weekend, if there's any news on Analyzed. Fingers crossed!'

And seconds later, she was out of there, leaving Iris in the gloom of a rainy June night, all alone with her thoughts. As per usual.

She slid the envelope Kim had left for her across the desk and opened it.

Happy Birthday from the team here at Sloan Curtis!

Well, well, well. Kim had got them all to sign it. Hannah, Emma, even that loud, obnoxious Greg from Statistics – every single one of her work chums. Under extreme duress, no doubt. Iris knew perfectly well they all called her the Dreadnought Iris behind her back.

Still, though. Sad as it may have sounded, this was probably the single nicest thing to have happened to her all day.

She glanced at her desktop, refreshed it and knuckled down for yet one more hour of work, before finally calling it a night.

And she honestly couldn't remember ever having felt so lonely.

Chapter Thirteen

Connie

Connie was delighted with herself. And sure, why wouldn't I be, she thought, merrily humming away, as she carefully dabbed a nice bit of powder on her face along with a slash of scarlet red lipstick. She was wearing her favourite summery dress, too, which was long, pink and flowery and she honestly felt better and more positive about her life than she had done in the longest time.

It was a special day, a real day to remember, or so she hoped. True, she had butterflies deep in the pit of her stomach when she thought of what actually lay ahead. But when she reminded herself that today marked the first proper day's work she'd done in years, it really did put the pep in her step and the smile back on her face. Not that you could call this work, at least, not really. Sure what was she being paid to do but sit and chat? It was hardly the same as being out ploughing a field of potatoes, now was it?

Kim, like the good girl that she was, had even treated Connie to a bit of an aul' makeover at a fancy hair salon in town beforehand, where she'd insisted Connie go for a full head of highlights, as well as a right good chop to go along with it.

'Takes years off you, Mam!' she'd said, paying the nice receptionist at the salon and barely even blinking at the price, which was well over three figures. Mother of God, Connie thought, sure I could have done a home dye job easily at the kitchen sink, for a fraction of that. But Kim had put her foot down, and had insisted.

'I *have* to treat you, Mam,' she'd said. 'This is a real breakthrough day and I'm so proud of you. Not only are you going back to work again—'

'Ahh now, love, don't say work,' Connie had tried to argue. 'Sure all I'm doing is giving you a bit of feedback on your dating appy thing . . . whatever you call it . . . that's all.'

But Kim was having none of it. 'You're being paid to do this, aren't you, Mam?' she'd said, as they stood in the salon's elegant reception area where they had all kinds of fancy coffee makers and where you could help yourself to as many fresh Danish pastries as you liked. 'So therefore, it's work, isn't it? Money in your back pocket. Now what's so wrong with that? All good, if you ask me.'

Afterwards the two of them strolled out of the David Marshall salon together, and Kim had insisted on treating her mam to a lovely Americano coffee in Hogans Bar, right across Fade Street, which was narrow and cobblestoned, stuffed full with restaurants, pavement cafés and flower sellers, every single one of them doing a roaring trade.

'Howaya, Kim,' the barman had called out cheerily the minute they crossed the threshold of Hogans. It was just coming up to lunchtime, and as the place was quiet, he was all over Kim. 'Haven't seen you in here for a while. I hope you're not cheating on us now, with some other, cooler hotspot you've found to hang in!'

Bit cheeky of yer man, Connie had thought, but she kept her mouth zipped shut.

'Don't you worry, Derek,' Kim called back, as she scanned around the place picking where to sit. 'I'll be back in here this weekend and that's a promise.'

'Ah here, love,' Connie couldn't resist lobbing in, raising her eyebrows a bit. 'Is there a single barman in the whole of Dublin that doesn't know you by name?'

'Givvus a break, Mam,' Kim laughed. 'Sure someone has to keep all the pubs and clubs in this town going, don't they?'

'Few nice early nights would do you no harm, missy,' Connie chided her, half joking, all in earnest. 'It's going to be a crazy few months ahead for you with all of this . . . this . . . new online dating . . . whatever you may call it . . .'

'App, Ma. Analyzed. That's what it's called.'

'Well, it's all like a foreign language to me, but I can tell you one thing – you will need to be firing on all cylinders in the weeks to come. You've got all that going on, not to mention the great job you have. That's quite enough for one person. You just listen to your aul' mammy for a change. Bit less partying and a bit more work would do you no harm.'

'Never mind about me, Mam, what about you?' Kim asked, as the two of them settled into a lovely window table for two with a view right out over Fade Street. 'You're all set, then? Today's the day,' she added, with a big cheery thumbs up. 'Your very first proper date courtesy of Analyzed. I'll tell you one thing: he's a very lucky man, whoever this fella turns out to be. How fabulous are you looking, going off to meet him? You'd think you were mid-fifties tops, never mind over seventy.'

'Ahh now, go on out of that,' Connie chided, starting to feel nervous now that the time was getting nearer and nearer. It was only lunch, she reminded herself, just a little bit of lunch; that was it, that was all. One hour and no more. A casual, Saturday-afternoon lunch in a little deli place that Kim had suggested – nothing fancy. No linen napkins, no menus, none of that; this was all going to be as relaxed and laid-back as you liked. Worst-case scenario, she'd thank her date very politely, scamper out of there as quick as she could and still be home in loads of time to watch Ant and Dec later on that evening.

'No need to be nervous, Mam,' Kim reassured her. 'Just remember, I'll be on standby the whole time, hovering, just in case you need to be bailed out. You know the drill – text me if you feel awkward or icky, or if he turns out to be a fecking pain in the arse, and I'll zip in to rescue you, like one of the Avengers. I'm your back-up, and I won't let you down.'

'There's a good girl.' Connie smiled fondly across the table at her. 'You're a great young one, you know that?'

'Come on then,' said Kim happily. 'Get that coffee into you, and I'll walk you to the deli where you're meeting him. And who knows? The second big love of your life could just be sitting there waiting for you.'

There was only one part of this whole experiment that Connie had been less than happy about, to put it mildly.

Which was a few days ago, when that horrible Iris one had insisted on meeting up with her face to face. 'Just so I can talk you through exactly what's involved here,' she'd said bossily down the phone to Connie. 'It's important that I set the parameters for you, Mrs Bailey, before you begin to use Analyzed. That way, there'll be no grey areas. Best all round, don't you think?'

Last thing Connie would have wanted, a 'face to face' with that rude, awful woman. But then she reminded herself that she was being paid to do this, and had she ever needed the extra bit of cash more?

'Just give Iris a chance,' Kim had said to her encouragingly, during one of her 'wolfed back' dinners, when Connie tried to get her to eat as much hearty, nutritious food as she could, before the girl was straight back out the door again. 'Remember that you're dealing with probably the loneliest saddo in the whole world, and then she won't irritate you so much. That's what I always try to do, anyway.'

'Do I really have to?' Connie asked, a bit like a sulky child. 'Could you not just say that I'm . . . gone away, or something?'

'Come on, Mam, that's not like you,' Kim replied, sounding surprised. 'You're the one who's always saying it costs nothing to be nice, and that everyone deserves a bit of kindness.'

'Sorry, love, but I just can't take to Iris. Never could and never will. How you and Hannah and all your lovely pals in work put up with her is beyond me.'

'Well, I'll tell you something about her that'll make you see her in a whole new light,' Kim said. 'Last week when we launched the app, it actually turned out to be her birthday. Anyway, I found her sitting in her office all alone, with no friends, no family, absolutely no one to go out and celebrate with. Iris obviously hasn't a soul in her life at all, which is kind of pathetic, when you think about it. So just let her into the house, throw a cuppa tea and a few McVitie's at her and look on it as your good deed for the day.'

Sure enough, Iris had come hammering on Connie's front door at the crack of dawn last Saturday morning, saying that it was 'convenient for her' as she was 'on her way to the gym anyway'. No word about whether or not this was a good time for Connie, not a single thing. Iris had arrived bang on the dot of 8 a.m., dressed in those shiny black leggings, trainers and a tight Lycra top, things that you saw so many middle-aged women wearing these days, like they were deliberately trying to show off what skinnymalinks they all were.

'Come on in, you're most welcome,' Connie had said, not meaning a single word of it. She was caught off guard, and had answered the door still in her dressing gown, feeling at a distinct disadvantage. Not only that, but a quick peek into Kim's bedroom told her that the girl hadn't come home yet; her bed was unslept in, so she'd absolutely no back-up, now when she needed it.

'Would you like a nice cup of tea?' Connie asked Iris, ushering her into the kitchen and immediately putting the kettle on.

'Only if you have herbal, thank you,' said Iris, glancing around the kitchen in a very disapproving manner, Connie thought, having a good gawp at just how old and tatty and worn the whole place looked. Snooty cow. Iris was tall, tall, tall, and so thin and bony that it seemed the woman was permanently looking down her nose on everyone and everything.

'Only good old-fashioned builder's tea in this house, I'm afraid,' said Connie, hoping it didn't sound like she was apologising, because she most certainly was not.

'In that case, I won't trouble you for anything, thank you, Mrs Bailey.'

'Well then, won't you at least sit down?' Connie said, as politely as she could.

'No, thank you,' the stuck-up madam replied, probably because she didn't happen to like the look of the vinyl chairs. 'I have a hot yoga class in exactly thirty minutes, so this is just a fleeting visit. As you are aware, I need to discuss our arrangement, just to make completely sure that you're crystal clear on what will be required of you.'

'I thought it was all very straightforward,' Connie said, a bit puzzled now. 'All you want is an aul' one like me to test out your . . . dating thingy . . . whatever you call it . . . and then tell you if there's any trouble with it.'

And believe me, madam, I'll be the very first to tell you, she thought, folding her arms and standing proud, determined not to be intimidated by an aul' witch like Iris in her own home, thanks all the same.

But Iris just gave a patronising little snort. 'It's actually a little more detailed than that, Mrs Bailey,' she said. 'As you know, Kimberley and I have been working around the clock on Analyzed for some time now . . .'

'Kimberley?' Connie interrupted. 'Who's this Kimberley when she's at home? Oh, I think you must mean *Kim*.'

There was a tiny head bow from Iris, in acknowledgement that she'd made a rare mistake, but not a word of apology out of her, nothing.

'As I was saying,' she said, 'Analyzed has only just been approved as an official app for Apple iPhone users, so it's vital not only that it's successful, but that it works as smoothly as possible. We all share the common experience of using dating sites that disappoint and that, as you are doubtless aware, is what I'm out to correct.'

'With Kim's help, of course,' Connie said. A bit rude, she knew, but to hell with it, she couldn't help herself. Why shouldn't Kim get full credit for all the hard graft she was putting in?

'Your daughter's assistance is most certainly invaluable,' Iris replied, which mollified Connie a bit. 'But if we could just get back to the point, please? Although I'm supremely confident of the detailed, in-depth questionnaire all prospective new members to Analyzed must complete, we still need feedback. The more, the better. Our app is brand new to the market, and the more information we can garner about how it works now, in these early days, the stronger we'll grow. It's vital that we winnow out the time-wasters from the more serious daters, so as you can appreciate, Mrs Bailey, what's needed here are rock-solid, trustworthy critiques. How else can we know what's working and, more importantly, what isn't?'

'Kim has already filled me in on all of this, thanks very much,' Connie replied, calmly and clearly. Just so Iris knew she wasn't some thick who had to have everything spelled out to her in letters written six foot high. Honestly, she thought. What did she take her for anyway, a complete eejit?

'Yes, of course,' Iris replied, 'but I still felt it important that you and I meet and speak about this. You yourself, Mrs Bailey, would naturally be required to complete the questionnaire too,' she went on, 'so you can be matched as successfully as possible. As already stated, I would require a detailed report from you concerning the whole user experience: matching with someone, booking a date and most importantly of all, the whole suitability of the match. I'm particularly interested in knowing how you find the more subjective questions on our app, such as your idea of perfect happiness, or the virtue you consider the most over-rated. The more complex, tricky questions. And of course, it goes without saying that if you have any issues getting to grips with anything, you have only to ask for help.'

Oh, would you ever listen to yourself, Connie thought crossly. Why did she always have to sound so up herself and superior? Of course, she knew it was mean and unchari-table of her to even think it of another fellow human being, but honestly. Was it any wonder that Iris had been on her own for so long? Seriously, was there a single fella out there who'd put up with that awful, domineering, bossy manner of hers?

Somehow Connie very much doubted it.

'I wanted to meet you today, Mrs Bailey,' Iris was still spouting on, 'to respectfully ask that you not make the mistake of confusing these dates with social occasions. I am very much paying you to work and to pass on the most detailed feedback possible. Therefore I think it quite reasonable to request that you refrain from alcohol consumption while working for me, as it were. Also, it may sometimes feel desirable to you to leave a date early, particularly if it's not panning out as planned. I would request that you not do so. All meetings should at least be of a reasonable length, you do understand?'

Don't drink? Don't leave whenever you want to leave? Connie thought she was hearing things. Was there any limit to how rude this one was?

'As long as you keep at the forefront of your mind that these meet-ups are professional engagements,' Iris was blathering on, totally unaware that she'd caused such deep offence, 'I anticipate that all should go well.'

Then she shot a quick glance down at one of those Fitbit thingies she had strapped to her wrist, the ones that told you your pulse and showed you your emails as well as the time. 'Now if you'll excuse me, Mrs Bailey, I really must dash, or I'll be late for my gym class.'

Two seconds later, she swept out of there like a tornado and was gone, leaving Connie feeling as if she'd just been run over by a double-decker bus. Mother of God, she thought. Why was it that she only came up with all the great things she should have said back to that awful, awful woman the minute she was gone out of her front door?

The smart alec indignation stayed with her for the rest of the whole day, and felt the exact same as when her ulcer was at her.

♥

Back to Hogans Bar, and Kim was looking at Connie half expectantly, half worriedly.

'Ready for kick-off, Mam? Because you know, we really need to get moving here. In my experience, dates get narky if you keep them waiting.'

Connie fumbled around with her lipstick and played for time, before they got up to leave.

'Starting to get a bit nervous now?' Kim said, looking keenly at her.

'A little bit, love.'

'It's only natural, Mam. It's just because this is your first proper date with a single man in, how long? Forty years? You probably had to have chaperones back in those days to keep an eye on the two of you, before you went for a perambulation through the park to take in the air.'

'Less of your cheek, thanks very much, missy,' Connie retorted.

The two of them stepped out of Hogans into the warm July sunshine, and headed in the direction of Nassau Street, which was as busy and crowded as you'd expect on a sunny Saturday afternoon. For some reason, everywhere Connie looked, all she seemed to see were couples, either holding hands or else walking arm in arm together, enjoying every minute in the lovely sunshine. *The whole world seems to be in love*, she thought, which made her smile.

She had a sudden pang of grief when she thought of her Jack, and how the two of them would have been every bit as loved up as any of these young couples, back in the day. They'd had all those wonderful years together; more happiness in four decades of marriage than most people ever got to see in an entire lifetime. Was it a bit greedy of her now, she wondered, to be going back for second helpings? And what would Jack make of all this? She could almost hear his voice going round in her head. 'You're going to meet some total stranger you never set eyes on before in your life? Are you gone soft in the head, Connie girl, or what?'

Steered on by Kim, who seemed to power-walk everywhere she went, they finally arrived at the door of KC Peaches restaurant, one of those deli places where you served yourself from a hot counter, if you were after something decent, or else you just ordered a drink from the coffee bar, which was brimming over with lovely cake slices to go with it.

It was coming up to lunchtime, and peeking through the windows, you could see the place was already packed inside, as KC Peaches grew busier by the second. Hordes of people, all considerably younger than Connie, swished past her and Kim to get inside, while at the same time customers were coming out carrying takeaway bags and boxes with reusable cups of tea and coffee, or else hot noodle pots which smelled delicious and reminded Connie that she was actually starving.

They were in the way now, and needed to move.

'Do I really have to do this, love?' Connie said to Kim, with a note of pleading in her voice this time that had never been there before.

'Yes, Mam, you really have to. You already arranged to meet here, and it would be the rudest thing in the world not to show up. Trust me, will you? I go on dates like these all the time and it's really not a big deal.'

'But look how jammers it is in there,' said Connie, playing for time once more. 'I mean, how am I supposed to even know what this fella looks like?'

'You'll know, Mam. You've already seen his photo. And not only that, but he's going to recognise you too. Come on, you've come this far. You've done all the hard work, you filled out the whole Analyzed questionnaire, and that was a tough enough job, wasn't it?'

'It certainly was,' Connie muttered, as the sound of bus after bus thundering past almost drowned them out. That bloody form was a complete nightmare, is what she could have said, but didn't, for fear of hurting Kim's feelings, when the girl had put so much hard work into this aul' dating thing in the first place. Honest to God, some of the questions were pure mad altogether. Like what do you consider the most overrated virtue? Sure what kind of a question was that? Any virtue at all is a good thing, she'd written in her reply, and Iris could shove it up her arse if she didn't like it.

What is the last cultural experience you had, was another one. Does watching *Agatha Christie's Poirot* count, she'd written in her reply, which as far as Connie was concerned was a telly show that was cultured enough for anyone. Which historical figure do you most identify with, another right head-melter of a question. Who cares, was what Connie wanted to write, but then she thought of Kim, and restrained herself.

Mrs Claus, she wrote, and what did it matter if the woman never really existed in the first place? *You can be sure that she's the one who keeps the show on the road in the Claus household and makes sure Santa gets his act together to keep all those children happy on Christmas morning. Without Mrs Claus, the chances are Santa and the elves would spend most of their time lolling around the workshop, drinking beer from the tins and watching Championship matches.*

'The hard work is over, Mam,' Kim was saying, as yet another bus whooshed past them on Nassau Street. 'Now this is the pay-off. This is the bit you're going to enjoy. This is the fun part.'

Doesn't feel very much like fun to me, Connie thought anxiously, as a lovely young couple brushed against her on their way out of the deli bar, both eating gorgeous-looking ice creams from little containers and seeming so in love, it would have put a smile on her face on any day other than this.

'Mam,' Kim said, warningly now. 'The longer you put it off, the harder you're making it. He's probably in there now, every bit as nervy as you are. Just make a bit of small talk for the first few minutes and you're home and dry.'

'Could we not just . . .'

'So what's it to be? Go in there voluntarily, or else I shove you in?'

With little choice in the matter, Connie blessed herself, gave Kim's hand a tight little squeeze for good luck, took a huge deep breath as if she was about to jump off a diving board into a swimming pool, and without any more of her nonsense, opened the door and stepped inside.

Chapter Fourteen

Kim

Saturday, 5 p.m.

Later on that same afternoon, Kim was back at home, sprawled out on the sofa in the living room, laptop balancing on her tummy, catching up with a bit of work on the Analyzed app. In more positive news, ever since it launched the whole project seemed to have taken on a life of its own.

Users were flooding in. They'd now reached over six thousand, which for a brand-new app, just over a week old, was pretty good going. Feedback was overwhelmingly encouraging too, even though so far it had mostly been word of mouth, from Kim's gang of workmates.

'Hugely well done on Analyzed.' Hannah had smiled at her, warm and generous as ever. 'If I can find a guy who says his last cultural experience was *The Greatest Showman*, then I'll know I'm home and dry. Bonus points if he can sing.'

Her pal Emma was slightly more guarded. 'It's good,' was all she said, nodding at Kim. 'Makes you think. Really think. None of the others do, but this one does.'

'Well . . . thanks,' said Kim. 'Any of the questions driving you nuts, or tripping you up? If there's anything shit about it, you have to tell me. The more feedback we get, the better.'

Emma thought for a second. 'Which living person do you most despise?' she said thoughtfully. 'That should separate the men from the boys. Ditto, "what do you regard as the lowest depth of misery?"'

'And what do *you* regard as the lowest depth of misery?' Kim asked her teasingly.

But Emma said nothing. Just stared off into space for a bit, then went back to her desk. Still waters, Kim thought, certainly did run deep.

The good news was that overall, Iris seemed pretty . . . well . . . OK, really, at the whole way Analyzed was shaping up. You could tell, because she was barking up Kim's arse considerably less than she normally would; always a good sign. She'd confided in Kim that she'd earmarked herself to 'road test' the forty-to-sixty age range, and Kim would be all ears to know how that one would pan out.

Meanwhile she herself was down to give feedback on the younger age groups, and although she was well used to dating online, somehow it felt very different when it was an app you'd actually worked on yourself. More at stake, for starters. What would their users be like? Misfits? Nutjobs? A right shower of eejits, as her mam would say?

Well, there was only one way to find out, which is exactly what she was working on that sunny Saturday afternoon.

5.59 p.m.

Something was wrong, though, weirdly wrong, and it took a moment before it eventually dawned on Kim.

6 p.m.

Where the feck was Connie?

6.01 p.m.

No answer from her mobile. Kim tried calling it repeatedly – nothing. So she left a bright, breezy voice message: 'Hi Mam, it's just me checking in with you. Guess your date must be going pretty well, because you're still not home yet. Givvus a text message, or better yet call if you can, just to let me know how you're getting on. Love you!'

6.37 p.m.

Still nothing – no word, no reply to a single one of her messages, not a sausage. Their living room looked right out over the street outside, in a quiet little residential area where you could hear every passing footstep loud and clear. With every passer-by with a walk even remotely similar to her mam's, her heart leaped and she bounded out to the front door to see who it was.

So far, just a Deliveroo guy, Mrs Mooney from three doors down carting home her shopping in a Tesco's bag, and a guy from UPS Delivery with a giant parcel for Alex across the road, a thirty-something flight attendant with a well-known shopping addiction.

7.21 p.m.

Well, this can only be a good thing, Kim reasoned with herself as she paced around their tiny house, calling

Connie time and again and trying not to get too panicky when the phone wasn't answered. After all, if anything bad had happened, she'd have heard by now. Wouldn't she?

7.22 p.m.

Now a fresh bout of anxiety hit her. KC Peaches, the deli where she'd dropped her mother off all those hours ago, would probably be long since closed by now. Feeling her heart starting to palpitate, Kim googled their land-line number and tried calling it. It rang and rang and was eventually answered.

'Hi there,' she said, a bit breathlessly, 'I really need your help . . .'

'Sorry,' came a woman's voice, sounding brisk, efficient and very definitely Eastern European. 'Now, we are closed. Reopen tomorrow. Ten a.m. Thank you for calling.'

'No, please, just wait one sec before you hang up,' Kim tried to interrupt. 'I wanted to ask about an older lady who was with you at lunchtime . . . short fair hair, in a bright pink flowery dress . . . do you remember seeing her, by any chance? Any idea when she might have left?'

A snort of derision.

'Many, many people here at lunchtime. All seats taken and queues out on to the street.'

'Yes, but this particular lady would have been at a table for two, with a man about the same age . . .'

'Reopen 10 a.m. tomorrow, thank you for call.'

And just like that, she'd hung up.

7.39 p.m.

This felt wrong on so many levels. Nearly eight hours on a lunch date? Kim was pretty expert when it came to this kind of thing – but never, in all her years, had she seen this before. Kim, who had seen fecking everything.

7.44 p.m.

A whole barrage of texts started pinging through. Kim dive-bombed on her phone, hoping and praying this was it, this was Connie saying all was well and that she and her date had gone on for a bite to eat, or maybe she'd bumped into an old friend in town. Some simple explanation to put all of this to rights again.

Hi everyone, looking forward to seeing you all at 8 p.m. Hope we're not barred from The Liquor Rooms after the last time!

Shit, poo and bollocks, Kim thought. Not Connie at all. Instead it was a WhatsApp message from an old gang of her college mates, who she was due to meet up with later on that night. She'd completely forgotten, but she'd definitely be there as soon as her mother materialised. Did she ever need a drink more, after all this shagging worry? Then she reassured herself: her mam was probably in a taxi and on her way home right now and would walk through the front door any minute. Probably.

She messaged back to her pals on WhatsApp.

*Bit delayed this end lads, but I'll see you all later –
and mine's a very large pint of cider, ta.*

Then a random thought struck her. Wasn't it supposed to
be the other way around? Shouldn't it be the parent at home
worrying as to where the feck their offspring had disappeared
off to? How did their roles get reversed like this? A sharp
pang when she thought of all the worry she must have put
her mother through over the years. And now on top of everything else, she had a horrible dose of the guilties to deal with.

7.59 p.m.

OK, this is not good, Kim thought, really kicking herself now.
She had of course closely vetted the elderly man her mum
had been due to meet. Thanks to Analyzed, she was pretty
well abreast of a lot of intimate details about him. She knew
he was a seventy-year-old widower called Ronnie O'Regan,
with a grown-up son. She knew he considered the lowest
depth of misery to be leaving the immersion on all night, and
that under 'when and where were you happiest?' he'd said
his wedding day, all of forty years ago. That single answer
had been the deciding factor as far as Connie was concerned.

'That's exactly what my answer is too!' she'd said,
delightedly. 'The day I married your dad was still the best
day I ever had. I'm going to give this man a whirl, Kim,'
she'd added decisively. 'Doesn't it sound like we really
have a lot in common? Imagine, I'm getting paid to do
this, and I might even meet a nice, decent fella into the
bargain. Isn't that the best thing ever, now?'

8.15 p.m.

Kim knew absolutely everything about this date her mam was going on: the when, the where, the who and the why. But did any of that matter now that her mother appeared to have gone missing? She was cursing herself for not sitting at a table close by her and this Ronnie fella and keeping a close, watchful eye on them at all times. What the feck had she been thinking? She should have stood guard over the pair of them, videoing them on her phone, purely to have something to show the cops, if needs be.

Holy shite, she thought, weak-kneed by now with worry. The cops.

Was this really the way she was thinking?

8.39 p.m.

A flurry of even more texts, but they were all from the gang in The Liquor Rooms, telling her to hurry the feck up.

> **Come on Kimmy, get here quicker would you? It's not a proper party till you're here . . . we need all your funny stories to get the ball rolling!**

My mother might well have been abducted by a serial killer, Kim thought, power-walking out the front door, slamming it behind her and marching along the street until she flagged down a vacant taxi. *And all you lot can think about is getting the stand-up comedian there to entertain you all? Get the feck over yourselves, would you? Some of us have real problems here.*

8.45 p.m.

She gave the driver KC Peaches' address, figuring there was no harm in going there anyway, even though the place was closed, to scout out any neighbouring bars or restaurants or even clubs where her mother might have gone.

Her mother, in a club? Had Kim really just had that thought? Christ, it was like in the past few hours Connie had just had a complete and utter personality change.

9.15 p.m.

In a mad, blind panic by now, Kim was trawling through all the side streets in and around Nassau Street, dropping in and out of literally every single venue that was open, showing them a photo of Connie on her phone and asking something she never thought she'd have to. 'Excuse me, have you seen this woman?'

Beyond caring how it looked, she found herself barging through hordes of Saturday-night revellers, peering through restaurant windows, asking every waiter and maître d' she could find had they by any chance seen a blonde-haired older lady in a pink flowery dress, possibly being bundled into the boot of a car on her way to the Dublin mountains, to be buried alive?

9.58 p.m.

More texts.

Kim! You're dead late – even for you – where are you? Your pint of cider is here, waiting for you!

Kim knew her friends only meant well, but right now, all she could think was, please piss off and leave me alone, the whole shagging lot of you.

10.07 p.m.

Her phone rang and she nearly dropped it, in her fumbling haste to answer. This time it was a blocked number – news, news, news, she hoped and prayed.

'Ciao, *buona sera* . . . I am Luigi . . .'

Luigi? Who the hell was Luigi?

A man's voice, Italian, only very broken English.

'Yes? Yes?' said Kim eagerly, having to turn into a door-way and clamp the phone tight to her ear, so she could hear properly.

'I call you from Pizza Action *ristorante* . . . *È tua madre* . . . it's Mamma . . .'

Kim hadn't a single word of Italian, but she sure as hell understood that one single word, 'mamma'.

'My mother?' she stammered, the breath catching at the back of her throat. 'She's with you? She's OK?'

'*Troppo da bere* . . . she's maybe a little . . . little . . . maybe too much of the *vino rosso* . . .'

Red wine. Her teetotal mammy, who prided herself on only ever having the tiniest snifter of sweet sherry on Christmas Day? WTF was going on here?

'My mum is OK, though?' Kim said, a cold clutch of fear stabbing her in the chest. 'I mean . . . nothing bad has happened to her? She's not hurt or anything?'

'No . . . not hurt . . . but maybe hurting a leetle tomorrow . . . in the head . . .'

'Gimme your address and I'll be right there,' Kim interrupted, hailing down another taxi and hurling herself into the back of it.

Whatever restaurant this Luigi guy was calling her from was deafeningly loud, but in the deep background she swore she could hear a woman's voice belting out 'Top of the World' by the Carpenters.

Which happened to be her mother's signature party piece.

10.22 p.m.

Pizza Action! (the exclamation mark was the least of Kim's worries), was right down in the bowels of Temple Bar, which on any given Saturday night was invariably party central. Tonight was no different, and it took Kim's taxi ages to weave its way through the huge throngs of boozers, revellers, lads out on stag nights and at least three gangs of hen nights, all in a flutter of pink feather boas, veils, plastic tiaras and L-plates.

It was a warm, balmy evening and everyone seemed to be spilling out onto the narrow cobblestone streets, with

146

music blasting out from just about every bar, and the deafening sound of chatter and guffaws of laughter all around. The taxi had ground to a halt, stuck in complete gridlock, so Kim paid him and hopped out, nearly tripping over herself to find this bloody restaurant.

10.31 p.m.

Pizza Action! was bang slap in the dead centre of Meeting House Square, and Kim had to barge, push and shove her way through all the street party crowds to get to it.

She heard the commotion before she saw it.

'*I'm on the . . . la la la laaaaaaaaa . . . then something about looking at the world from above . . . laaaaa di laaaaa . . .*'

She'd have known that voice anywhere. Sure enough, it was a bit more slurred and a lot more raucous than normal, but there was no mistaking who it was. But just then, as she 'excuse me'd' her way through a big gang of lads in Liverpool shirts, all clustered together drinking beer from plastic pint glasses, Kim could have sworn she heard a man's voice.

'Come on, Connie, you've been singing that song for ages now, why don't we give them a duet? Bit of Frank Sinatra and Nancy, sure you can't go wrong with that, can you?'

This time, Kim heard a deep, rich baritone ringing out loud and clear.

'Altogether now . . . *When . . . I first laid eeeeeeeeeeeyes on youuuuuuuuuuuu . . .*'

Finally, finally Kim could see the source of the racket. There was an outdoor seating area right outside Pizza Action!, and even though it was jam-packed, every single eye in the place seemed to be centred on an elderly man with a shiny bald head and a handlebar moustache. He was short, round and jolly-looking, and was standing up on some outdoor bench seating, entertaining everyone there with his rendition of God knows what. He seemed to be doing well, too, getting rounds of applause and even requests thrown at him, but it was only when he moved out of the way that Kim saw who was sitting tucked in beside him the whole time.

There she was. Her mam, slumped over the table with a half-drunk bottle of red wine in front of her and another empty one right beside that. Her mother, always so neat and pristine whenever she was out and about, now with her hair skew-ways, make-up long since rubbed to nothing and eyes half-shut, like she was about to conk out at the table any minute. She was trying to support her head in her two hands, but was barely able to, as it kept lolling forward on her.

Kim wove her way over to her, a weird mix of relief, delayed shock and scarlet-for-you mortification making her feel nauseous.

'Mam!' she yelled. 'What the feck is going on here? How much have you had to drink?'

'Oh, Kim! What a nice surphhhrise . . .' her ma said woozily, sounding as groggy as someone coming round from a general anaesthetic. 'Shhhhhhhhit down and have a little drinkie. Then you can meet Ronnie . . . RONNNNNNIE!

This is her, this is my daughter I was telling you all about . . . come and say hello!'

Next thing, a waiter bustled over, sweating profusely and nearly stumbling over Connie's bag and coat, which had just been abandoned on the floor.

'You are her?' he said to Kim in a voice she recognised. 'Daughter I speak to on phone?'

'Yes, yes, and thank you for calling me when you did,' Kim said breathlessly. 'I was out of my mind with worry—'

'RONNIE?!' Connie screeched so loudly, the restaurant could hear, 'shhhtop shhhinging for a minute and meet my Kim! Still single . . . you know . . . can you believe that?!'

'The mamma have a little too much drink . . . we worry about her here . . . she not well . . . need to go home . . . sleep for long time . . . paracetamol . . . lots of pain drug she will maybe need . . . bucket beside bed . . . *lei non sta bene . . . molto vomito . . .*'

Kim certainly didn't need the word 'vomito' translated for her. 'Come on, Mam,' she said, taking control and strong-arming her mam up into a standing position. 'You've had enough for one night – we are so out of here.'

Connie's head rolled dangerously and Kim needed all the help the poor waiter could give her to struggle towards the restaurant entrance.

'*Nooo!*' Connie screeched at the top of her voice, and every eye swivelled their way, just in case there were a few diners that mightn't have been aware of the drunk woman in the corner making a holy mortifying show of herself. Normally this was the kind of thing Kim didn't give two shites about; many's the time she herself had to be 'escorted off the premises' when she was acting the maggot and out of order. But this? When it was your own mam, it was different and it was minging. They were a sideshow, and you couldn't not be aware that every person in the place was gawping at them.

'I don't *waaant* to go home, Kim!' Connie wailed. 'Me and Ronnie are having fuuun! Doesn't he have a lovely voice? One more drinkie, just the one . . .'

Ronnie was still belting out his aul' fella party piece, but as soon as he realised they were leaving, with Connie yelling her head off, his singing stopped abruptly. Next thing, he was clambering down from the bench he'd been perched on and was straight over to them; round and smiley with the baldie head and the handlebar moustache sitting so perfectly, Kim could tell he must have slept with a hairnet around it. Like Hercule Poirot. He slipped his arm around Connie and tried his best to persuade her to stay.

'Don't go now!' he said, as the poor, long-suffering waiter tried to hold Connie upright and Kim anxiously scanned the narrow street outside for a passing taxi, desperate to get themselves home. 'Come on, ladies, how about one for the road? A little nightcap? You still haven't heard me sing "Born Free" – and that's my signature tune . . .'

Thanking her lucky stars, just then a taxi rolled up, and as Kim and the poor, harassed waiter desperately tried to bundle her mother into the back seat, Kim turned to face the elderly man, old enough to be her grandad. She stood tall, all five foot two of her, horribly aware that every eye was boring into them.

'And you, I take it,' she said frostily, 'must be Ronnie?'

Chapter Fifteen

Iris

Weekends were always the worst for Iris. No matter how hard she tried to fill in the days, she still ended up feeling sad, lonely and utterly fed up by the time Sunday night rolled around. This particular one stood out though, because the previous evening at work, she'd accidentally walked in on an exchange that she wasn't meant to hear, but did. Nasty comments normally didn't bother her. Unpleasant nicknames in work? Water off a duck's back. But this? This one stung. Really, really stung.

Iris had been working late that particular Friday, as per usual, but with the main office deserted and the place more or less to herself, she took a quick moment to slip out to the bathroom on the staff corridor outside. Locked in her little cubicle, next thing she overheard the clickety-clack of heels on the tiled floor, and voices full of excited chat about their plans for the weekend.

Two women. One with a strong Northern accent, which meant it had to be Belinda, the company Head of HR, a brisk, no-nonsense type who was around Iris's own age and who she'd always got on well with. The other woman was soft-spoken and calm, sounding very much like Janice, the company's Senior Cyber Exposure analyst, who Iris barely knew, as she'd only joined the company a few weeks previously.

'So will we just meet up at the party tomorrow night?' Belinda was saying, as they banged cubicle doors, ran taps and generally made their presence felt. 'Or do you want to go for a quickie little drink beforehand?'

'I think everyone is meeting in The Grayson hotel on St Stephen's Green,' Janice said in that quiet whisper of a voice of hers. 'Then it's only a short stagger across the road to The Shelbourne hotel for the party. We have to bear in mind that on a glammed-up night like this, we'll all be in our highest heels. None of us will be able to walk too far.'

Iris flushed the loo and thought no more of it. So, there was a party tomorrow night that she knew nothing about. What was new about that? She was seldom invited to social occasions outside of work, so this was no big deal.

But then she overheard something that stopped her dead in her tracks.

'Paul is really going all out for this big fiftieth of his, isn't he?' Belinda said, stomping her way into the cubicle right beside Iris's and locking the door behind her. 'He seems to have invited the world and its sick dog. Over two hundred and fifty guests, if you don't mind. That's twice as many as I had at my wedding.'

'Oh, apparently he's taken over the ballroom at The Shelbourne and we're all invited,' Janice agreed, raising her voice to be heard over the sound of a hand dryer outside. 'The entire senior staff of Sloan Curtis. Even me, and I'm hardly in the door a wet week. All anyone can talk about is what to get him for a present. Did you get the WhatsApp message about us all chipping in for a travel voucher for Paul and his family? I know his wife Annie is talking about a trip to Mauritius, so we thought a voucher for a travel agent might come in handy.'

No, Iris thought, slowly digesting what she'd heard. No, she most certainly didn't get a WhatsApp message from anyone. Nor did she get an invitation to Paul's fiftieth bash the following night, which apparently all of the senior staff at the company had been asked to. Except for her. Normally, she'd have batted something like that away, but this one really cut deep. She knew Paul well; they'd been hired together, all of fifteen years ago now, and their careers had more or less kept pace with each other. Of course Iris hadn't deluded herself into thinking that they were best buddies or anything, but nonetheless. She'd always thought they'd got on pretty well. That they were allies, and maybe even friends. Yet now he was throwing a huge party and never even thought to ask her.

The wife's doing, maybe? What was her name again, Annie? Iris had a distinct memory of chatting to her at a Christmas party the previous year, and Annie happening to mention that she was a stay-at-home mum. All Iris had asked was whether or not she found that fulfilled her. A perfectly reasonable question, surely?

In fact, now that she thought about it, she'd also possibly passed a comment about how she'd go out of her mind if she was stuck at home with kids, all day, every day. Well, was there anything wrong with that? It was only the truth. Great umbrage seemed to have been taken, though, because Iris had a clear memory of Annie immediately moving away from her and subsequently blanking her for the rest of the night.

Back to the present, and she couldn't stay hiding away in the cubicle forever. So she decided to stand tall and put a brave face on it.

'Hello there, ladies, how are you both this evening?' she said as brightly as she could, washing her hands and splashing water everywhere, in her haste to get out of there as fast as possible.

'Oh, it's you, Iris.'

'Working late again?'

Janice and Belinda were both polite. Muted. But no more than that.

'Have a good weekend,' Iris even managed to smile back at them as she left the bathroom.

Back to her desk in a lonely, empty office, back to the harsh realisation that yet again she'd been overlooked, ignored and left out in the cold. Back to yet another long weekend stretching out in front of her with nowhere to go and no one to talk to. Everyone else on the planet seemed to love their weekends, to live for them, make plans for them, enjoy every minute of them.

But not her. Never her. Ever.

♥

The following day, as the dreaded weekend rolled around, Iris tried her hardest to fill the time as best she could. Same as she did every other weekend. On Saturday morning she stayed in bed for as long as possible, to try and make the day that bit shorter. Got up, made coffee, had a bowl of muesli, then scrubbed her immaculate home from top to bottom, even though it was already gleaming to begin with.

Iris didn't allow dust, dirt, mess or clutter and the bright, airy two-bedroomed town house where she lived in Portobello, right beside the canal, was always pristine. She'd bought it straight off the plans when the property market bottomed out some years ago, and as she'd proudly boasted to all her colleagues at the time, 'a brand-new build in such a central area is a very sound investment and should yield a good return on my capital outlay in years to come. You'd all do well to do as I did, you know. Buying an apartment in this economy is just for losers – they're projected to lose 2.3 per cent of their saleable value over time. You need to get smart, like me.'

She remembered more than a few frosty glances aimed her way after she'd said it, from colleagues who she'd subsequently found out had *all* invested in apartments. Invested big, she discovered. But what was Iris supposed to do about it? She'd only been telling the truth. If they were that bloody thin-skinned, then they really needed to toughen up a bit, just like she'd had to.

With the early part of the morning accounted for, Iris jumped straight into her car to get to her yoga class. There was a bit of small talk with the others in the class both before and after, but it was tough going for her, because all anyone could ask was, 'Any nice plans for the weekend?' 'Busy enough, yes, thanks,' Iris would answer as politely as possible, all the while wishing they could find some other topic to discuss.

She did her weekly supermarket run, loaded up the car and by the time she got home again, it was already lunchtime. *Doing very well here*, she congratulated herself. *You see? Half the day already killed.*

Then, mug of coffee in hand, she kicked off her gym trainers and padded her way into her little home office, which she'd converted the spare bedroom into. A wise move, too, she always told herself. After all, when did she ever have overnight guests to stay? When this was a bedroom, it had never been slept in, not once, so a home office made sense.

She went on Analyzed, as she pretty much did around the clock, ever since they'd first launched. To check in, to update, to make notes, to watch, to monitor, to learn. Just like a new parent with a baby, she thought, with a tiny smile. If she wasn't hovering over the site, then she was busy thinking about new and varied ways to improve and perfect it.

Naturally Iris had done her homework, and knew that for any brand-new app, between five hundred and a thousand downloads a day would be considered respectable. Upwards of a thousand a day would mean you really had something rock solid to work with, and if by some miracle you were attracting from five thousand upwards, then you were seriously on to something potentially very exciting.

So far, Analyzed had been downloaded close to six thousand times. Six *thousand*. She had to blink, she had to keep staring at the screen in front of her, she had to make sure she wasn't seeing things. Six thousand was nothing short of a minor miracle. It was astonishing. It was really something to be very proud of. That meant that, so far, they'd found six thousand lonely hearts out there. Six thousand people who she had the potential to possibly help.

Excited and heartened by this, Iris picked up her phone to text the only other person who she knew would feel as elated by this as she did.

Hi Kim, Iris. News. We're not quite at six thousand downloads yet, but at the rate we're growing, I'm quite confident that we'll get there.

No answer from Kim, but doubtless she had a considerably more hectic weekend than Iris did and wasn't sitting at home, alone and working, with the whole evening stretching out ahead of her.

Ordinarily, Iris dreaded a Saturday night at home. Ordinarily, she did anything and everything she could to try to fill the void, including going on dates with men who she seriously doubted she had anything in common with. Just for company. Just for someone to talk to.

But this Saturday night was different. That evening, Iris treated herself to a takeaway from one of her favourite restaurants, FX Buckley, ordering a delicious fillet steak cooked medium rare, just the way she liked it, with a side of the most indulgent French fries she'd ever tasted, along with a rich, fruity glass of Rioja, from a bottle which had been sitting in her kitchen for months and which she'd been saving for a very special occasion. A complete and utter calorie-fest, she knew, and although she'd pay the price at her gym the following day, for once she allowed herself to relax.

With her tummy full to groaning, she sat back on her elegant cream silk sofa, listening to Rachmaninov's second piano concerto, glass of wine in hand.

She had thought this particular Saturday night would be even worse than normal. She thought she'd be consumed with thoughts of Paul and his big, lavish fiftieth, every single senior staff member from work there, partying away like there was no tomorrow.

Strangely though, she wasn't. As Iris chilled out on the sofa, all she could think was, *right now, there are six thousand like-minded souls out there, lonely and searching, just like me.*

And for the first time in as long as she could remember, she actually felt something approaching happiness.

Chapter Sixteen

Connie

'Wakey, wakey, Ma.'

Connie opened her eyes and peered up, aware that there was someone hovering right over her. Kim, with what smelled like a mug of coffee in one hand and what looked like a large packet of paracetamol in the other. It was hard to be sure, though; her eyes were all blurry and unfocused and the bright morning sun streaming through her bedroom window was actually hurting her head. Oh God, even blinking was sore.

Connie groaned and tried to sit up, but failed miserably. She slumped back on the pillow, and that's when it hit her. The most blinding headache she'd ever experienced in the whole of her life.

'Kill me now,' she said in a growly voice that sounded three times deeper than normal. 'Just kill me now.'

'How are you feeling?' Kim asked, plonking the coffee and tablets on Connie's bedside table. 'Because you sound like Barry White. Or Leonard Cohen. On a bad day.'

Connie tried to string a sentence together, but her mouth was all dry and parched. It felt like she was trying to talk through layers of carpet underlay.

'Oh Kim, love,' she croaked, 'I'm really not a bit well today. I think you might need to ring Dr Maguire and ask her to take a look at me. Maybe I have the flu or pneumonia or something, and that's why my headache is so bad. I can't move. Not a muscle. Every single part of me hurts.'

On cue, their next-door neighbour started to rev up a leaf blower out in his back garden and the noise was deafening.

'Oh, make it stop!' Connie whimpered weakly, thrashing against the pillow and trying to pull the duvet over her head. 'Go out there, love, and for the love of God, make it stop! Tell Oliver next door that your mother is lying here on her deathbed.'

Kim almost snorted laughing.

'I'm being serious, missy,' Connie insisted. 'I really think I could be at death's door, here. In about five minutes you could be ringing for a priest. The laugh will be on the other side of your face then, you cheeky article.'

'Did it occur to you,' Kim said, folding her arms, 'that you might just have a good old-fashioned hangover?'

'This isn't a hangover!' Connie wailed. 'No hangover on earth could possibly be this bad! Maybe this is . . . I don't know . . . maybe the start of a brain tumour?'

'Take it from me, Ma,' Kim said firmly, 'this is what every hangover in the world feels like. Believe me, I know what I'm on about.'

Silence from Connie, as some of the memories of last night began to catch up with her. *Oh, sweet God*, she thought. *Was I really singing? In public? In a restaurant? Did a waiter really come over to ask if there was anyone he could call to help get me home?* And what about that man she had been with? Try as she might, Connie had completely blanked out every single thing about him.

Except maybe for aftershave. She had a definite memory of the smell of aftershave off him. He smelled like coconuts. Nice and clean and freshly scrubbed up. She could remember next to nothing else about him . . . except that he had a really complicated-looking moustache, and that he smelled really lovely when they first met and he stood up to shake her hand. She got the waft of coconuts and thought he must have had a good aul' wash before he came out to meet her. Which was . . . nice, she supposed.

But then the rackety leaf blower from next door revved up again, deafening her and making her poor throbbing head pound.

'Oh, for the love of Jesus!' she snarled savagely this time, most unusual for her. 'Kim, get out there and tell Oliver I'll give him my next week's widow's pension . . . I'll give him anything he wants, if he just stops. For God's sake, it's July, how many dead leaves can there be?'

'Drink the coffee,' Kim sighed wearily, 'take two paracetamol now and then two every four hours for the rest of the day. You're going to feel like shite today, but with a good, carb-heavy dinner tonight, I might actually get my mother back by tomorrow. Not this grouch-bag who can't stop snapping at me.'

Connie racked her brains to try to think of a smart answer, but her brain was on a go-slow. Oh, this was sheer hell; she couldn't even open her eyes properly. Every time she tried to, it hurt. Normally, she loved this little bedroom, with its pink and yellow flowery wallpaper, matching curtains from IKEA and a lovely duvet set with primroses and giant dahlias all over it. Not today, though. Today, just looking at all those bright, garish colours was pure torture.

'You've got to trust me here, Mam,' Kim said, wagging her finger. 'I've had enough hangovers in my time to know what I'm talking about. Coffee and paracetamol right now, and that's not negotiable.'

Feeling weak as water, with her head throbbing every time she tried to move, somehow – with a lot of help from Kim – Connie managed to haul herself up into a sitting position. Kim peeled off two painkillers from the pack and handed her the coffee, which looked and smelled so strong, Connie thought, you could have trotted a mouse across it. But egged on by Kim, she did at least manage a few tiny little sips, to wash down the tablets.

Bad idea. Very Bad Idea.

A minute ago, Connie didn't think she could move, but as a wave of nausea took hold of her, she sprang to her feet, managing to croak just one single word at Kim.

'Bathroom.'

Now. Urgently, she tried to say, but wasn't able to.

Even though Kim tried her best to help and haul her out of the bedroom door, it was too late. Connie turned around to Kim to say something, but all that came out of her mouth was a big, spewing waterfall of vomit. All over Kim, all over her nightie, all over herself, all over everything.

♥

'I'm never drinking again.'

'See that, right there? That's known as the world's greatest lie.'

'No, Kim, I really mean it. Not even a little snifter of sherry on Christmas Day at Betty's drinks party. From here on in, your mother is teetotal.'

It was later that Sunday night, and Connie was sprawled out on the sofa in the living room, with the debris from some pizzeria place in town strewn all over the coffee table in front of her. At Kim's insistence, they'd ordered in a takeaway for dinner, and although in the whole of her strength Connie wouldn't have heard of eating junk food when she could easily rustle up one of her nice Mammy dinners of roast chicken, gravy and all the trimmings, just for today she was too ill to care.

'So do you feel a bit more human now, Mam?' Kim asked her, from where she sat in the armchair opposite, polishing off the last of the pepperoni and mozzarella pizza she'd just had, with enough garlic bread on the side to do a family for a week.

'I hate to say it, love,' Connie told her, 'but actually . . . yes. I'm starting to feel a little bit more like myself now, thanks be to God.'

'Well, that's the best news I've heard all day. You've been like a nest of wasps since you woke up.'

'Oh, don't talk to me. It's a wonder I didn't end up in the ICU. You know, I actually thought I'd die earlier today, and I think it must have been a terrible dose of food poisoning that I had. Sure how else could you explain how sick I was?'

Kim was wiping her fingers on a big lump of kitchen roll to get rid of the greasy, tomatoey stains, but she paused to eyeball Connie when she heard that particular beaut.

'Oh yeah, sure, Mam,' she said drily. 'Maybe you somehow picked up some freak bout of food poisoning that's doing the rounds, maybe that's what was wrong with you. Or maybe it might have had something to do with the gallon of wine you were skulling back last night? Just maybe?'

'Very smart, missy,' said Connie tartly. 'Now be a good girl and turn on the telly. Then you can start clearing up these empty pizza boxes and make your Mammy a nice cuppa tea, while you're on your feet.'

'You certainly look a lot better, after the grub,' Kim said, scanning her up and down like a hangover expert. 'And you're bossing me around again, so you sound more like you too.'

'Compared with this morning? I'm a new woman, thank you, pet.'

'Right then,' said Kim, stretching out for her laptop, which was on the coffee table in front of her, then opening it up and tapping away. 'In that case, time for a bit of work.'

'What? Did you just say work? In my condition?'

'Well, what did you expect?' said Kim. 'Iris is paying you to give her feedback on any date you go on, so now's the perfect time to do it. While it's still all fresh in your mind.'

'Oh, Kim,' Connie groaned, 'why does it have to be now? Just as *Line of Duty* is about to start?'

'No such thing as a free lunch,' Kim said. 'OK, Ma, so here goes. Question one, describe your first impressions of your date. So there you go, a fairly easy one to kick off with.'

'First impressions?' said Connie, looking a bit bewildered. 'Well . . . emm . . . Ronnie was . . . nice, I suppose.'

Kim frowned over her laptop at her.

'Nice?' she repeated. '"Nice" isn't good enough, Ma. Iris is going to need an awful lot more than "nice".'

'He smelled lovely,' Connie added helpfully.

Kim rolled her eyes. 'I'm delighted to hear he didn't stink of stale BO,' she said, 'but how your man smelled isn't really what we're looking for here. What we need to know is exactly what you thought of him when you first walked into that restaurant. In detail, Ma.'

Connie sat back wearily and rubbed at her forehead like it was still at her. 'Well, the thing is . . . I don't really remember, love. And my head hurts. Can we do this another time?'

'Oh, come on, all I'm asking you is to tell me what happened! It was only lunchtime when you met him, you were stone-cold sober then. You can do it, Mam. It's only going to take a few minutes.'

'Well . . .' Connie began warily, 'I do remember we were both really nervous when we first shook hands. The two of us said it to each other at the exact same time and then we both laughed, and that kind of broke the ice a bit.'

'OK, this is a bit better,' said Kim, tapping away on her laptop at speed. 'Keep going, you're off to a good start.'

'So we might have started with a tiny little drink at that place where we first met,' said Connie in a small little voice.

'You started boozing that early in the day?' said Kim, peering over her laptop. 'Wow. Not even I'd do that.'

'It was all Ronnie's idea, though. We'd both been so nervous, he suggested it. A glass of Prosecco, he said, just to chill us out. That's all.'

'OK, you're doing great here,' said Kim, typing away furiously, 'keep those details coming.'

'Well . . . then I'm almost sure we had a second glass each,' Connie said, staring into space, as she racked her brains to dredge up more. 'I remember thinking he put it so nicely. "I've just met a lovely lady," is what he said, "so this second glass is to celebrate that." Wasn't that nice of him, now?'

'Keep going . . .'

'Then . . . I remember we realised neither of us had eaten, so we shared a pot of tea between us and a few sandwiches.'

'And? More specifics, please.'

'I can't be sure, now, but I think I might have had the cheese and onion, because I ended up with fierce indigestion. You know the way onions always play havoc with my ulcer. Dr Maguire is always saying to me, "Connie, when will you ever learn?"'

'Ma,' Kim sighed, really trying to be patient. 'Again, when Iris asks you for your report, I don't think your ulcer is the kind of thing she has in mind.'

'Oh,' said Connie, sitting up, 'and Ronnie definitely had the BLT sandwich. I distinctly remember because we had a giggle over how enormous it was – sure it would easily have done the two of us.'

'Ahh, here!' said Kim, losing it now. 'I have to email this to Iris tonight and when she asks me how your date went, she's unlikely to want to know what kind of sandwiches you both had.'

'Oh, I see,' said Connie apologetically. 'Sorry.'

'So let's get back to this Ronnie,' said Kim, reading off the screen in front of her. 'Question two. Did he in any way differ from the profile he presented to you on Analyzed, and if so, please provide details about said inconsistencies.'

'Different from his profile?' said Connie, confused. 'I suppose that means did he tell any lies I might have caught him out in?'

'Now you're getting it,' Kim nodded. 'So did he?'

'Emm . . . well, on that appy thing he did mention he was retired, but it turns out that he wasn't really telling me the whole truth there,' Connie replied, delighted with herself that she was actually able to remember something useful.

'So he lied on his profile?' Kim asked, her ears pricking up.

'Not in a bad way, though,' Connie said defensively. 'Not like some of those awful dates you tell me about, where married men pretend to be single and it turns out they've wives and a whole clatter of kids. Nothing like that at all.'

'So what was Ronnie's big lie then?' said Kim, frowning. 'Because when I met him, he looked more or less the same as his profile photo and he certainly didn't look like he'd fibbed about his age, either.'

'He told me that he used to work as a professional driver.'

'Do you mean like a courier? Or a private driver for hire?'

'No, I mean a bus driver. On the 38A to Blanchards-town. Imagine me remembering a detail like that,' Connie beamed. 'Even Iris will be pleased.'

'Mam! What Iris is trying to flush out here is online deceit, not what number bus your date drove.'

'Be patient, I'm getting to the point here, love,' said Connie. 'So then Ronnie told me he retired from Dublin Bus, but he hated being home all day, every day with nothing to do. Especially when Barbara died. That's his wife, by the way,' she added helpfully. 'Anyway, one of his friends said he should help him out with a business he was setting up, so that's what the two of them did. And now they run a great little business together. They're nearly turning down work, Ronnie was telling me.'

'What's the business?'

'They run a chip van. His friend Barney drives it and Ronnie helps out with all the deep fat frying. Most of the time, they park it outside big concerts and football matches, but he said they often do a roaring trade at the beach too, in fine weather.'

'So Ronnie said he was retired, but it turns out he's still working,' Kim sighed, abandoning her typing. 'Doesn't exactly make him Richard Nixon, now does it?'

'He promised me a battered cod and a large single next time we go out,' said Connie dreamily. 'Wasn't that nice of him? That was your dad's very favourite chippy dinner, too. Kind of like a sign from above, when you think about it, isn't it?'

'What do you mean, next time you go out?' said Kim, looking sharply across the room at her.

'Turns out Andrea Bocelli has a concert here in Dublin next week, and you know how much I love him. So Ronnie said he'd take me to the show. I was thrilled, I always wanted to hear Andrea Bocelli sing live. Wasn't that a lovely invitation to get?'

'He's taking you to an Andrea Bocelli concert?' Even Kim looked impressed at that.

'Well, not actually *to* it as such,' said Connie, 'but Ronnie said the chip van will be parked right outside and if I sit in the passenger seat beside him with the windows rolled down, we get to hear the whole thing for free. Wait till I tell Betty, she'll be mad jealous. She loves Andrea Bocelli even more than I do.'

Kim folded her laptop shut and sat back, sighing wearily and rubbing her eyes.

'Mam,' she said, 'you do realise what you've signed up for here? That you've agreed to go on multiple dates with multiple men, not just the one?'

Chapter Seventeen

Iris

Barely ten days into project Analyzed and already they had climbed to over twelve and a half thousand downloads. This, Iris thought, wasn't just healthy, or positive, or encouraging – this really meant they had somehow tapped into something pretty special. This meant it wouldn't be long before advertisers came calling. Which meant that, with any luck, she could hopefully recoup some of her start-up costs, which had been considerable. But best of all, it meant that her initial hunch had been right and that Analyzed seemed to be going about the delicate business of matching people up in a manner that, for once, really seemed to work.

That particular morning, even Iris was smiling. She smiled all the way into work, she greeted each of her colleagues with a particularly cheery 'good morning, nice to see you', and when she ran into Paul, the birthday boy, as he stepped into the lift beside her, she even found it within herself to wish him a belated Happy Birthday.

'I hope you had a fantastic celebration at the weekend?' she asked sincerely, as the lift door glided shut and they both stood side by side.

'Emm . . . yeah . . . good, yeah,' said Paul, going a bit red-faced and shifting around uncomfortably, now that he'd come face to face with the one senior staff member in the whole company he'd neglected to invite.

Iris just smiled benignly at him, genuinely beyond caring now.

'How is Annie?' she asked. 'And all the kids? I believe you hope to take a holiday to celebrate your big roundy birthday?'

Again, Paul looked flummoxed and started to sweat a little. 'Yup, yup,' he said nervously. 'That's the plan, all right.'

'Whatever you decide to do,' Iris smiled cheerfully, as the lift arrived at their floor and they both stepped out together, 'I wish you all a wonderful time.'

'Well . . . thanks very much,' said Paul, looking flabbergasted that she was actually being so gracious about it. 'That's very good of you.'

Iris didn't even have to fake her smile, as they parted company on the third floor.

Then, that particular lunchtime, she briefly slipped away from the office and zipped across the road to a very popular salad bar, where the menu covered everything from Asian street food to Iris's personal favourite, a light Cobb salad, made with egg whites, avocado, a Saint Agur blue cheese and a simple Dijon dressing; a good, nutritious, protein-based meal. It was always mayhem at lunchtime, but if you were organised, as naturally she was, you could order ahead and thus avoid the worst of the queues.

Which is where she overheard a most interesting snippet of conversation.

'It's so completely different, it's brilliant!' It was a young woman a few people ahead of her with her back to her, who had shoulder-length light blonde hair and who spoke in a gentle Donegal accent. Without even seeing her face full on, Iris instantly knew this to be Hannah Davison, who worked under her direct supervision and who seemed to be a genuinely lovely person, and a good, conscientious team player to boot.

She was chatting to Greg Wilkinson, who worked in Statistics and who Iris knew to be ambitious, vocal and always outspoken. If there was any kind of team issue going on, there was a 72.85 per cent probability that Greg would be the one to come hammering on her door about it, like an unelected office spokesperson.

'Come off it,' he was saying to Hannah. 'We all know those dating apps are one and the same, and they're all crap. Same old, same old – you even meet the same people on them time and again – or at least, I always do.'

'That's what I thought too,' Hannah said enthusiastically, 'but honestly, Kim is right, this one really does stand out. It's all down to the profile you fill out. It's so minutely detailed, you really have to dig deep and think hard to answer some of their questions. You can't just skim through it, or cheat it, not like on every other dating site out there. I was at it all weekend, but I posted mine up last night and I've already got three matches . . .'

'No offence,' said Greg dismissively, 'but that's really not a lot, considering. On Tinder, you could get three matches within an hour, and that's on a slow night.'

'Yeah, but those matches never go anywhere, do they? Have you ever met a partner there? I certainly haven't, and I've been on it for years. These three Analyzed matches actually sound like they might be promising. Like the guys I'm being matched with *get* me, and I get them too. That's the thing about Analyzed, it does a lot of the heavy lifting for you.'

'So what's different about it?' Greg asked, as Iris silently prayed they wouldn't get served too fast; this was one conversation she *really* needed to eavesdrop right to the end of it. Although she was standing several people behind them in the queue and pretended to have her face buried deep in her phone, so it wouldn't look too obvious that she was straining to catch every single word.

'What's different about this one,' Hannah replied, as the queue inched forward again, 'is that before I even have a conversation with anyone I've been matched with, already I have such a clear picture of them, I feel like we've already met. I know their cultural influences, I know about their parents and family, their hopes and ambitions for the future, what makes them tick, and best of all, what their happiest day was. Amazing how much you can tell about a person by the way they describe their happiest day,' she added dreamily, as Iris kept her head down to try and hide her smile. 'One guy said it was the day he was made godfather to his best mate's little girl. Right off, I know this fella is a family man, committed, loves kids – it could take me months of dating to find out that much, but now I already have that information, before I even go in. Isn't that amazing?'

Just then, their order arrived, so they paid and made to leave, thankfully not spotting Iris in the long, snaking queue on their way out.

God bless you, Hannah Davison, Iris thought, as the two swished past her. She knew for a fact that a lot of senior staff, even some at board level, had already got their eye on Hannah Davison for bigger and better things. But after this? Iris would personally put in a glowing recommendation that Hannah be instantly promoted, and given a good, hefty 10.5 per cent pay rise to match.

The girl had single-handedly just made her entire day.

♥

It was late that evening, and Iris thought she had the office to herself, when Kim unexpectedly bounced in brandishing a final bound copy of the infamous McKinsey report.

Still on a high from the positive feedback Analyzed seemed to be generating, Iris sat back, thanked her very politely for all her hard work, then enquired as to how she'd enjoyed her weekend.

'You're in great form,' Kim said, looking at her in surprise.

'You have, I take it,' Iris replied with a wry smile, 'seen for yourself the amount of downloads we're generating to date?'

'Not too shabby, is it?' Kim grinned back. 'And you know, our hit rate seems to be climbing by the hour. Plus, have you seen some of the reviews we're clocking up? So far, there's nothing less than five stars, which is pretty astonishing for any dating app, let alone a brand-new one. You know what users are like online, they'd savage you over nothing. I once saw a review of a dating site that gave it zero stars because this user was matched up with too *many* dates. If they can find the tiniest thing to whinge about, people will.'

Iris's stomach started to rumble, so she quickly glanced down at her watch; past seven thirty already. That slightly light-headed feeling she had reminded her that she hadn't eaten a single scrap, bar that light salad she'd had at her desk at lunchtime.

'You and I have lots to discuss,' she said to Kim. 'But I wouldn't mind grabbing a bite to eat first, and I'm guessing you must be hungry too.'

'Cool,' said Kim, brightening. 'How about I run down to that new deli along the street and get some takeaway pasta salad there, to keep us going? And two cans of Red Bull? That's my go-to for a late night. Unless you'd like me to order in another pizza?' she added cheekily.

But Iris shook her head and stood up, grabbing her handbag and getting ready to go.

'Never mind pizza at our desks,' she said crisply. 'Tonight, I'm taking you out for a proper meal. In a proper restaurant, and none of your pasta salads or fast food, thank you all the same. This is my treat, and I'm terribly sorry, but it's not negotiable.'

Twenty minutes later, Kim and Iris were both tucked into a gorgeous window seat for two in Soul, a hugely popular fish restaurant where you could never get a table ordinarily, but given that it was so early in the week, they somehow managed to wangle the best seat in the house.

They ordered, and Iris even insisted they both have a glass of wine to go with it.

'Wow, you're really pushing the boat out here,' said Kim, drinking in the plush surroundings, impressed. 'I haven't the first clue about wine, so I'll leave the wine list to you. As long as it's wet and alcoholic, I'm happy.'

'Oh, it's just a small way to thank you for all your hard work,' Iris said, 'and to mark Analyzed getting off to such a great start. Not every day you launch a new app that actually appears to be catching on.'

'Isn't it amazing?' Kim beamed proudly, sitting forward and chatting animatedly. 'Every time I refresh it on my phone, we've got even more downloads. From all ages, and all walks of life too – just like you wanted. You built it, Iris, and they came. In droves.'

The wine arrived, a crisp Chablis which was a particular favourite of Iris's, and they clinked glasses to celebrate.

'And now to the small matter of dating feedback,' Iris said, sitting back and enjoying a tiny sip of the wine. 'Your mother, I understand, had an Analyzed match and a date at the weekend? So how was it? Has she written a full report yet?'

Kim took a massive big gulp of the Chablis before answering. *No, no, no*, Iris wanted to say to her. *This is meant to be sipped and savoured, not drunk like it's a can of Fanta.* She held her tongue though and smiled politely.

'She's working on it,' Kim said. 'But she and her date certainly seemed to hit it off – they even plan on seeing each other again soon.'

'But your mother will still continue to explore the sixty-plus dating age group for us?' Iris asked worriedly. 'By my estimation, it's probably going to be the toughest one to generate accurate feedback about. Older people tend to be slower to date. They're set in their ways and fearful of change. All perfectly understandable, I suppose.'

'Mam is absolutely delighted you're paying her to do this,' said Kim, glugging back yet more of the wine till she'd almost drained her glass. 'And I'm delighted she's getting out and about again. Don't you worry, I'll make sure she sticks with the brief and keeps up with the multi-dating – even if none of these aul' fellas work out for her.'

'I'm very glad to hear it,' said Iris, as their starters arrived, scallops with grapefruit for Kim and a tomato tartlet for herself. 'Although I'm loath to hear our users referred to as "aul' fellas",' she added drily, flicking her linen napkin before laying it neatly across her lap.

'Wow, this grub really is something,' Kim said, enthusiastically tucking in. 'And the wine is something else, too. I could get used to all this posh fine dining, you know.'

'Anything that gets you away from takeaway food at your desk can only be a good thing.'

'So now, of course,' said Kim, with her mouth full, 'you and I have to step up to the plate. It's our turn. Like we agreed – you with the over-forties and me with the twenties to thirties. So come on, Iris, over to you. Tell me what it is that you're looking for in a partner – I'd really love to know.'

That was easy to answer, given the amount of thought Iris had put into it over the years.

'Companionship,' she answered, without a single scrap of hesitation.

'Hmm . . . odd one,' Kim said thoughtfully, chewing on a scallop.

'Odd, how?'

'Well, normally people say they want to meet their soulmate, the love of their life. They want mad, passionate sex and fireworks and a real whopper of a proper love story. To say you're looking for *companionship* is kind of . . .'

'Yes? Kind of what?' said Iris, peering over her glasses at her.

'Kind of vanilla, is what I was trying to say,' Kim trailed off.

'Kim, you're young,' Iris sighed. 'You have your whole dating life stretching ahead of you and right now, you're in a buyer's market. Youth, as we all know, is currency – every man online seems to want to be with a younger model. But trust me, when you get to my age, you'll find that what you look for in a partner changes radically. A companion suddenly seems very desirable and not in the remotest way "vanilla". So to answer your question more thoroughly, I suppose what I'm really looking for is someone to banish the loneliness.'

Kim stopped eating and looked across the table at her.

'You're lonely?' she asked gently.

In a million years, Iris wouldn't have dreamed of answering such a deeply personal question, particularly from a junior subordinate in work. Maybe it was the Chablis, maybe it was because today had been such a good day, or maybe it was that the more she grew to know Kim, in spite of herself, the fonder she was becoming of her.

'Yes,' Iris nodded truthfully. 'Yes, I am. Very much so.'

'Wow,' said Kim, sitting back and stifling a belch. 'It's just that you seem . . . well, you're always on the go, go, go, for one thing. You're probably in the office more than the CEO, and you just . . . you always seem too busy to need a companion.'

Iris took another sip of wine and sat back reflectively.

'Busyness,' she said after a thoughtful pause, 'can be a highly effective panacea against loneliness. You'll find that people who deliberately keep themselves busy tend to be the very ones who do it for a reason. It's a case of doing anything rather than going home alone – yet again.'

Kim looked at her with a mixture of interest and concern, and Iris was sorry she'd let her guard down to share even that much. *Don't you dare pity me*, she thought. *You're in your twenties now, you're surrounded by friends day and night, what would you know? Just come back to me in another two decades, and let's see how your life has panned out then.*

'You know, I'm someone who did everything that I was supposed to in life,' Iris went on to clarify, pushing away the debris of the tomato tartlet she'd been nibbling at. 'I worked hard in school, got top grades, went to college, I even did a Masters at Oxford. Then I went out there and got the best job I possibly could and from there, just kept working and climbing and ticking all the boxes in life that you're supposed to tick. I did what I was told, Kim, really believing that if I just played by all the rules, the rewards I wanted would come to me. A loving home, husband, kids. The whole package. But they didn't. And now, here I am, in my forties and alone. Believe me, never in my wildest dreams did I ever think that I'd end up . . . well, in my forties and alone. So let me serve as a sort of cautionary tale for you and hear my words, Kim. Do not, repeat, do not end up in your forties and alone.'

So now that awful sympathetic look on Kim's face had gone and Iris was profoundly grateful for it.

'Right, then,' Kim said, getting her phone out and scrolling through it. 'To work. Enough talk, whingeing will get you nowhere. So come on, let's get cracking.'

Iris looked back at her blankly.

'Well, we're both monitoring Analyzed every single chance we get, aren't we?' said Kim. 'So surely you must have checked out the guys in your age range by now? Just to scope out the talent?'

Iris stumbled over that one.

'Well, it's just that I've been so busy overseeing the whole site . . .' she began to say, but Kim was having none of it.

'For feck's sake, Iris. The whole reason you started this project was because you'd had one shitty date too many. So what's the point of trying to improve the dating lives of countless strangers if you can't do the same for yourself?'

'Well, yes, of course,' said Iris. 'Just not right now . . . I want to wait till Analyzed is well established first . . .'

'My arse,' said Kim. 'We're doing this now, and that's all there is to it. After all, twelve thousand users can't be wrong, can they?'

Iris said nothing, but felt a rush of deep gratitude towards Kim.

'Actually, scratch that,' said Kim. 'Because you won't believe what I'm seeing right now.'

'Which is?'

'Oh, nothing at all,' Kim replied airily. 'Just the fact that we're now at eighteen thousand users and still climbing, that's all.'

'Eighteen thousand?' said Iris, shocked. '*Eighteen*? Here, show me that.' She grabbed Kim's phone, almost as if she didn't believe it and had to see for herself. She clicked onto Google Play – and there it was, in bold black and white.

'Every single time I go to log in, we're still growing,' said Kim, taking the phone back from Iris.

Iris sat back, utterly at a loss for words.

'We're not even two weeks old,' she said quietly, 'and somehow we've attracted this many . . .'

'I know,' Kim nodded.

'I mean . . . five hundred downloads in a single day for a new app like ours is generally considered a success. This is . . . *phenomenal* . . .'

'I know,' Kim repeated.

'This means we can possibly start to expand the app wider, possibly even overseas . . .'

'And more to the point, I'll tell you exactly what it means for you, Iris.'

'Which is?'

'It means that out of those eighteen thousand, somewhere out there, after so many false starts and disappointments, there really, truly is someone for you. No more loneliness. No more lonely nights. No more.'

To her surprise, Iris found herself smiling. It was a kind sentiment, kindly meant, and all she could hope was that Kim would be proved right. She pulled herself together, sat up straight and waved over at the wine waiter to catch his eye.

'And even more to the point,' she said, 'I'll tell you exactly what it means for you, Ms Kimberley Bailey.'

'Tell me,' Kim grinned.

'It means to hell with us having just one glass of wine. Tonight, only a bottle is good enough.'

'Well, now you're speaking my language.'

Chapter Eighteen

Kim

It was fast becoming a verb. Analyzed. Not just online, in the many hundreds of positive reviews that had been left on the app, but all around the Sloan Curtis offices, too, where friends and co-workers Kim didn't even know would stop to chat to her, discreetly saying, 'You know, I've just been Analyzed and matched with someone very promising. I heard you were involved, so I wanted to catch you to say a quick word of thanks.'

'It's Iris Simpson you should really be thanking, not me,' Kim would always say. 'It's all down to her, really. It was her vision, her idea – I only came on board at the very end, to help out a bit with the digital side of it, that's all.'

But just at the mention of Iris's name, people's faces would never fail to glaze over. Why was that, Kim often wondered? Why did Iris always have this effect on people? OK, so the woman had a habit of rubbing everyone up the wrong way, but now that Kim was spending so much time in her company, she was slowly starting to understand where Iris was coming from. The more she got to know Iris, in spite of herself, the fonder she was becoming of her. There was a real human being under all that frostiness and bossiness and superiority, if you just took the trouble to look.

If people would only give her half a chance, Kim thought, they'd see a whole new side to her that you'd never know was there.

'Her office is on the sixth floor,' Kim was always at pains to say to anyone who spoke to her about Analyzed, 'and I know she'd love your feedback. To hear you've met someone on the site would make her whole day.'

No one ever did, though. Not once, not ever. Kim even had it out with her own gang of sesh buddies in the bar of the Spencer Hotel, where she, Hannah, Emma and Greg had gone for a quick after-work drink one sunny, summery evening.

Except with this lot, as Kim knew only too well, 'just the one' never, ever meant just one drink. Just the one late night, and just the one minging hangover the next day, maybe.

'So, how's your new best friend Iris?' Emma asked her pointedly in her low growl of a voice. Kim's bum had barely even grazed the bar stool she was perching on and already they'd started Iris-bashing. It was only just midweek, but the Spencer was a popular spot with the after-work crowd from the Financial Services Centre and the whole place was buzzing.

'New best friend?' said Kim, sensing where this was going and steeling herself.

'It has been noted,' Greg chipped in, loosening his collar and tie, peeling off his work jacket and flinging it over a bar stool, 'that you and the Dreadnought Iris are thick as thieves these days. You're never out of her office, you're starting to work just as late as she does, all cosied up, the two of you, side by side . . . oh, our spies are watching you, Ms Bailey!'

'Dinners out in fancy restaurants together?' Emma said, with a disparaging sneer to her tone. 'Lunches at her desk every day? Seems to me like we're losing you, Kim. You've got bigger fish to fry now.'

'It's only just because the two of them are working on this app together, that's all, isn't it, Kim?' said Hannah defensively, bless her, the only one to take Kim's side in . . . well, Kim wasn't quite sure what they were all driving at just yet. So she sat back, folded her arms and let it roll.

'You'll be spending weekends together soon,' Emma said witheringly.

No, Kim thought. I'm definitely not imagining it – *Emma's in one of her legendary snots with me, best by far to let her have her say and get it off her chest.*

'Oh God, I just had a horrible thought!' said Greg. 'Suppose you started taking the Dreadnought Iris out with us for drinks after work? Not sure I could handle that. In fact, I need a pint right now, just to blot out the image.'

'OK, OK, everyone,' Kim said, making a 'calm down' gesture. 'Let's just take a moment here. Do you ever ask yourselves why you're all down on Iris so much? I mean, what did she ever do to you that was so awful?'

'She bollocked me out of it for a miscalculation on the Sisk insurance report,' Emma said tightly. 'In front of half the office, too. It was mortifying.'

'And I got strips torn off me for being half an hour late,' said Hannah. 'Even though the Luas I was on was involved in an accident, so it wasn't technically my fault.'

'Iris is our team supervisor,' said Kim. 'You can't get annoyed with her just for doing her job.'

'Yeah, well, I just don't like her, simple as that,' said Greg, folding his arms and frowning, as he really gave it thought. 'Never have, never will. There's something about her manner I can't abide.'

'. . . and that horrible condescending tone she gets when she's pulling you up on something . . .'

'She never gives positive feedback . . . but dear God, she's so quick off the mark to give you a dressing-down if she stumbles on something you did wrong . . .'

'She never engages with you . . . just strides past you without even a hello, how are you. It's beyond rude . . .'

'OK, I get it,' said Kim, taking it all in. 'So maybe Iris isn't exactly a people person. But did it ever occur to you that underneath all that coldness, there's a good soul in there, buried deep?'

'Buried very fecking deep,' said Emma cuttingly.

'And if you're going to go preaching at us to start giving her a second chance,' said Greg, 'then you're wasting your time with me.'

'And me.'

'Sorry, Kim,' Hannah said, but not unkindly. 'There's very few people in this world that I don't like, but Iris . . . she's an awful piece of work, and nothing you say will make me change my mind.'

Fair enough, Kim thought, as yet another gang of colleagues from Sloan Curtis drifted into the bar and joined them. *Then maybe it's not your collective minds that I need to change at all. Maybe it's something, or rather someone, else entirely.*

♥

The following night, it was Kim's turn to step up to the plate. Her very first date via Analyzed, and for once in her dismal dating career, this time her hopes were high.

'Lots in common with this young man, I hope?' Iris said, standing over Kim at her desk as Kim brushed her choppy, shoulder-length hair and lashed on a tiny bit of make-up, squinting into a compact mirror so small she could barely see a thing. It was just after 7.30 p.m., the office was largely deserted and she was all set to meet her date at eight.

'Well, he says his greatest fear is unemployment, and he thinks the lowest depth of misery is having a full day ahead of him with absolutely nothing to do. Sounds like my kind of guy – I go off my head on holidays, unless there's a serious bit of nightlife going on,' said Kim, trying to contour her cheeks, something she'd never attempted before in her life. She'd seen a YouTube video on it though, and for feck's sake, she figured, how hard could it be?

'Well, I look forward to a full report about it tomorrow,' Iris said tartly.

'To hell with this anyway,' said Kim, flinging down the contouring stick in exasperation. 'Who invented this contouring lark? In fact, I don't think I'll bother with make-up at all, he can take me as he finds me.'

With that, she stood up, grabbed the backpack that went everywhere with her and whipped off her neat navy-blue work jacket and shirt, to reveal a tight little halterneck top underneath.

'Well, well, look at you,' said Iris, taking in her transformation. In the space of about four minutes flat, Kim had gone from looking like what she was, an actuary working for a large global conglomerate, to full-on, festival-chic clubwear. 'Now off you go, and just remember this nugget of advice at all times, and all will be well.'

'What advice?' said Kim, already halfway out of the office on her way to the lift bank.

'That your date this evening is purely an exercise in data compilation, for the purposes of feedback and nothing more. It's most certainly not about enjoying yourself or having fun, you know.'

But she was smiling as she said it.

It was Kim who'd picked the venue; Sophie's at The Dean, a really cool rooftop bar and restaurant on the top floor of a hotel on Harcourt Street, just a short taxi ride from the office. There were even swings there, actual wooden swings, just as you stepped out of the lifts and before you went into the bar itself. Which is where Kim was to be found, perched up on one of them, backpack at her feet, swinging away to her heart's content and whistling a happy little tune, as she waited for her date to show up. Every time the lift opened, she looked up in case it was him, but so far it was all couples and gangs of friends who she reckoned were coming here straight from work for a night on the lash.

But then the lift doors glided open, and Kim's heart sank. It was a guy on his own all right, who looked like he might be here to meet someone; he had that anxious, jumpy look on his face that fellas got when they were stressed about a first date. The nerves were practically pinging off him. But he looked older, so much older than Kim would have thought – mid- to late thirties, maybe, with thinning grey hair and round-rimmed glasses that gave him the look of a grown-up Harry Potter. He was wearing a suit and tie, carried a heavy-looking briefcase and, in short, looked like an insurance broker or maybe even someone more senior to Kim who worked at Sloan Curtis; basically the total, polar opposite of what her type usually was.

He marched straight past her on his way to the bar, almost as if she wasn't even there, then did a double take and an about-turn on his heel like something out of a cartoon.

'Excuse me,' he said politely, in a voice so cultured and articulate, he sounded like he was about to read the *Nine O'Clock News*. 'At the risk of being presumptuous, may I ask if I'm addressing Kim Bailey?'

'That's me all right, yeah,' said Kim, slowing the swing down and clambering off it to scoop up her backpack. 'And you must be Harold West.'

'Delighted to meet you,' he said, giving a pompous little bow and stooping down to shake her hand formally.

'Is it Harry for short?'

'I prefer Harold, actually.'

'Oh,' said Kim flatly. 'OK.'

He held open the door for her and she walked ahead of him through to the bar, starting to dread this and feeling like she was about to do the world's weirdest job interview.

It went from bad to worse. Given half a chance, Kim was nothing if not a total chatterbox. She rarely shut up talking; even her mother used to say she woke up first thing every morning talking, talking, talking. But even she was struggling for things to say on this excruciating date.

'So what kind of music are you into?' she asked, racking her brains for something – anything – to say. She and Harold had been seated at a fabulously sunny table for two right by a window, and the real killer was that they were surrounded by people more or less Kim's own age all having the best laugh ever. Already she'd spotted several out-and-out rides hovering over by the bar, and if she could only shake Harold off, she'd be over there like a bullet; she'd insert herself right into the thick of them, skull back the cider and actually start enjoying the night for a change.

Meanwhile, she and her date sat in a painful, long-drawn-out silence.

'Do you mean pop music?' Harold asked her. 'Only I'm more of a classical merchant myself, you know. My mother is an opera singer, a soprano. It's quite exciting, actually, as she's currently in rehearsals at the Royal

Opera House in Covent Garden for a production of *Madame Butterfly*. She has played the title role before, many years ago, but this time she's playing Butterfly's mother,' he added helpfully, as if this might mean anything to Kim, who just sat opposite him looking longingly over in the direction of the bar.

'It sounds wonderful,' she said unenthusiastically. 'You must be so proud of your mum.'

'Same question, back to you,' Harold said, with a little half-smile.

'Fontaines D.C., BTS, but strictly for irony, Taylor Swift when I'm home alone, Drake, and Eminem for a bit of old-school stuff,' she shrugged. Then she glanced across the table at Harold, who was blinking back at her through the Harry Potter glasses, looking lost and confused, almost as if she was speaking a foreign language.

'I'm afraid I'm not quite familiar with any of the bands you mention,' he said, 'though I've no doubt they're all superb, in their own way.'

A waiter came over to clear away the dregs of their main courses, which they'd somehow stumbled through, and offered dessert menus, which they both politely declined. The sooner we finish up eating, Kim thought, trying to stifle a yawn, the sooner I can make my escape. The waiter was fussing and faffing about with plates and glasses when Harold excused himself for a moment – she presumed to run to the bathroom. She also didn't really care.

Her eye followed Harold the whole way across the bar, noticing how tall and lean he was, with that sloping kind of walk that people with really long legs all seemed to have. There was nothing wrong with him per se, she thought, mulling over what she'd report back to Iris in the morning; Iris, who'd surely want to know every single last detail about the date. Harold seemed like a good person, polite, interested and friendly. But there was absolutely zero spark between them, and that was as much Kim's fault as it was his. The guy is a young fogey, she decided. Still only in his thirties, and yet acting like someone generations apart from her. Bet he wears pyjamas, she thought. Bet he likes to take afternoon naps whenever he can. Bet he's always losing his car keys. Bet he reads the *Guardian* and watches *Antiques Roadshow*.

'Forgive me for having to leave you alone,' Harold said, coming back to the table quicker than she thought and slipping into his seat.

'Harold,' Kim said, sitting forward and stretching her hands out on the table in a 'game's up' gesture. 'Can I ask you something?'

'By all means,' he smiled.

'OK, here goes. How would you say this date is going so far?'

Feck it anyway. Kim was nothing if not a straight talker, and wasn't tonight all about garnering accurate feedback for Analyzed anyway?

He blinked back at her through the glasses.

'Oh,' he nodded, a bit taken aback at her bluntness. 'I see. Right-i-o. Well, let's see now . . .'

As he fumbled for the right words, Kim jumped in ahead of him.

'Because my answer would be, "not very well",' she said, looking him right in the eye.

'Oh. Yes, I see,' he nodded.

'Can I ask you something else?'

'Absolutely, by all means,' Harold said, taking out a neat cotton hanky and dabbing minuscule beads of perspiration from his forehead.

'What was it on my profile that made you want to meet up with me?' she asked out straight. 'The reason I matched with you is because you'd said your idea of hell was having nothing to do, and that, I could certainly relate to. So out of all the women out there, what was it about my profile that made you think, yeah, I wouldn't mind matching with this one?'

Harold locked his two hands together and sat forward to face her.

'As a matter of fact, I remember distinctly,' he said, with a crooked little smile. 'It was your answer to the question, "how would you like to die?"'

'Seriously?' said Kim, racking her brains as to what she'd written. For the life of her she couldn't remember. She'd had a few drinks when she filled out the online questionnaire; she could have written anything.

'You said you'd like to die in the loving arms of your boyfriend, and for the very last words you heard on earth to be, "she can't be dead; she's far too young and beautiful!"'

'Is that what I put?' she said, surprised.

'It made me chuckle,' Harold explained. 'And I so rarely laugh. So that's why, I suppose.'

'Do you think you'd ever want to meet up with me again?' she asked, fully certain as to what her own answer would be.

'I think that, in order for any date to be deemed a success,' he said, after a thoughtful little pause, 'it must surely be mutually enjoyable to both parties. Don't you agree?'

Kim nodded.

'And on mature reflection,' Harold went on, 'if you'll forgive my bluntness, I doubt that this evening will go down as one of the most enjoyable either of us has ever had. Am I correct?'

'Dead right,' Kim said, relieved that they were at least on the same page.

'With that in mind,' Harold went on, twiddling with his hanky now, 'I've already taken the liberty of paying our bill.'

She went to protest, but Harold held up a firm hand.

'I wouldn't dream of allowing you to pay, when, regrettably, I seem to have bored you for the evening,' he said, with a little shrug of his shoulders. 'That's what I was doing just now. I felt it was the very least I could do. And forgive me if I let you down or disappointed you in any way.'

'Oh . . .' said Kim, temporarily wrong-footed. She'd been blunt with Harold, but hadn't expected him to be quite so blunt in return. Plus, she wasn't used to generosity on this kind of scale. She'd been drinking vodkas with dinner and in a fancy place like this, God knows what they cost.

With that, Harold took out his phone and clicked on a taxi app.

'You must allow me to order you a taxi, to take you safely home,' he said kindly.

'Oh . . . there's no need, honestly,' Kim protested. It was still early, barely ten o'clock, and she'd no intention of going home just yet. When Harold left, her plan was to have a nightcap at the bar and get flirty with some of the crew hanging out there, who looked like her kind of people.

But Harold was having none of it.

'May I ask your address, if it's not too presumptuous?' he insisted. Then hastily added, 'I promise I'm not a stalker, or anything of the kind. I just want you to get home safely, that's all. Besides, it's raining,' he added, and when Kim looked out the window, sure enough, it was pitch dark and there was a heavy summer deluge pelting down.

With little choice in the matter, she reluctantly gave her address and minutes later, was outside on the street, as he shook her hand and wished her a fond farewell.

'Good luck, Kim Bailey,' he said, holding open the taxi door for her and sheltering her under a giant umbrella.

'And to you,' she smiled back at him, clambering inside. Harold had said he lived in the city centre and would walk home, so as the taxi splashed off, she got a good last look at him, strolling through the sheets of rain, with that distinctive, sloping, long-legged walk.

A perfectly nice guy for someone else, she thought. Just not me, not ever, not in a zillion years.

Then she thought about Analyzed and about the hundreds and hundreds of five-star, glowing reviews they'd been attracting, and she wondered.

Was it possible, she thought, as a nasty little worry started to form, that the app just wasn't as deadly accurate as everyone was saying it was? Was it even possible, she wondered, hating herself for articulating the thought, that the whole project was a flash in the pan? One that had the potential to be a spectacular, overhyped, out-and-out, holy mortifying flop?

Chapter Nineteen

Connie

'Now, Ma, you remember what I told you?'

'I know, I know . . .' Connie replied sulkily.

'You're meant to be out there, multi-dating,' said Kim. 'And you know what that means, don't you?'

'From what you've told me, it means being mean and deceitful to a perfectly nice gentleman who I happen to like very much.'

'That's absolutely not what it is at all, Ma!' Kim said, starting to lose patience. 'This is the way things are done now. This is how it works. When you're dating online, as the whole world seems to be, it's not smart to just tie yourself down to the one fella – at least, not in the early stages. You have to cast your net wide and really see what's out there, before you commit to each other. It's what everyone does.'

'You can say what you like,' Connie sniffed, 'but it doesn't feel right to me. It feels like I'm doing the dirt on poor Ronnie behind his back. When he's being so good to me, too!'

'Come off it, Ma,' Kim said, rolling her eyes. 'You can be sure of one thing with this Ronnie fella – he's probably online right now, doing exactly the same thing we are. Meeting other people, messaging them, chatting to them – that's what's considered the norm.'

'Well, it doesn't feel normal to me.'

Kim was quite wrong about all this, Connie thought primly to herself. Ronnie wasn't that kind of chap at all; he was an old-school gentleman, just like her Jack had been. Once he was seeing a lady, that was the end of that, and there was no way in hell he'd dream of going back onto these aul' websites to start eyeing up other women.

'Besides,' Connie said, as a fresh argument struck her. 'You're the one who was always on and on at me to try out these dating sites in the first place, weren't you, missy? Your poor dad was barely cold in his grave before you were at me to start getting back out there again. And now that I've actually done what you told me to, you're still not happy. Of all people, you'd think you'd be delighted that I met a dote like Ronnie – and on my very first go at the online dating, too!'

Kim ignored her, and tried a different tack instead.

'There is also the small matter of payment,' she reminded Connie, giving her a cheeky little wink. 'The more of these dates you go on and the more feedback you give Iris, the more you get paid. You have to admit, Ma, not a bad way to earn a nice few quid for yourself, now, is it?'

'It's not right, love,' Connie said firmly. 'Making money by cheating? You can tell that Iris one to shove her cash. I'd rather not have it at all, than do the dirt on Ronnie behind his back. Not when the two of us are getting on so famously. You know, he rings me every single morning, right after you go out to work, just to ask me how my day is going so far and to check I'm not feeling all lonely on my own. Then last thing every evening, before I go to bed, he calls me again, just so he can say night-night and the two of us can have a nice chat about our days. It's so lovely,' she added, beaming and not able to help it.

Connie was sitting side by side with Kim at the kitchen table, with an iPad propped up between the two of them, as they scrolled the whole way down through that website or app or whatever you were supposed to call it. But Kim just didn't seem to get how the older generation worked, did she? So she could go on and on till the cows came home about 'getting out there' and 'casting your net wide', but it just felt plain wrong to Connie and that was the end of it.

'Take a look at this fella here, now,' said Kim, bringing up yet another man's profile and photo. 'Here's a guy exactly the same age as you, and it sounds like the two of you have loads in common.'

'Naaa. I don't like the look of him,' said Connie dismissively.

'You shouldn't judge a book by its cover,' Kim persisted. 'Besides, what's so wrong with the way he looks? He looks perfectly fine to me.'

'No, he doesn't,' Connie sniffed. 'He looks like a vegetarian. Like Jeremy Corbyn. I could never trust a man who didn't eat meat.'

Kim shook her head, but didn't pursue it. Instead, she brought up another profile, this time of a man with a big bushy beard that went all the way down to his collarbone.

'OK, what about this fella here?' she said, shoving the iPad under Connie's nose and tapping off the screen.

'Look! He says his favourite movies are *Butch Cassidy and the Sundance Kid* and *The Sting* – and you're always saying they're the best films ever made. Doesn't it sound like the two of you would have loads to talk about?'

'If you think I'm meeting up with that aul' eejit,' Connie said, barely even glancing at the screen, 'you've another thing coming. A beard? Eughhh. Disgusting. Your uncle Mick had a beard, God rest him, and you could tell what he'd had for his breakfast, lunch and dinner just by looking at the state of it.'

'You're not exactly making this easy, Ma, are you?' said Kim wearily. 'OK, here's a doozy for you . . . take a look at this guy here. A retired doctor, doesn't that sound promising to you? Four grandchildren, loves travel and loves his garden . . .'

'Ronnie's a great gardener too, you know,' Connie said, drifting off into a happy little reverie. 'He and I really do have everything in common that way. It's amazing, really. Grows his own spuds and all, so he says. He promised me a bag-load of them, next time I see him.'

'Never mind about Ronnie,' said Kim, starting to get a bit cross now. 'What about Dr Handsome that's right here in front of you, looking to meet someone special? I'm warning you, Ma, if you don't snatch him up, then someone else will.'

'I'm so looking forward to the Andrea Bocelli concert with Ronnie, too. Won't that be such fun? And romantic.'

'Ma, look!' Kim said, ignoring her. 'This doctor here says he's happiest whenever he's in Rome on holidays, and you're always saying Italy was the best hollier you and Dad ever went on. You're always banging on about how you'd love to go back, and you only ever order lasagne when you're out. Come here till you get a look at his photo.'

But Connie was far too wrapped up in happy daydreams about Ronnie. Why couldn't Kim understand? This multi-dating nonsense was a terrible way to carry on altogether. And she knew in her waters that there was no way in the world that Ronnie was out there doing the same thing. She trusted him, and that was something Kim's generation just didn't understand. For all their talk about 'multi-dating', and how normal it was now, they could learn a lot from their parents and grandparents when it came to proper, old-fashioned commitment.

'So come on, Ma,' Kim was saying, interrupting her chain of thought. 'What do you say we message this doctor fella and see how the two of you get on? I'll do it for you, if you don't want to.'

Connie knew she wouldn't get two minutes of peace until she played ball, so she put on her reading glasses and took the iPad from her, so she could have a decent look at this doctor, whoever he was.

'Him? Oh, Jesus, no way,' she said, handing the iPad straight back again.

'What's wrong with him?' said Kim.

'Lookit, says it right there, at the very top of his profile,' said Connie.

'Says what?'

'He's from Kerry.'

'Why have you got a problem with that?'

'Because I don't like the accent, that's why.'

'What's wrong with a Kerry accent? You're from West Cork, and that's only a stone's throw from Kerry.'

'And another thing,' said Connie, pointing down at the screen. 'He's separated – look, he says so right there.'

'Why is that an issue?' said Kim. 'Sure half the country is separated.'

'Yeah . . . well . . . it would be . . . against my religion to start seeing a separated man,' she replied, clutching at straws.

'Excuse me?' said Kim, looking at her mother like she had a screw loose. 'You know loads of separated people, and it doesn't stop you seeing any of them. Your pal Betty is divorced, and you're always saying getting rid of her lousy husband was the makings of her.'

'It's against the teachings of the Church,' said Connie, blessing herself and trying to look holy.

'Ma, the last time you were inside a church was on Dad's last anniversary, and that's nearly a year ago now. Who do you think you're trying to kid here?'

Just then, Connie's phone started to ring – saved by the bell. Literally.

Better yet, it was him – Ronnie.

'Oh, will you excuse me, Kim love?' she said, sweet as you like. 'That's Ronnie on the phone, and I really need to take this.' Then her whole tone and character changed as she purred down the phone in her 'posh' voice. 'Yes, who is speaking, please? Oh, hello Ronnie, it's you, what a lovely surprise! No,' she said, looking disparagingly down at the iPad Kim still held in front of her, 'no, you're not interrupting anything here at all, Ronnie. It's wonderful to hear from you, and I'm greatly looking forward to our big night out!'

Kim glared hotly at her and rolled her eyes up to heaven, but Connie didn't care. Instead, she got up and left the kitchen to step out into the garden, banging the door behind her, so she and her brand-new boyfriend could have all the privacy in the world.

♥

The following Saturday, Connie was meeting her friend Betty for lunch in the St. George Hotel, right in the heart of the city centre. It was a grand, old-fashioned hotel with a lovely lounge up on the first floor, where they did gorgeous sandwiches with nice big pots of tea and if you asked for refills, they didn't charge you.

'I'm so sorry for dragging you all the way into town on such a busy Saturday afternoon,' Betty said breathlessly, arriving late as usual, and laden down with heavy-looking shopping bags from Brown Thomas. 'What with me being a career girl now, unfortunately I'm not able to meet you on weekdays anymore. Weekends are the only bit of time I have free these days – I'm not a lady of leisure like you, Connie! Work, work, work, you know how it is,' she sighed theatrically.

Connie smiled sweetly back at her and stood up to give her a little peck on the cheek. Betty was by far her most glamorous and most competitive friend, always bragging and boasting about her two kids: Pamela, who was married with a family and who was basically her mother all over again, and Nigel, Betty's pride and joy and who was never out of all the gay bars in town, according to Kim, and 'out' to everyone bar his mother.

Ordinarily, Connie never failed to come away from meeting Betty feeling drained and cross and patronised, but just this once, she knew exactly how to handle her.

'Not at all, Betty,' Connie smiled back at her oldest frenemy. 'I'm just delighted to see you. Now sit down and tell me all your news, I can't wait to hear.'

Connie braced herself. No harm to let Betty get all of her bragging and boasting over and done with, and then maybe she'd be able to tell her own bit of news.

'Well,' said Betty, fluffing out her finely bobbed, snow-white hair, carefully coiffed at incredible expense by a colourist you had to wait four months to get an appointment with, as she never failed to remind Connie. 'The grandkids have me *exhauuusted*, you know how it is.' But then she instantly clamped her hand over her mouth as if she'd just put her foot in it. 'Ooops! How tactless of me. Of course, you *don't* know how it is, do you, Connie?'

'Well, Kim is only twenty-six,' Connie said politely, 'plenty of time for all that later. So how are little Douglas and Lillian?' She kept on smiling and tried to look as interested in this as she could, given that, from what she could see of Betty's grandchildren, they were two of the most spoiled brats you'd ever meet.

'Well, they only ever want to be with Gan-Gan, that's their new name for me, isn't it adorable?' Betty replied, picking up a menu and scanning down through it. 'But with Pamela so busy with work – she's been promoted in the bank, did I mention that?'

Connie shook her head.

'Oh, Pamela is practically running her whole branch single-handedly now. She takes after me – a bit of a career girl!' Betty trilled at her own joke, then did a double take when she had a closer look at the menu. 'Oh, dear – I hope the food here is within your budget, Connie, love? I keep forgetting you're jobless. Sorry – retired, I meant to say,' she threw in, with a condescending little smile. 'There are plenty of days when I envy you, let me tell you. All that lovely time to yourself – I never seem to get a minute these days, what with being general manager of the store. Honestly, I just feel so stressed with all of the incredible pressure I'm under. You don't know you're born, Connie!'

Betty might have made it sound like she was running a company the size of Google, but as Connie had to remind herself, she was actually volunteering behind the counter in a small, smelly local charity shop.

Just then a friendly, smiley waitress came over to take their order; a fish pie for Connie, with just a Caesar salad for Betty.

'Have to watch the calories, you know how it is,' Betty said, patting her tummy as she ordered. 'I've got so many nights out coming up, and I need to fit into all the brand-new clothes I've just bought,' she added, waving down at the shopping bags strewn around her feet. 'But you go right ahead and enjoy all those lovely carbohydrates, Connie. You're so lucky, you can go home later on and get into a nice, comfy tracksuit if you feel like it. I envy you!'

'Actually,' Connie smiled sweetly, unable to hold her tongue for very much longer, 'the reason I'm having such a big lunch now is because it's probably the only chance I'll get to eat all day. What with getting my hair done this afternoon, and all.'

'You're getting your hair done?' said Betty, raising an eyebrow. 'You hardly ever get your hair done. Unless it's Christmas, or something.'

Connie smiled and decided she was really going to enjoy this.

'Oh, just a blow-dry, Betty. Only I want to look my best for my big night out this weekend.'

'Big night out?' said Betty, frowning. 'Big night out where? Bingo, or something?'

'No, not at all,' said Connie, getting into her stride. 'As a matter of fact, I'm going to the Andrea Bocelli concert tomorrow evening. Can you believe it? I'll be sure to let you know what it's like. I know you're a huge fan of his.'

'You're going to Andrea Bocelli?' Betty said, looking very far from pleased about it. 'I don't know how you managed to get tickets, they've been sold out for months. Nigel tried so hard to get two seats in the VIP area, so he could treat me. Well, you know how generous he is, but even he couldn't get tickets. And Nigel is friends with everyone in the know. If he can't get tickets, then no one can.'

Connie sat back and, God forgive her, savoured every minute. Feck it anyway, she thought. Betty never stopped putting her down, no harm for her to win this round. Course, she didn't mention that she wasn't actually going *to see* the concert as such; that she'd be listening to it from a chip van parked outside. She wasn't a complete thick. Instead, she tried to hide her smirk, while Betty kept on needling at her.

'Is Kim bringing you?' Betty frowned across the table. 'Did she win the tickets in some kind of competition? I'd hardly have your Kim down as a Bocelli fan.'

'Oh no,' Connie blinked back, the very picture of innocence. 'Nothing like that at all. I've been invited on a date, as it happens.'

At that, Betty looked sharply up at her.

'A *what*? A *date*-date? You can't possibly mean a normal date, though. With a *man*.'

'Oh, but that's exactly what I mean,' Connie smiled.

'Don't be ridiculous,' said Betty. 'Do you mean with one of your brothers? Or a cousin up from Cork, or something?'

'No, Betty, love. I mean with a very nice gentleman who I've recently met up with. And it's not our first date either, you know. We were out last week for lunch. Except it was a lunch that turned into dinner, we were getting on so famously. Like a house on fire.'

Connie thought it best to leave out the part about Kim having to come into town to collect her because she was so stocious drunk. And it was worth it; the look of disbelief on Betty's face was pure comedy gold.

'You met a man?' Betty managed to stammer, as their tea arrived. 'How? Where?'

Thank God for Kim, Connie thought, who'd briefed her very carefully on what to say to this one.

'We met online,' she answered truthfully. 'Through a new start-up venture that Kim is closely involved with. All very exciting, isn't it? It's called Analyzed and Kim said to tell you that you should definitely sign up to it – that over-seventies such as yourself and myself are more than welcome. Course, you pay a few quid to download it, but she says she'll gladly give you a discount.

'Now, are you ready for a good, strong cup of tea? Betty, love? Are you all right? Why has your face gone a funny colour?'

Chapter Twenty

Iris

The online reviews. Oh dear God, those online reviews. Every spare chance she got, Iris would log on to Analyzed, just to scroll through them and savour them and gloat over them, reading and rereading every single one she possibly could.

Honestly, some of them she could have written herself. This, for instance, from a woman about her own age.

'I don't think I've ever been so accurately matched before, not in the whole course of my entire dating career, which, by the way, has been long and pretty dire. I'm forty-two and separated with three kids, so it's been a nightmare for me trying to spark up any kind of new relationship. Up till now, most of the guys I met online would just ghost on me the minute they'd discover I had three kids under the age of six.

'I first heard from a friend about Analyzed. She was raving about it, saying that it was completely different to all the other dating apps out there. So I thought what the hell, and decided to give it a go. Straight away, I matched with a guy about my own age and background and it was as if he and I just spoke the same language, right from the off. Same backgrounds, same hobbies and interests; we both love art-house movies and we're both driven demented by

people who talk at the cinema. Anyway, he and I met for a casual drink one night last week, we literally didn't stop chatting all night and it's been like that ever since. A soulmate. I finally really, truly feel like I've met my soulmate, something I never felt with my ex-husband, even after twelve years of marriage.'

That review alone, from an anonymous user, put the biggest smile on Iris's face. And it got better from there.

'You've got to check out Analyzed! Never in my wildest dreams did I ever think I'd meet someone I could be so compatible with . . .'

'Trust me, Analyzed goes so much deeper than the other dating apps out there . . . you have to invest a lot of thought into their incredibly detailed questionnaire, but it's time very well spent . . .'

There were users of all ages and from all walks of life who'd downloaded the app, just like Iris had hoped and prayed that they would. From college students to pensioners – you only had to read the reviews to see for yourself the breadth of the age range here. Users were generous enough to post reviews based on their experiences, so Iris figured the very least she could do was read every one of them and see where there was room for improvement. Some were joyous and made her beam with pride and happiness; others were gut-wrenchingly honest, like this one, which her keen eye lit on.

'So, I'm twenty-one, a straight, white cis guy in my final year studying psychology at UCD and I honestly never thought I'd make it all the way through college without ever once having a proper girlfriend. Twenty-one

years old and a complete romantic failure, that's what I thought. I'm young, I'm a student, I should be having the time of my life – how was it possible to feel so alone and miserable?

'I spotted Analyzed online and as a psychology student, it appealed to me, so I signed up to it and quickly matched with three women, all fantastic, but with one of them, I just felt a really deep connection, the kind I've never felt before.'

Then one from an old-age pensioner, a man in his late seventies, a widower with grandkids who described himself as 'an ageing hippy eco-warrior and a bit of a recycling bore'. His very first sentence was what caught Iris's attention.

'The loneliness in my dismal, empty shell of a home was killing me slowly. Since my late partner and life-buddy passed away, I never thought that the quiet could be so excruciating. Recently, however, my son encouraged me to sign up to this new website, which is generating quite positive feedback, according to him. So I thought, why not, what's to lose? Pretty early on I spotted a lady who'd described her ideal quality in a man as 'free-spirited'. Well, I live on a houseboat, so I thought, surely I qualify? We began messaging via the site and quickly realised we had such a lot in common.'

On and on he gushed, sounding warm and happy and in the fabulous first flush of new-found romance.

I'm helping people here, Iris thought proudly. I never thought I'd say the words, but I actually seem to be making a difference, even just a small one, in people's lives.

Analyzed was still such a new site, her fervent hope was that the app would only grow from here, and hopefully help even more users to find love and romance and all the good things that made life worthwhile.

Iris was working on the site late that Saturday night when something dawned on her. This was the longest period of time she'd gone in years without a date. She'd been so busy trying to make sure her users were happily matched up, that she'd completely forgotten all about herself.

♥

That particular Sunday, a most unusual and unexpected invitation came Iris's way. Kim had rung her earlier in the day, and out of a clear blue sky, she invited Iris over to her house for Sunday lunch.

'We've so much to talk through,' Kim had said, 'particularly about our digital content, so why not? The Mothership does a whopper of a Sunday spread here, she always cooks enough to feed an army, even though there's only the pair of us. You'd be more than welcome. Plus, Mam will be able to tell you all about her first Analyzed date when she sees you. So come on, Iris, jump in the shower and get your arse over here. See you in about an hour, and you'd better arrive good and starving. Mam's doing a big vegetarian banquet in your honour.'

Just a few short months ago, if someone had told Iris that she'd be driving to Kim Bailey's home on a sunny

Sunday afternoon, as an invited guest for a family meal, she'd have thought them insane. When, she wondered, pressing the doorbell on the Baileys' neat little suburban house, was the last time she'd sat down to a proper home-cooked Sunday lunch? Not since her own mum had passed away, and she'd barely been sixteen years old then.

Truth be told, Iris had been grateful beyond words to get Kim's kind invitation. Without fail, a Sunday would dawn and she knew with 97.5 per cent accuracy that the day ahead would be a nightmare. Saturdays were horrible in their own way too, but at least then she could keep herself busy and occupied, hopping to her various gym classes, zipping into the office to get ahead on work for the following week, and maybe treating herself to a little shopping excursion, or a movie screening, if she felt brave enough to slip into a cinema alone, surrounded by couples or else friends on a best buddies' night out. Sundays were a whole different brand of torture altogether. Sundays tended to be family days, and when you were without either a partner or a family, where did that leave you? How were you supposed to fill the long, lonely hours?

Kim answered the door, dishevelled-looking, with not a scrap of make-up on, her hair piled high on her head in a messy topknot and wearing a slouchy, grey, tired-looking tracksuit. But her face instantly brightened when she saw who it was, something that touched Iris deeply. Just the fact that someone was actually pleased and happy to see her made such a big change.

'Iris!' Kim grinned delightedly. 'You're here – perfect timing. Now get your arse into the kitchen and prepare to stuff your face.'

'It's so very kind of you to ask me,' Iris said, handing over a bottle of Sancerre, her favourite 'special occasion' choice of wine, along with a huge bunch of white lilies that she'd stopped off to buy along the way.

'Wow, thanks so much,' Kim said, gratefully taking the wine and kissing the bottle, like she was in love with it. 'Badly needed in my case, the hangover on me is sheer murder today. Hair of the dog, that's your only man. *Mam!*' she screeched at the top of her voice, '*Iris is here, and look what she brought us!*'

'Iris, you're most welcome,' Kim's mother said, bustling out of the kitchen and wiping her hands on her apron before shaking Iris's hand.

'So kind of you to include me, Mrs Bailey,' Iris smiled. 'Something certainly smells divine. Here you go, some flowers for you.'

'Ahh, you're very good, thanks, they're gorgeous. But we'll have none of that Mrs Bailey nonsense, though. The name is Connie. Come on inside and sit yourself down. There's nothing fancy for lunch now, it's just plain, simple home cooking, that's all.'

Iris followed both mother and daughter down the narrow little hallway into the kitchen and gratefully took the seat she was offered at a long, pine kitchen table that looked like it had been *in situ* for decades. There were even sums scratched into the wood, in what she could only presume was Kim's childish writing. Connie made the biggest fuss of Iris, insisting she take off her jacket and have a glass of wine before lunch.

A strange thing; was Iris imagining it, or did the woman seem much warmer towards her today? More relaxed and welcoming? Last time she'd left this house with the distinct impression that Connie Bailey was one of the legions of people who most definitely did not like her. Today, however, she was like a completely different person.

'Mam has a hot date later on this evening,' Kim said, with a sly little wink. 'All thanks to Analyzed, isn't that right, Mam?'

From where she was, standing over at the oven, Connie flushed deeply, then opened it up to produce the most delicious-smelling, garlicky aubergine and mushroom pasta bake, trimmed with stuffing and roast vegetables; the whole works.

'He's bringing me to a concert tonight,' she said to Iris, absolutely delighted with herself. 'Andrea Bocelli at the Aviva Stadium. Aren't I lucky?'

'Very lucky indeed,' Iris smiled. 'So tell me all about this mysterious "he",' she asked, genuinely curious.

'Oh, he's completely wonderful,' Connie happily gushed away, scuttling over to the table with the pasta bake while it was steaming hot and starting to dish out big, thick, succulent-looking helpings. 'He's called Ronnie. Ronnie and Connie, isn't that gas? And . . . *YOU!! You lazy-looking article! What do you think you're doing, sitting there like Lady Muck?* Get up out of that, and drain the carrots – give me a hand, instead of lolling around the place expecting to be waited on hand and foot!'

'Oh,' said Iris, a bit taken aback, but rising to her feet. 'Sorry about that. Yes, of course, I'm delighted to help.'

'She means me,' said Kim, rolling her eyes and hauling herself over to the big Aga in the corner of the kitchen.

'So anyway, getting back to Ronnie,' Connie said, all sweetness and light once more. 'He calls me all the time, day and night, doesn't he, Kim?'

'Weirdly, yeah,' Kim nodded, putting on a pair of oven gloves and draining a potful of carrots into a serving bowl. 'No bloke *I've* ever met ever calls me that much.'

'It's just so nice to have the aul' bit of male attention again,' Connie chirped. 'Puts a spring in your step. My late husband Jack was my very first boyfriend, you know, so this is all a bit of a new adventure for me. Have to say, I'm enjoying it very much. And I have you to thank for it all, Iris, love.'

'Oh, well, thank you,' said Iris, amazed at just how hospitable and friendly Connie was being today. She wasn't used to being spoken to like this, and for the life of her, couldn't remember the last time anyone had ever referred to her as 'love'. Had anyone ever uttered the words, 'Iris, love' before? Somehow she doubted it. Not in decades, anyway.

'Ronnie and I have so much in common, you wouldn't believe it,' Connie went on, serving Iris up an extra-large helping of pasta bake, liberally sprinkled with parmesan cheese. 'Even the little things, and they matter so much, don't they?'

'I've always found that to be the case,' Iris nodded.

'For instance, we both love crime fiction,' Connie chatted away, 'and we both hate people who chew their food too loudly. And people who wear perfume or aftershave that's too strong. AND people who interrupt you all the time.'

'Those traits are deeply irritating,' Iris said politely, 'I have to agree.'

'In fact, when Ronnie and I first swapped notes, our list of pet peeves was far longer than our list of things we both love.'

Iris smiled, as Connie poured her out a ridiculously large glass of wine, then pointedly poured out the tiniest little thimbleful for her daughter. 'Now if I could just find a lovely man for my Kim here, we'd be laughing.'

'No joy on my first outing on Analyzed,' Kim shrugged, coming back to the table with the serving bowl piled high with carrots and passing it over to Iris, so she could help herself. 'It's all a numbers game, I know that, although it's a game I've been playing for a long, long time now and still not a peek of a half-decent boyfriend out of it. Like, one that lasted more than two or three dates at most, that is.'

'So why do you think that is?' Iris asked, deeply interested.

'Wish I knew the answer to that one,' Kim said with a grin. 'Relationship fizzle, that's my trouble, that's the Curse of Kim for you. Oh sure, they all seem to like me initially and they have a great laugh and they think I'm a bit of craic, but then within no time, I spot them straight back online, looking for someone else.'

'Well, maybe if you acted more like a lady,' Connie said, her tone instantly sharpening, 'and took a bit of pride in yourself, you might do better. I might sound old-fashioned, Kim, but men want to be with someone they see a long-term future with, not just some class of a good-time girl.'

Good-time Girl, Kim squinted back at her. 'Where are we living anyway, mother, in a western movie above the saloon?'

'I'm in the right, aren't I, Iris?' Connie insisted. 'Back me up here, there's a good woman. Tell this article to change her image, stop acting like one of them ladettes and clean up her act. Then maybe she'd change the class of fella she's meeting quick enough. Kim might actually listen to you, on account of you're her boss and all, because she certainly won't listen to a word I tell her.'

Iris could do nothing but give a weak little nod, because, really, who wanted to referee in a mother–daughter squabble?

'Come off it, Mam, fellas don't give a rat's arse about that kind of thing,' said Kim, glugging back the minuscule glass of wine in front of her, then immediately reaching out to top it up. But Connie was ahead of her, giving her a light smack on the wrist.

'You'd quite enough last night to keep you going for the whole weekend, missy,' she said crossly. 'Go and get water out of the tap if you're thirsty.'

Kim pulled a face at her, and went back to stuffing herself with pasta bake, covered in her mother's roasted veg.

Iris hid a little smile – mothers and daughters, she thought. When she saw how the whole dynamic played out in adult life, she began to realise just how much she'd missed out on all these years. She continued tucking into the aubergine pasta, which was delicious, listening intently to all the back-and-forth joshing and sniping and teasing that went on between Kim and her mum. On the surface, you'd think they were arguing, but you didn't have to look too far to see the deep affection underneath.

Well, well, well, Iris thought. *This must be what it's like to come from a normal, functioning family.* How lucky were Kim and Connie, to share such a loving bond? Her thoughts wandered to her own late, lamented mother, twenty-five years gone now. Was this how she and Iris would be acting now, had her mum not passed away so young? Lightly bickering over a gorgeous Sunday lunch, squabbling and argumentative on the surface, yet with the love for each other palpable, just beneath?

I miss my own mum, she thought, feeling something she rarely allowed herself to indulge in – self-pity. *I miss this. I miss having one single relative in my corner, who'd nag at me for wearing the wrong clothes and having one drink too many and still somehow love me all the same, and who'd stand up for me.* Next time she got Kim alone, Iris vowed, she'd make a point of hammering it home to her just how damn lucky she was.

'Anyway, missy,' Connie went on, still finger-wagging at Kim, 'instead of going out on dates in those ridiculous strappy tops that you can see your belly button in, looking like a lady of loose morals, as we used to say in my day, you might start paying a little bit more attention to how you dress. Look at Iris, now, see how well turned-out she is?'

Iris glanced down at what she was wearing: her 'uniform' of black woolly trousers and a black cashmere polo neck to go with it. She was about to say that this was exactly what she wore every other day of the week, but was fast finding out that with Connie, it was very difficult to get a word in.

'If you went out looking a bit less like you'd gone out in your underwear,' Connie was saying, 'and a bit more like Kate Middleton, then you'd be grand.'

'Thanks but no thanks, Mam,' Kim said with great finality. 'If I was ever thick enough to listen to you, you'd have me going around like a nun, dressed in black and covered from head to foot.'

'And another thing,' Connie went on, 'maybe if you didn't go out every single night with the intention of getting scuttered out of your brains, you might do a bit better for yourself, Missy.'

'Give it a rest, Mam,' Kim groaned. 'My hangover is too bad to take in one of your lectures. Besides, any guy I meet can take me as he finds me, simple as.'

'I don't care what you say, men don't like drunk women.'

'Oh yeah? Because you're one to talk, Mam.'

Iris jumped in here, judging it best to change the subject.

'Wasn't there anything positive about your date the other night?' she asked Kim, turning her full focus on her, genuinely interested.

'Oh yes, that nice man you met in The Dean Hotel?' Connie chipped in. 'Because he sounded like a grand young fella to me. Saw you safely to a taxi and everything, didn't he? Paid for the dinner and all. From what you said, he came across like a real gentleman. But sure that's my Kim for you,' she added, raising her eyes to the ceiling dramatically, 'she'll run a mile from any half-decent fella, and yet she'll make a right eejit of herself over a heartbreaker who'll treat her badly. Seen it a hundred times.'

'Ahh drop it, Mam, will you?' said Kim, abandoning her food, holding onto her throbbing head, then giving her eye sockets a nice, soothing rub with her knuckles. 'Like I said, there was nothing wrong with your man the other night, Harold, that's his name, except that he bored the arse off me.'

'You mind your language in front of our guest,' Connie snapped at her. Then she lit up as a fresh idea came to her. 'Ronnie has a son about your age, you know. If he's single, I could always try matching you up with him? Seeing as how you're next to useless at picking out fellas for yourself.'

'Thanks, but no thanks, Mam,' said Kim drily.

'Actually, Iris, love.' Connie beamed across the table at their guest. 'You'll get to meet Ronnie later on. He's calling to collect me before the concert. He has to get there early, you know, as he has a little bit of work to do there.'

'Running a mobile chip van,' Kim said, going back to her Sunday dinner, but this time horsing into it, like this was her death row meal and she'd never see food ever again. 'Just in case listening to Mam made you think Ronnie was the onstage warm-up man for Andrea Bocelli. And by the way, Mam? If he collects you in the van, any chance he'd throw a batter burger and a few onion rings my way? Or a spice bag that I can have for later? You know how hungry I always get with a hangover.'

'You cheeky article,' Connie snapped at her, 'do you see now, Iris, what I have to put up with? Did you ever see such disrespect?'

But it was done affectionately, Iris observed. As was all their light bantering and bickering.

And in that moment, she missed her own mother more than she had done in decades.

♥

'So what do you think, ladies?' Connie said, beaming from ear to ear, thrilled with herself as she twirled round in front of Iris and Kim, proudly showing off the blue pleated skirt she'd just changed into, along with a crisp white blouse and a neatly ironed blue cardigan the exact match of the skirt.

She'd left the table straight after dessert, so she could go upstairs to prep and preen herself; she'd been gone for ages, and now here she was, all set for her big date with Ronnie, who was due to call any minute.

'You look lovely,' Iris said, sincerely meaning it. 'Blue really is your colour. Brings out your eyes.'

'Stop being so bloody polite, Iris,' said Kim, sitting back at the kitchen table, which was piled high with dirty dishes, with her feet up on the chair. 'You're like the Queen, Mam. No matter what you wear, it makes absolutely no difference. You always end up looking the very same.'

'Just for that, smarty pants,' said Connie, instantly shifting back into nagging mode, 'you can get off your lazy bum and start loading up the dishwasher. I want this place spotless by the time I get home, do you hear me?'

Kim pulled a face at her, and then Connie turned to Iris, all sweetness and light again. 'I hope you enjoyed your dessert, Iris, love?'

'It was gorgeous, thank you,' Iris smiled.

'You can't beat a nice slice of Viennetta, can you?'

Just then, the doorbell buzzed, sending an almost electric current through Connie, as she stiffened and froze. 'Oh, Jesus, that's him now! Stay where you are, Iris, I really want you to get a good look at him. Kim? Make yourself useful and get the door. And you're to be nice to him!'

'I'm always nice,' said Kim defensively, slowly hauling herself up and padding down the hall in her socks to answer it.

The kitchen door was half closed over and Iris and Connie locked eyes with each other, both tuning into what was being said at the hall door.

'Hi, Ronnie,' Kim was greeting him, 'come on in, she's just in the kitchen.'

'Ahh, howaya, Kay, love,' Iris heard a man's deep voice saying. 'Good to see you again. That was some night last week, huh?'

'I think the less said about last week, the better.'

At that, Iris sat up straight and really started paying attention. There was something in Kim's tone of voice which didn't sound like her at all.

'Ah sure, meself and your mam got on like a house on fire,' this man was saying, as Kim led him down the hallway. 'And wait till you see, we'll have a great night out tonight too. I'll make sure of it, don't you worry, Kay.'

'It's Kim, actually.'

Then Kim dropped her voice, so Iris really had to strain to overhear. No, it seemed, she hadn't been imagining things. Kim was ice-cold now and almost seemed to be threatening him – so unlike her usual buoyant, happy, upbeat self. Thankfully Connie didn't appear to have heard a word, as she was now fussing and faffing in front of a tiny mirror over beside the kitchen window, carefully reapplying lipstick, then fluffing out her fine, feathery hair, humming happily to herself.

But Iris could hear the little radio drama that was playing out in the hallway, loud and clear.

'You listen to me, Ronnie, and you listen well,' Kim was saying, her voice low and almost threatening. 'I've no problem with you taking Mam out for a few drinks and a late night – God knows, I do it myself often enough. But if you even think of getting my mother into the state you got her in last week, you'll have me to answer to – do you understand? She was poisoned for about two days afterwards. She could barely even remember that night.'

'Ahh, keep your hair on, Kay,' this Ronnie answered back. 'At least your mam is getting out these nights, and she has a proper boyfriend now. Not like plenty of others I could mention.'

'Excuse me?' said Kim, rounding in on him. 'Were you having a go at me just there?'

Iris had been riveted to this, but at that moment Connie turned away from the mirror and breezed out of the kitchen, completely oblivious to the undercurrent of tension that was making itself felt.

'Ronnie, there you are!' she trilled, as he kissed her lightly on each cheek, Mediterranean-style. 'Are you and Kim having a nice little chat? That's lovely, I so want you both to be friends. Now come on inside and say hello to our guest, Iris.'

Connie wobbled back into the kitchen on her high heels, followed by a short little man with a shiny bald head and one of those complicated handlebar moustaches that looked like a great deal of work had gone into its maintenance.

Introductions were made, and Iris stood up to shake hands. She towered over this Ronnie, who appeared to be eyeing her up and down, getting the full measure of her.

'Iris is a friend of Kim's,' Connie said, as Kim stood by the door, arms folded, frowning crossly. 'They work together, in fact.'

'No offence, Iris, love,' said Ronnie, 'but are you not a bit old to be a pal of Kay's? I mean, Kim's?'

'Real charmer, aren't you, Ronnie?' Kim said, her voice dripping with dry sarcasm. There was a tiny, taut little pause as everyone read her tone.

Then Connie snapped out of it, quickly leading him out of there and safely back through the front door again.

'See you later, girls! Don't wait up!'

There was a long, long pause before Kim spoke.

'Don't get me wrong, Iris,' she said tightly, sitting back at the kitchen table again. 'There's good stuff about Analyzed. A lot of good stuff. But the genie's out of the bottle now. And holy fuck, it sure as hell has a lot to answer for.'

Chapter Twenty-One

Connie

'Amore mio . . . tu sei quello per me . . .'

'Oh, I love this song so much!' Connie squealed like an overexcited fangirl. 'My Jack sang it in the shower all the time. Well, he tried to sing it, given that the poor man didn't have two notes in his head. It means "you are the one for me", in English. Listen to it, Ronnie, isn't it only beautiful?'

'Roll down the window there, love,' said Ronnie, making the biggest fuss of her, 'so you can hear it that bit louder.'

The two of them were sitting very companionably side by side up in the front of the chip van, as Ronnie stretched across the passenger seat where Connie was perched to yank the window down even further. Sure enough, the sounds of Andrea Bocelli's angelic voice wafted in much more clearly, and Connie honestly thought she was in seventh heaven.

It had been a magical evening, and may God forgive her, but Connie kept thinking to herself, 'Wait till I tell Betty all about this!' Betty of all people would be pea green with envy. Of course, she and Ronnie strictly speaking weren't exactly *inside* the Aviva Stadium, where the concert was taking place, but as Ronnie kept reminding her, sure hadn't they still got the best seats in the house?

'And you can help yourself to a bag of chips any time, if you fancy it,' he'd offered, very generously too, she thought. 'Or a Magnum out of the freezer. No expense spared for my big date tonight, wha'?'

Mind you, when they'd first got to the concert car park, poor old Ronnie had to knuckle down to some very hard work; honestly, Connie had never seen anything like it in her life. No sooner had they pitched a good parking spot and pulled over, than a long queue formed at the van's serving hatch, everyone looking for singles of chips and batter burgers before the show.

'You'd never think the classical music brigade would be so mad about spice burgers, would you?' Ronnie had called out to her from the back of the van, where the poor man was run off his feet frying, serving customers, taking cash and giving back change. A real one-man band, Connie thought. Of course, when she'd seen for herself just how hectic it was for him, she immediately offered to help him out.

'I could make myself useful, you know!' she'd said, but like the gentleman that Ronnie was, he wouldn't hear of it.

'Are you soft in the head or what, love?' he'd said, horrified at the very thought. 'You're my guest, so you just sit up at the front of the van there, and enjoy your tin of Fanta.'

It wasn't usually like this though, he'd explained to her; his pal Barney normally worked alongside him and between the two of them, they could usually manage the pre-show rush. However, given that Ronnie was 'on a date with a lady friend tonight', Barney apparently had handed over the keys of the van to his pal so he and Connie could have a nice bit of privacy to enjoy the concert together.

'Barney didn't fancy playing third wheel with the two of us, you know yourself, love,' as Ronnie had cheerily told her.

Connie couldn't remember the last time she'd felt so happy. Throughout the whole concert, when the demand for chips had calmed down, she and Ronnie were getting on famously. In between Andrea Bocelli's songs, as thunderous applause rang out, the pair of them had great chats about her Jack and his late wife, Barbara, and what they'd make of it if they saw the pair of them out on a date.

'When Kim first talked me into doing this dating thing,' Connie said, as the crowd in the stadium cheered themselves hoarse, 'I felt awful about it – nearly like I was cheating on poor old Jack's memory, if that makes any sense. But then, as soon as I met you . . .' She broke off there, staring fondly across at Ronnie. He was back sitting in the driver's seat beside her, glugging a tin of Coke and tapping his fingers on the steering wheel, to the beat of the music.

'. . . I completely changed my mind,' Connie said, finishing her sentence. 'Because I think my Jack would have got on great with you. You'd be exactly the type of fella he'd love to go for a pint with.'

'Ahh, what a lovely thing to say,' Ronnie beamed back at her.

'So what about your Barbara? Do you think she'd approve of you going out dating again?'

'God rest the poor woman's poor soul,' Ronnie said, blessing himself and falling silent for a bit, staring thoughtfully out through the windscreen as his jovial mood suddenly seemed to shift down a gear. 'Taken from us too young. She's six years gone now, and there's not a day goes by that I don't shed a little tear over her.'

Was he shedding that little tear now? Certainly looked like it, Connie thought, reaching out to give his hand a comforting squeeze.

Not over her yet, she thought. *Not by a long shot.*

Something she'd have to bear in mind. Just in case this budding little romance ever went anywhere. Because the more she got to know Ronnie, the more she really, really wanted that to happen.

Sure there was no harm hoping, was there?

You had to say this about Andrea Bocelli. He sure as hell gave great value for money, and after no fewer than three encores, the show finally came to a thunderous ending. He'd saved the best for last, with his beautiful rendition of 'The Prayer', a song that always made Connie cry. Happy tears, though, she thought, dabbing her eyes as she looked fondly across the van at Ronnie. He stank of chips and vinegar and deep-fat-fried onion rings, and she didn't mind a single bit.

'Right then, showtime,' he said, snapping into action as the post-concert crowds started to descend on the van, all looking for late-night suppers to take home with them. It was, if possible, even more insanely busy than it had been before the show, and it just felt plain wrong to Connie that she was sitting up in the front passenger seat, twiddling her thumbs, as poor old Ronnie worked his socks off. Mother of God, it was like a sweatshop back there.

'Ahh, here this is pure madness,' she said, making a snap decision, flinging open the van door and clambering down, while trying not to let her skirt blow up over her head in front of an ever-growing queue of hungry people. She went straight round to the back of the van and hammered on the door till Ronnie opened it up for her.

'What are you at, love?' Ronnie said, while simultaneously scooping up fresh-cooked chips into brown paper bags, lashing salt and vinegar all over them, handling cash payment for it and taking an order from the next in line. 'You're my guest for the night, I'd be miles happier if you went back up to the front seat and relaxed.'

'You must be joking,' Connie said firmly, climbing up inside the van beside him. 'Me, sitting up the front like Lady Muck while you're slaving away here on your own? Sure didn't I work in Flynns hotel for decades? Trust me, Ronnie, I know my way around a chip pan and a deep fat fryer better than anyone you ever met. Now,' she said, turning round to face the queue, 'who's next in line? Yes, madam? What can I get for you this evening?'

It was well past midnight, and the pair of them were exhausted. It had been non-stop in the van, and neither of them had drawn breath. Connie had completely taken over the cooking end of things, where, she had to say, Ronnie was making a bit of a pig's ear with the batter burgers, and his idea of portion control was out the window.

'What are you doing, doling out bags of chips that size?' she chided him, as soon as she took in the state of the van. 'Do you want your punters to be sick? And you have to give out little side portions of coleslaw in plastic containers. Why have you none here? Irish people love a bit of coleslaw with their chippy suppers. And where's the bread and butter? Supposing punters fancy a chip butty? Did you think of that?'

Meanwhile, Ronnie took over the cash end of things, and between the two of them, they had everyone served and heading home happy by the time the Guards came over to tell them the stadium was closing its gates for the night.

'You were a little gem tonight,' Ronnie smiled at her, as he peeled off his apron, dabbed the sweat from his baldie forehead and helped Connie climb down out of the van. It was pitch-dark now, and the giant car park was completely deserted, apart from one or two lone cars.

'Never would have managed without you, Connie, love,' he said, as the two of them paused to breathe in the cool, refreshing night air. Oh God, Connie thought, the state of me. Her good blue rig-out was spattered with grease, and there wasn't a single part of her that didn't stink of onions and deep fat frying oil.

'We make a great team, don't we?' he said.

'Ahh, sure it was nothing,' Connie flushed. 'Glad to be useful, that's all. And if you think that rush hour was bad, you should have seen Flynns hotel on the day of a big international match, you'd have died!'

Ronnie looked fondly down at her, then slipped his arms around her waist and cuddled her in closer to him.

'Ahh Jesus, Ronnie,' Connie protested, 'the stink off me . . . even my hair is smelly!'

'Go on out of that, you smell gorgeous,' he grinned, leaning down to her for a big, wet kiss.

Connie was going to kiss him back, but then, out of the corner of her eye, she noticed something. A man, youngish, not that much older than Kim, with a tight haircut and one of those goatee beards, had just stepped out of a big black jeep parked close by and seemed to be staring, just staring over at the two of them, with his arms folded. A punter who wanted chips, maybe, and who was checking to see if the van was still open? He seemed to give up pretty quickly though, because moments later, he jumped back into his jeep and zoomed off.

She was on the verge of saying it to Ronnie, but just then, he kissed her, warmly and softly, and all thoughts of eejits in parked cars looking for chips at this hour went clean out of her head.

Chapter Twenty-Two

Kim

'Because you know, Iris, this isn't just out of the ordinary, or a flash in the pan . . .'

'I am naturally well aware of this,' Iris replied sharply.

'I thought this was going to be some tiny little venture that fizzled out in a short time, the way most of them do . . .'

'But we didn't, did we?'

'You do know that investors are going to start knocking at your door very soon? And you're gonna have to take those meetings . . .'

'Of course. And should such a miracle happen, I'll need you there, in the room with me. We've come this far together, Kim, so let's keep going wherever the journey takes us – together.'

The two of them were sitting out on the Sloan Curtis rooftop one sunny lunchtime, where their colleagues were clustered around them on various bench tables, yakking, chatting, laughing, having a rare old time. Meanwhile Kim went back to wolfing down an oversized submarine roll, while Iris nibbled thoughtfully on a rice cake and sipped at a herbal tea. It was packed on the rooftop, as it normally was come 1 p.m. every day in summer, and when Kim spotted Iris sitting all alone in the shade, she didn't hesitate to join her.

'It'll mean you can recoup your costs,' she went on, 'and maybe even grow Analyzed that bit more . . .'

'Which in turn means that I need to prepare, like I've never done before in my whole life,' said Iris, thinking aloud. 'And you can help out here. We're going to need to target all of the appropriate investors, create a pitch deck, detail precisely how we would use investment funds to grow . . .'

'Course I'll help,' said Kim. 'We're actuaries. We know how this shit works.'

Iris smiled at that. Amazing, Kim thought, looking over at her, how much even just a smile softened her face so much. One of these days, she might even say it to her. *Smile more, finger-wag less. You'll be so glad you did.*

'To be honest with you,' Kim added, 'I think investors would be insane to turn us down. We're growing at the rate of knots here. In fact, you know what?'

'What's that?'

'I think we're going to have to take on extra staff. I can barely cope with the digital end of things as it is, and you've hardly seen the light of day since this took off.'

'Even more astonishingly,' Iris nodded in agreement, 'I've been so run off my feet overseeing the whole site, I have yet to go on one single date. One. I think it's my longest time ever without an online date of some kind. I certainly never saw that happening.'

'Ironic, isn't it?' Kim sighed, staring blankly ahead. 'The whole reason for Analyzed in the first place was to help users find accurate matches, and yet the only two people I know who've yet to meet anyone are you and me.'

She was just about to make a fresh point to Iris when a familiar voice broke in.

'Excuse me, ladies, could I interrupt you both for a wee moment?'

The two of them looked up to see Hannah standing there, in an elegant tea dress that was blowing in the summery breeze.

'Of course, honey, sit down,' said Kim, patting the empty bench beside her.

'No, not at all, honestly,' Hannah said, shaking her head, 'I didn't want to disturb you. It's just, when I saw you both out here together, I only wanted to say ... well ... a huge, big thank you. Thank you so, so much.'

Kim could second-guess what was coming next, and gave Hannah a supportive little half-wink.

'Oh? Yes?' said Iris, looking at her quizzically. 'Why is that?'

Be nice, Kim willed her silently. *Hannah's reaching out to you here. For the love of God, don't go all 'Dreadnought Iris' on her.*

'Well, all because of Analyzed, I think I've met the first semi-decent guy I've come across in a very long time,' Hannah said shyly, tucking her long fair hair behind her ears and flushing to her roots.

At that, Iris took off her pointy glasses, crossed her legs and folded her arms, listening intently.

'Of course, we've only been on three dates so far,' Hannah went on to explain, as Kim smiled back at her friend. 'So it's still very early days.'

'And all went well?' Iris asked, squinting up at her and shielding her eyes from the glare of the sun.

'Oh, so much better than just "well",' Hannah said warmly. 'Joey and I – that's his name, by the way – matched because I loved what he'd written in his profile about his happiest day – which was the day he was made godfather to his best friend's baby boy. Anyway, I messaged him to say how touched I was by that, because I have a five-year-old goddaughter and she's the light of my life. So the two of us just bonded from there, really. Long before I even met Joey, I felt like we had a really special connection. Our first date went on for hours longer than I ever thought it would.'

'Considering you're a Donegal supporter in the All Ireland and he's a diehard Dubs fan through and through,' Kim teased, 'I thought there'd be skin and hair flying between the pair of you. I nearly had the Guards on standby.'

'And the latest with Joey,' Hannah said shyly, 'is that he wants me to meet his family, the godson included. I can't remember the last time a guy actually asked me to meet his folks. Not since I first moved to Dublin, anyway.'

'Well, that's wonderful to hear,' Iris smiled back at her. 'How kind of you to share it with me.'

'Least I could do,' said Hannah.

'I know from long and bitter experience,' Iris said wisely, 'that when dates go wrong, it can be quite soul-destroying, but when they go right, there's nothing quite like it, is there?'

Well done, Kim thought, all her focus on Iris. You see? *How easy it is just to be pleasant and give people the time of day?*

'Anyway,' Hannah said, getting flustered now, as it seemed everyone rose en masse to get back to their desks, bang on the dot of 2 p.m. 'I only wanted to thank you, Iris. I know from Kim that Analyzed was all your baby – and how hard you both worked on it, too.'

She went to leave, then turned straight back again, a fresh thought occurring to her. 'Oh, I'm so sorry, I forgot to say that just in case I'm a wee bit late getting the Delta report back to you, it's not because I was off dating and letting my work deadlines slip. I'd hate for you to think that, because it's not the case at all. It's because there was a bit of a delay with the risk assessment file.'

'Never you mind about the Delta report,' said Iris, sounding every bit as gracious and benevolent as a queen on a throne. 'You just enjoy this precious time together with the new man in your life. It's Joey, isn't it?'

Hannah nodded.

'Well, thank you for your feedback, Hannah. It means a great deal to me.'

Hannah smiled, winked at Kim and had just moved off when, shock horror, Paul, one of the head honchos at Sloan Curtis, wafted over to join them.

We're certainly popular today, Kim thought. Paul was one of the board of directors; a brusque, gruff type who wore stinky aftershave and who thundered around the offices like he owned them. Kim wasn't one to be easily intimidated, but Paul would scare the shite out of anyone.

In all her years at the company, she'd barely spoken two words to the mighty Paul, but now here he was, chatting to her. Even more surprising was that he was being as warm and friendly as you like.

'Well, well, well, ladies, here you both are,' Paul said jovially, 'the burgeoning success stories of the mobile app world, or so my sources tell me.'

Both Kim and Iris just looked blanky back at him, wondering where this was going.

'Analyzed?' Paul went on to explain. 'You pair are the joint powerhouse behind it, I gather?'

At that, Kim couldn't keep silent.

'Actually, it's all credit to Iris here,' she said, probably the first sentence she'd ever spoken to Paul since she'd been hired. 'It's her baby, her brainchild, 100 per cent all hers.'

Iris said nothing, just shyly lowered her head like someone utterly unused to compliments, gathering up her bag and empty cup, ready to leave.

'Well, in that case, Iris,' Paul said to her, 'I owe you a personal debt of gratitude.'

'Oh, really?' she said, stopping dead in her tracks now.

'My son,' Paul said. 'My wife and I used to despair at the way he worked his way through girlfriends. None of these girls seemed to last longer than a week, but lately he's been saying how popular your app is among his college pals and, long story short, he actually seems to have met someone really lovely on it.'

First Iris looked shocked, then surprised, then really, seriously pleased. 'I'm glad,' she said simply. 'Helping other people, that's all I ever wanted to do.'

'Name of Catherine,' Paul went on. 'Annie, that's my wife, Annie and I have even met this Catherine and she just . . . fits in with our family, is the best way to describe her. Well mannered, polite, easy to get along with, and even I can see that she's good for our boy. You know, when she first came to our home, she brought flowers for Annie and a bottle of wine for me? Amazing,' he said, shaking his head in wonder. 'In fact, I said to my son, "Just make bloody sure you don't mess this up."'

They both thanked him profusely, Paul drifted off and the minute his back was turned, Kim gave Iris the hugest, biggest high five.

'You see?' she said. 'This is all I hear everywhere I go. It's working. It's really, really working.'

'It really seems to be, doesn't it?' Iris said, shaking her head, as if she still couldn't believe it.

'Although,' Kim added, frowning, 'I should probably qualify that. What I mean to say is, that for everyone else other than us, it's working. As long as your name isn't either Kim Bailey or Iris Simpson, then you're home and dry, baby.'

Please don't turn out to be any of the following, Kim found herself praying silently later on that evening. *A weirdo, a pervert, a married man who thinks he's a separated man, a separated man who thinks he's single, a single man who thinks he's God's gift, or else a multi-dater who has no intention of being anything else, because this way, he has the best of all worlds.*

Just then, he arrived at the packed, jostly bar where they'd arranged to meet, which was a little outside of town in the suburb of Tallaght – a fairly unusual place to pick for any date, and it had struck Kim as odd. Ninety-nine per cent of the time, any potential date would arrange to meet up with her in the city centre, where it was central and reasonably convenient for both parties.

Not that meeting up in a suburb that cost upwards of forty euro in a taxi just to get there was going to be a deal-breaker for her, certainly not at this stage in her dating life cycle, when she'd pretty much seen it all. Generally, Kim's policy on dates was thus: unless in the case of exceptionally bonkers carry-on, she would usually put up and shut up. Feck it, was her attitude; as long as she got a laugh and a few drinks out of any night out with a fella, then it was time well spent, as far as she was concerned.

But this was different. This time, Kim had been through the whole painstaking Analyzed process and right now, the stakes were high. So here she was, sitting up on a bar stool at a high table, surrounded by Thursday-night drinkers all out for a good time, just like she hoped to be.

Kim had been scrolling away on her phone, but managed to spot him before he spotted her. Fella a few years older than her, thirty according to his profile, with pale Irish gingery hair, freckles and a wide, crinkly smile that made him look seriously cute in his photo. Mind you, it was his answer to the question *what is your most marked characteristic* that first caught her attention. This guy's answer?

No matter how bad things get, I can still always find some way to raise a laugh out of it. There's nothing so tragic that you can't find something to laugh at.

Which was something Kim related to so strongly, she could happily have had it printed on a T-shirt. Had she finally met a kindred spirit, thanks to Analyzed? Tonight would tell.

Ginger-haired Guy seemed to be moving her way, but just then Kim's heart sank. He seemed to have a woman with him, about thirty or so too, pretty and petite with frizzy brown hair, wearing a pretty pink summer floral dress that swept all the way down to her ankles, with seriously cool platform trainers.

Rats, Kim thought. He's definitely part of a couple. Such a pity, because this guy actually looked cute, not to mention a dead ringer for the date she was waiting to meet. She stopped staring and went back to her phone, but to her surprise, the same ginger-haired, freckly-faced guy came up and tentatively approached her.

'It's Kim, isn't it?' he asked a bit hesitantly, with his frizzy-haired partner just hovering at his shoulder.

'Ehh . . . yeah . . .' she said.

'Hi. I'm him. Louis. Your date? We both got Analyzed?'

'Oh,' she said, taken aback. 'OK. Well, good to meet you, Louis. Here, grab a seat, sit down.'

'And this is Louise,' he said, proudly introducing his companion, who smiled happily and reached out to shake hands. 'Louis and Louise. Gas, isn't it?'

These two are together, Kim wondered? No. She must have got that wrong. Friends, probably, or else they were after-work colleagues, and this Louise just wanted to come along to scout out Louis's date for the night. Bit odd, but then each to his own, she figured.

But that's where the whole night started going pear-shaped. Louise pulled up a bar stool and not only joined them, but kept pointedly holding hands with Louis, touching him, even leaning her head on his shoulder at one stage, all while they were still on their first drink. Kim cracked a few jokes, told a few funny stories, and even though they both laughed, it was hard to ignore what was going on right in front of her.

Am I in the way here, she began to wonder? *Is this Louise one marking her territory with Louis?* The two of them seemed so couply and compatible, and the body language between them was something else.

Ahh, to hell with this anyway, Kim thought, plonking her drink down on the table in front of them and speaking up.

'So, can I ask you both something?' she said, straight out.

'Actually,' Louis said, looking lovingly down at Louise and slipping his hand through hers. 'I think we're the ones who'd like to ask you something.'

I don't know what the hell is going on here, Kim thought, *or what I've walked in on, but I don't like it one bit, and I am so outta here. Just as soon as I finish my cider.*

'What do you think of her?' Louise asked Louis, speaking about Kim in the third person, almost as if she wasn't there.

'I think she's perfect,' said Louis. 'Just what the doctor ordered.'

Kim's brain tried to process what she was hearing, except this time, the two of them turned to her, saying, 'So would you be up for it?'

'Excuse me?' Kim said, her worst fears beginning to materialise.

'Back to ours? Just the three of us?'

'The three of us?' said Kim. 'That is what you just said? I'm not hearing things?'

'Well, yeah, why not?' said Louis. 'You did say on your Analyzed profile that there was nothing you hadn't seen and nothing you wouldn't be game for, so that's why we chose you.'

'You seem pretty game for a laugh,' Louise added. 'And you did say that at this stage in your dating career, you wanted to meet someone new, to experience something you never had before.'

'Yeah,' Kim spluttered, 'by which I meant a half-decent fella who wouldn't start acting the maggot on me! That was NOT my subtle way of saying that I wanted to have a fecking threesome!'

At that, both Louis and Louise's faces fell.

'Oh, right,' they both said flatly, in perfect unison.

'Surely you realised,' said Louise, starting to sound irritated now, 'that when we suggested meeting out here in Tallaght, there was a very specific reason for it?'

'Yeah,' said Louis. 'Because we live so close by. We thought a few drinks here to loosen us all up a bit, get to know each other better, then back to ours.'

Now they were both glaring hotly at her, as if she was some kind of a spoilsport killjoy.

But Kim didn't even let them say another word. Instead she glugged back the dregs of her cider and made for the exit, not even bothering to say goodbye, she was in such a rush to get out of there.

Well, at least there's one small consolation here, she thought, the whole taxi ride back home. The one good thing to come out of all this. Which, of course, was the great story she'd be able to entertain them all with when she got into work first thing the following morning.

They've never heard anything quite like this beaut before, she thought, instantly cheering up in the back of the taxi. Wait till you see, she'd have the whole lot of them in stitches. Best story she'd have told them all in weeks.

♥

But Kim couldn't have been more wrong about that.

'And it turned out the two of them were only after a threesome! Can you believe it? Only my second go on Analyzed and I match up with these pervs?'

Sure enough, there were a good few of her sesh crew clustered around her desk having the chats, Hannah, Greg and Emma among them. Weird thing though, instead of the loud guffaws that Kim had been anticipating – and looking forward to – today it was different. Was she imagining it, or were her mates all looking at her with something like . . . sympathy? Pity? WTF?

'You poor thing,' said Hannah softly. 'What a lousy thing to happen.'

'You must be doing it wrong,' said Emma, folding her arms and squinting at her from under all that black eyeliner. 'Come on, you're the only person I know who's not finding success on this app. And you're one of the co-founders.'

'Yeah, you of all people should get how it works,' said Simon, a serially single guy from Statistics, who they'd all crushed on at some point and who Kim had enjoyed a series of drunken flings with when he first joined the company, about a year ago. 'Even I met someone promising on Analyzed, and I'd given up all hope.'

Ouch. That fecking stung. One by one they all drifted away, not the reaction Kim was used to. Kim, who was normally the centre of attention, the class comedian, Sloan Curtis's resident stand-up.

'*Et tu, Brute?*' she said to Greg, the last man left standing by her desk, one hand shoved deep into his pocket, cradling a coffee with the other.

He shrugged. 'Ask me this time tomorrow.'

'Big date tonight then?'

'Yet again – thanks to Analyzed,' he grinned, rocking up and down on his heels and looking pleased as punch.

'Oooh, really? Fill me in,' said Kim. 'Who is she? Guessing she had good answers to your questions, then?'

'Her name's Mia,' said Greg. 'And put it this way: for the question, "when were you happiest", her answer was the day Ireland won the Grand Slam.'

'OK. Nice one,' Kim nodded. Greg was a massive rugby fan, and when the Six Nations was on, would regularly spend a small fortune travelling abroad to a match at the drop of a hat.

'*And* she's in training for the Dublin marathon. So at least I should have lots in common with Mia. Sounds like a keeper, doesn't she?'

Greg was a veteran of five Dublin marathons and one year, had famously run it on zero sleep after a late, boozy night out with Kim and the gang. More astonishingly, he still managed to finish the shagging thing in a very respectable time, while Kim stayed home in bed, eating chocolate and whining about her hangover.

'Best of luck with it. With Mia, I mean,' said Kim, watching him leave as he drifted back to his desk at the far side of the office. Christ, she thought. Literally all my pals are in the throes of a new romance. Even my mother. Absolutely everyone except me.

But if Kim thought she could escape home for a bit of peace and respite from all this love bollockology and all the budding romances she was starting to get a bit vomity-sick of hearing about, she was sorely mistaken.

She was just about to let herself in through the hall door after work that evening, when it was opened up for her from the inside. Ronnie. Like he lived here. Like he'd moved in.

With the shiny, baldie head on him and that ridiculous-looking moustache.

'Ahh, Kay, there you are now,' he said, sweating from the forehead down. 'Bit unusual for you to be home this early, isn't it? Your ma says you normally don't crawl home till all hours.'

I'm entitled to come home any time I bloody well feel like it, Kim wanted to snap at him, but she bit her tongue.

'Young one like yourself, Kay,' Ronnie went on, waddling down the hall ahead of her, 'you should get out more, meet a nice boyfriend for yourself. Your poor ma is despairing, you know. Says you seem to date all the time, and yet not one of them turns into a boyfriend. Not a single one. "If that's the case, Connie love," I said to her, "then it's your daughter that's the problem, not all the fellas she keeps meeting. She's the common denominator here."'

At that, Kim physically started to seethe. She rarely got cross or cranky or narky, but right now, she was all three.

'I'll thank you for keeping your nose out of my private life, all the same,' she barked at him. *Jesus*, she thought. *Who do I remind myself of?* And then it came to her: Iris at her very worst, Iris back in the bad old days, the same Iris she was gently trying to soften around the edges a bit.

'Only trying to help, Kay,' Ronnie shrugged. 'You're a terrible worry to your ma, and I don't like seeing her fretting over you like that. Still living at home at your age? When I was in my twenties, I was a married man, with my own house, an' all.'

'Ronnie,' Kim said, keeping her voice dangerously low. 'Not that this is any of your business, but it's actually me who pays all the bills here and puts food in the fridge and looks after my mother cash-wise. So if you're going to throw things like that at me, you should at least get your facts straight. I'm the one supporting my mam here, not the other way around. Got it? Now I swear to God, one

249

more offensive remark like that out of your mouth and I'll have no difficulty asking you to leave.'

Ronnie was totally unbothered by her little speech.

'You'd be a lot less narky if you had someone special in your life, Kay, that's all I'm saying.'

'It's KIM! For feck's sake, how hard is that to remember? KIM!' She'd seriously lost her rag now, and was about to escalate this to a full-blown ding-dong, when just then, Connie appeared at the top of the stairs, all dressed up to the nines in her good pale blue suit with the summery sandals she only ever wore on fancy occasions, like weddings, or that time she was summoned for jury duty.

'Ahh, there you both are,' she smiled blissfully. 'I'm so glad the two of you are getting to know each other better, I so want you both to be friends.'

'And here she comes, my beautiful dinner date,' said Ronnie, clutching his hands to his heart, making like he was about to keel over at the very sight of Connie inching her way down the stairs, super-slowly on account of her arthritic knee.

'So where are you off to tonight?' Kim asked. 'Another night in the back of the chip van, getting my mam to work for you for free?' Feck it, she couldn't resist lobbing in the barb. Low-hanging fruit, and so on.

'Kimberley! I don't care for your tone,' said Connie, in her posh, put-on voice that she only ever used when she was out to impress. 'As a matter of fact, Ronnie is taking me out for a lovely Italian meal tonight.'

'Yeah, in fact we better get moving,' Ronnie said, heading for the front door and holding it open for her. 'The early-bird voucher I have expires at 8 p.m. and I don't want to get stuck paying the full whack.'

'Last of the big spenders,' Kim muttered under her breath.

'Don't wait up, Kim! This could be a late one!'

Laughing and tittering their heads off, the two of them skittered out the door, whamming it firmly shut behind them. Leaving Kim alone – all alone with the whole evening stretching ahead of her.

She rolled her eyes, then made for the kitchen, to see what grub was in the fridge that she could possibly cobble a dinner out of. Feck all, as it turned out. Oh, beautiful bowls of fresh pasta salad and a cold chicken with stuffing, she'd gladly have horsed into. But all of them were plastered in yellow Post-its saying, 'Don't touch, Kim, this is for Ronnie's supper!'

Just gone half seven. The earliest she could remember being home in months. She picked up her phone to order a Deliveroo, when next thing a message pinged through from Iris.

You free to talk now? Have some news concerning investors for Analyzed. Good news too.

At that, Kim slumped down at the kitchen table and flung the phone as far away from her as she possibly could.

Fecking Analyzed. Right now, she was seriously wishing she'd never heard of the shagging thing.

Chapter Twenty-Three

Iris

It was a crazy-busy lunchtime later that week, and Iris was a bag of nerves. Mind you, he was the one who'd approached her first, not the other way around. He was the one who'd initiated contact with her, who'd made all the running, who'd suggested where and when they would meet – he'd even gone to considerable trouble to outline his reasons for picking Iris, of all people. Out of the thousands of potentials out there, it seemed that she was the one he'd really wanted to meet up with in person.

He'd chosen the venue too, saying that meeting for the first time via Zoom or a Skype call didn't really cut it for him. Person to person was always better for this sort of thing, he'd insisted, and even though slipping out of the office for lunch was seriously problematic for her, she weighed it up and decided to go for it.

Kim had been largely instrumental in this too.

'This is one meeting you have to take,' she'd said, as soon as the arrangement was mooted.

'I would be considerably happier if you were there with me,' Iris said, raising an eyebrow, as she patted on some tinted moisturiser at her desk, with Kim hovering right at her shoulder. 'We're a team now, it feels wrong to go in there alone.'

'I'll be just on the other end of the phone if you need me,' Kim said, dismissing it. 'For now, though, he suggested a one-to-one with Analyzed's founder, and that's you. So away you go, listen to what he has to say and . . . sparkle!'

'Did you just say . . . *sparkle*?' Iris said, wondering if Kim had momentarily lost it. 'Hello? Do I strike you as the sparkly type? Have you and I actually met?'

Kim grinned.

'You know what I mean, just go in there, smile, shine, be positive – and enjoy.'

'I'm not quite sure how much enjoyment there is to be had from a meeting with a putative investor,' said Iris in her crispest tones as she rose to leave, 'but we shall see.'

Kim walked Iris through the office, into the lift and all the way down to the main entrance at ground-floor level. Funny thing, Iris thought distractedly, just how many people were greeting her with warm smiles and big hellos these days. Never used to happen before. People she didn't even know were saying hi, which was certainly a first. Since when did she get so popular?

The two turned to face each other at the giant glass entrance doors.

'Well, best of luck then,' said Kim, giving her a cheery thumbs up.

'Oh, and one more thing I neglected to ask you,' Iris said, halfway out of the revolving door, as something struck her almost as an afterthought.

'Yeah?' said Kim, turning on her heel.

'How are you getting on with Analyzed this week? Any interesting dates come out of it for you yet?'

Kim had been smiling and in her usual bouncy form, but at that, her whole mood seemed to shift.

'Don't ask,' she groaned. 'Just don't even ask.'

'So the upshot is, we're offering you €500k, in return for 40 per cent of Analyzed.'

Iris, who was sitting across the table from him, took her glasses off and tried to process what she was hearing. His name was Will, Will White, and he was young, late twenties tops, focused and straight to the point, which Iris greatly appreciated. Polite and businesslike, he'd made a point of rising to greet her when she first arrived at the smart, chic restaurant where they'd arranged to meet, one of those restaurants with a celebrity chef in the kitchen, award-winning menus and every single table occupied. As with most busy professionals, he'd allowed just a sufficient amount of time for small talk before diving straight down to business. Something she respected.

'You will, of course, need to think about this,' Will said, as their bill arrived and he insisted on paying.

'And discuss it with my colleague and digital manager,' Iris said. 'But yes, I will give it considerable thought and come back to you with a firm yes or no.'

'In my experience, we need to move fast on this,' Will said. 'That's the thing about start-up apps. Very often they can flare hot for a finite period of time and then fizzle out.

Just to remind you, there's half a million euro on the table here. My company's strength is in developing apps and taking them to the next level. I appreciate that Analyzed has started local, but in the long term, we could potentially be talking global here.'

'It's certainly a lot of money,' Iris said, thinking aloud. 'So clearly you anticipate a projected revenue stream that would give you a return of 29.4 per cent. That's considerable.'

This time, Will let out a low little whistle. 'Did you just do that calculation in your head?' he asked. 'Impressive.'

'It's what I do. I'm an actuary.'

'Well, you certainly know your stuff.'

'Just one more question,' Iris said, as the restaurant began to clear and they both rose to leave. 'Why Analyzed? What was it about us that made you want to meet me, to talk in person?'

They were just stepping out of the restaurant and onto the busy street outside, but at that, he stopped to really consider the question.

'Iris,' he said after a pause, 'you don't need me to tell you that there's literally thousands of dating apps out there, some successful, some not so. Each one seems to have its own unique selling point and its own very specific target market, particularly age-wise. It's a massive growth area online, and so that was the initial attraction for us. But what made Analyzed really stand out was the fact that it's appealing to all age groups and demographics. I've seen college students on it, thirty-somethings who are probably at their dating peak and who really want to settle down, and then the middle-aged cohort, many of whom are separated or even divorced, with families, which of course can make it more difficult to find a partner.'

'Our age range goes even higher than that,' Iris said proudly. 'I know of many in the sixty-plus age group who have an activity hit rate of 62 per cent on our app. You'd be surprised,' she added with a little grin.

'They've possibly got that bit more time on their hands,' Will agreed.

'In fact, my digital manager's mother is in her seventies and she's one of our biggest success stories.'

'And like all the best ideas, yours was simple. Ask the right questions, to find the right partner. And it's caught on, and it's growing all the time.'

'Thirty-four-point-seven per cent in the past week alone.'

'So if that's what you can achieve in barely two months, can you imagine where we can take you in the next three to five years? It seems there's a lot of lonely people out there.'

I know, Iris thought. *I'm one of them.*

Then she paused to correct herself mentally. *Or rather, I used to be.* Because when had her life ever been so full or so busy as it had been since Analyzed was first launched?

'So it's all just very impromptu now, nothing fancy at all,' Hannah was saying, in that beguiling Donegal accent of hers. 'Our house is only a wee two-up, two-down that I share with three other girls, and it wouldn't be in the poshest part of town, or anything like that. Nothing like what you'd be used to, Iris.'

'I see.'

'But the one thing the place does have going for it,' Hannah went on, 'is that the garden is really lovely. And the forecast is to be fine and sunny for tonight, so we thought, why not? Just a little barbecue for all the team, and a few drinks, have a bit of a laugh. All very last-minute and casual, you know how parties like this work.'

Iris didn't have a clue how these things worked, but she said nothing. Mainly because she was still unsure as to where Hannah was going with this. Was this what she thought it was? Was she really being invited into a colleague's home for an actual party?

'So I'll write down the address for you,' Hannah said, 'and we hope to see you there – any time after seven is great. And you're to bring nothing, only your good self, do you hear me now?'

Iris was completely stupefied, and couldn't find the words to answer. This certainly made a first. Never, in her fifteen years of working for Sloan Curtis, had anyone ever invited her to a party before now. Never.

Just then, Kim bounced over to where the two of them were standing together at the top of the conference room, where a big strategy meeting for the whole team was about to kick off. As usual, just barging straight in without a preamble.

'Of course Iris is coming tonight!' Kim interrupted. 'Don't you worry, Hannah, I'll make sure of it. See you later, and by the way, mine's . . .'

'Don't you worry, a large pint of cider will be on standby, waiting for you,' Hannah laughed, before drifting off to take her seat at the table, along with the rest of the team who were assembling.

'She really wants me to be there?' Iris muttered to Kim, looking stunned.

'Well, don't sound so surprised,' said Kim. 'Thanks to you and your work, Hannah is the happiest she's been since she moved to Dublin, with a big ride of a fella hanging off her arm. Course you're invited.'

It wasn't often she was lost for words, but that particular afternoon, Iris was.

She was working late, *quelle surprise*, and so ended up being among the last to arrive at Hannah's neat little red-brick house in a well maintained, recently gentrified part of town. *I'll stay for an hour*, she thought, rapping on the door. *Just to be polite. Just to show how much I appreciate getting this invitation in the first place.*

But nothing could have prepared her for the warmth of welcome she received.

'Iris, you found us!' said Hannah, throwing open her hall door and stretching out to give her a big warm hug. Iris almost had to take a step back, she was so shocked. Someone was actually hugging her? For real?

'Come on in, let me get you a drink,' said Hannah, guiding Iris through the tiny little hallway. From there, you had a clear view right the way out to the garden, which was sun-soaked, packed to the rafters and with the most delicious smoky smell wafting back into the house, as the barbecue got into full swing. 'I hope you're hungry,' Hannah added cheerily. 'Greg is on barbecue duty tonight, and he fancies himself as a real Jamie Oliver, but you'd be well advised to make sure your burger's not too pink before diving in. When it comes to Greg, we've all learned that one the hard way.'

She led Iris on into the garden, and Iris was genuinely touched at how many people there turned around to give her a friendly wave. Especially seeing as she was probably the oldest person there by a good fifteen years. Again, another first. Normally, at lunchtime in the office, no one ever looked twice at her, and most of the time, she sat and nibbled at a few rice cakes alone with her laptop, invisible to the masses.

Not tonight, though.

A cluster of people who she knew from her department, but who she'd never really spoken to socially before, all began to gather around her and in no time, Iris found herself in the highly irregular position of being the dead centre of attention. Even Greg Wilkinson, who rarely spoke to her unless he had something to complain about, wafted away from his barbecue duties purposely to chat.

'Hey, Iris,' he said, folding his arms and looking so at odds with how he normally did, with a spatula in one hand and wearing a neon-pink frilly apron. 'It seems I owe you a very big thank you.'

'Let me guess, you got lucky on Analyzed then?' Iris smiled back.

'Early days, of course,' he grinned, and yet again, this was new. Greg had to have been working on her team for about six or seven years now, and never once in all that time had she seen him crack even the merest hint of a smile.

'Let's just put it this way,' he said, 'it's taken me a very long time to meet someone as passionate about running marathons and doing triathlons as I am. Most women think I'm a complete nutjob, but . . . I feel like I've finally met a like-minded soul. Her name is Mia, and so far, it's bloody great.'

'That's wonderful to hear,' said Iris, genuinely touched. 'Is she here? I'd really love to say hi.'

'Sure, wait right here and I'll bring her over. She'd be intrigued to meet the founder of Analyzed. She and I both reckon you're the Jack Dorsey of tomorrow.'

Greg drifted away in a cloud of barbecue smoke, calling out to a tall, athletic-looking blonde woman who was sitting on a bench at the back of the garden. 'She's here, come on, come over and say hi!'

Just then, that dark-haired member of Iris's team, Emma, a woman about Kim's age who always wore the most ludicrous Doc Martens into work, along with nightclub amounts of black eyeliner, sidled up to have a chat. Normally Iris was acutely aware of a distinctive vibe emanating from Emma, a pronounced, low-level hostility. But tonight, she was all sweetness and light itself.

'So how does it feel to be Miss Popular?' Emma asked, in that husky smoker's voice. A strange question, and for a second Iris almost wondered if Emma could possibly be speaking to her, when Kim bounced out of the house, dressed in denim shorts and an acid-yellow halterneck top, sunglasses perched on her head, carrying a trayload of cocktails in the most lurid shade of turquoise Iris had ever seen.

'Hey, you made it!' she yelled at Iris the minute she spotted her. 'I'm thrilled you came – aren't Hannah's parties the best? Come on, I just made us all Blue Lagoons, grab one quick before they're gone. Vodka and curaçao, you're gonna love it.' Then, raising her voice to address the whole garden, she said, 'Oi! You lot! Iris is here, and you all better be nice to her now, before she gets famous and even richer than Mark Zuckerberg!'

It wasn't just a ripple of applause that followed. It seemed like the whole garden turned to Iris and cheered her. This was the sort of whooping and clapping from the rafters that Iris had never once experienced in her life.

It bowled her over.

'Wow,' she said to Kim, genuinely touched to tears. 'Just . . . wow.'

'Why are you surprised?' Kim asked, as she started passing around the cocktails. 'Thanks to you, Sloan Curtis has practically turned into an episode of *Love Island*. And you and me, my friend, are the only two gooseberries on the whole show. We need to find partners for ourselves next, and that's not negotiable.'

Iris had only planned on staying an hour max at the barbecue, but as the evening wore on, there was no question of her leaving, none at all. Certainly not when Hannah and her brand-new boyfriend urged her to taste the cocktails, and surprisingly, they began to have the most pleasing effect, making Iris feel woozy and happy and absolutely not like going anywhere. Then Greg served her up a burger with coleslaw and all the trimmings, and if it looked a bit pink in the centre, then Iris was tactful enough not to say anything.

As darkness fell, one of Hannah's flatmates, a soulful, Joni Mitchell type, produced her guitar and, urged on by Kim, started up a sing-song. All the chatter and laughter quietened down as people lolled about drunkenly on the rugs that were dotted all over the grass, and she launched into a beautiful, sweet-sounding Katie Melua number. The whole mood of the party shifted to a cooler, late-night, more mellow vibe, and Iris sat back on the garden bench she'd been perched on, cocktail in hand, eyes closed over, just listening to the purest and most angelic singing voice.

Wow, she thought, marvelling that a) she'd stayed out past eleven at night; b) she was squiffy enough that she'd have to abandon her car and take a taxi home; and, most astonishingly of all c) she'd actually had the best time she could remember in ages.

'Can I talk to you for a sec?'

Iris squinted up through the twinkly fairy lights that illuminated the whole garden to see that it was Emma, in those awful-looking Doc Martens, hovering over her.

'Certainly,' said Iris, patting the empty seat beside her. 'Here, sit down.'

Emma threw herself down onto the bench and immediately started puffing on an e-cigarette.

'Thing is, Iris, I've had more than a few scoops by now . . .'

'Haven't we all?'

'. . . and normally, I wouldn't even dream of saying this, only that's the effect a bucketload of Kim's cocktails will have on you.'

'Good, aren't they?' Iris said with a little half-smile.

'Bit too bloody good,' Emma replied, sucking away at the vape. 'Anyway, you're here tonight and everyone is glad you came, and all I wanted to say was that . . . well, if I ever came across as being nasty or moody or a bit sarky with you in work . . .'

Which you have been, many, many times, Iris thought. *I conservatively calculate that in approximately 75 per cent of our dealings with each other, you've been little short of passive-aggressive.*

Of course, Iris said nothing out loud. It wasn't that sort of evening. Besides, she was enjoying herself far too much to bring in any negativity.

'Then I'm really sorry,' Emma trailed off. 'People are always telling me that I give off the wrong impression, so if I ever did it with you, then mea culpa.'

Iris sat quietly for a moment, drinking in the night air and the music and the whole chilled-out vibe before she replied.

'You know something, Emma?' she said softly. 'Then you and I have that much in common. I'm always giving people the wrong first impression, too.'

'What I meant to say,' Emma qualified, her hand twitching nervously on her short, spiky hair, 'is that I never really realised how sound you were before this. Because it turns out that you are, Iris, you really are. And so I'm sorry – for ever coming across as disliking you or even being hostile.'

'Me and all,' came a man's voice from right behind them. Iris twisted round to see Greg there, helping himself to a tin of beer from a makeshift bar behind the bench.

She just blinked back at each of them in turn, not quite certain what the right thing to say here was. But then, she was so out of practice socially, how was she to know?

'You know what?' Greg went on, ripping open the tab on the beer and glugging back a mouthful. 'Kim's been telling us for a while now that we're all wrong about you.'

'And it turns out she was dead right,' Emma said, nudging Iris drunkenly. 'In fact, you wanna know something? It actually turns out you're kind of cool. In your own Iris-like way, of course, but still.'

'You're one of us,' Greg nodded sagely. 'Most definitely one of us.'

Iris knew only too well that as backhanded compliments went, this was right up there. She also knew there was a 92 per cent probability this was the alcohol talking and little else. Doubtless, all would be forgotten at the office, and normal hostility would be resumed. But so what, she thought, feeling tipsy and happy and content and popular. For however long it lasted, it sure as hell felt good.

'Well now,' she said, aware that the two of them were looking at her, waiting for a response. 'That's certainly good to hear. And for my part, if I've ever come across as being a little . . . you know . . . the Dreadnought Iris-like with either of you . . .'

Emma buried her face in her hands, mock theatrically. 'Oh, would you stop! I swear it wasn't me who thought up that shitty nickname, I swear, it was Gregory there behind me, looking as innocent as an altar boy.'

'That's right, rat on me to the boss, why don't you, you spiky-headed minx!'

Iris just smiled and dismissed their good-natured banter with a wave of her wrist.

'No biggie,' she said, a phrase so unlike anything she'd normally say and one she'd recently picked up from Kim. Like she was learning so much from Kim these days.

Emma slipped her arm lightly around Iris's shoulder.

'You're part of the gang now,' she said.

'And like it or not, you're going nowhere,' said Greg.

A silence descended as a gentle round of applause broke out for the singer, and from the bottom of the garden, Kim shouted out a request for some class of pop song Iris had never heard of. Something more upbeat and bouncy, with a refrain that claimed that if you liked something, then you really ought to put a ring on it. Utterly bizarre. All of the young ones who surrounded her seemed to be very familiar with it though, as every head bobbed along enthusiastically.

Meanwhile, Iris just sat back and allowed the pleasantness of the evening to wash all over her.

You know what? Maybe I was wrong, she thought. *Maybe it wasn't a loving, steady boyfriend that I was looking for at all. Maybe it wasn't a partner or a husband or even a family that I spent all these long, long years searching for.*

Maybe it was just friends – full stop.

Chapter Twenty-Four

Connie

'Now of course, this is really only a flying visit,' Connie chirruped, all delighted with herself.

'Just as well,' her friend Betty replied a bit snippily. 'I am at work, you know, dearest, so socialising really isn't a good idea just now. I'm sure you understand. Even though it has been quite some time since you yourself held down a job. I really am up to my eyes here today.'

'Is that right now?' said Connie, looking all around her in mock surprise. 'Because I seem to be the only customer in here.'

Pointedly, she glanced around the charity shop where Betty worked, which, sure enough, was tumbleweed-empty. The shop was so run-down, too, Connie thought disgustedly; in near-permanent semi-darkness and with mould on the walls – an absolute disgrace. And for some reason, the place always stank to high heaven of damp. It was stuffed to the rafters with all manner of tat and junk like you just wouldn't believe. The place was piled to ceiling height with cardboard boxes full of magazines so old, Princess Diana was still alive in them, banjaxed NutriBullets, ancient mobile phones the size of a car battery and souvenir tea towels from the last Pope's visit.

It was such an embarrassment, in fact, that kids locally had nicknamed the shop Dead Old Lady Dresses.

'Just because there aren't any customers in the store doesn't mean I'm not busy,' Betty said, with a rock-hard, forced smile. 'I'm doing the books here, if you must know. Which is highly skilled work, requiring a great deal of concentration. So if you're just in for a chat, Connie dearest, perhaps we can leave it till another time?'

'Oh no, not at all, Betty,' Connie smiled sweetly. 'I'm actually here to buy. Well, I thought to myself, there's poor old Betty all on her lonesome in that tiny little charity shop, I should really do the kind thing and pop in to support her.'

'Well, I suppose the prices here are certainly within your budget,' Betty fake-smiled back. 'So what can I help you with? New housecoat, maybe? We got a donation just this morning of a load of surgical stockings from the nuns across the road in the Sisters of Charity. Perhaps something along those lines? We have all the larger sizes here, so we should definitely find something to fit.'

Connie pretended to muse on this for a bit, then shook her head firmly.

'I don't think so, Betty. Not really suitable for where I'm off to. You hang onto them for yourself, sure you can't have enough, can you?'

You could see that it physically choked Betty to ask the question, but curiosity got the better of her, and she couldn't resist.

'So where is it you're off to, Connie? Mass? Bingo? A good funeral, maybe?'

Connie just smiled and took all the time in the world before answering.

'Not at all,' she said. 'Ronnie and I – that's my boyfriend, by the way—'

'Yes, so you've told me,' Betty said drily. 'Many, many times. There's not too many of us around here who aren't aware that you've got a new boyfriend, Connie. Drives a chipper van, isn't that right?'

Connie let that one pass, and instead went for the big pay-off.

'Anyway, Ronnie is taking me away for the weekend,' she said triumphantly. 'To Brittas Bay, if you don't mind. For a nice bit of sea and sunshine, as he says. Isn't that just lovely of him? You'll really have to meet him one of these days, Betty, the two of you would get on so well. You never know, he might even have a nice friend for you. Then we could go out in a foursome – wouldn't that be gas, now? Like old times.'

'Brittas Bay?' sniffed Betty. 'Wicklow? Not taking you too far, is he? I thought you were going to say Paris, but Wicklow? Sure Brittas is only down the road. Mind you, I suppose he can't drive too far in that chip van of his, can he?'

'Oh, the van isn't actually his at all, love,' Connie said, putting her straight before she rubbed it in even more. 'It belongs to a friend of his, Barney. Ronnie just gives him a hand in it the odd weekend, that's all.' Then breaking off dreamily, she added, 'He's such a dote like that. The kind of fella that would do anything for you. He might even help you tidy up the place here a bit, if you were stuck?'

Betty chose to ignore that one.

'Hmm,' she said, as though really giving this thought. 'Wicklow. I'm afraid the only place I know in Wicklow is the Powerscourt Hotel, five-star, you know. My Nigel treated me to a spa weekend there for my last birthday. A fortune, of course, but worth every cent. You're hardly staying there though, are you? This Ronnie would need to sell a fair few singles of chips before you'd stretch to even one night at the Powerscourt Hotel.'

'It's a secret where he's taking me,' Connie smiled. Which was only a white lie, she told herself. Truth was that Ronnie was taking her to a caravan park for the weekend, where his pal Barney owned a mobile home that he was lending them. But if she told Betty she was going to a caravan park, she'd never hear the end of it. Also, she didn't put it past Betty to start spreading rumours that Ronnie and his pals were Travellers.

'Ronnie said just to leave it all to him,' she said, 'and that he'd take care of everything. I can't tell you how fabulous it is to be spoiled rotten by a man like this – I'd highly recommend it.'

'Makes a change for you anyway,' Betty said waspishly.

'Mark my words, Betty. The sooner you get yourself on that Analyzed dating thingy, the sooner you'll get yourself matched up too. Oh Betty, you wouldn't know yourself – have you any idea how wonderful it is, after all these years, to fancy someone again? Do you remember all those butterflies-in-the-tummy feelings we used to have as teenagers? They never really go away, you know. That's the most astonishing thing of all. I feel like I'm seventeen years of age again, and it's so wonderful.'

'I'm afraid career girls like me have precious little time to trawl the internet, trying to pick up random men who drive chip vans,' said Betty sourly, temper clearly getting the better of her. 'And now, if you'll excuse me, I'm afraid I really do need to get back to my bookkeeping.'

'Not at all,' said Connie. 'Don't worry a bit about not serving me or anything, I've had a good look round and to be honest, I doubt there's anything suitable. No offence to the Sisters of Charity or anything, but nuns' cast-offs really aren't what you want to be seen in on the kind of weekend we're planning.'

Betty flushed red with temper and Connie air-kissed her goodbye, before bouncing out of the shop, feeling on top of the world.

And why wouldn't she be? It wasn't often that she won game, set and match against Betty Darcy now, was it?

'Now it's not the Ritz-Carlton, nor nothing like it,' said Ronnie, as he and Connie drove down the N11 in his little Nissan, with the pine air freshener the shape of a Christmas tree bouncing around on the rear-view mirror and the sound of the Mellow Oldies radio station in the background playing a nice, soothing Simon and Garfunkel song, 'Feeling Groovy'. Which pretty much summed up how Connie herself felt, that balmy Friday afternoon.

'Sure it's only a little caravan really,' Ronnie went on to explain, 'that's all. There's a tiny little kitchenette and two bunk beds, and that's about it. I'll take the top bunk, so you needn't be worrying about climbing up ladders or anything like it, with your dodgy knee. It's a grand aul' break for us though, isn't it, love? And not costing a single penny either.'

'You're far too good,' Connie beamed lovingly across at him from the passenger seat. Although if the truth be told, she wouldn't have minded if the two of them had shared a single bed, even if it was a bit of a squash. The kind of weekend she had in mind involved precious little sleep. And hadn't she splashed all her pension money for the week on matching underwear from Marks and Spencer's specially? She and Ronnie had kissed, many times now, but oh dear, she sighed, starting to feel like she was getting the first proper hot flush she'd had in years. What she wouldn't give for more. Just at the thought of Ronnie's chunky, tanned arms holding her tight in bed, she went scarlet red and flushed right up to her hairline. Even her palms began to sweat at the thought of Ronnie's bare body against hers. She had to fan herself with a copy of the *Racing Post* she found lying at her feet and roll down the car window just to cool down a little.

It took just over an hour to get there, and when they did, it turned out the mobile home was absolutely gorgeous, more like a proper little one-bedroomed flat, really, than the sort of caravan Connie had geared herself up for. There was a lovely bright living area, with a telly that even got *Sky News*, and a tiny kitchenette just beside it, but with everything you could possibly need there, even a proper oven, then right beside that, there was a little bathroom with a shower, with the one and only bedroom at the very back. Outside, there was a lovely sun-soaked decking area, which backed on to a load of neighbouring decking areas with the most wonderful views all the way out to the sea.

No sooner had they arrived than some of the neighbours started knocking at the back door to say hi, and to ask the two of them to join everyone else for drinks later on that evening.

'So we can all give you both a big warm Wicklow welcome,' said a woman called Marjorie, who was about the same age as Connie, with real healthy-looking tanned skin, all dressed in white linen that looked like it cost a fortune, with huge big chunky, arty jewellery in bright turquoise clamped around her neck. It looked fabulous on this Marjorie one, but Connie knew she'd be a holy show in it. Marjorie was warm and welcoming though, and Connie was thrilled with the invitation.

'Couldn't think of anything we'd enjoy more,' she answered for both herself and Ronnie, delighted beyond words at how the weekend was shaping up so far. And especially happy with the way she and Ronnie were automatically being considered a proper couple, being asked to do proper couple-y things with other proper couples.

The whole evening turned out to be out-of-this-world wonderful. The mobile home neighbours, the Wild at Heart Wicklow Gang, as they apparently called themselves, were a sort of club who met up like this for drinks and nibbles and chats regularly throughout the summer.

And sure enough, later on they all sat in the middle of the mobile campsite on cushions and garden chairs, with those stunning sea views right across Brittas Bay to gape at. They chatted away, sipping wine while nibbling at sausage rolls, cheese platters and guacamole dips that each of them had produced from their little homes, like a sort of communal street party, except they didn't need the excuse of a royal wedding to celebrate.

The mobile gang were meeting Ronnie for the very first time, but couldn't have been more inclusive or welcoming to him, or to Connie either, for that matter. There were a dozen of them or so in total, aged from about sixty upwards, every one of them actively retired, and yet by the look of them, Connie thought admiringly, all fit as fiddles thanks to their daily swims down at the bay. As twilight fell, the neighbours sat in a comfortable circle, with Dean Martin playing out from someone's mobile, on one of those aul' Spotty-whatever-you-call-it playlists that Kim was always going on about.

As they were all of an age, they were having a very enjoyable bitching session about them snowflaky young ones, and how they wanted every statue they ever set eyes on toppled over and what an absolute disgrace they all thought it was.

'Sure people can get "cancelled" now over the tiniest little thing they might have said thirty years ago,' said a man called Terry, who seemed to be in charge of the music and who must have been a big Rat Pack fan, because all he played for the whole night was Frank Sinatra, Sammy Davis Jr or Dean Martin. Pure bliss, Connie thought.

'And don't get me started on how hard it is to ask for an ordinary cup of coffee in a coffee shop now,' Marjorie chipped in, to lots of understanding nods from around the circle.

'With all their talk of Americanos and lattes and decafs,' said a very chatty man wearing a cravat and blazer, who lived in the mobile right beside the one Ronnie and Connie were in.

'And whatever you do,' said a younger man beside him, who Connie thought might be his boyfriend, 'don't dream of asking for milk to go with it. Otherwise they bombard you with more questions than you'd see on a medical form. "Do you want it flat white or semi-skimmed or low-fat," or, God help us, "almond milk or soya?"'

'Whoever heard of almond milk anyway?' Connie chipped in, feeling brave enough to contribute after her second glass of rosé wine. 'Sure that's only for young ones looking for notice.'

'If you all want to have a good bitch about something,' said a woman who had to have been in her early eighties if she was a day, but who'd been bouncing around refilling the paper cups everyone was drinking out of non-stop the whole evening. 'Then you should see the carry-on of my grandkids. The way they're on their iPhones and iPads all the time? Now I know that's the world they've been born into, but honestly. I've sat at dinner tables where both my grandson and granddaughter won't say a single word to me or, God forbid, their parents, yet they're texting and tweeting away to their pals like their lives depended on it. Pure rudeness, if you ask me.'

Nods of approval from around the circle, but then something very, very strange happened. A flashy-looking black jeep pulled up into the car park just outside the mobile park and a youngish guy hopped out, looked around, spotted the Wicklow gang enjoying a few drinks and a chat, then immediately strode towards them. Everyone else seemed to notice him too, because the chat broke off as they looked to see who this newcomer was, and wondered what the hell it was he wanted.

'New arrival?' Connie asked innocently. Maybe one of the people who managed the park? This young fella certainly had the look of someone who ran the place; he was well groomed and businesslike, dressed neatly in a collar and tie with a nicely trimmed goatee beard, as he marched briskly up the little pathway that lead to the park entrance. They'd a great view from where they were all sitting, and everyone was transfixed by him.

'Never seen him before in my life,' said Marjorie, shaking her head and looking puzzled. 'And I've been coming here for over forty years.'

There was only one person around the circle who looked concerned, and that was Ronnie. Up till then he'd been as relaxed as you like, shooting the breeze and holding Connie's hand; but the minute he spotted this guy approaching, he sharply pulled his hand back. He'd started sweating, too, Connie noticed – again, strange. Whereas five minutes previously, he was sprawled out on a garden chair, legs wide apart as he sat back and soaked up the last of the evening rays, now he was shifting around awkwardly, looking like he'd rather be anywhere else.

'Are you all right, Ronnie?' she asked him worriedly.

He ignored her and jumped straight to his feet.

'S'cuse me for a minute, folks,' he said apologetically to the group. 'Just got to . . . ehhh . . . take care of a bit of business, you know yourself.'

With that, he left the circle and walked all the way down the sandy path to meet this young fella, whoever he was. Everyone got back to the far more agreeable business of chatting and bitching – everyone except for Connie. Instead, she went very quiet, her eyes never leaving Ronnie the whole time. He approached the stranger and, even though it was impossible to tell from this distance what was being said, one thing was for certain. The discussion was heated, with Goatee Beard Man jabbing his finger in the air a lot and Ronnie doing that 'calm down' gesture with his two hands. It was all over quick enough, though as the young fella hopped back into his jeep a few minutes later and zoomed away again, in a big cloud of sandy dust.

Meanwhile, Ronnie ambled back to the gang, his usual, easy-going self, absolutely delighted with life again.

'Sorry for the interruption there, folks,' he grinned, taking his seat beside Connie, as relaxed as he ever was. Balance seemed restored to the world once more, and all was well.

'So who was that?' Connie asked, dying to know.

'Ahh, nothing to worry about, love,' said Ronnie, gripping her hand again and giving it a reassuring little squeeze. 'That's just one of Barney's sons. Turns out the mobile was double-booked, and he thought he had it for the weekend. He hadn't realised his da had promised it to us instead, but once I explained that we'd be gone soon enough, he was cool about it.'

'Oh, I see,' said Connie, pondering all this.

'We might need to head back home tomorrow, though,' Ronnie said, 'if you don't mind leaving a day early, that is?'

'No, of course not,' Connie said disappointedly. 'It's only fair, I suppose, seeing as how his family own the place and we're only here out of the goodness of Barney's heart. At least we still have tonight, don't we?'

'That's my girl.' Ronnie smiled at her, and Connie's heart danced.

'What's the lad's name?' she asked, out of idle curiosity more than anything.

'Who?'

'Barney's son, of course.'

But Ronnie had to think before answering.

'Ehh . . . Michael,' he said, after a pause. 'Sorry, love, the aul' memory isn't what it was, and sure I haven't seen him since he was a teenager, kicking a football around Barney's back garden. Anyway, thanks for being so understanding about leaving a bit early. You're a smashing girl, Connie Bailey, do you know that?'

But there was more disappointment ahead. If Connie thought there might be a bit of 'the other' between her and Ronnie that night, she was sadly mistaken. When the Wicklow gang eventually called it a night, it was well past midnight, as they all gathered up their garden chairs and said their fond goodnights and everyone drifted home, each towards their own individual mobile. She and Ronnie let themselves into theirs and as soon as they were safely inside, Connie turned to give him an affectionate little kiss.

She hoped that might lead on to more – truth be told, there was a very comfortable-looking sofa in the living area. What was to stop them having a bit of fun there? Connie badly wanted a bit of fun. Sure hadn't she gone and bought all that expensive new underwear specially? Very gently, though, Ronnie broke away from her, unlocking her arms from around his neck and headed for the fridge, where he took out a tin of beer for himself.

'Tell you what, love,' he said, ripping open the can and taking a big gulp of it. 'I'll let you go into the bedroom first and get yourself into your night gear, ready for bed. I'll be in after you shortly.'

'Come on in with me and help me get undressed,' Connie said, in what she hoped was a seductive voice, but then she was so out of practice at this lark, she could have sounded more like Marge Simpson, for all she knew.

But Ronnie was already on his way back to the TV, where he clicked it on, and kept on scrolling till he found a sports channel with a soccer match in full swing.

'You go on ahead there,' he said, throwing himself down onto an armchair. 'I just want to see who won the Man U game against Aston Villa. And take your time,' he called after her, as she padded into the tiny little bedroom on her own, bitterly disappointed.

An hour later, he still hadn't come to bed, as Connie lay on the bottom bunk, her mind racing. There was some dull, niggling thought nagging at the back of her head that she was trying to catch a hold of, but couldn't.

She could still hear the match blaring out of the TV and there was still no sign of Ronnie, and she was still lying there like a statue, in her brand-new nightie from Marks and Spencer's, with the matching dressing gown hanging neatly on the back of the door.

What the hell had she been trying to remember anyway?

It was hours later, in the dead middle of the night, before it came to her.

It was that young fella with the goatee beard. Connie had seen him before, she was sure of it. The night Ronnie had taken her to the Andrea Bocelli concert. It was the black jeep she remembered. The very same one she'd seen that guy driving this evening.

She was certain it was him. Rock-solid, 100 per cent certain.

Chapter Twenty-Five

Kim

Come on, Kim willed her not-yet-arrived date-to-be. *Be nice, be normal, be interesting, be funny, be cool, be easy-going.* That's all. Not a lot to ask for, surely? *Oh yeah*, she thought, adding another mental note, *and please be someone who, for once in my miserable years-long losing streak at the dating game, might turn into a proper actual boyfriend.* Just this once. Just for a fecking change, that's all.

Because if this one doesn't work out, she thought worriedly, *then it means there's definitely something wrong with me. I'm the common denominator, so therefore, I have to be the problem.* Kim was rarely down, but this was seriously getting to her. Just about everyone else around her was happily coupled off now, and it was hard to put into words how crap it was to be the last woman left standing. Like being chosen last for team sports in school.

It was early September now, just over two months since Analyzed had first been launched, and Hannah was still very much with that sweetheart of a fella, Joey. Meanwhile Greg seemed to be seeing that fitness nut Mia round the clock these days. The two of them were even planning a trip away to Berlin together – well, more like a torture trip to Berlin, really, if you were to ask Kim, seeing as how they were planning to run a marathon while they were there. Even Emma, who was serially single and who practically pleaded the Fifth if you even dared ask her if there was anyone on the scene, was cautiously admitting to 'having someone on the back burner – possibly'. When pressed for further details, she'd just smile mysteriously and say, 'Ask me in another two dates and we'll see where we are then. And now, change the subject or I'll smash your face.'

So it's my turn, Kim thought. Because it has to be. Because it's Time's Up on being serially single and the butt of everyone's gags around the office.

By now, it had gone beyond a joke about the Curse of Kim. For someone like her, who'd worked so hard on the digital end of Analyzed, not to have any joy on the shagging thing herself was starting to get mortifying. Kim was used to being the class clown at work, and now she was a pity case and it was beyond shite.

Right now, she was a twitching bag of nerves, feeling jumpy as feck as her eye darted around the tapas bar where they'd arranged to meet up. The bar was on Coppinger Row in the heart of the city centre, a narrow, pedestrianised little alleyway packed to the gills with restaurants and bars, with gorgeous, sun-soaked outdoor seating, so you could grab a table outside, drown a pint of cider, as Kim was now doing, and watch the world go by.

She was lost in her thoughts, staring the whole way down Coppinger Row, idly picking out any passing rides from the crowds and wondering if by any miracle they might be the fella she was there to meet. Next thing, she spotted someone reassuringly familiar coming down the narrow little laneway. It was his distinctive walk she recognised first – that stooped, slightly sloping, long-legged walk. As if she needed further confirmation, sure enough, he was wearing Harry Potter roundy glasses, with that neat, short-back-and-sides haircut and the expensive looking suit that made him look like he was the CEO of somewhere very big and impressive and important.

He must have spotted her in the crowd, too, because next thing, he waved and ambled over to her.

'Well, good evening, Ms Bailey,' he smiled warmly. 'How delightful to bump into you like this. Can't Dublin be such a charming village that way?'

'Good to see you too, Harold,' Kim laughed, surprising herself at how genuinely pleased she was to see him. But then he was a nice guy, she remembered. Not unattractive either, she thought, eyeing him up as she tried to remember what it was about him that made her run screaming to the hills the night they'd first met.

'A most pleasant and agreeable surprise indeed,' Harold went on. 'I do hope the evening is treating you well?'

And there it was. Now it came back to Kim exactly why she'd rejected him in the first place. That whole 'young fogey' thing Harold had going on. The slightly pompous way he talked, like he'd stepped out of an Edith Wharton novel. His clothes were all perfectly normal to look at, but there was just something about the way he wore them that made him look like he was born a century out of his time. That he really should be riding around on a penny farthing. A good person otherwise, she thought, just not in a million years for her.

'I'm actually out on another date this evening,' she confided in him, as they chatted over the table-height rattan parapet that divided the tapas bar from the alleyway. 'So wish me luck, won't you?'

'Oh now, someone like you doesn't need luck at all,' said Harold, with a formal little half-bow. 'In fact, may I say that whomsoever your date is, he's a very lucky chap indeed. A charming young lady like you? I should think he ought to consider himself royally blessed.'

Kim grinned back at him. 'How about you, Harold? Where are you off to this evening?'

'It's rather exciting, actually,' he said, instantly lighting up. 'As you may perhaps recall, my mother is an opera singer. She's in London at present, but she managed to secure a ticket for me to see *Madame Butterfly* at the Gaiety Theatre this evening. I'm overjoyed to see the production, as it's been completely sold out for months now.'

'Are you taking a date?' Kim teased. 'Go on, you can tell me.'

But Harold just shook his head.

'Not this evening, I'm afraid,' he said. 'Sadly, it was only a single ticket, but still. Given the demand to see the show, I'm perfectly happy to sit there alone. In fact . . .'

Just then, he took an actual fob watch on a chain out of his pocket to check the time. Jesus, Kim thought. The White Rabbit in *Alice in Wonderland* had nothing on Harold.

'. . . with no rudeness intended,' he said, taking in the time, 'I'm afraid I really must dash.'

'Go,' Kim smiled, fondly waving him off. 'Enjoy. Have fun. Good to see you!'

Harold waved goodbye and sloped off, just as a voice from directly behind Kim made her jump.

'Hi . . . emm . . . Kim? Hi . . . it's me . . . I'm your date for the evening!'

Excitedly she twisted around on her seat, hoping against hope that he'd turn out to be good-looking and charming and the whole total package.

But there was feck all to prepare her for this.

'Seriously?' she said, when she saw who was hovering nervously just at her shoulder. '*Seriously*, it's you?'

'Surprise!' he said, doing a very annoying 'taa-daah!' gesture with his hands, that gave her a strong urge to throw the dregs of her cider over him. This was a surprise, all right. But certainly not a good one. Kim glared hotly at him, too infuriated to string a sentence together.

'I was hoping you might be glad to see me again,' he said nervously. And well he might be nervous, too, given the nasty little scam he'd just played on her.

'What the feck do you think you're playing at?'

'Well,' he said, shuffling around awkwardly on his feet, 'you see, thing is, I always felt you didn't really give me enough of a chance the last time we met. Because I think about that date a lot, you know. You're a really cool, funny person who's up for a laugh, and I don't meet many cool, funny women like you. I thought we had a real connection.'

'So you stalked me online again and you thought you'd approach me under a fake name, fake email and made-up profile?' Kim almost spat at him, incandescent with fury.

Not only that he'd taken her like that, but that she'd bloody well fallen for it. 'Have you any idea how duplicitous this is? And how mental that makes you, to chance your arm like this? What did you think I was going to do anyway? Go running into your arms, all delighted to see you? After what happened the last time we went out?'

'Now, you might at least give me a chance to explain about last time . . .' he tried to say, but Kim was having none of it.

'Oh yeah,' she said, her voice dripping with angry sarcasm. 'You were driving me out to a restaurant somewhere and your car got pulled over by the cops . . .'

'Yeah, but you still haven't heard my side of it . . .'

'*Your* side of it?' Kim spewed back at him, aware that other diners were gaping over, enjoying the floor show. *Let them stare*, she thought, way too furious to give a shite. 'What's your side of breaking your parole? Can I just remind you that you were led off in handcuffs? Only for the fact that the cops took pity on me, all on my own on a country road in the middle of nowhere, and offered me a lift home, I was a goner.'

'Yeah, but you see, I have to explain to you how the whole parole system works,' he said, scratching at a new-looking giant tattoo on his forearm. Doubtlessly got in prison, Kim thought, seething crossly.

'Oh, tell it to your free legal aid team,' she barked back at him, scooping her backpack up off the floor, tossing twenty euros on the table to cover the drink she'd had while she was waiting, then stalking out of there.

'Oh, and if he attempts to steal that cash,' she said loudly to the other diners, who were staring at her anyway, 'feel free to call the cops. They'll know exactly where he is. Chances are he's wearing an ankle monitor anyway.'

'Kim, be fair, will you?' he called after her, but she was already striding furiously out of there. 'Give me a chance! It was only a suspended sentence, and breaking and entering is a victimless crime!'

'Save it for the next judge you're up in front of,' she yelled over her shoulder, to a gentle ripple of applause from the tapas bar, as he continued shouting out her name, entertaining the crowds as she wove all the way down Coppinger Row.

That Saturday morning, Kim was still in bed, dead to the world and enjoying her usual weekend lie-in, except for the unfamiliar and slightly eerie sound of dead silence from around the house. Normally the usual weekend morning background noise involved Connie bashing pots and pans in the kitchen downstairs, singing along at the top of her voice to her favourite golden oldies station on the radio and shouting so loudly down her mobile to whatever neighbour she was phoning, it was a wonder she didn't just save herself the bother and have a full conversation through the walls.

Totally unused to it, the quiet unnerved Kim, and it took a split second before her still-fuzzy brain remembered what was going on and it all came back to her.

Connie was down in Wicklow for the weekend, wasn't she? With that baldie-headed gobshite, Ronnie, much to Kim's growing concern. Fully awake now, Kim waited a second for all her worries to flood back to her, which they did quick enough. In droves. The nub of it was this: the fact that her mam and Ronnie seemed to be spending so much time together was worrying her sick, and the more she tried to analyse why she felt like this, the more confused she became.

Why did she dislike Ronnie so much anyway? From day one, she'd taken an instant dislike to him, and getting to know him more only exacerbated that horrible, uneasy feeling. So what the feck was wrong with her anyway? Hadn't Kim been the one who was at Connie non-stop to sign up to dating sites and get back out there again, and start expanding her social horizons? And now the woman was doing exactly that. So why was Kim so down on this budding new relationship? Because it was moving a bit too fast? Because she didn't quite trust Ronnie and felt she still hadn't got a handle on the guy?

It isn't like I've never been guilty of carry on like that myself, now is it, she thought crossly. Feck's sake, she was known to have had conversations with fellas about the possibility of moving in together after just a few months of dating – she was hardly one to talk about things moving too fast, now was she?

Then another, more depressing thought struck her. Maybe, she thought, slumping back down under the covers and pulling the duvet over her head, maybe it was possible that she was feeling a little bit jealous and a whole lot left out? Not only that all her friends were in new and budding relationships, but that even her seventy-something mother seemed to be in the throes of a steady romance, being whisked out for romantic dinners and weekends away by the sea. Even if those dinners were cheapie early birds in a local pizzeria that came heavily discounted with vouchers and the seaside weekend was in a borrowed mobile home, barely an hour down the road in Brittas Bay.

Meanwhile Kim was left rattling around an empty house, home alone and with shag all to look forward to this weekend. Well, unless she set up another Analyzed date, doubtlessly letting herself in for nothing only another crappy anticlimactic let-down. Not tempting, she thought.

She was just about to drift back into a second sleep and hopefully shut out the whole world, when from downstairs there came a deafeningly loud rapping at the hall door.

'Piss off, whoever you are,' she grunted, rolling over, with no intention whatsoever of hauling herself out of bed. But then, the doorbell rang out. And again. Then a third time, except now, whatever git-head arsehole was at the door was just keeping their finger on the bell non-stop – clearly not going anywhere till they gained access.

Oh, feck this anyway, Kim sighed, forcing herself into an upright position and wearily hobbling out of bed. There'd be no peace until she got rid of whoever it was. Could it be something she'd ordered online and forgotten all about? She often shopped online late at night after a few drinks, then found herself at a complete loss when boxloads of clothes from ASOS or Boohoo would land on her doorstep.

The doorbell pealed out yet again and this time, Kim snapped.

'Gimme a chance, will you?' she yelled out, padding down the stairs in her bare feet. 'I'm coming!'

Jesus, she'd murder whoever it was. Although deep down she reckoned there was a good chance it was only her mam's pal Betty dropping in for a cuppa, and for yet more of her passive-aggressive competitive talk about how amazing her kids were compared to Kim, and how her own life was far more fabulous than Connie's.

Kim stood on tiptoe to undo the bolt at the top of the hall door and open up, but to her surprise, there was a total stranger standing there. She was still half-asleep, and had to have a good squint at him through her messy fringe before she could be sure. But no; it seemed whoever it was, she definitely didn't know him. This was a guy about her own age, tall and lean, with a goatee beard, dressed in jeans and a T-shirt, with his arms folded like he was all geared up for a battle royal. There was a black jeep parked on the pavement outside, new and expensive-looking. Whoever this fella was, he was frowning crossly and looked as furious as Kim felt. A new neighbour, maybe, come to complain about . . . well, about what, exactly?

'Can I help you?' she asked woozily, her brain trying to process what the hell was going on here.

'Are you the daughter?' he asked her.

'I'm sorry?' she said.

'Because I'm the son. And I think it's high time you and I had a little chat.'

Chapter Twenty-Six

Connie

'It's such a shame we have to leave so early,' Connie was saying, as she and Ronnie drove down the motorway, all set for home. 'I'd really love to have stayed the extra few days, just like we'd planned.'

Stony silence from Ronnie. Instead, he just kept completely focused on the road ahead, as the air freshener shaped like a pine tree bounced annoyingly around the dashboard.

'Maybe you and I could come back another time?' Connie asked gently, sliding her hand over his on the gearstick. 'That's if your pal Barney was ever kind enough to lend us the mobile again.'

More silence.

'Because all the Wicklow gang seem like dotes,' she persisted. 'Be so nice to spend more time with them and get to know them better, wouldn't it?'

This time, Ronnie grunted, which she took as a yes. God Almighty, she thought. Ronnie was normally so full of chat and craic. Normally she couldn't get a word in edgeways. Normally you couldn't shut him up. So what was wrong with him this morning?

'Did you sleep all right, love?' she asked him, a bit concerned as a fresh thought struck her. Maybe that's all that was wrong with him, a bad night's sleep. He hadn't even come into the bedroom at all the night before; first thing that morning, Connie had found him crashed out in the armchair in front of the TV, with three empty tins of beer at his feet and the TV still blaring away, except with some class of a Saturday-morning kids' show on. They didn't even get to have brekkie, either; Ronnie was so anxious to leave that Connie barely got a cuppa tea into her, and he himself refused to eat a scrap – not even a quick bowl of Crunchy Nut Cornflakes that Connie had found tidied neatly away at the back of a kitchen cupboard.

'Ahh, I slept a bit,' Ronnie shrugged, not getting into it anymore. By now, Connie had had quite enough of the long-drawn-out silences, so to hell with it, she grabbed the bull by the horns and asked him straight out.

'I'll tell you the truth now, Ronnie,' she said softly. 'I'm worried about you, very worried. You're so quiet today. Not a bit like yourself at all. Is something the matter? Is there something on your mind? You can tell me, you know that. Sure you can tell me anything.'

Ronnie let out a heavy sigh.

'It's just the date, that's all,' he eventually said. A break-through, Connie thought, finally he's speaking to me again.

'What about the date?'

'This time of year,' he said, 'never the easiest for me.'

'Why is that?'

But now, he looked like he was grasping for the right words and having a very hard time finding them. He was sucking in his cheeks, breathing in short, spiky jabs, and looking like he might be on the verge of tears.

'Ronnie?' Connie said, seriously concerned. 'Do you want to pull the car over? Take a minute to gather yourself? What is it, love? You can tell me anything, you know that.'

There was a grass verge ahead, so Ronnie pulled over, rolled down the window and stared straight ahead of him, looking miserable and alone and lost.

'It's my Barbara,' he eventually said. 'Today's her anniversary. Six years gone and . . . and still . . . God, I miss her so much . . .'

Oh, the poor man, Connie thought. He's distraught. Ronnie choked and fumbled about for the right words, but Connie was well able to guess the rest. Hadn't she been through bereavement herself, for her Jack? She got it, she understood, and now all she could do was reach over to Ronnie, give his hand a supportive little squeeze and reassure him.

'I know, pet,' she said, 'believe me, I know how hard it can be.'

'She was the love of my life . . .' Ronnie said, all choked up.

'Of course she was.'

'And I could do nothing for her, at the end . . . nothing at all . . .'

'Oh now, I'm sure that's not true! I'm sure you were a great comfort to her.'

'Her last months in that hospice were the worst of my life . . . I'll never get over it. I'll never get over the pain of losing her like that.'

'Let it out, that's a good man. You just let out all the tears, and you'll feel so much better. Sure I get like this over Jack all the time. Still, you know, to this day. All I have to do is hear a song that reminds me of him on the radio, and I'm in a puddle of tears.'

'Fecking cancer,' sniffed Ronnie, gratefully taking the hanky Connie passed over to him and blowing his nose noisily. 'You know, if we'd only caught it earlier, she'd still be here today.'

'I'm sure . . .'

'Because she and I had years ahead of us, happy years. We could have travelled, gone on cruises, visited places we'd never been before and always wanted to see.'

'Oh Ronnie love, it's heartbreaking, I know it is. But you know what they say, grief is the price we pay for love. Now today is a day to remember Barbara, maybe bring a few flowers to her grave and say a few prayers. I can go with you, if you like?'

'You're very good,' he replied, wiping his eyes and starting up the car engine again. 'But honestly, this is something I need to deal with on my own. I'll drop you home first, and then I'll visit her grave. I just need to spend today nice and quiet, remembering her. Don't you worry, love, I'll be back to normal in a few days.'

They drove on in silence. *Six years, and he's not over her*, Connie thought gloomily. And for her, that was sad beyond words.

Not easy, was it? she told herself as they drove home in silence. *Trying to forge a new relationship with someone who was still in love with a ghost.*

Chapter Twenty-Seven

Kim

'Please tell me you're joking. This has to be a joke,' was all Kim could say, repeating herself over and over.

'I wish I was, but I'm not.'

'Fecking hell,' she whistled.

'I know.'

'I mean . . . I did suspect something, all right, but nothing like this. Never this.'

'It wasn't easy for you to hear,' he said tightly. 'That I can appreciate. Believe me, it wasn't easy to tell you either.'

'Jesus,' Kim said, sliding down onto a kitchen chair, while her unexpected visitor stood over by the kitchen door, hands shoved in his pockets, rocking back and forth on his feet, as if he were hating every single second of this.

'Would you like me to get you some water?' he asked her. 'You look a bit shook, if you don't mind my saying.'

'It's OK, thanks,' she replied, still trying to get to grips with it all. 'Yeah, it was hard for me to hear all right, but you know what's going to be a million times worse?'

Her visitor, who it turned out was called Simon, nodded, accurately predicting what was coming next.

'I can guess,' he said drily.

'Now I have to tell my mam. And it's going to be horrible for her. Just horrible. She's the kind of person who only ever sees the good in people, and this will be such a betrayal of trust for her. I mean . . . the *duplicity* of it. The two-facedness. I can hardly wrap my head around it myself. What an actor that man is. Seriously, someone hand him an Oscar.'

'If it's the slightest consolation,' Simon said, 'your mother isn't the first.'

'Really?' Kim looked up at him in sharp surprise. 'You mean he's done this before?'

'Oh yeah,' Simon nodded, his jaw set. 'That's how, this time, I already knew some of the giveaway signs to look out for.'

'So what were the signs?' Kim sat forward now, interested. How had the fecker got away with it for so long, without getting caught out?

'Oh, lots of things,' Simon replied. 'I haven't lived at home for years, so I don't see my dad as often as I used to. But when this whole thing between him and your mam started, I'm guessing just a few weeks ago now . . .'

'Just over two months ago, to be exact,' Kim said bitterly. She of all people should know. Because that was when she and Iris first launched Analyzed and all of this crapology with Ronnie kicked off in the first place. Jesus, if she'd known what was ahead of her then! She'd have run screaming in the opposite direction, dragging her mother along with her.

'Anyway,' Simon went on, 'I started noticing things – little things at first, but then the signs got bigger and harder to ignore. For starters, when he first met your mum, he began to smarten up his appearance. Going to the barber for hot shaves, the kind of thing he never did. Then he started dressing differently, too – wearing neat suits with open-neck shirts – I'd swear one time he even went and got himself a spray tan. I was laughing at him, I said to him, "Dad, you're going around the place like the oldest swinger in town." I'm not laughing now, though, am I?'

'Neither am I,' said Kim wryly. 'So how did you first find out about my mam? Not to mention where we live?'

'Easy enough,' Simon shrugged. 'Dad's next-door neighbour Barney owns a chipper van and Dad helps him out in it the odd time, if there's a particularly big match on, that kind of thing.'

'Yet another lie,' Kim said, thinking aloud.

'Oh yeah?' said Simon, raising an eyebrow.

'Dirty fecker told Mam he co-owned that chip van.'

Simon rolled his eyes. 'Then clock it up to his whole catalogue of lies,' he said. 'Because believe me, you haven't heard anything yet.'

Kim steeled herself.

'Anyway,' he said, 'a few weeks ago, Dad asked if he could borrow the van, so he could work by himself at the Andrea Bocelli concert. That immediately alerted me – Dad never knowingly went to a classical music gig once in his entire life. I knew something was up, I just smelled it. So I drove to the concert grounds, and sure enough, there he was, with your mam beside him. First time I'd set eyes on her. So then everything dropped into place. I followed them back here and decided to hold off confronting him for a bit longer, just to be absolutely certain. Just in case your mum turned out to be a friend of his and nothing more. Not exactly Hercule Poirot levels of detection on my part, but at least I got to the bottom of it.'

Kim had to take a very, very long pause before she was cool-headed enough to answer.

'I know this is your dad we're talking about,' she eventually said, 'but the absolute useless, lying, cheating *gobshite*. When I get my hands on him—'

'With the greatest of respect,' said Simon stiffly, 'but as his only son, I get first dibs when it comes to tearing strips off him.'

'So what happened last night?' she asked. 'At that mobile home in Brittas Bay?'

'Pure dumb luck on my part. I called into Dad's yesterday evening after work with groceries for him, but he wasn't there. By sheer chance, Barney was out the front mowing his lawn, so I asked him if he'd seen Dad around. And that's when Barney told me that he'd lent Dad his mobile home for the weekend – so I hotfooted it there and had it out with him.'

'You saw Mam there too?' said Kim, a knot forming in her stomach as it really started to dawn on her what lay ahead.

'Sitting with a group of people about their own age, having a great laugh and a chat,' Simon answered. 'Dad begged me not to make a show of him in front of so many people, so I agreed to back down – on one condition. That he came straight home today and told your mum the truth, the whole truth and nothing but.'

'And you say this has all happened before?' Kim asked, her mind swimming at the sheer brass neck of Ronnie, as much as anything else.

'More than once,' Simon told her straight.

Then an even worse thought hit Kim as she sprang to her feet and started to pace around the kitchen.

'Shit, shit, shit,' she muttered in frustration. 'You do realise that the two of them could walk through the hall door any second now?'

'Good,' Simon nodded. 'Bring it on. Because this, I want a ringside seat for.'

'It's going to break Mam's heart.'

'Dad's not going to like it either, but you know what? The truth will out eventually, and sometimes we have to be cruel to be kind.'

'Well, seeing as how you're here, Simon, can I at least offer you a coffee?'

'Thought you'd never ask,' he said, giving her a tiny hint of a smile, then pulling up a chair and gratefully sitting down. 'And just so you know, after today? I'm going to confiscate Dad's iPhone and iPad and burn them. If that's what it takes to keep him away from these bloody dating apps, then that's what I'll do.'

Kim stuck a pod into the Nespresso maker, but judged it best to say nothing.

'Analyzed,' Simon went on, as the coffee brewed away with a low hum in the background. 'That's where the trouble first started, you know.'

Not a word out of Kim. Instead, she just busied herself with cups, spoons, a milk jug and anything else that clattered and made a lot of noise.

'Have you heard of it?' Simon asked her.

She didn't actually lie; she just chose not to answer.

'Milk? Sugar? Do you fancy a bit of brekkie, slice of toast maybe?'

'Sorry,' Simon said, with an apologetic little smile. 'That was very presumptuous of me. Assuming someone like you was trawling through dating sites like that.'

'No worries,' Kim said blithely, bringing two big mugs of strong coffee to the table and leaving one in front of him.

'It's just that bloody website – that's where they initially met.'

'Really?' she blinked back innocently.

'It's a brand-new one,' he said, gratefully taking a sip of coffee. 'And the whole gimmick is that it asks you all these deep probing questions, real amateur psychology stuff. Like, "what do you regard as the lowest depth of misery", and "what is your current state of mind".'

'Oh yeah?' said Kim.

'Anyway, Dad stumbled across it completely by accident, and unbeknown to me, he signed up to it. So now, here we are. You know how the rest turned out,' he said, with a wry smile.

'What about you?' Kim asked, genuinely curious. 'Do you use dating sites yourself?' Why not, she thought. Simon was around her own age, he wasn't wearing a wedding ring and certainly didn't act all 'married', banging on about his partner and family non-stop, the way guys in relationships inevitably did, in her experience.

To her surprise, he just pulled a face and rolled his eyes.

'How long have you got?' he asked her. Kim was about to probe further, when just then, she heard the sound of her mum's key in the front door.

Holy Jesus, she thought. Showtime.

Chapter Twenty-Eight

Iris

At precisely the same time, Iris was on the receiving end of a surprise too, albeit a far more pleasant one. She was home, beavering away on her laptop in her little converted office, when the email pinged through.

And there it was. An Oxford email address she instantly recognised, from her oldest friend Anna.

My dear Iris

It's with the greatest pride that I'm getting in touch with you today.
    You never said. You never told me.
    Modest as ever, when I was in touch with you for your birthday, you never even referred to it. Yet it turns out that you and your wonderful new dating app are quite the buzzword around the college campus over here. Long before I knew of your involvement, I had heard so many of my students chatting animatedly about a dating site which was new to the market and which was proving to be uniquely popular among both undergraduates and postgrads, too. I even walked in on one of my tutorial groups, to overhear them all chatting about Analyzed, which in turn was tossing up all manner of philosophical debates and discussions along the lines of, where were you happiest? Or, how would you like to die?

Far, very, very far from the normal topics of conversation among my students, let me reassure you.

An Irish woman is behind this, you know, one of my students told me. Educated here, too. At this very college. About twenty years ago now – way back in your day, miss, before any of us were born. Apparently she's an applied maths graduate. Made the honour roll and everything. Well on her way to making millions by now probably, my student nodded sagely.

Well, doesn't all this sound remarkably like someone I know, I thought? After all, how many Irish women studying that very subject have made the honour roll in the past two decades? Only one that I know of, and she's reading this right now. So I logged on to Analyzed to see for myself, and lo and behold, there it was, the name Iris Simpson buried deep in the 'contact us' section right at the end.

Well, my heart almost burst with pride, and I had to get in touch to congratulate you heartily on a job very well done. I wish you were here for yourself to see how astonishingly popular your app is proving to be. It's nigh on impossible, I know, for any app designer to identify what strange alchemy makes most start-ups die a death, whereas a handful of others seem to just catch a wave, making it appear almost effortless. And yours is most definitely one of the latter, Iris.

With all this going on, as you can imagine, you've been on my mind such a great deal lately. Every time you and I are in touch, we vow to meet up soon, we faithfully promise that one of us will visit the other, and yet we never do. We're as guilty as each other on this score, and I exonerate us both of all blame; after all, for ladies such as ourselves, who work so damn hard and who rarely seem to get time off, life is busy and the best-laid plans of mice and men, etc. etc.

And so I finally get to the point, after such a lengthy preamble. I'm very cheekily taking the bull by the horns here and can only hope it's not presumptuous of me. As it happens, I have an embarrassing amount of holiday long overdue to me, so I earmarked the last weekend of this month and – if agreeable to you – I will happily book a flight to Dublin, so I can hopefully get to meet up with you. My plan then is to whisk you out to dinner so we can talk, talk, talk the night away. I so want to hear all about your life and your work at Sloan Curtis, about Analyzed too, of course, and what inspired you to set it up. Most of all, I want to hear all about your private life, and I'll try not to bore you to tears about mine. Any boyfriends/dates/partners out there for someone as special as you?

So what do you say, Iris? One word from you and I'm booking this and taking you out and nothing in the world will stop me.

Your old buddy, who misses you.

Anna

There was a PS right at the very bottom, one that caught at Iris's heart, so accurately did it mirror what she herself had been feeling since all this first started. It was as if she and Anna had already slipped back into that old, indefinable habit they'd always shared. That of almost being able to read each other's thoughts, without the need for either to articulate as much as one single word.

You know something? Anna had written. *Analyzed has generated so much buzz around the topic of asking the right questions to find the right person. But supposing it's not a boyfriend or girlfriend some of us need? Supposing it's just friends, full stop?*

Chapter Twenty-Nine

Kim

Back in Kim's kitchen, the sound of her mother's door key scratching in the lock was all you could hear, as Kim leaped up to her feet, her heart pounding in double quick time.

'I need you to do me a favour, Simon,' she asked him.

'Of course.'

'Give me a minute alone with Mam – let me speak to her first. Your dad, I'll happily leave to you.'

'Gladly,' Simon replied, standing up tall and steeling himself. 'Good luck, then.'

Kim bolted out to the hall, where Connie had already opened up the front door and was now struggling to haul her bags inside. As it happened, she'd brought enough luggage to do her for a fortnight, never mind a weekend, but instead of helping her, Kim ignored every single one of the bags, abandoning them on the doorstep, where they were strewn about everywhere.

'Here I am, love,' Connie said breathlessly, 'and I've got so much to tell you!'

'Leave your bags there for a minute, Mam,' Kim said gently. 'And come inside and sit down. I've something to tell you and it can't wait.'

'Just let me wave Ronnie goodbye,' Connie said, as a little Nissan zoomed off at scarily high speed down the road. 'God love him, the poor man doesn't even have time to come in for a cuppa tea.'

Of course he doesn't, Kim thought crossly. *Makes perfect sense. Doubtlessly he's spotted Simon's jeep parked outside, put two and two together and decided to get the hell out of there, like the cowardly git that he is. Leaving me and Simon to clean up his mess.*

'Oh, it's so good to be home,' Connie said, giving her daughter a big, warm hug before Kim led her into the kitchen. Simon instantly came over to her, and reached out to shake her hand politely.

'Oh, hello there,' said Connie, looking a bit confused by this total stranger in her house, on a Saturday morning. 'Are you a friend of Kim's? Nice to meet you. You look a bit familiar, now I wonder why that is?'

'Mum, this is Simon,' Kim said, pulling out a chair and easing her mam down. 'And we've got something to tell you. Something that you're not going to like.'

'It's about Ronnie,' Simon began, taking the seat opposite Connie and looking her right in the eye.

Kim shot a significant look across the table to Simon – *go easy on her. Let her down gently.*

'What about him?' Connie said, looking from one of them to the other, bewildered.

'He's actually my dad,' Simon replied.

'Your *dad?*'

'That's right. And I don't know what he did or didn't tell you about my mum.'

'Barbara, yes,' said Connie, in a small voice, starting to sound worried sick now. 'Your dad was just telling me that today is her anniversary, the poor woman. Six years gone, I believe.'

'I'm so sorry to have to tell you this,' Kim said, 'but I'm afraid it's not her anniversary at all. Ronnie was telling you lies.'

She glanced over to Simon, who took up the baton. 'Kim is right,' he said, very, very gently. 'My mother is very much alive, as it happens.'

Connie just looked at him, her mouth forming a perfect letter 'o'.

Kim judged it wisest to step in here.

'It turns out that Barbara is actually in a nursing home, Mam,' she said softly. 'It seems she's been there for several years now, and that's the only reason why Ronnie is living on his own and claiming he's single.'

'Mum has Alzheimer's,' Simon explained. 'Sadly, it got so we couldn't care for her at home anymore, so she's now in St Michael's nursing home out in Bray. She's been there for years.'

Connie looked blankly at each of them in turn.

'Barbara?' she said weakly. 'Are we talking about the same Barbara here? You're telling me she's alive?'

Simon sucked in his cheeks and nodded yes. 'My mother is actually physically healthy,' he said. 'But of course, it's heartbreaking for us to see her cognitive deterioration. And I know this isn't easy for you to hear, Mrs Bailey, but you do understand why I had to tell you, before this went any further.'

Kim looked across the table to her mam, who'd gone ghostly white.

'So . . . Ronnie was making this up all along? All this time he was only telling me lies?'

'I'm afraid so,' said Simon.

'Oh, dear God,' Connie repeated over and over. 'He had me convinced. You should have seen him. On the drive home now, he was telling me all about Barbara's anniversary. He was even crying – he was so upset, we had to pull the car over!'

'I know this is a tough blow, Mam,' said Kim, 'but Simon is right. Isn't it so much better to find out sooner rather than later?'

'You're not even the first,' Simon said gently. 'Believe it or not, Dad's actually done this kind of thing before. Pretended to be a widower, so he can hook up with women his own age. I don't even know why he does it – if he just told the truth, it would be a lot more palatable. It's a rotten, awful thing to do, it's deceitful on every level and believe me, Mrs Bailey, I have no words to apologise to you for what he's put you through.'

But Connie was crying now. Hot, angry, bitter tears.

Kim stood to her feet. 'I know you mean well, Simon,' she told him, 'but I really do think you need to leave now. Mam's in shock, and she needs time to get her head around all this.'

'Of course,' Simon nodded understandingly. 'I'll go. And once again, Mrs Bailey, on behalf of my family, I really am so, so sorry.'

Connie didn't answer him. Instead she just stared straight ahead, with tears rolling down her face, not even bothering to wipe them away.

Chapter Thirty

Iris

'I mean, the whole reason you went and set up Analyzed in the first place was because you wanted it to be different from all the other dating apps out there,' said Kim, staring into space.

'Agreed,' Iris nodded, carefully laying out a plateful of elegant antipasti on the glass coffee table in her sitting room. It was the first time she'd entertained an actual guest in God knows how long, and she was going all out to make Kim feel welcome. How did her home look to an outside eye, she fleetingly wondered? Bit cold and clinical and minimalist, compared with the chaotic clutter at the Baileys' house? But then Kim was upset, she reminded herself. She needed a friendly shoulder to lean on that evening, and was hardly likely to comment on the interior design.

'Which in turn, was a whole lot of the reason why I first came on board, after one shitty date too many.'

'Nor were you alone in that,' said Iris understandingly.

'And yet, here we are. Back to square bloody one. You and I are having shag all luck on the site—'

'Although to be reasonable,' Iris interjected, 'I haven't used Analyzed to try to meet someone yet. Because frankly these days I barely have time to get into the office to do a day's work. Running the site is effectively turning into a full-time job.'

'Well, so far all I've met are a couple who were looking for a threesome and an ex who got pulled over by the cops and arrested last time we went out. Hardly a walking ad for Analyzed, now, am I?'

'Tell me how your mother is,' said Iris, changing the subject as she reached out to top up Kim's wine glass. By the look of the poor girl, she badly needed it too. Kim was pale and rattled and shaken-looking, and when she'd phoned Iris earlier that Saturday afternoon, she'd sounded desperately upset – a million miles from her usual effervescent, bouncy self, brimming over with energy and enthusiasm. Accurately sensing that something was up, Iris had asked if anything was the matter, so Kim filled her in.

'I see,' Iris had said, never one for fake, gooey sympathy. Instead, she'd responded as practically and as down to earth as ever.

'In that case,' she'd told Kim down the phone, shades of her old bossiness coming back, 'I suggest you spend the afternoon looking after your mother. Lots of sweet tea and a good lie-down, that's what she needs. Later on, you yourself are going to need some headspace, so why don't you call over to me this evening? Then we can talk some more.'

Which was precisely what the two of them were doing now. Iris had laid out a tasty Mediterranean supper: bread, cheese, hummus dips and olives, the whole works. She herself was tucking into everything hungrily now, while

Kim just played with the tapas nibbles and knocked back her wine like it was a double brandy and she was shell-shocked.

'A bigamist,' Kim said flatly. 'I mean, can you believe it? A bigamist. I'd read that this kind of thing went on a lot back in, like, the old days, like in wartime, long before the digital age. Apparently back then it wasn't hard to reinvent yourself and make a whole new family, while your first family were none the wiser.'

'I don't doubt it,' Iris said, listening intently.

'And by Jesus, this Ronnie fella is a world-class liar – I think he's one of those people who's so bloody good at it, he actually comes to believe the lie himself. Mam says he had her 100 per cent convinced that today was the anniversary of his wife's death. Tears streaming down his face when he told her, the whole works. Real BAFTA award-winning stuff.'

'A sociopathic liar is what you've just described,' Iris said, 'although technically Ronnie hasn't committed bigamy per se, considering he hadn't married your mum.'

'Oh come on, does it matter?' Kim said, slumping back wearily against Iris's beautifully elegant cream cushions and looking utterly defeated. 'The fact is, the two of them met on our dating app, Ronnie spun a whole web of lies for Mam and she fell for it, hook, line and sinker. It's heartbreaking. It took so much gentle persuasion and outright nagging on my part to even get Mam to go out on a date in the first place. She trusted in us, she trusted in our app. And the very first time she does, something like this happens.'

Knowing Kim needed to get it off her chest, Iris kept listening and nodding and topping up her glass at appropriate intervals.

'The poor woman is at home now,' Kim went on, 'and to say she's crushed is an understatement. It's the sheer deceit of it all, the two-facedness. I'm used to this kind of shitology, I've been dating online for long enough, but for someone like Mam? This is going to take her a long, long time to get over. I can't stay here too long this evening, I'm almost afraid to leave her on her own. Not after this.'

Iris nodded sympathetically.

'It seems no matter how deep and probing the questions we ask to screen our users,' she replied, 'we still can't legislate for duplicity.'

'You might well call it duplicity,' Kim said bitterly. 'But I call it good, old-fashioned lying, cheating and acting the maggot. Jesus, if I ever get my hands on that bollocks Ronnie, I really will swing for him. We should have a "name and shame" feature on Analyzed, you know that? A sort of rogues' gallery, where users can post photos of anyone at all who's led them a merry dance. Serves the feckers right, too.'

'Were it not for the fact that we'd doubtlessly be sued from here to next Tuesday,' Iris said, tongue firmly in cheek, 'then yes, I agree. Not the worst idea I've ever heard, Ms Bailey.'

'So now what?' Kim said, head back against the cushions, staring blankly across the living room to where Iris's

312

tasteful artwork dotted the walls. 'Where do we go from here?'

'I suggest you have another drink first,' Iris said. 'Because when I tell you what I have in mind, I think you're most definitely going to need it.'

Chapter Thirty-One

Kim

The following Monday lunchtime, Kim found herself side by side with Iris in a huge conference room, taking their seats at a table opposite another guy, who was introduced to Kim as Will White and who seemed to be pretty senior at Investco, the company where this big, scary meeting was to take place.

Investco was on Harcourt Street, just a short taxi ride from the International Financial Services Centre, where Sloan Curtis were based. The company took up an entire Georgian building, so it wasn't nearly as cool or cutting-edge when it came to office design as Sloan Curtis was, with its glass walls and floor-to-ceiling windows and light, light, light everywhere. Here at Investco, Kim and Iris were ushered into a stucco-ceilinged, ground-floor room, stuffy and airless, with Georgian windows that overlooked all the hustle and bustle on Harcourt Street directly outside.

The room began to fill up, with men predominantly, all of whom were introduced to both Kim and Iris as company lawyers, investment advisers and various other Investco bigwigs. Iris shook every hand and seemed to have a knack for memorising names on the spot, while Kim followed her lead and hoped the meeting wouldn't drag on for the entire afternoon. It was so hot and sultry in that room, it was starting to stink like a sweatshop, and she longed to be outside on the street, breathing in cool gulpfuls of fresh air. And downing pints of cider too, of course, but that would just have to wait, for the moment, anyway.

Iris acted as cool and composed as ever, as she faffed about importantly with her laptop and all manner of spreadsheets, waiting for everyone to take their seats so the meeting could kick off. Meanwhile Kim herself obediently took the seat beside her, feeling sticky in her work suit and desperately uncomfortable in her stiff-backed, Victorian chair, without even a biro to twiddle and distract her.

'Good afternoon, everyone,' this Will White said, as the room began to quieten down a little and everyone shushed and gave him the floor. 'Thank you all for assembling here at short notice.'

Iris just sat back and folded her arms, cool as a breeze, drinking it all in. But then, she had Kim fully prepped and warned well in advance of this meeting.

'Just remember this and all will be well,' she said to Kim, as the two sat in the back of a cab on the way there. 'Investco are the ones who initially approached us last week, not the other way round. They're the ones who put an offer on the table, and now they're the ones who want to meet to see if we can take it to the next level. They know Analyzed is hot to the market, and they're anxious to grab us early, and as cheaply as possible, before other investors begin to gather. Which, the way things are going, is only a matter of time.'

'So what's the plan for this meeting?' Kim asked her, wishing she was wearing shorts and a T-shirt on a humid day like this, and not a woolly suit with a pair of bloody tights.

'The plan is this,' said Iris, sounding brisk and business-like and not a bit like the new improved Version Two of herself that had been such fun to be around over the past few weeks. This Iris was driven and determined and completely focused, like a mother tiger protecting her digital 'baby' from anyone or anything who'd do it harm.

'We say as little as possible,' Iris went on. 'Instead, we just sit back and hear exactly what this lot have to say. We have their offer on the table, which is a generous one – half a million in return for a percentage of Analyzed. It's good, and of course, we're interested.'

'We'd be mad not to be,' Kim chipped in.

'But there's always scope to do better, isn't there?' Iris insisted. 'You and I have our counter-offer prepared and ready to go, and unless they're willing to consider it, then we walk.'

'We walk?' said Kim, looking at her in surprise. 'You mean we just turn our backs on half a million quid?'

'That's exactly what I mean,' said Iris. 'In the secure knowledge that we can – and will – do better. As my lawyer so wisely says, never accept a first offer. If they really want a piece of Analyzed, trust me, they'll go higher. If not, we go elsewhere, simple as that. Investco are a good company, and while I'd like to do business with them, they're far from being the only show in town.'

'Bloody hell,' said Kim, fanning herself, then lowering the window so she could take a gulp of air. 'You need nerves of steel for this kind of lark.'

'Think and act like a poker player,' said Iris calmly, 'and all will be well.'

'So, say we do end up walking out on this meeting,' Kim asked, as the thought struck her, 'then what do we do next?'

'Then we go back to Sloan Curtis and back to our day jobs, of course,' Iris replied, checking her already immaculate lipstick in an elegant little compact mirror, before snapping it tightly shut. 'We will naturally pursue other investment offers and take it from there. Although if you're very good and behave yourself,' she added, with the hint of a tiny wink, 'I might buy us each an ice cream afterwards.'

Back to Investco, where Will White was addressing the room.

'So you and I have had a preliminary meeting,' he was saying, with a respectful nod towards Iris, who again, didn't attempt to respond. 'We've already discussed Investco's initial interest in Analyzed. The reason I invited you here today was to meet our team and see if we can strike a deal.'

Again, just a tight little nod from Iris, as Kim eyed Will White up and down, trying to figure him out. He seemed young, ambitious, clean-cut and not bad-looking, she thought. Basically an interchangeable carbon copy of 99.9 per cent of the fellas she met every day over at Sloan Curtis.

'I hope you've had a chance to discuss our offer with your own legal representatives?' he asked politely.

'Naturally,' Iris replied, giving nothing away. Wow, Kim thought, her eyes darting across to Iris with fresh admiration; she seemed to be the only person in the room not sweltering in the sticky heat and looking all red-faced and uncomfortable. Instead, she was sitting tall, cool, pale and composed – a consummate pro who actually seemed to be enjoying herself.

Just look at you, Kim thought, lost in wonder. *I'd hate to be on the side that's negotiating against you, you'd run rings around them. You'd eat them for breakfast without breaking a sweat.*

Right at that very moment, and much to his embarrassment, Will's phone rang out, to irritated looks and a few *tsk tsk*s from all around the table.

'I beg your pardon, please excuse me,' he began to say, flushing red and fumbling through his jacket pocket to switch it off. But then he realised who it was that was calling and his whole tone changed. 'Apologies, everyone, but I need to take this. It's our CEO.'

Iris nodded and sat back, helping herself to a glass of sparkling water as Will slipped away from the table and took the call quietly in the corner of the room, but with the whole room tuning in.

'Yes, Mr West . . . yes, we're all assembled here now, in the conference room. Of course . . . if you had the time, that would be great . . . I think we'd all be prepared to wait a few moments . . .'

Kim's attention drifted out the window, where a taxi had just pulled up and someone seemed to be getting out and coming up the steps to the door of Investco. She couldn't see who it was, but Will was certainly acting like a Very Important Person indeed was on the way. Quickly, he wrapped up the call and came back to the table to address the room.

318

'I hope you'll all forgive the interruption,' he apologised to everyone, and to Iris in particular. 'It seems a meeting our CEO had earlier ended sooner than he thought it would, so he'll be joining us this afternoon after all.'

'Good,' said Iris crisply. 'Your CEO should be here – proper order, in fact.'

'Mr West is also our co-founder,' Will explained, 'and he's showing particular interest in this project and how we can bring it to a global market. He'll be here any moment – he's literally just arriving now.'

They didn't have to wait too long either. Moments later, the conference room door opened, and every eye turned to have a good gawp. In he came, as people rose to their feet to shake hands and greet him and arse-lick and all the usual shitology, Kim thought, that went on when the top brass graced you with their presence. Just like in Sloan Curtis. The whole room became a jumble of hellos and good to see yous and introductions and friendly handshakes. Kim stood up and was about to join in the melee and introduce herself, but then she saw who it was there, and instead, stood rooted to the spot.

The CEO caught her eye and she caught his and for a minute, the two of them just stared at each other in mutual surprise.

'Harold?' said Kim, scarcely able to believe what she was seeing.

'Kim . . . Bailey?' he replied, looking and sounding equally taken aback. Then the two spoke together.

'What on earth are you doing here?'

Chapter Thirty-Two

Connie

Connie sat in the café part of their local bookshop, waiting for Betty to make her grand entrance. It was a gorgeous little café, right beside the charity shop where Betty worked, and it had been a long-standing arrangement between the two of them that they'd meet there for a bite to eat that particular evening.

Of course, Connie had wanted to cancel. Last thing she was in the humour for was Betty and all her bragging and boasting and her relentless put-downs. Not after what she'd just been through over Ronnie and what a bombshell it had been.

Every time she thought about that man, her eyes automatically welled up and her bottom lip started to wobble. The cruelty of it. The meanness. The selfishness. The total lack of consideration for that poor wife of his, who'd done absolutely nothing wrong. Half of her had a good mind to drive out to the nursing home Barbara was in, and let her know exactly what her husband was getting up to behind her back. But then she reminded herself, sure wasn't the poor lady suffering from Alzheimer's, so what good would that do anyone?

When Connie thought of the high hopes she'd had for her and Ronnie, too! We're at the exact same phase in life, she'd happily figured just a few short days ago. We've both had great marriages, we've both been blessed with an only child each and sure they're grown adults now, so the pair of us can do what we like, go wherever we want and just enjoy every minute in each other's company.

She'd missed so much about having a man around the place, too, she thought sadly, as a very nice, smiley waiter came over to leave menus on the table. Companionship, great chats about the old days, someone who'd ring her up first thing in the morning and last thing at night, just to see how she was, just so they could fill each other in on how their days had been. And yet the whole time, Ronnie had been lying to her. Sheer, outright porky-pies. To hear him talking about his wife's death and how much he missed her? Oh dear God, what a performance. The lying fecker would have given Daniel Day-Lewis a right run for his money.

'I liked him,' she'd spent the whole weekend wailing at Kim. 'I even thought he was the kind of fella your dad would have got on with, and there's no higher praise than that.'

'I know it's shit, Mam,' Kim had said, in between long, soothing, sympathetic chats and making endless pots of tea. 'Break-ups are a load of poo, and it doesn't get easier. But just think, Ronnie was the first fella you met online. Who knows? Maybe if you dipped your toe in the pond again, you might meet someone even better for you. Someone properly single, for a change.'

'Hell will freeze over before that ever happens,' Connie had snapped, then immediately felt guilty for biting the head off Kim, when the girl was only trying to help. 'I tried your aul' app thing,' Connie went on, 'and I'm very sorry for you and Iris, love, but what a total load of rubbish. I only hope neither of you lose money on it. Honestly, what class of a way is that to meet someone nice? It's far too easy for anyone to feed you a big load of lies. And then,' she added, sounding morose and depressed, 'eejits like me, gullible aul' ones who believe anything they're told, completely fall for it.'

'You just need a bit of time, Mam,' Kim had counselled. 'Let's see how you feel when you've had a chance to get over Baldie Head.'

'Don't you be calling him a Baldie Head!' Connie said sternly. 'I'm allowed to call him Baldie, but you're not. Ronnie was so lovely – and so good to me too.'

Of course, that had started her off on a fresh bout of wailing and gnashing of teeth, but Kim was well able for her.

'And I'm sure he's very good to his wife too,' she'd fired straight back. 'The one whose whole existence he lied to the gills about, just in case you've forgotten.'

To her great shame, Connie had spent the rest of the weekend like a bag of wasps, utterly miserable and wallowing in it and refusing point-blank to be cheered up.

'And another thing,' she'd sniped at Kim only just that morning, before the girl scooted off to work for the day – and more than likely for most of the night too.

'What's that?' Kim had said, horsing down a bowl of Cheerios as she stood over the kitchen sink, with not even enough time to sit down at the table for two seconds together.

'I'm meant to be having a bite to eat with Betty later on,' Connie griped, pulling her dressing gown tightly around her, 'and I don't want to go. You can tell her I'm sick or something. Say whatever you like, I'm not in the mood for her.'

'Hiding away isn't the right thing to do, Mam. You've got to get out there and face the world sometime, so why put it off? Betty's your friend, she's hardly going to gloat when you tell her you and Ronnie broke up, now is she?'

But that's exactly what I did to her, Connie thought. When she and Ronnie first got together, she'd done nothing but lord it over Betty, like she was the first woman in the whole world to have a new man in her life.

So now all she could think sadly was, doesn't this big dose of humiliation serve me bloody well right?

♥

'So sorry to keep you waiting,' Betty said, breezing in to the little bookshop café where they'd arranged to meet, dead late as usual. 'We're so busy in the shop today, you've no idea. It was a nightmare for me to try to get away, the customers wouldn't let me lock up, even when it got to 6 p.m. closing time. They kept clamouring to get in!'

Connie rose to give her a hug, then sat back down again. Might as well get this over with, she thought, steeling herself to grab the bull by the horns. As it worked out, though, Betty paved the way very nicely for her.

'So,' she said, her tone shifting so she almost sounded dour about it, 'you were away with your new man for the weekend. Go on then, you might as well tell me how it went.'

Get it over and done with, that was her tone, so Connie took her chance. Thank God for Kim, she thought, who had her well prepped and primed on exactly what to say to this one.

'I'm very sorry to say that Ronnie and myself have decided to call it a day,' she replied, hoping it didn't sound too rehearsed, like words were put in her mouth. 'It turns out that he and I are very different people on very different paths, and while I wish him well, I think it's best we go our separate ways.'

Then she picked up the menu to fan her face, delighted she'd managed to get at least that much off her chest. Now for the gloating and rubbing salt in the wound from Betty, she thought.

To her astonishment, Betty wasn't a bit like that at all.

'Oh my poor girl,' she said sympathetically, moving her chair to Connie's side of the table and slipping a comforting arm around her. 'I'm sorry. I'm so, so sorry. Tell me what happened – but only if you want to, of course.'

Connie looked at her in mute surprise. She scanned Betty's face, looking for a hint of an aul' gloat, but there was none, zero. This seemed to be real, genuine sympathy here. For the first time in a long time, Betty seemed to be acting like a proper, actual friend and right now, Connie was deeply grateful for it.

'It hurts, Betty,' she said, as the tears began to start up, in spite of her best intentions. 'It really hurts. He told me all manner of lies and the worst part is that I believed him, I really did. Oh, I made such an eejit of myself over that man!'

'We're all eejits when it comes to men,' Betty said wisely. 'Makes no difference whether you're seventeen or whether you're in your seventies, like us.'

'Turns out he's married,' Connie started to sob properly, cross with herself for it, when she vowed she'd act all cool and casual in front of Betty, of all people. But of course, the minute even Ronnie's name was mentioned, it all rushed back to her, a fresh kind of torture every single time she thought of it.

And so the floodgates opened and it all came gushing out, in torrents.

'He swore blind to me he was widowed, and it turns out the wife is in a nursing home. His son told me, so I had it straight from the horse's mouth. And do you want to know what the worst part is? I've been calling Ronnie ever since, to try and have it out with him, just to see what he'd say to me, but the bloody coward won't even answer the phone.'

Betty pulled a face and kept her arm good and tight around her pal. It felt warm, comforting. Felt like exactly what Connie needed just then.

'Take it from me,' Betty said wisely, 'that's nothing. Sure look at what I went through with that aul' shite of an ex-husband of mine? Cheated on me with the half of Dublin, and of course, the last one to find out was me.'

Now it was Connie's turn to be shocked.

'Dear God, Betty, love,' she said, looking at her in bewilderment. 'You never said your Jeremy was messing on you behind your back – why didn't you tell me at the time?'

'Very long story,' Betty said drily, rolling her eyes. 'Jesus, I wish we had a decent drink right now. We could both do with it. What are we doing in a café? We need gin. Lots of lovely, lovely gin.'

'Whenever you'd talk about Jeremy,' Connie said, in amazement, 'you'd always put on this perfect shopfront. Even back when you were going through the separation and all that malarkey with solicitors and accountants, and selling the house and dividing everything between you both. Whenever you and me would meet, you'd just say that you were miles better apart, and that this was the best thing to ever happen to you. You never told me any of this before.'

Betty said nothing, just fluffed her hair and twiddled with her sunglasses.

'You and I are supposed to be friends,' Connie said gently. 'What's the point of our being proper pals unless we can be honest with each other?'

Just then, the waiter came over to take their order.

'What would you ladies like to drink, tea? Coffee? Water? Would you like to see the pastry menu?'

The pair looked at each other like two shifty schoolgirls.

'We're terribly sorry,' Betty said, rising to her feet, 'but I think we're both going to need something considerably stronger than a jam sponge and a pot of tea. Connie? Grab your bag. I know exactly where we're going, and no, I will not be taking no for an answer.'

Chapter Thirty-Three

Iris

'Harold, I'd like you to meet Iris Simpson, founder of Analyzed,' Kim said, making the necessary introductions, before the meeting finally kicked into gear. Harold reached out to shake Iris's hand, immediately launching into a full litany of apologies for his late arrival.

'Dreadfully rude of me to barge in like this,' he said to her, removing his glasses and doing a polite little head-bow. 'But as your charming colleague Kim may have told you, I've been taking a close personal interest in Analyzed – right from the off, as it happens.'

'That I can certainly vouch for,' Kim grinned, but tactfully said no more than that.

'Good, good.' Iris nodded approvingly. Naturally she already knew who Harold West was, knew all about him, as it happened. As did anyone in her position who read the business pages as avidly as she did. But she was particularly pleased that Kim appeared to know someone at such a senior level who was closely involved in the negotiations. Maybe now they had a shot at really nailing this. Harold had a wonderful reputation as a financial investor, he already seemed onside, and it gave them such an advantage that he was prepared to attend the meeting personally.

'We only bumped into each other very recently, in fact,' Harold said, with a respectful little nod towards Kim.

'That's right,' Kim replied. 'I was on what turned out to be the world's shortest date ever and you were going . . . to the opera, wasn't it?'

'Oh, really?' Iris asked, her interest piqued and her attention momentarily sidetracked. 'Which opera?'

'*Madame Butterfly* at the Gaiety Theatre,' Harold replied, smiling now, and warming to a subject he seemed to know quite a lot about. 'A wonderful production, too, I'd highly recommend it. The performances were out-standing, with full credit to their conductor. It really is quite breathtaking. It runs for another week and if you can make it, you really should.'

'I'm seeing it this evening, as it happens,' Iris said with a smirk. 'It's my favourite Puccini opera.'

'Oh, good for you,' said Harold, delighted. 'I really think you'll enjoy it, particularly if you're a Puccini fan.'

'I booked it a very long time ago,' Iris said, 'and yes, I'm greatly looking forward to it.'

'You were so lucky to get a ticket, you know,' Harold chatted away, 'there were only single seats available the night I saw it.'

Iris was going to the show on her own, as it happened, and found it interesting that Harold had done exactly the same.

Then Will White interrupted them, calling everyone to order.

'Ladies and Gentlemen,' he said, over the clamour of chatter in the room, 'if we could all take our seats, please, then we can finally get started.'

Harold took a seat directly beside Iris, with Kim on her other side.

'I'd be intrigued to know what you think of the production after you've seen it this weekend,' Harold said, still deep in conversation with Iris.

'I most certainly will let you know,' she replied, while all around them there was a kerfuffle as people took their seats. 'And just out of interest,' she added, 'I once had the pleasure of seeing Maria de Maderas, a wonderful soprano from Barcelona, sing the title role in *Butterfly*, many years ago now. It's a performance I think I'll carry to my grave, that's how utterly in command of the stage she was. She was sublime – quite extraordinary. She made me cry and that never, ever happens.'

'I can vouch for that,' Kim chipped in.

But now Harold was giving Iris quite a strange look, as everyone else quietened down and helped themselves to large glasses of iced water, waiting for the two of them to finally shut up.

'Maria de Maderas?' Harold said to Iris. 'Did you just say Maria de Maderas?'

'That's right,' she nodded. 'Are you a fan of hers?'

'Maria de Maderas,' Harold said, looking at her in amazement now, 'happens to be my mother.'

'No!' said Iris, momentarily shocked, as Kim nudged her to wind up the small talk so the meeting could kick off.

But this didn't seem to concern Harold in the slightest. Instead, he sat back, folded his hands across his tummy and chatted away, like someone with all the time in the world, seemingly oblivious to the fact that a whole roomful of people were starting to get impatient.

'Actually,' he said, 'my mother will be appearing in *Butterfly* at Covent Garden again very soon. Next month, in fact.'

'I didn't know that,' Iris said, utterly intrigued. 'Which role is she playing this time?'

'Butterfly's mother,' said Harold. 'Almost forty years to the day since she played the title role of *Butterfly* on the very same stage.'

'How extraordinary,' Iris said, as she whipped off her glasses, seriously impressed that Harold came from such a cultured family, with such a distinguished operatic pedigree. 'You must be so proud of her.'

'Oh, I am,' he smiled modestly, 'and I'm delighted to say I'll be there on the opening night.'

'Do you know, I think I'm actually jealous,' Iris smiled back, growing more and more convinced by the second that the stars were aligning and that Investco were people she really wanted to do business with. This surely was a sign, wasn't it? Kim shot her a significant look that seemed to say, *shut up, will you?* But Iris remained unperturbed. Harold was the CEO around here, and if he wanted to chat all day about Covent Garden operas, then that was absolutely fine with her.

'So if I can draw everyone's attention to the prospectus in front of you all,' Will piped up, accurately reading the room and seemingly more aware than his boss of the growing tetchiness around the table. 'Then maybe we can begin?'

♥

Facts and figures were whizzing back and forth across the table, but fortunately facts and figures were where Iris excelled.

'As you know,' Will was saying, confidently giving a preamble as to why they were all there in the first place, 'we feel that, for a start-up, our standing offer is extraordinarily generous. We're offering €500k in exchange for 40 per cent of the company. If you'd all be so good as to turn to page three of your prospectus, you'll see the advance broken down into instalments on a month-by-month basis.'

He stopped there, to clear his throat and take a sip of water, so Kim jumped in.

'Yeah,' she said, flicking through the prospectus. 'But where does it say in this yoke exactly what we'd get in return for that 40 per cent?'

Iris silently blessed Kim for her refreshingly down-to-earth attitude, but for the moment, she herself stayed silent.

'It's all there from page fifteen onwards,' Will answered. 'In fact, if I can bring everyone's attention to this section of your prospectus, you'll see exactly how we plan to take Analyzed global, on a step-by-step basis.'

'Because here at Investco,' one of their legal team butted in, a man in his late thirties who'd been clicking a biro non-stop in the most annoying manner ever since the meeting started, and addressed Harold and Harold only, no one else, 'we believe that we're the right people for you at the right time. You need our expertise here. You ladies have done incredibly well so far, but now it's time to call in the big guns. No one will do a better job than us at taking your company to the next level. I'm sure Harold would agree.'

What an insufferably little toady you are, Iris thought, taking him in. *Not to mention patronising to both Kim and I.*

Harold said nothing, and then Iris realised that everyone seemed to be looking at her, waiting to see what she'd have to say in response.

'Your offer is a generous one,' she replied briskly, 'but the stake you're looking for is considerably higher than we envisaged. In short, no deal. Yes, we're only a startup, but may I point out that we're growing at a rate of 37.5 per cent week on week? By my calculation, if we project this into the future, then one year from now we'll exceed 1.75 million users, and that's worldwide. Ladies and Gentlemen,' she added, '40 per cent of Analyzed is just too much for us to rescind.'

One by one, she eyeballed everyone around the table. The vast majority on the Investco side looked red-faced, sweaty and clearly wanting nothing more than to reach a deal, wrap this up and get out of there as quickly as possible. Harold, on the other hand, was sitting back with his hands crossed over his lap, cool as a breeze and looking like all he was short of was a Panama hat and a walking stick to transform him into a younger version of James Joyce.

'I'm actually with Iris on this,' Kim chipped in, as Iris shot her a look of gratitude, deeply glad of the back-up. 'We'd be nuts to sign away almost half of a company that's growing so fast. We don't want to end up kicking ourselves in a few short years. We can't be bought cheaply, I'm afraid. Can we, Iris?'

'It's quite out of the question,' Iris replied.

Now there was silence from around the table, with everyone on the Investco side looking anxiously at each other. Everyone except for Harold, who continued to sit there impassively.

Will blinked first.

'Would it be OK with everyone,' he said to the room, 'if we had a brief recess to confer with each other?'

There were mumbles of agreement around the table as, en masse, the Investco side rose from their seats to take a little time out. Again, everyone except Harold.

'Actually,' he said, without breaking a sweat. 'I don't believe that's strictly necessary. I've read this pretty thoroughly,' he added, referring to the prospectus, 'and I feel we can do better for you. Considerably better. So, Ms Simpson, Ms Bailey, how do you feel about this? Seven hundred and fifty thousand euro, in return for 33.3 per cent of the company. Is that something that might pique your interest just a little more?'

Chapter Thirty-Four

Connie

'Bloody online dating,' Connie was happily bitching away, very pleasantly sozzled on her second gin and tonic, thanks very much, and feeling no pain whatsoever. 'That's the root cause of all this, you know. You're a wise woman, Betty, love, to stay well away from all those dating site – they're nothing but trouble, take it from me.'

'Are you joking me?' said Betty, waving at the barman to bring over two more drink refills. 'I've no intention of ever going on a date again – after what I went through with that eejit ex of mine? Who I hear is miserable now with his new "partner", as he refers to her. May she plague the living bejaysus out of him, and it serves him right.'

'Jeremy is miserable now?' Connie blinked back at her.

'So I hear,' Betty said, with a conspiratorial little nod. 'Apparently the new girlfriend is in her forties, you know, and is all into camping and mountain-climbing and kayaking. Imagine Jeremy up a mountain. Or out camping! Him that complains if he has to walk as far as Tesco.'

'They don't have proper toilets on any of those campsites, I heard,' Connie said supportively.

'And Jeremy has IBS.'

'Good enough for him, then.'

More giggles from the pair of them, now happily ensconced at a cosy corner table in a bar right opposite the café they'd met in earlier. Moving across the road there, Connie thought, was the best thing they could have done. In fact, the more she thought about it, the more she reckoned that tonight really was turning out to be one for the books.

Connie had known Betty for well over forty years and never once, in all that time, had Betty even hinted that there was even the slightest trouble between her and her ex-husband. Never did she even suspect that Jeremy had a brand-new partner, either – Betty had never breathed a single word. Instead, she'd just smile at the world, and if anyone asked her how things were at home since her marriage break-up, she'd say, 'wonderful. Couldn't be better. I'm on top of the world!' Then she'd clam up, just like that. Now, of course, Connie was kicking herself for not asking more, but back then, Betty would have taken the nose off you.

Not tonight though. This was fast turning into the best night out Connie had had in a long, long time. Like discovering a brand-new friend, a really fabulous friend, except this person had actually been in your life all this time, it's just that you never really knew them before. Not really. Not in the way friends were supposed to know each other warts and all.

'So what's Jeremy's new partner like?' Connie asked, intrigued.

'Cheap,' said Betty, taking a sip of her gin. 'Tarty-looking, covered in fake tan and wears jeans with rips in them. Forty, trying to look twenty, but all she really ends up looking is ridiculous.'

The two of them burst into peals of giggles at that, then clinked glasses and drank some more.

'I really wish you'd told me at the time,' Connie said, suddenly ashamed of herself. 'There you were, going through so much and you never said a single word.'

'Well . . .' said Betty, as the mood between them seemed to shift a bit. 'It didn't seem right somehow. No one likes a moaner, do they? And what good would all the moaning and whingeing in the world do anyway? Jeremy had met someone else and he was gone out of my life and that was the end of that. Besides . . .'

'Besides what, love?' Connie asked gently.

'Well, how could I possibly have offloaded on you, of all people? You had your Jack, and the two of you always seemed so content with each other. It wouldn't have been right.'

'I never even suspected what you were going through,' Connie said. 'Not for a moment. I'm a bad friend, Betty, thoughtless and insensitive, and now that we're being straight with each other, there's no words to tell you how sorry I am.'

'Oh now, there's no need for any of that at all,' Betty insisted. 'Sure we've always had each other, and it's lovely to be able to reconnect now, properly. And this time, as we really are.'

'You always had your "best side out",' Connie went on. 'I think that's why I didn't pick up the phone to you when your marriage broke up, or why I didn't call in to see you nearly as often as I should have. You see what I mean? I'm a lousy friend.'

'You most certainly are not!' Betty insisted. 'What about me, when you first got together with Ronnie? I don't mind telling you, I was pea green with jealousy. Out of the blue, you seemed to have met a decent fella who was taking you to the Andrea Bocelli concert. I nearly wanted to vomit when I heard, so if anyone's a bad friend here, it's me!'

A lovely wave of wooziness came over Connie, as she plonked her gin down and decided it was time for some truth from her, for a change.

'Technically, yes, Ronnie did take me to the concert all right,' she said, 'but only to sit in the passenger seat of his chip van in the Aviva Stadium car park, listening to the concert with the windows down. So you had feck all to be jealous of.'

'You're kidding!' Betty said, clamping her hand over her mouth, getting a fresh bout of the giggles.

'Not only that,' Connie went on, starting to join in the sniggering as the ridiculousness of it dawned on her, 'but after the concert, I ended up working in the van, side by side with Ronnie, frying chips and burgers and onions. Well, I tell you, I came home stinking like a drive-through McDonald's. The bang off me! My hair was destroyed, and my good blue skirt hasn't been the same since.'

More giggles, and then it was Betty's turn for a truth bomb.

'Well,' she said, 'you know how I was always telling you my Pamela kept getting promoted in the bank, and that now she was practically running the place?'

'Course,' said Connie. 'You said she was made manager of a branch down in Athlone.'

'Total fabrication. Pamela was actually made redundant months ago now. So that's why I told you she was working outside of Dublin – I was afraid you'd call into her old branch and wonder why she wasn't there anymore.'

'Ahh, for God's sake, Betty,' Connie said, horrified, 'you could have at least told me about Pamela. The poor woman. I would have totally understood, I know how awful it is. Sure wasn't I made redundant myself, not so long ago?'

'But how could I?' Betty asked, staring ahead of her. 'There's your Kim, still only in her twenties and doing so brilliantly in work with the great job she has. How could I compete?'

'Oh now, love,' said Connie. 'Why do the pair of us need to compete at all? Isn't life tough enough without that?'

A pause as their fresh drinks arrived.

'Wouldn't life be so much easier,' Betty mused, staring into space, 'if we just started telling each other the truth?'

'So much simpler,' Connie nodded in agreement. 'There was me, mad jealous of you and your perfect life and your perfect job . . .'

'Job?' Betty sneered. 'You call that a job? In that dump of a charity shop? It's a wonder I haven't got scabies from working in there, the state of the place. I only go in there a few days a week to get me out of the house, that's all.'

'At least you've got something to do and somewhere to go,' Connie said. 'Here's me, rattling around the house all by myself, day and night – I'd kill for even a part-time job.

A proper decent one that might make me a nice few quid on the side. I think that's a lot of the reason I went headlong into that ridiculous dating site in the first place – sheer boredom. I'd nothing else to do and no one else to chat with all day, so I thought, why not?'

'What kind of a job would you be looking for?' Betty asked, eyeing her keenly.

Connie had to take a moment to give some thought to that one. She glanced around the bar they were in, which was high-ceilinged, old-fashioned and so busy there wasn't a single table free, with, she noticed, the poor lounge staff practically run off their feet. They were stressed, they were hassled, they were getting orders wrong, they needed proper management.

'Well,' she eventually said, taking it all in, 'somewhere like here, for instance. After all, I was all those years working as a waitress in Flynns hotel, and I really loved every day of it there. The laughs I used to have with the staff! So I suppose something along those lines would be the dream. But who's going to hire a waitress in her seventies? Believe me, I've tried, and there's nothing out there. Not for me, anyway.'

'I used to love popping into Flynns for my tea,' Betty enthused. 'You were so great at your job, too. I used to watch you yakking away to all your regulars like they were old pals. You'd even remember what they liked to order before they'd barely even sat down.'

'What about you, love?' Connie asked, genuinely interested. 'If you're not happy in the charity shop, where else would you like to work?'

Betty sat back, took another sip of her gin and fluffed out her hair again, really giving it thought.

'Well, you know me,' she said, 'I love a bit of glamour. I always thought I'd adore a job where I could dress up to the nines and chat away with all the various people I met. Like . . . like . . . for instance . . .'

'Like working front of house in a restaurant?' Connie suggested.

'That's exactly what I'd love!' Betty said, instantly lighting up. 'I'd be rubbish in the kitchen, but good at showing people to their tables and taking bookings, that kind of thing.'

'You'd be wonderful at it, too,' said Connie, sincerely meaning every word.

'So we sort of complement each other that way, don't we?'

'Something to think about for the future? Maybe?'

'You never know.'

Chapter Thirty-Five

Kim

'So, come on, tell me, I'm dying to know! What do you think?' Kim asked Iris, as the two of them sat side by side in a taxi, finally heading back to Sloan Curtis. Thank Christ, she thought, their big, scary investors' meeting had finally wrapped up, so at least they could have a quiet post-mortem in peace. In peace with, mercifully, air-conditioning.

'Well,' Iris said, calmly flicking through the prospectus they'd been given at the meeting, 'we'll obviously need to reflect on it over the coming days. But you know, considering what they're offering, 33.3 per cent is a pretty reasonable stake to ask for in return. Just doing a quick mental calculation, that means Investco are projecting a year-on-year growth rate of 65.3 per cent, yielding a projected revenue stream for Analyzed of 52.1 per cent. For a brand-new start-up, that's considerable.'

'Ahh, you eejit,' Kim said, shaking her head. 'Their offer is great, I know it is. No matter what way we crunch the numbers, it works for everyone. What I meant to ask was, what did you think of Harold?'

'Do you mean Harold West?' Iris blinked back at her in surprise.

'Well, how many other Harolds did you come across this afternoon? Course I mean Harold West, who else did you think I was talking about?'

'Why do you want to know what I think of him?'

'Well, he's a nice guy, isn't he?' Kim said lightly.

'He seems a most effective CEO,' said Iris, considering the question. 'Perhaps someone we can even do business with. Perhaps. It was hugely helpful that you'd met him previously. May I ask where the two of you met?'

'Via Analyzed,' Kim said proudly. 'Remember me telling you about him? He was the very first fella I met, thanks to the app. He took me for dinner and insisted on paying and everything. Very classy. Just not my type, at all.'

'No, no, I can see that quite clearly,' Iris said distractedly, scrolling down through all the messages and missed calls on her phone. 'You and he would be most unsuited, that's as plain as the nose on your face. A flaw in the algorithm there, I think. One we'll have to address in the not-too-distant future. We don't want that happening too often, it's not good for our reputation.'

'Oh, for feck's sake, Iris,' Kim said exasperatedly, snatching the iPhone out of her hands, so at least she could grab her full attention. 'Do you see what's going on here? See what you and me are doing? This is what's known as "girl talk".'

'Excuse me?' said Iris, looking up at Kim.

'I know it's strange and new to you,' Kim went on, 'but trust me, it's how we women communicate when we're alone, and you'll get used to it and you'll love it. We're yakking about fellas we've just met. And it's perfectly normal and it's how we rock. We can talk about projected revenue streams and ironing out flaws in the app another time, but for now, will you just tell me what you thought of Harold?'

'Why would it matter what I think of him?' Iris asked her, with genuine surprise. 'As long as you and I can potentially do business with him, then what do individual personalities matter?'

'Iris!' Kim said, at the end of her rope now, practically yelling in the woman's face in exasperation. 'Do I have to spell it out to you? Harold is a good guy, and all I'm saying is that the two of you already seem to have a lot in common. Opera, for starters. And I bet there's loads more, if you just gave him a chance. Question is, could he be the type you'd ever fancy?'

Now Iris was looking at her in utter bewilderment.

'Why would you think Harold West would be the type I'd find attractive?' she asked, puzzled.

'Well, I have to ask, don't I?' said Kim. 'Because when it comes to men, I haven't a clue what your type actually is. You said you were looking for companionship, but other than that . . .'

'Oh, all right then.' Iris sighed reluctantly, as if she knew she wouldn't have a minute's peace till she got this out of the way. 'If you must know, then Harold West seems like a perfect gentleman, polite and professional. Which is pretty much all I ask of anyone I'm considering doing business with.'

'And?' Kim said, feeling like she was pulling teeth here.

'And while it's delightful that we share a deep love of opera,' Iris said, 'if you're asking me would I consider

Harold as a potential partner, my answer is twofold. First, he's a little young for me – I'm a good few years older than him. Secondly, what could possibly be more fool-hardy than to embark on a new relationship with some-one you work with? A total recipe for disaster, let me tell you. So in short,' she went on, taking her phone back from Kim and scrolling down through all her missed calls and emails, 'are you out of your mind? An investment firm are currently dangling €750k in front of us and all you want to know is, do I find their CEO attractive? Have you com-pletely lost your reason?'

It was just coming up to 10 p.m. that night when Kim finally arrived home, after the longest, hottest, most bone-wearying, banjaxing shag of a day she could remember in months. Course, she and Iris had ended up working late together, on a conference call with their accountant, thrashing out the small print on the Investco offer. Ordi-narily Kim liked numbers and maths and 'doing sums in her head', as her mam put it, but after a non-stop twelve hours of it, she was crying out for home and a takeaway and something trashy to watch on Netflix. Pointless even to ask all her sesh buddies if anyone was going for a few Friday-night scoops; the whole lot of them were out on dates, in their fast-growing new relationships. Everyone except for her.

Kim sighed wearily, paid her taxi driver and was just coming down her street, fumbling around in her backpack for her door keys and wondering if she'd order from the Thai place she liked on Deliveroo, or else sesame chicken strips and garlic fries from the takeaway down the road, when she became aware that there was someone standing right at her front door, with his back to her. It was late, and what little light there was was dim, so she had to squint to be sure, but no – there was definitely someone there all right.

Tall guy, bending over on the doorstep, so his arse was pretty much all she saw of him. Am I being burgled, she wondered? Have I just caught them in the act? It was only when he stepped away that she realised what was going on; whoever this guy was, he was actually dropping off a giant bouquet of gorgeous, expensive-looking flowers. At nearly ten o'clock at night. Weird, she thought, as she waved and called out to him.

Which is when she spotted a black jeep parked just a few houses down from hers, and the penny finally dropped.

'Simon?' she said, coming up to her front door. 'What the hell are you doing here? And with flowers?'

'Didn't want to disturb you,' he grinned back modestly. 'I never even rang the doorbell. I only wanted to drop these off, that's all.'

'Flowers?' Kim said, flabbergasted. 'For . . .'

'Actually for your mother,' he explained. 'Just by way of a little apology to her, to say I really am so sorry for what she's been through. For the awful shock she must have got last week.'

'Oh, well . . . thanks,' said Kim, scooping them up off the doorstep and burying her nose in a bunch of purple hydrangeas and lillies. They smelled gorgeous, too. A sweet, summery, lingering smell. 'That's really kind of you. Mam will be pleased.'

'How is she doing?' Simon asked her, still standing opposite her on the doorstep, seemingly in no rush to leave.

'Come on in and ask her for yourself,' Kim said, letting herself in and beckoning Simon to follow her. But when she got inside, the house was still in pitch darkness; wherever Connie was, she most definitely hadn't come home yet.

'Well, this can only be a good sign,' Kim said, thinking aloud, as she led Simon down the hallway and on through to the kitchen. 'Mam went to meet a pal after work earlier, so I'm guessing it turned into a bit of a Friday-night session for the two of them. I'm glad. I'm glad she's out, and I hope she's enjoying herself.'

'No worries at all,' Simon said, standing awkwardly in the kitchen doorway, hands shoved deep into his pockets, as Kim found a vase, filled it up with water and arranged the flowers in it. 'Please tell your mum I'm sorry I missed her.'

'Course I will,' Kim said. 'So, how is your own mum doing?'

'Well, thankfully she's oblivious to all the shenanigans Dad was getting up to behind her back,' he replied, almost shrinking the doorway just by standing in it, he was that tall. 'Alzheimer's is hell, and there's been plenty of times when Mum doesn't remember who Dad is, or who I am for that matter. But when something awful like this happens, it's a kind of blessing in a way. At least

Mum is protected from knowing Dad was openly seeing other women behind her back.'

'I'm glad to hear she's OK,' Kim said, coming back to the table with the flowers and placing them right in the centre. 'At least that's something. The poor woman is blameless in all of this.'

'My dad, though, is a very different story,' Simon went on, folding his arms, as his whole expression changed. Kim stopped faffing around and looked him right in the eye, bracing herself for this.

'Did you have it out with him?' she asked.

'Did I what?' he said wryly. 'I told him in no uncertain terms that you and I had had a full and frank conversation about what he'd been up to, so everyone was well aware of what was going on. I said that under no circumstances was he to ever attempt to contact your mother again.'

'Good,' Kim nodded.

'I hope he's at least done that much?'

'Not a peep out of him all week,' she said. 'Nothing. Because if he did? He'd have me to answer to, and no messing. I'd throttle Ronnie for what he put Mam through. Gladly.'

'I don't blame you,' Simon nodded tightly. 'Anyway, it's good to hear that he's leaving your mum in peace, at least.'

'Have you been keeping an eye on him since we last spoke?' Kim asked, sure that someone like Simon definitely had been. He seemed like a responsible type of guy; trustworthy, the kind that kept his word and didn't tolerate messing of any kind.

'Been watching Dad like a hawk, monitoring his phone and his computer, that kind of thing.'

'Glad to hear it.'

'I'll tell you something, though,' Simon added, his jaw tightening, 'There's times when I feel like a parent with a child, except weirdly, I ended up being the parent here and Dad is the child.'

Kim smiled at him, recognising the feeling only too well.

'And I've disabled Dad's account on that dating app that was the root cause of all this. Analyzed, the one I was telling you about,' Simon threw in helpfully.

She chose not to answer that one, and instead busied herself pretending to rearrange the flowers, that were already perfect.

'And you'd probably do well to warn your mother to steer clear of it too,' Simon went on, again, to stony silence from Kim.

'Those dating apps have a lot to answer for,' he said, still not letting it go.

Shut up, will you? she willed him, to no avail, while pretending to be completely absorbed in admiring the white lilies that were buried deep in the bouquet he'd brought.

'Apps like that one, for all that they pretend to be different because they ask more detailed questions, still make it far too easy for messers and cheaters to get away with it. They should be named and shamed, if you ask me.'

'And you've never tried online dating yourself then?' she asked, genuinely curious. Simon was attractive enough, she thought, looking at him dispassionately, as if they'd just met for the first time in a bar, and she was sizing him up. Conventionally tall, dark and not at all bad-looking, he was dressed in creamy trousers with a pale blue shirt, and if she were to describe him to Hannah or any of her work buddies, she'd say he looked like he'd fit right in on the sixth floor, where Paul the CFO and all the head honchos had their offices. The important ones, the ones who counted. The ones who barely said hello to Kim or anyone on a lowly level in the Sloan Curtis hierarchy.

'I think we've all tried online dating and dating apps at some point,' Simon said. 'But now, I don't go near them.'

Means he has a girlfriend, she thought.

'One bad experience too many,' he said aloud.

'Hey,' she grinned, 'I'll have you know you're talking to the queen of crappy dating experiences. Someday, if you have about five hours to spare, I'll fill you in.'

'My advice to you?' he said. 'Whatever you do, don't go near Analyzed. Of the whole lot of them out there, it has to be the worst.'

'Really?'

'Definitely.'

'Oh, you know,' she said airily, unable to keep quiet for much longer, 'I'm sure Analyzed isn't all bad.'

'You're sticking up for them?' said Simon, raising an eyebrow and looking at her with great interest now.

'No! No, not at all,' she was quick to claw back. 'It's just that . . . well, Analyzed is still fairly new to the market, you know. I'm sure the team behind it realise that there's all kinds of teething problems and a lot of shitology that still needs to be ironed out.'

She trailed off then, aware that Simon was continuing to look at her, tilting his head, as if he was really trying to get the measure of her.

'It's an Irish team behind Analyzed, you know,' he tossed in. 'I work in fintech; that's financial technology, secure payments online, that kind of thing, and I can tell you, their rapid growth is all anyone can talk about. They're the digital success story of the year – so far, anyway.'

'Oh yeah?' Kim said casually, heading for the fridge, where a menu from a local takeaway place she was fond of was half hanging off, barely held up by a magnet. 'Hmm, I'm starving . . . nothing like a Friday-night takeaway, is there?'

'Analyzed are quite the buzzword in financial circles,' he went on, still looking very strangely at her. 'Everyone wants to know more about who's behind it, and what their next move is going to be.'

Oh, what the feck, she thought. Pointless keeping quiet anymore. It was like he'd half guessed anyway, so she may as well come clean. She turned away from the fridge to face him and sighed deeply.

'Simon,' she said, 'why don't you sit down? There's something I need to get off my chest with you.'

Chapter Thirty-Six

Connie

Connie tra-la-la'ed her way in through the hall door, very pleasantly tipsy after the few gin and tonics she'd enjoyed with Betty. Not so squiffy that she'd have a hangover the next morning, though. Never again – not after the last time she went down that road with that gobshite would-be bigamist, who's name she refused to even invoke. He whose name shall never be spoken, as Betty referred to him in her put-on 'posh' voice, which of course, only made Connie giggle.

She was on a lovely, delicious high, mainly thanks to the fabulous chat she and Betty had been having for the whole night. The honesty, the frankness of it had felt like a real breath of fresh air. It was probably the first proper chat the two of them had had in years, without any of that awful one-upmanship or all the showing off the pair of them had been guilty of over the decades. She was so excited, too, about all the wonderful plans she and Betty had been brewing up together for the future, and she couldn't wait to see Kim's face when she told her.

Skipping down the street and coming up to her hall door, Connie spotted a black jeep parked outside the house, but she thought no more of it. Sure weren't there thousands of those ugly-looking things on the road these days? Yes,

Ronnie's son drove one of them, but so did hundreds of other people all over the city. It was just a coincidence, nothing more.

'Kim?' she called out as she let herself in, peeling off her jacket and dumping her handbag and keys on the hall table. 'It's me, I'm home – finally – and I've got loads to tell you! Where are you, love?'

She could hear loud guffaws of laughter coming from somewhere, then Kim's voice, telling one of her dating disaster stories. Then Connie got a whiff of a lovely, garlicky smell and followed her nose into the living room, where sure enough, Kim was sprawled out on the sofa, with the coffee table in front of her laden down with what looked like Thai food: chicken dishes that looked gorgeous, lovely lean strips of beef on a bed of onions and enough side portions of rice to feed the whole street.

There was a fella sitting on the armchair beside her, tall, skinny and very familiar-looking – it was only when he stood up to shake Connie's hand that she put two and two together and remembered exactly who he was.

'You?' she said, just staring at him. 'You're the son, aren't you?'

'That's right, Mrs Bailey,' Simon said respectfully, 'and please forgive me for barging in on you like this . . .'

'Simon brought you lovely flowers, Mam,' Kim tried to say, with her mouth full.

'By way of an apology,' Simon finished the sentence for her. 'Hearing what you had to hear last week must have been such a shock for you.'

'It certainly was,' Connie said primly, clasping her two hands in front of her, unsure how she felt about the son being here in her house.

'I felt like the worst in the world having to break such awful news,' Simon went on. 'And I only wondered how you were now, that's all.'

Connie looked at him for a long time, weighing up what to say, before the smell of that delicious chicken started getting the better of her. So she sat down on the armchair opposite and helped herself to a couple of chicken strips before answering.

'I'm feeling much better this week, thank you, Simon,' she said. 'No thanks to your father. Course, I know what happened wasn't your fault, and you're very good to check up on me and I know he's your dad and all that, but still. What Ronnie did was shameless and no good will come to him because of it, I can tell you that for nothing.'

'You'll be glad to know I tore strips off him,' Simon said. 'Put it this way, hell will freeze over before he ever tries to deceive any other unsuspecting ladies the way he did with you.'

'I'm very glad to hear it,' said Connie. 'And now, let's never speak of it again. Kim, love, pass me over a bit of dinner, will you? I'm starving – and you'll never guess what I have to tell you. It's you and Simon who are in for a shock now, not me!'

'What's up, Mam?' Kim asked, grabbing a spare plate and piling it high with stir-fry beef with bell peppers, pad thai and a Thai chicken lettuce wrap.

'Me and Betty have cooked up a very exciting little plan together,' said Connie, clapping her hands.

'Oh yeah?' said Kim. 'To do what? Go on a cruise? Join a golf club? Do walking tours around Dublin, maybe?'

'Oh, there'll be none of that boring, active retired aul' nonsense for us,' Connie said with a dismissive wave of her hand. 'No, this is something far more exciting, as it happens.'

Now both Simon and Kim were looking expectantly back at her.

'We're going to open a little pop-up café together!' she squealed back at them. 'Isn't that great news? Betty is going to ask her son Nigel to finance it, and we thought we'd take a nice short lease on one of those vacant shops down in the village, to see how we get on. She'd do all the front-of-house stuff and I'd do the catering, because I'd love it. Sure we'd only be serving teas, coffees and home made cakes and tarts to start with, and I could do that blindfolded.'

'It's a brilliant idea,' Simon said enthusiastically. 'People will pay a fortune for barista coffee these days – you should see what we pay down where I work in the Financial Services Centre. My weekly coffee bill is extortionate.'

Connie smiled warmly at him, starting to like him more and more the better she got to know him.

'Wow, Mam,' said Kim, her eyes popping. 'That I did *not* see coming. Great news, though and you'd be brilliant at it. You're a born natural. I remember you in Flynns hotel. You played a blinder.'

'You know what, pet?' Connie beamed back at her, thrilled with the bit of encouragement. 'You've been on at me for ages to start getting back out there again and living my life, and now here I am – finally doing it! Just not with a man. But isn't this so much better?'

Chapter Thirty-Seven

Kim

Hours later, after an unexpectedly enjoyable night, and when Connie had long since peeled herself off to bed, then and only then was Kim showing Simon out the door and back into his jeep. She walked him down the street to where he'd parked and he thanked her profusely every step of the way.

'I mean, it was just after ten when I landed on your doorstep,' he said, 'and it's two in the morning now – can't believe I stayed so late!'

'You're more than welcome,' said Kim, wrapping a little woolly cardigan she had on tightly around her, as the night air had grown chilly. Autumn was in the air, there was no doubt.

'Anyway, it's your fault when you think about it,' he teased her lightly, turning to face her as they reached the car.

'Oh yeah?'

'I was enjoying all your dating disaster stories far too much to get going any earlier. The one about the guy getting picked up by the Guards is a classic – you're wasted in Sloan Curtis, you know that? You should be doing stand-up down at the Comedy Cellar.'

He stood by the door of his car, seemingly in no rush to go anywhere.

Kim smiled up at him. And up and up. Jesus, why did he have to be so tall? But still. *You're a sweet, lovely guy*, she thought. *And I'm not used to sweet, lovely guys.* She didn't know how to behave around them, except to crack gags and hope they'd like her for it.

'Anyway,' Simon was saying, arms folded as he rocked awkwardly back and forth on his feet. 'Thanks for dinner – it was gorgeous. Can't beat a Friday-night takeaway, can you?'

She racked her brains for a one-liner to come back with, but couldn't think of a single one.

'Well, have a nice weekend,' she smiled, hating herself for how nerdy and boring she sounded.

'And you too,' he said, still not leaving. 'And . . . hey . . . you know what I just thought of?'

She looked up – and up – at him. *If I ever see him again*, she thought, *I'd need to wear the highest pair of heels I own, just to come up to the guy's collarbone.*

'What's that?'

'Maybe you and I should swap numbers?'

'Oh?' she said, hopefully. 'Why's that?'

'Well, just in case my dad ever tries to contact your mum again. So you can let me know and we can put a stop to it right away.'

Kim was about to say, God help Ronnie if he ever does try to contact Mam again. She'd tear strips off him, then go through him with a bread knife. But she managed to keep her mouth shut, fished out her phone and gave Simon her details.

'Cool, thanks for that,' he twinkled down at her. 'Well, I've taken up quite enough of your evening, so I suppose I'd better . . .'

'Bye, Simon,' she said, turning round and walking back to the house. But she was smiling as she said it.

Chapter Thirty-Eight

Iris

Iris's phone had rung at the very worst possible time for her. She was in the last place she'd ever have expected to find herself, a sort of home store which she'd often over-heard colleagues speak about gushingly by the name of IKEA. It was proving to be a most strange and peculiar new experience for her, albeit not an unpleasant one. Given that it was the weekend, it was busy, but even Iris was impressed by how well organised and streamlined it was, with orderly queues everywhere, and everything was beautifully laid out in easy-to-navigate showrooms. A model of Swedish efficiency, she thought.

Of course, this was normally the kind of place Iris would have avoided like the plague, but needs must, and besides, this was quite different. This was something of a homewares emergency. Her dear old friend Anna was coming to visit the following weekend, and Iris needed to buy everything required to entertain a guest. Some class of a put-up bed for starters, then bed linen, spare towels, actual kitchen utensils for a kitchen that was hardly ever used – the whole works. In all the years since Iris had first bought her townhouse, never once had a single guest come to stay, and it was a whole new experience for her.

By the end of the week, she thought, I'll need to learn to cook, entertain properly and convert my home office into a welcoming little guest room. Not too tall an order, surely?

She was just debating between a model of bed with a peculiar name and another by an equally unlikely one when her phone rang out. Not a number she recognised, but half thinking that it could possibly be Anna calling her from Oxford, she answered right away.

A man's voice, polite and cultured.

'Ms Simpson?' he said apologetically. 'Please forgive me for disturbing you at the weekend.'

There was only one person within Iris's orbit who spoke so respectfully. Only one.

'Harold?' she asked. 'Harold West? Is that you?'

'Yes, indeed,' came the friendly response. 'But rest assured, this is most definitely not a work-related call. Nor am I in any way attempting to sway your decision towards accepting Investco's offer, goodness no. I shouldn't dream of ever doing anything so unorthodox.'

A family wheeling an overstuffed trolley, with a gang of bored, squealing kids in tow, trailed past Iris and she had to strain to find out what this was all about.

'How can I help you, Harold?' she said, confused.

'Well, thanks to my mother,' he said, 'I've managed to secure two tickets to this evening's performance of *Turandot* at the National Concert Hall. You did mention that you were a Puccini fan, so I wondered if perhaps you'd care to join me?'

For a moment, Iris couldn't answer. Was this it, she wondered? Was this what it felt like to have a man call you up and ask you out on an actual date?

There was only one person in the whole world she felt she could ask. She got back to the privacy of her car, loaded up the boot with all her new purchases and made the call.

'Well, well, well,' was Kim's response, and Iris swore she could hear the smirk in her voice, even over the phone. 'I hate to say I told you so, but Iris? I did tell you so.'

Chapter Thirty-Nine

Four months later

Christmas at Sloan Curtis, and the decorations were out in force. There were real Christmas trees on every floor and the conference room, where the party was taking place, was no exception. A giant tree stood in the corner, filling the air with a gorgeous fresh pine smell, and everywhere you looked there was tinsel and glitter and full signs of festivity.

But that wasn't the main thing you noticed. Mainly because in pride of place, dominating the entire room, was a giant banner that said, in bright neon-pink lettering . . .

WE'll ALL MISS YOU, IRIS!

It was a whopper of a party, and there was no expense spared. Caterers had been called in and were now circulating the packed room with trays of festive grub: miniature turkey and cranberry bites, along with mouth-watering baby-sized mince pies. A makeshift bar had been set up in a corner of the room, and given that the whole office was officially closing for the holidays that same day, everyone was liberally helping themselves to anything and everything on offer.

Paul, company CFO, was mid-speech, addressing the throng from the centre of the room, microphone in hand, his voice booming and reverberating off the walls.

'. . . So of course, like the rest of us, I first became aware of Analyzed and its incredible growth rate through good old-fashioned word of mouth. My son, as it happened, who met his girlfriend via the app, had been raving about it non-stop. "You know what, Dad," he gleefully told me, "even old people like you can go on Analyzed." Of course, I tried not to take that too personally.'

He paused for laughter there, and sure enough, there were a few obedient titters from around the room.

'I realised early on that there was an Irish team behind the app's incredible success,' Paul boomed on, 'but like so many of us, was staggered to learn that its founder was none other than our very own Iris Simpson.'

Now there were cheers and full-on whoops from around the room and a round of applause that lasted so long, Paul had to wait till it died down before he could continue.

'Aided and abetted by Kim Bailey, of course, who I'm reliably informed is our resident office stand-up comedian . . .'

More cheers from around the room as Kim took a pretend-y bow, then, to even more laughter, held up the two full glasses of champagne she was drinking at the same time.

'However, the stellar success of Analyzed took everyone by surprise. For a company less than one year old to have grown to more than a million users is truly astonishing – we're all so proud of you, Iris! But now, of course, the inevitable has happened, and Iris has decided the time is right to leave us, so she can focus on growing Analyzed as a full-time career. Naturally, we are gutted to lose her, and all I can say now is, we wish you continued success in everything you do, Iris, and please don't forget us now that you're on your way to being a multimillionaire. So now, everyone, please join me in raising a glass to the lady of the hour – Ms Iris Simpson!'

Now the cheers were deafening and wherever you looked, people were in high good humour, loving the party and the festive spirit that was all around.

There was just one person standing quietly in a corner, sipping on a mulled wine and drinking it all in, completely overwhelmed by what she was seeing and feeling and experiencing. Dressed in her customary black, and barely able to process every strange new emotion pulsing through her.

Was she really standing here, Iris wondered, the dead centre of attention and the toast of the whole room? The very same Iris Simpson who used to eat lunch alone day in and day out? The same person who people barely spoke to, unless they really had to? It was nigh on impossible for her to believe that lonely woman who was never invited anywhere had somehow along the way morphed into Miss Popularity. How, she wondered over and over, did that most unexpected miracle happen?

'So how does it feel?' Kim bounced over to ask the guest of honour. 'Look! The entire company has turned out to celebrate you!'

'Why don't you ask me yourself in six months' time?' Iris smiled quietly. Mainly because in exactly six months,

Kim's contract with Sloan Curtis would have expired, so she was free to leave the company and join Iris to work full-time on the adventure story that Analyzed had become. Kim had already handed in her notice, and Iris was beyond thrilled that her dear friend and partner in crime would be joining her in the not-too-distant future.

'I'm counting the days.' Kim grinned back at her, flushed from all the freebie champagne she'd been glugging back. 'I'll be so sad to leave here, of course, but hey, the pals I've made will always be my pals. And yours too, of course.'

'Well said,' Iris replied.

'With you top of the list there,' Kim winked.

'Friends,' Iris said thoughtfully, as in the background, the party really got into full swing. 'Do you know something, Kim? I set up Analyzed with the sole intention of finding a partner, and you know what? It turned out that the biggest hole in my life was because I was utterly friendless.'

'Except you have a partner now, don't you?' Kim teased.

'As I've repeatedly told you, dearest,' Iris replied, clamming up a little, the way she always did whenever this particular topic arose, which was pretty much round the clock, given how much she was seeing her new partner these days, 'while Harold is an absolute sweetheart, he and I are very happy to take things nice and slowly.'

'Ahh, get off the stage!' Kim said lightly. 'You always say that, and yet here we are, months on, and you're still seeing him. You got to admit Iris, you like him. Go on! You can tell me.'

'Watch this space,' was Iris's prim reply, the same stock answer she fell back on every time, even though she knew deep down she wasn't really fooling anyone.

'And you certainly can't say that you're friendless,' Kim said stoutly, putting her arm warmly around Iris's shoulders. 'Not anymore!'

Just then the whole gang, Hannah, Emma and Greg, all wafted over to join them.

'You see?' Kim said to Iris. 'The gang's all here – just for you, babes.'

'We're all going to miss you so much!' Hannah said, giving Iris a big warm hug.

'I'll miss you too,' Iris said, sincerely meaning it. 'But you know I won't be going far away.'

'Thanks to Investco and the fabulous new office they've leased for us!' Kim squealed. 'Oh lads, you have to come and see the new place – you're all going to want to pack in your jobs here and come and work for Analyzed immediately!'

'You never know,' said Emma thoughtfully. 'Maybe one day we will.'

'Anyway,' said Hannah, 'we all clubbed in to buy a little something for you, Iris, just to say goodbye. Greg – have you got it there? Go on, give it to her.'

Sure enough, Greg produced a beautifully gift-wrapped little bag and handed it over to Iris, who looked puzzled and shocked at such generosity.

'You can blame Emma there if you don't like it,' Kim teased. 'She's the one who chose it.'

'Piss off, you,' said Emma drily. 'But seriously, Iris, I saw this in the design centre and it just . . . I don't know . . . it seemed to have your name on it. We got it engraved and everything.'

Iris opened up the gift box and almost wept when she saw what was there. It was a solid-silver pendant necklace with the Analyzed logo on one side and a simple little message on the other.

For Iris, with love from all your friends at Sloan Curtis.

Everyone was looking expectantly at her, waiting for her reaction, but for once in her life, she was too choked up to say a single word.

'It's perfect,' she managed to get out, between the most inconvenient tears which were springing to her eyes. So unlike me, she thought. 'I absolutely love it. Thank you all, so much. You're such special people, and you're all very dear to me.'

'Hey, don't you start crying,' said Greg, 'or you'll set the rest of us off too.'

Later on, Iris and Kim headed out into the chilly night air to the Trocadero restaurant for a very special celebratory meal with a very special group of people. It was only a small gathering, Kim figured, but tonight was a Very Big Deal and she wanted the people who were closest to Iris to be there, just for her. She had organised it all, and it was to be a total surprise for Iris, although Kim had to lie through her teeth just to get the woman there in the first place.

'Come on,' she'd said to her, as soon as the drinks party at Sloan Curtis wrapped up, 'we need a bit of food, and I just called the Troc, who said they've got a table for two free – so why not? Just you and me, what do you say?'

'But don't you want to join all your pals at whatever nightclub they're going on to?' Iris asked her innocently.

'Food first,' Kim said sternly, 'late-night haunts after. Now come on, I've got a taxi outside for us downstairs, so what are you waiting for? You must be starving – I know I am.'

Twenty minutes later, Kim had finally got her there and even though the Trocadero, which was a landmark Dublin institution, was packed out, they were immediately ushered to a plush, red-velvet booth table, right at the back of the restaurant and tucked well out of sight, so it was lovely and quiet and private – Kim, of course, frantically texting the whole way there to make sure everything, and everybody, was in place.

'Surprise!' everyone called out, and the satisfaction Kim got from seeing Iris's jaw drop in total shock was beyond price. *This is great*, she thought, *this is so cool. This is the real thing – genuine, totally un-faked surprise.*

'You're here!' was all Iris kept saying, over and over again, looking utterly stunned, Kim thought delightedly. 'You're all actually here . . . I can't believe it!'

Of course, Iris had spotted her old friend Anna's distinctive copper hair first and her heart had leaped.

'Anna!' she said, as her pal rose to give her a big, warm bear hug. 'You came over to Dublin specially for tonight? I can't believe it!'

Although, truth to tell, these days Anna often zipped over to Dublin for weekends, particularly after that wonderful first visit she'd had a few months back, where she and Iris had talked late and long into the night and where the two old friends had really, properly reconnected. Mind you, Iris still had to return the visit and take a mini break over in Oxford, but then, given how flat-out busy she was, that was something Anna knew she'd have to work on.

'Of course I came over,' Anna smiled, in that soft-spoken, beguiling Belfast accent. 'This is an epic day for you – try keeping me away! Besides, I've been having such a lovely time here, chatting to Harold about all matters cultural.'

'Anna and I quite agree about one thing,' Harold said, rising to his feet and giving Iris a cute little kiss on the lips. *God, they're so adorable together*, Kim thought. *Formal, yes, super-polite, of course – this was, after all, Iris and Harold you were dealing with – but still. So, so cute too.*

'A trip to Oxford for both of us is most definitely on the cards,' Harold was saying, 'and the sooner the better. Perhaps something we might think about for New Year's Eve, Iris dear? What do you think? Wouldn't that be something special?'

Iris laughed, loving that idea and basking in the warm glow of this happy evening. How loved she felt. How rare and precious that was for her.

She put down all the many, many gift bags she'd been given at Sloan Curtis, then worked her way round the other side of the booth to greet Connie, who was all dressed up in her 'good' suit, enjoying a gin and tonic and studying the menu closely and looking pink-cheeked and absolutely delighted with herself.

'Connie, you came,' Iris said, hugging her tight, as Kim slipped into the spare seat beside her mam. 'I'm so pleased you're here, it wouldn't be the same without you.'

'Oh, sure I'm only thrilled to be here, Iris love,' Connie beamed. 'I'm so proud of you and everything you've achieved – it's wonderful, and I know Kim can't wait to join you full-time at that fancy new Analyzed office . . . so exciting for you both!'

'How are things at the CupCake Café?' Iris asked her, taking a free seat beside Harold and continuing the chat across the table.

'Well, of course, it's still all very early days.' Connie just loved to get chatting about her pet topic. 'But I was telling Harold here that we really are out the door at lunchtimes. Some days, there's even queues down the street, can you believe it? For a tiny little pop-up stall like ours? The cupcakes are very popular too, I can't keep up with demand. Kim will tell you – my whole house is turning into an episode of *Bake Off*.'

'I've put on half a stone since the café opened,' Kim chipped in. 'That's proof of how bloody good those cakes are.'

'Betty, that's my business partner,' Connie said proudly, 'deals with the customers as well as all the accounts, and I look after the catering end of things and . . . well, so far, so good.'

'I'm particularly partial to your delightful chocolate-chip cupcakes,' Harold smiled kindly across the table.

'Hey, you're in danger of turning into Mam's best customer at this stage,' Kim grinned back at him. Because no matter how busy Harold was, and doubtlessly urged on by Iris, he would regularly make time to visit the CupCake Café, and rarely left without a large box of takeaway goodies for the whole team back at Investco.

'You never know,' Harold went on, 'in time, perhaps you and your chum Betty might consider expanding into the more savoury elements of the market? Sandwiches and lunchtime fare, that sort of thing?'

'Not a bad plan, Mam,' Kim nudged her mother encouragingly. 'Maybe something to think about, in the new year?'

'I have to visit this place while I'm here,' Anna smiled quietly. 'I've heard so much about it – I think I'd die and go to heaven if I could bake cupcakes properly. You'd do a bomb over in Oxford, Connie – all those hungry students. You'd have to franchise out the café in no time.'

Connie wasn't too sure what franchising was, but still, she knew Anna meant well. She sat back proudly as the chat weaved on, everyone in high good spirits, everyone out to enjoy the night and celebrate one person only.

Because this night was all about Iris.

♥

It was well past midnight by the time they were all spilling out onto the icy-cold street outside, where, with typical thoughtfulness, Harold had pre-ordered a fleet of taxis to whisk everyone home. Anna said her goodbyes warmly and fondly, hugging Iris goodnight as she jumped into a taxi to take her back to her hotel, making all sorts of vows and promises to meet up the following day.

'My flight home isn't until tomorrow evening,' she said, 'so maybe we can visit this famous CupCake Café I've been hearing so much about?'

'Only if it's all on me,' Iris smiled, hugging her back, still overwhelmed that her best friend had flown all the way over, just to be there for her on her special night.

'Don't be daft, ladies!' Connie trilled, as Kim helped her up into the taxi right behind. 'You can order whatever you like – it's all on the house.'

Then Iris and Harold each turned to give Kim a big goodbye kiss on the cheek.

'Chat tomorrow?' Iris said to Kim, as she and Harold clambered up into a waiting taxi. 'I'm sure you're going on somewhere now to meet up with the gang, and an old fart like me will want to hear all the gossip, with no detail spared.'

'I'm planning on having a whoperoo of a hangover in the morning,' Kim said cheekily, 'but yup, I'll be sure to call you the minute I surface – at the crack of lunchtime.'

Iris and Harold's taxi sped off next, just as Kim's phone pinged – yet another text message coming through. Her phone had been hopping the whole night long, but it was only now she actually got to look at all her messages and missed calls.

Predictably, there were loads from the gang, her sesh pigs, all along the lines of *Kim! What's keeping you?*

We're all in The Workman's Club for a late drink, hurry up, the craic is mighty and we need you here! Bring Iris too!

'Are you coming home with me, love?' Connie asked, rolling down the window of her taxi. But Kim seemed to have forgotten about the bitterly cold, sub-zero temperatures and just kept on scrolling.

Sure enough, there was a clatter of messages and texts and missed calls all from a certain someone. Which made her smile.

You still at the Troc? Will I come and get you? My Christmas work do is wrapping up now and it's boring beyond words – would love to see you. You'd brighten up any night.

Kim smiled to herself and was about to text back, when with impeccable timing she heard her name being called from the other side of the street. She immediately looked up and there he was, ambling around the corner to Andrew Street and the Trocadero. Wearing a heavy navy overcoat with a wool scarf, his hands tucked into his pockets against the freezing night air. She smiled and gave him a tiny little wave.

'Your timing is perfect!' she called out, as he grinned and waved back at her, picking up his pace.

'Ahh, there's Simon now,' Connie said, sounding pretty pleased about it. 'Simon, love?' she called out through the window of her taxi, just as he arrived over to them.

'Well, good evening, ladies,' he twinkled, leaning down to give Kim a kiss, before turning his full attention to Connie.

'Don't you look fantastic this evening, Connie? Love the suit on you.'

'Oh, you're too sweet,' she blushed prettily.

'So how was the party?' he asked. 'And the dinner afterwards?'

'We've had the most wonderful evening,' Connie said. 'But you know, I think it's time I headed home for my bed. No doubt the pair of you are going on somewhere. Maybe to a club to meet up with your pals?'

'Sounds good to me,' said Kim, feeling unusually shy around Simon and still not quite sure why. They'd been sort of seeing each other on and off for a few weeks now, and lately, he was hinting that they might start 'going exclusive'.

No fella had ever said that to Kim before, not once, not ever. Having a man in her life who seemed kind-hearted and funny and sexy and a whole lot of other things besides was a brand-new experience for her. She wasn't used to this – being treated well, being romanced, being with someone who actually wanted to be with her too. It was new, it was different, it was scary . . . but if she was being honest with herself, it was just a little bit wonderful too.

Simon took Kim's hand and held it tight, as Connie's taxi started off into the night.

'Well, goodnight, the pair of you,' she called out through the open window. 'Have fun! Mind you bring her safely home for me, Simon. And I'm sure I'll see you over the weekend – come for Sunday lunch, as usual!'

And with that, she was gone.

Connie knew she should probably give the pair of them their privacy, but the nosy part of her couldn't resist. Looking over her shoulder through the back window of the taxi, she was just in time to see Simon lean down to kiss Kim properly now, just as the icy wind whipped up and a snow flurry that had been threatening all day began to fall.

Good, she thought, happy to see that for once, Kim seemed to be stepping out with a perfectly nice young man, a real gentleman. Unlike her usual carry-on, where she'd run a mile from a genuinely good fella and go off with a bad boy instead, who, of course, would smash her heart into smithereens. Many's the time Connie had despaired of her – but not now.

After all, she thought charitably, Simon was a grand young sort, who never called to their house without lovely flowers for herself and a nice bottle of wine for Kim. Hardly his fault that his dad was what he was, now was it? Besides, the last bulletin they heard about Ronnie, the aul' eejit was now pretty much living down in Wicklow full-time, still working the chip van and well out of Connie's orbit, thanks very much.

The taxi driver had a Christmas radio station on in the background and just then, a song Connie knew well came on, an old favourite of hers. The tune got to her and she couldn't stop herself from singing along.

'Sleigh Bells ring are you listening . . . in the lane, snow is glistening . . . a beautiful sight, we're happy tonight . . . walking in a winter wonderland . . .'

'Jeez, you're in good humour tonight, missus,' said her taxi driver, looking at her in the rear-view mirror as

Connie warbled away. 'You must be looking forward to Christmas, yeah?'

'I am,' Connie sighed contentedly. 'And to the new year, too. For the first time in a very long time, I really think this is going to be a good one.'

Acknowledgements

Thank you, Marianne Gunn O' Connor. Always and for everything.

Thank you, Pat Lynch.

Thank you Sarah Bauer and all the wonderful team at Bonnier Zaffre in London. Thank you Katie Meegan, Kate Parkin, Francesca Russell, Jenna Petts, Jenny Page, Perminder Mann, Stephen Dumughn, Felice McKeown, Vicky Joss, Holly Milnes, Elise Burns, Stuart Finglass, Mark Williams, Vincent Kelleher, Sophie Hamilton, Margaret Stead, Kelly Smith, Alex May, Eloise Angeline, Laura Makela and Laura Marlowe.

You are and remain, the undisputed Dream Team.

Thank you, Vicki Satlow.

Thank you to everyone at Gill Hess here in Dublin, Helen McKean, Simon Hess, Declan Heeney and Eamonn Phelan.

Thank you to all my author and actor pals. I cherish our nights out and long, long chats so much.

Thank you Sinead Moriarty, Liz Nugent, Monica McInerney, Patricia Scanlan, Sheila O'Flanagan, Carmel Harrington, Caroline Grace Cassidy and Ciara Geraghty.

Special thanks to my family and friends, Paddy Carroll, Sam Fitzsimons, Richard Carroll, Maria McCann, Clelia

Murphy and Neil Cassley, Clarabelle Murphy and Savina Farrell, Frank Mackey, Tony O'Doherty, Karen, Caroline and Isabelle Finnegan, Marion O'Dwyer, Susan McHugh, Sean, Luke and Oscar Murphy, Pat Kinevane, Fionnuala Murphy, Noelle Brown, Robert Dogget, Ken Hutton, Rory Cowan, Mark Lambert, John Murphy, Sharon Smurfit, Kim Thorpe, Adrienne Lynch, Pat Moylan and of course, all the 'Gamester gang,' Brian and Miriam Rogers, Hugh McCusker, Sharon Hogan and Lee Kerrigan.

Hello dear reader!

Is it not the most wondrous thing in the world to be emerging from the horror show that the past two years has been for all of us? Post pandemic, there are three things I will never, ever take for granted as long as I live.

1) Live entertainment.
2) Being able to hug people again after so long apart, (yes, I am a hugger.) Lastly though, and above all,
3) bookshops being open again.

I don't know about anyone else reading this, but reading is without question what got me through lockdown. Reading anything and everything I could get my greedy paws on. Old classic favourites, my beloved Jane Austen's and PG Wodehouse for the darker days, when we all needed to smile, dystopian thrillers to try to make sense of what was going on in the world when it all got too much for me and of course my beloved 'tribe' of fiction authors, everyone from Sheila O'Flanagan to Marion Keyes and back again.

And it so happened, that on one of my many, many reading binges, I accidentally came across a story online that sent a chill right to my very core. I won't divulge any further, let's just say it gave me the inspiration for the very first chapter of this book. Because this particular sorry tale I'd read happened to be about online dating. And the sheer horribleness of it.

That's the thing, you see. For all the successful 'happy couple' stories that come out of meeting online, believe me, there are an equal and opposite number of horror stories. Online dating seems to have had an absolute field day during the pandemic, where meeting people in the old-fashioned way, in a club or bar or even just through pals, was completely off the table.

Which of course, is exactly the kind of thing that would get any author thinking.

The thing is, we're living through a digital age, and while much of it is wonderful (oh, Netflix, how I worship at thine altar) there comes a point where it seems that algorithms are dictating anything and everything that's presented to us. From the movies we stream to the TV series we binge on, there's always some pesky algorithm that thinks it has us pegged. They're the taste-controller of the modern age and there's not a whole huge amount any of us can do about it.

So, I thought, suppose you had a character who's had one too-many romantic let-downs on one-too-many online dating sites and who's fed up to the gills with some random algorithm dictating her preferred choice of partner to her. And suppose this particular character decided she was going to do something about it once and for all? What then?

And no, I'm not telling you any more! All I can say is that this book means so much to me; I loved writing Iris, and her flintiness and her sour outlook on life and getting to the bottom of what it was in her life that made her that. And Kim just strolled into my mind fully formed, the woman I wish I could be; feisty and tough and funny and fearless. A woman without a pause button.

When you're working on a book, I'm fast learning, each one has its own alchemy, that special 'secret sauce' that just makes the characters start telling you their story, instead of the other way around. And so it was with this little book baby. I loved every second of working on *The Love Algorithm* and I can only hope and pray you enjoy reading it too.

Warmest wishes – and happy reading, and welcome back to the world.

You were much missed,

Claudia
🐦 @carrollclaudia
📷 @claudiacarrollbooks

If you enjoyed

The *love* Algorithm

Why not try these other fabulous books by
Claudia Carroll . . .

You've got someone in your life driving you nuts?
I'll get rid of them for you.

Meg Monroe is a Fixer.
Got a: Dodgy ex? Errant employer? Clingy former friend?
Meg, using the time-honoured arts of charm, manipulation
and persuasion, can make them disappear. Forever.
In-demand and devilishly discreet, Meg has a 100% success
rate. That is, until a previously-disappeared (or so she
thought) case turns up on her doorstep, threatening to
bring her entire operation crumbling down.

There is not a single case that Meg cannot fix.
Well, until now . . .

'An immensely talented writer'
Sinéad Moriarty

There are so many stories hidden behind closed doors . . .

It's late at night and the rain is pouring down on the Dublin city streets. A mother is grieving for her dead child. She stands silently outside the home of the teenage boy she believes responsible. She watches . . .

In a kitchen on the same square, a girl waits anxiously for her mum to come home. She knows exactly where she is, but she knows she cannot reach her.

A few doors down, and a widow sits alone in her room. She has just delivered a bombshell to her family during dinner and her life is about to change forever.

And an aspiring theatre director has just moved in to a flat across the street. Her landlord is absent, but there are already things about him that don't quite add up . . .

Welcome to Primrose Square!

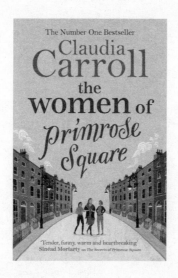

Frank Woods at number seventy-nine Primrose Square is about to turn fifty, and nobody seems to care. His friends are all busy; his wife and children have other plans. After years of being 'Mr Cellophane', he decides, finally, to do something for himself. But when he gets home to a surprise birthday party, it is his guests who get the real surprise.

Standing in the doorway is not Frank, but Francesca.

As she transitions, Francesca struggles to come to terms with her true self, and her relationship with her family is thrown into turmoil. At a loss of where to turn, she moves in with her cantankerous neighbour Miss Hardcastle, who hasn't left her home for decades. There she befriends fellow lodger Emily Dunne – fresh out of rehab, finally off the drink and desperate to make amends.

As gossip spreads through Primrose Square and every relationship is tested, nothing in this close-knit community will ever be the same again . . .